THE LE CARRÉ OMNIBUS

THE LE CARRÉ OMNIBUS:

comprising

CALL FOR THE DEAD

and

A MURDER OF QUALITY

by

JOHN LE CARRÉ

LONDON
VICTOR GOLLANCZ LTD
1969

© VICTOR GOLLANCZ LTD 1961, 1962

FIRST PUBLISHED JULY 1964
SECOND IMPRESSION AUGUST 1964
THIRD IMPRESSION SEPTEMBER 1964
FOURTH IMPRESSION APRIL 1967
FIFTH IMPRESSION APRIL 1969

575 00348 0

MADE AND PRINTED IN GREAT BRITAIN BY
THE GARDEN CITY PRESS LIMITED
LETCHWORTH, HERTFORDSHIRE

CALL FOR THE DEAD

CONTENTS

CONTENTS

A BRIEF HISTORY OF GEORGE SMILEY

When Lady Ann Sercomb married George Smiley towards the end of the war she described him to her astonished Mayfair friends as breathtakingly ordinary. When she left him two years later in favour of a Cuban motor racing driver, she announced enigmatically that if she hadn't left him then, she never could have done; and Viscount Sawley made a special journey to his club to observe that the cat was out of the bag.

This remark, which enjoyed a brief season as a *mot*, can only be understood by those who knew Smiley. Short, fat and of a quiet disposition, he appeared to spend a lot of money on really bad clothes, which hung about his squat frame like skin on a shrunken toad. Sawley, in fact, declared at the wedding that "Sercomb was mated to a bullfrog in a sou'wester." And Smiley, unaware of this description, had waddled down the aisle in search of the kiss that would turn him into a Prince.

Was he rich or poor, peasant or priest? Where had she got him from? The incongruity of the match was emphasised by Lady Ann's undoubted beauty, its mystery stimulated by the disproportion between the man and his bride. But gossip must see its characters in black and white, equip them with sins and motives easily conveyed in the shorthand of conversation. And so Smiley, without school, parents, regiment or trade, without wealth or poverty, travelled without labels in the guard's van of the social express, and soon became lost luggage, destined when the divorce had come and gone, to remain unclaimed on the dusty shelf of yesterday's news.

When Lady Ann followed her star to Cuba, she gave some

thought to Smiley. With grudging admiration she admitted to herself that if there were an only man in her life, Smiley would be he. She was gratified in retrospect that she had demonstrated this by holy matrimony.

The effect of Lady Ann's departure upon her former husband did not interest society—which indeed is unconcerned with the aftermath of sensation. Yet it would be interesting to know what Sawley and his flock might have made of Smiley's reaction; of that fleshy, bespectacled face puckered in energetic concentration as he read so deeply among the lesser German poets, the chubby wet hands clenched beneath the tumbling sleeves. But Sawley profited by the occasion with the merest of shrugs by remarking *partir c'est courir un peu*, and he appeared to be unaware that though Lady Ann just ran away, a little of George Smiley had indeed died.

That part of Smiley which survived was as incongruous to his appearance as love, or a taste for unrecognised poets : it was his profession, which was that of intelligence officer. It was a profession he enjoyed, and which mercifully provided him with colleagues equally obscure in character and origin. It also provided him with what he had once loved best in life : academic excursions into the mystery of human behaviour, disciplined by the practical application of his own deductions.

Some time in the twenties when Smiley had emerged from his unimpressive school and lumbered blinking into the murky cloisters of his unimpressive Oxford College, he had dreamed of Fellowships and a life devoted to the literary obscurities of seventeenth-century Germany. But his own tutor, who knew Smiley better, guided him wisely away from the honours that would undoubtedly have been his. On a sweet July morning in 1928, a puzzled and rather pink Smiley had sat before an interviewing board of the Overseas Committee for Academic Research, an organisation of which he had unaccountably never heard. Jebedee (his tutor) had been oddly vague about the introduction : "Give these people a try, Smiley, they might have you and they pay badly enough to guarantee you decent company." But Smiley was annoyed and said so. It worried him that Jebedee, usually so precise, was so evasive. In a slight huff he agreed to postpone his reply to All Souls until he had seen Jebedee's "mysterious people".

He wasn't introduced to the Board, but he knew half of its members by sight. There was Fielding, the French mediaevalist from Cambridge, Sparke from the School of Oriental Languages, and Steed-Asprey who had been dining at High Table the night Smiley had been Jebedee's guest. He had to admit he was impressed. For Fielding to leave his rooms, let alone Cambridge, was in itself a miracle. Afterwards Smiley always thought of that interview as a fan dance; a calculated progression of disclosures, each revealing different parts of a mysterious entity. Finally Steed-Asprey, who seemed to be Chairman, removed the last veil, and the truth stood before him in all its dazzling nakedness. He was being offered a post in what, for want of a better name, Steed-Asprey blushingly described as the Secret Service.

Smiley had asked for time to think. They gave him a week. No one mentioned money.

That night he stayed in London at somewhere rather good and took himself to the theatre. He felt strangely light-headed and this worried him. He knew very well that he would accept, that he could have done so at the interview. It was only an instinctive caution, and perhaps a pardonable desire to play the coquette with Fielding, which prevented him from doing so.

Following his affirmation came training: anonymous country houses, anonymous instructors, a good deal of travel and, looming ever larger, the fantastic prospect of working completely alone.

His first operational posting was relatively pleasant: a two-year appointment as "englischer Dozent" at a provincial German University: lectures on Keats and vacations in Bavarian hunting lodges with groups of earnest and solemnly promiscuous German students. Towards the end of each long vacation he brought some of them back to England, having already ear-marked the likely ones and conveyed his recommendations by clandestine means to an address in Bonn; during the entire

11

two years he had no idea of whether his recommendations had been accepted or ignored. He had no means of knowing even whether his candidates were approached. Indeed he had no means of knowing whether his messages ever reached their destination; and he had no contact with the Department while in England.

His emotions in performing this work were mixed, and irreconcilable. It intrigued him to evaluate from a detached position what he had learnt to describe as "the agent potential" of a human being; to devise minuscule tests of character and behaviour which could inform him of the qualities of a candidate. This part of him was bloodless and inhuman—Smiley in this role was the international mercenary of his trade, amoral and without motive beyond that of personal gratification.

Conversely is saddened him to witness in himself the gradual death of natural pleasure. Always withdrawn, he now found himself shrinking from the temptations of friendship and human loyalty; he guarded himself warily from spontaneous reaction. By the strength of his intellect, he forced himself to observe humanity with clinical objectivity, and because he was neither immortal nor infallible he hated and feared the falseness of his life.

But Smiley was a sentimental man and the long exile strengthened his deep love of England. He fed hungrily on memories of Oxford; its beauty, its rational ease and the mature slowness of its judgements. He dreamt of windswept autumn holidays at Hartland Quay, of long trudges over the Cornish cliffs, his face smooth and hot against the sea wind. This was his other secret life, and he grew to hate the bawdy intrusion of the new Germany, the stamping and shouting of uniformed students, the scarred, arrogant faces and their cheapjack answers. He resented, too, the way in which the Faculty had tampered with his subject—*his* beloved German literature. And there had been a night, a terrible night in the winter of 1937 when Smiley had stood at his window and watched a great bonfire in the university court : round it stood hundreds of students, their faces exultant and glistening in the dancing light. And into the pagan fire they threw books in their hundreds. He knew whose books they were : Thomas Mann, Heine, Lessing and a host of others. And Smiley, his damp hand cupped round the end of his cigarette, watching and hating, triumphed that he knew his enemy.

Nineteen thirty-nine saw him in Sweden, the accredited agent of a well-known Swiss small-arms manufacturer, his association with the firm conveniently backdated. Conveniently, too, his appearance had somehow altered, for Smiley had discovered in himself a talent for the part which went beyond the rudimentary change to his hair and the addition of a small moustache. For four years he had played the part, travelling back and forth between Switzerland, Germany and Sweden. He had never guessed it was possible to be frightened for so long. He developed a nervous irritation in his left eye which remained with him fifteen years later; the strain etched lines on his fleshy cheeks and brow. He learnt what it was never to sleep, never to relax, to feel at any time of day or night the restless beating of his own heart, to know the extremes of solitude and self-pity, the sudden unreasoning desire for a woman, for drink, for exercise, for any drug to take away the tension of his life.

Against this background he conducted his authentic commerce and his work as a spy. With the progress of time the network grew, and other countries repaired their lack of foresight and preparation. In 1943 he was recalled. Within six weeks he was yearning to return, but they never let him go :

"You're finished," Steed-Asprey said : "train new men, take time off. Get married or something. Unwind."

Smiley proposed to Steed-Asprey's secretary, the Lady Ann Sercomb.

The war was over. They paid him off, and he took his beautiful wife to Oxford to devote himself to the obscurities of seventeenth-century Germany. But two years later Lady Ann was in Cuba, and the revelations of a young Russian cypher-clerk in Ottawa had created a new demand for men of Smiley's experience.

The job was new, the threat elusive and at first he enjoyed

it. But younger men were coming in, perhaps with fresher minds. Smiley was no material for promotion and it dawned on him gradually that he had entered middle age without ever being young, and that he was—in the nicest possible way —on the shelf.

Things changed. Steed-Asprey was gone, fled from the new world to India, in search of another civilisation. Jebedee was dead. He had boarded a train at Lille in 1941 with his radio operator, a young Belgian, and neither had been heard of again. Fielding was wedded to a new thesis on Roland—only Maston remained, Maston the career man, the war-time recruit, the Ministers' Adviser on Intelligence; "the first man," Jebedee had said, "to play power tennis at Wimbledon." The NATO alliance, and the desperate measures contemplated by the Americans, altered the whole nature of Smiley's Service. Gone for ever were the days of Steed-Asprey, when as like as not you took your orders over a glass of port in his rooms at Magdalen; the inspired amateurism of a handful of highly qualified, under-paid men had given way to the efficiency, bureaucracy and intrigue of a large Government department —effectively at the mercy of Maston, with his expensive clothes and his knighthood, his distinguished grey hair and silver coloured ties; Maston, who even remembered his secretary's birthday, whose manners were a by-word among the ladies of the registry; Maston, apologetically extending his empire and regretfully moving to even larger offices; Maston, holding smart houseparties at Henley and feeding on the successes of his subordinates.

They had brought him in during the war, the professional civil servant from an orthodox department, a man to handle paper and integrate the brilliance of his staff with the cumbersome machine of bureaucracy. It comforted the Great to deal with a man they knew, a man who could reduce any colour to grey, who knew his masters and could walk among them. And he did it so well. They liked his diffidence when he apologised for the company he kept, his insincerity when he defended the vagaries of his subordinates, his flexibility when formulating new commitments. Nor did he let go the advantages of a cloak and dagger man *malgré lui*, wearing the cloak for his masters and preserving the dagger for his servants. Ostensibly, his position was an odd one. He was not the nominal Head of Service, but the Ministers' Adviser on Intelligence, and Steed-Asprey had described him for all time as the Head Eunuch.

This was a new world for Smiley: the brilliantly lit corridors, the smart young men. He felt pedestrian and old-fashioned, homesick for the dilapidated terrace house in Knightsbridge where it had all begun. His appearance seemed to reflect this discomfort in a kind of physical recession which made him more hunched and frog-like than ever. He blinked more, and acquired the nickname of "Mole". But his débutante secretary adored him, and referred to him invariably as "My darling teddy-bear".

Smiley was now too old to go abroad. Maston had made that clear: "Anyway, my dear fellow, as like as not you're blown after all the ferreting about in the war. Better stick at home, old man, and keep the home fires burning."

Which goes some way to explaining why George Smiley sat in the back of a London taxi at two o'clock on the morning of Wednesday, 4th January, on his way to Cambridge Circus.

CHAPTER II

WE NEVER CLOSED

HE FELT SAFE in the taxi. Safe and warm. The warmth was contraband, smuggled from his bed and hoarded against the wet January night. Safe because unreal: it was his ghost that ranged the London streets and took note of their unhappy pleasure-seekers, scuttling under commissionaires' umbrellas; and of the tarts, gift-wrapped in polythene. It was his ghost, he decided, which had climbed from the well of sleep and stopped the telephone shrieking on the bedside table... Oxford Street... why was London the only capital in the world that lost its personality at night? Smiley, as he pulled his coat more closely about him, could think of nowhere, from Los Angeles to Bern, which so readily gave up its daily struggle for identity.

The cab turned into Cambridge Circus, and Smiley sat up with a jolt. He remembered why the Duty Officer had rung, and the memory woke him brutally from his dreams. The conversation came back to him word for word—a feat of re-collection long ago achieved.

"Duty Officer speaking, Smiley. I have the Adviser on the line...."

"Smiley; Maston speaking. You interviewed Samuel Arthur Fennan at the Foreign Office on Monday, am I right?"

"Yes... yes I did."

"What was the case?"

"Anonymous letter alleging Party membership at Oxford. Routine interview, authorised by the Director of Security."

(Fennan *can't* have complained, thought Smiley; he knew I'd clear him. There was nothing irregular, nothing.)

"Did you go for him at all? Was it hostile, Smiley, tell me that?"

(Lord, he does sound frightened. Fennan must have put the whole Cabinet on to us.)

"No. It was a particularly friendly interview; we liked one another, I think. As a matter of fact I exceeded my brief in a way."

"How, Smiley, how?"

"Well, I more or less told him not to worry."

"You *what*?"

"I told him not to worry; he was obviously in a bit of a state, and so I told him."

"*What* did you tell him?"

"I said I had no powers and nor had the Service; but I could see no reason why we should bother him further."

"Is that all?"

Smiley paused for a second; he had never known Maston like this, never known him so dependent.

"Yes, that's all. Absolutely all." (He'll never forgive me for this. So much for the studied calm, the cream shirts and silver ties, the smart luncheons with ministers.)

"He says you cast doubts on his loyalty, that his career in the F.O. is ruined, that he is the victim of paid informers."

"He said *what*? He must have gone stark mad. He knows he's cleared. What else does he want?"

"Nothing. He's dead. Killed himself at 10.30 this evening. Left a letter to the Foreign Secretary. The police rang one of his secretaries and got permission to open the letter. Then they told us. There's going to be an enquiry. Smiley, you're sure, aren't you?"

"Sure of what?"

". . . never mind. Get round as soon as you can."

It had taken him hours to get a taxi. He rang three cab ranks and got no reply. At last the Sloane Square rank replied, and Smiley waited at his bedroom window wrapped in his overcoat until he saw the cab draw up at the door. It reminded him of the air raids in Germany, this unreal anxiety in the dead of night.

At Cambridge Circus he stopped the cab a hundred yards from the office, partly from habit and partly to clear his head in anticipation of Maston's febrile questioning.

He showed his pass to the constable on duty and made his way slowly to the lift.

The Duty Officer greeted him with relief as he emerged, and they walked together down the bright cream corridor.

"Maston's gone to see Sparrow at Scotland Yard. There's a squabble going on about which police department handles the case. Sparrow says Special Branch, Evelyn says C.I.D. and the Surrey police don't know what's hit them. Bad as a will. Come and have coffee in the D.O.'s glory hole. It's out of a bottle but it does."

Smiley was grateful it was Peter Guillam's duty that night. A polished and thoughtful man who had specialised in

Satellite espionage, the kind of friendly spirit who always has a timetable and a penknife.

"Special Branch rang at twelve five. Fennan's wife went to the theatre and didn't find him till she got back alone at quarter to eleven. She eventually rang the police."

"He lived down in Surrey somewhere."

"Walliston, off the Kingston by-pass. Only just outside the Metropolitan area. When the police arrived they found a letter to the Foreign Secretary on the floor beside the body. The Superintendent rang the Chief Constable, who rang the Duty Officer at the Home Office, who rang the Resident Clerk at the Foreign Office, and eventually they got permission to open the letter. Then the fun started."

"Go on."

"The Director of Personnel at the Foreign Office rang us. He wanted the Adviser's home number. Said this was the last time Security tampered with his staff, that Fennan had been a loyal and talented officer, bla . . . bla . . . bla . . ."

"So he was. So he was."

"Said the whole affair demonstrated conclusively that Security had got out of hand—Gestapo methods which were not even mitigated by a genuine threat . . . bla. . . .

"I gave him the Adviser's number and dialled it on the other 'phone while he went on raving. By a stroke of genius I got the F.O. off one line and Maston on the other and gave him the news. That was at 12.20. Maston was here by one o'clock in a state of advanced pregnancy—he'll have to report to the Minister tomorrow morning."

They were silent for a moment, while Guillam poured coffee essence into the cups and added boiling water from the electric kettle.

"What was he like?" he asked.

"Who? Fennan? Well, until tonight I could have told you. Now he doesn't make sense. To look at, obviously a Jew. Orthodox family, but dropped all that at Oxford and turned Marxist. Perceptive, cultured . . . a reasonable man. Soft spoken, good listener. Still educated; you know, facts galore.

Whoever denounced him was right of course : he *was* in the Party."

"How old?"

"Forty-four. Looks older really." Smiley went on talking as his eyes wandered round the room. ". . . sensitive face—mop of straight dark hair undergraduate fashion, profile of a twenty year old, fine dry skin, rather chalky. Very lined too—lines going all ways, cutting the skin into squares. Very thin fingers . . . compact sort of chap; self-contained unit. Takes his pleasures alone. Suffered alone too, I suppose."

They got up as Maston came in.

"Ah, Smiley. Come in." He opened the door and put out his left arm to guide Smiley through first. Maston's room contained not a single piece of government property. He had once bought a collection of nineteenth-century water colours, and some of these were hanging on the walls. The rest was off the peg, Smiley decided. Maston was off the peg too, for that matter. His suit was just too light for respectability; the string of his monocle cut across the invariable cream shirt. He wore a light grey woollen tie. A German would call him *flott* thought Smiley; chic, that's what he is—a barmaid's dream of a real gentleman.

"I've seen Sparrow. It's a clear case of suicide. The body has been removed and beyond the usual formalities the Chief Constable is taking no action. There'll be an inquest within a day or two. It has been agreed—I can't emphasise this too strongly, Smiley—that no word of our former interest in Fennan is to be passed to the Press."

"I see." (You're dangerous, Maston. You're weak and frightened. Anyone's neck before yours, I know. You're looking at me that way—measuring me for the rope.)

"Don't think I'm criticising, Smiley; after all if the Director of Security authorised the interview you have nothing to worry about."

"Except Fennan."

"Quite so. Unfortunately the Director of Security omitted to sign off your minute suggesting an interview. He authorised it verbally, no doubt?"

"Yes. I'm sure he'll confirm that."

Maston looked at Smiley again, sharp, calculating; something was beginning to stick in Smiley's throat. He knew he was being uncompromising, that Maston wanted him nearer, wanted him to conspire.

"You know Fennan's office has been in touch with me?"

"Yes."

"There will have to be an enquiry. It may not even be possible to keep the Press out. I shall certainly have to see the Home Secretary first thing tomorrow." (Frighten me and try again . . . I'm getting on . . . pension to consider . . . unemployable, too . . . but I won't share your lie, Maston.) "I must have all the facts, Smiley. I must do my duty. If there's anything you feel you should tell me about that interview, anything you haven't recorded, perhaps, tell me now and let me be the judge of its significance."

"There's nothing to add, really, to what's already on the file, and what I told you earlier tonight. It might help you to know (the 'you' was a trifle strong, perhaps)—it might help you to know that I conducted the interview in an atmosphere of exceptional informality. The allegation against Fennan was pretty thin—university membership in the '30s and vague talk of current sympathy. Half the Cabinet were in the Party in the '30s." Maston frowned. "When I got to his room in the Foreign Office it turned out to be rather public—people trotting in and out the whole time, so I suggested we should go out for a walk in the park."

"Go on."

"Well, we did. It was a sunny, cold day and rather pleasant. We watched the ducks." Maston made a gesture of impatience. "We spent about half an hour in the park—he did all the talking. He was an intelligent man, fluent and interesting. But nervous, too, not unnaturally. These people love talking about themselves, and I think he was pleased to get it off his chest. He told me the whole story—seemed quite happy to mention names—and then we went to an espresso café he knew near Millbank."

"A *what*?"

"An espresso bar. They sell a special kind of coffee for a shilling a cup. We had some."

"I see. It was under these ... convivial circumstances that you told him the Department would recommend no action."

"Yes. We often do that, but we don't normally record it."

Maston nodded. That was the kind of thing he understood, thought Smiley; goodness me, he really is rather contemptible. It was exciting to find Maston being as unpleasant as he had expected.

"And I may take it therefore that his suicide—and his letter, of course—come as a complete surprise to you? You find no explanation?"

"It would be remarkable if I did."

"You have no idea who denounced him?"

"No."

"He was married, you know."

"Yes."

"I wonder ... it seems conceivable that his wife might be able to fill in some of the gaps. I hesitate to suggest it, but perhaps someone from the Department ought to see her and, so far as good feeling allows, question her on all this."

"Now?" Smiley looked at him, expressionless.

Maston was standing at his big flat desk, toying with the businessman's cutlery—paper knife, cigarette box, lighter— the whole chemistry set of official hospitality. He's showing a full inch of cream cuff, thought Smiley, and admiring his white hands.

Maston looked up, his face composed in an expression of sympathy.

"Smiley, I know how you feel, but despite this tragedy you must try to understand the position. The Minister and the Home Secretary will want the fullest possible account of this affair and it is my specific task to provide one. Particularly any information which points to Fennan's state of mind immediately after his interview with ... with us. Perhaps he spoke to his wife about it. He's not supposed to have done but we must be realistic."

"You want *me* to go down there?"

"Someone must. There's a question of the inquest. The Home Secretary will have to decide about that of course, but at present we just haven't the facts. Time is short and you know the case, you made the background enquiries. There's no time for anyone else to brief himself. If anyone goes it will have to be you, Smiley."

"When do you want me to go?"

"Apparently Mrs. Fennan is a somewhat unusual woman. Foreign. Jewish, too, I gather, suffered badly in the war, which adds to the embarrassment. She is a strong-minded woman and relatively unmoved by her husband's death. Only superficially, no doubt. But sensible and communicative. I gather from Sparrow that she is proving co-operative and would probably see you as soon as you can get there. Surrey police can warn her you're coming and you can see her first thing in the morning. I shall telephone you there later in the day."

Smiley turned to go.

"Oh—and Smiley. . . ." He felt Maston's hand on his arm and turned to look at him. Maston wore the smile normally reserved for the older ladies of the Service. "Smiley, you can count on me, you know; you can count on my support."

My God, thought Smiley; you really do work round the clock. A twenty-four hour cabaret, you are—"We Never Closed". He walked out into the street.

CHAPTER III

ELSA FENNAN

Merridale Lane is one of those corners of Surrey where the inhabitants wage a relentless battle against the stigma of suburbia. Trees, fertilised and cajoled into being in every front garden, half obscure the poky "Character dwellings" which crouch behind them. The rusticity of the environment is enhanced by the wooden owls that keep guard over the names of houses, and by crumbling dwarfs indefatigably poised over goldfish ponds. The inhabitants of Merridale Lane do not paint their dwarfs, suspecting this to be a suburban vice, nor, for the same reason, do they varnish the owls; but wait patiently for the years to endow these treasures with an appearance of weathered antiquity, until one day even the beams on the garage may boast of beetle and woodworm.

The lane is not exactly a cul-de-sac although estate agents insist that it is; the further end from the Kingston by-pass dwindles nervously into a gravel path, which in turn degenerates into a sad little mud track across Merries Field—leading to another lane indistinguishable from Merridale. Until about 1920 this path had led to the parish church, but the church now stands on what is virtually a traffic island adjoining the London road, and the path which once led the faithful to worship provides a superfluous link between the inhabitants of Merridale Lane and Cadogan Road. The strip of open land called Merries Field has already achieved an eminence far beyond its own aspirations; it has driven a wedge deep into the District Council, between the developers and the preservers, and so effectively that on one occasion the entire machinery of local government in Walliston was brought to a standstill. A kind of natural compromise has now established itself : Merries Field is neither developed nor preserved by the three steel pylons, placed at regular intervals across it. At the centre is a cannibal hut with a thatched roof called "The

War Memorial Shelters". erected in 1951 in grateful memory to the fallen of two wars, as a haven for the weary and old. No one seems to have asked what business the weary and old would have in Merries Field, but the spiders have at least found a haven in the roof, and as a sitting-out place for pylon-builders the hut was unusually comfortable.

Smiley arrived there on foot just after eight o'clock that morning, having parked his car at the police station, which was ten minutes' walk away.

It was raining heavily, driving cold rain, so cold it felt hard upon the face.

Surrey police had no further interest in the case, but Sparrow had sent down independently a Special Branch officer to remain at the police station and act if necessary as liaison between Security and the police. There was no doubt about the manner of Fennan's death. He had been shot through the temple at point blank range by a small French pistol manufactured in Lille in 1957. The pistol was found beneath the body. All the circumstances were consistent with suicide.

Number fifteen Merridale Lane was a low, Tudor-style house with the bedrooms built into the gables, and a half-timbered garage. It had an air of neglect, even disuse. It might have been occupied by artists, thought Smiley. Fennan didn't seem to fit here. Fennan was Hampstead and au-pair foreign girls.

He unlatched the gate and walked slowly up the drive to the front door, trying vainly to discern some sign of life through the leaded windows. It was very cold. He rang the bell.

Elsa Fennan opened the door.

"They rang and asked if I minded. I didn't know what to say. Please come in." A trace of a German accent.

She must have been older than Fennan. A slight, fierce woman in her fifties with hair cut very short and dyed to the colour of nicotine. Although frail, she conveyed an impression of endurance and courage, and the brown eyes that shone from her crooked little face were of an astonishing intensity.

It was a worn face, racked and ravaged long ago, the face of a child grown old on starving and exhaustion, the eternal refugee face, the prison-camp face, thought Smiley.

She was holding out her hand to him—it was scrubbed and pink, bony to touch. He told her his name.

"You're the man who interviewed my husband," she said; "about loyalty." She led him into the low, dark drawing-room. There was no fire. Smiley felt suddenly sick and cheap. Loyalty to whom, to what. She didn't sound resentful. He was an oppressor, but she accepted oppression.

"I liked your husband very much. He would have been cleared."

"Cleared? Cleared of what?"

"There was a prima facie case for investigation—an anonymous letter—I was given the job." He paused and looked at her with real concern. "You have had a terrible loss, Mrs. Fennan . . . you must be exhausted. You can't have slept all night. . . ."

She did not respond to his sympathy: "Thank you, but I can scarcely hope to sleep today. Sleep is not a luxury I enjoy." She looked down wryly at her own tiny body; "My body and I must put up with one another twenty hours a day. We have lived longer than most people already.

"As for the terrible loss. Yes, I suppose so. But you know, Mr. Smiley, for so long I owned nothing but a toothbrush, so I'm not really used to possession, even after eight years of marriage. Besides, I have the experience to suffer with discretion."

She bobbed her head at him, indicating that he might sit, and with an oddly old-fashioned gesture she swept her skirt beneath her and sat opposite him. It was very cold in that room. Smiley wondered whether he ought to speak; he dared not look at her, but peered vaguely before him, trying desperately in his mind to penetrate the worn, travelled face of Elsa Fennan. It seemed a long time before she spoke again.

"You said you liked him. You didn't give him that impression, apparently."

"I haven't seen your husband's letter, but I have heard of

25

its contents." Smiley's earnest, pouchy face was turned towards her now: "It simply doesn't make sense. I as good as told him he was . . . that we would recommend that the matter be taken no further."

She was motionless, waiting to hear. What could he say: "I'm sorry I killed your husband, Mrs. Fennan, but I was only doing my duty. (Duty to *whom* for God's sake?) He was in the Communist Party at Oxford twenty-four years ago; his recent promotion gave him access to highly secret information. Some busybody wrote us an anonymous letter and we had no option but to follow it up. The investigation induced a state of melancholia in your husband, and drove him to suicide." He said nothing.

"It was a game," she said suddenly, "a silly balancing trick of ideas; it had nothing to do with him or any real person. Why do you bother yourself with us? Go back to Whitehall and look for more spies on your drawing boards." She paused, showing no sign of emotion beyond the burning of her dark eyes. "It's an old illness you suffer from, Mr. Smiley," she continued, taking a cigarette from the box; "and I have seen many victims of it. The mind becomes separated from the body; it thinks without reality, rules a paper kingdom and devises without emotion the ruin of its paper victims. But sometimes the division between your world and ours is incomplete; the files grow heads and arms and legs, and that's a terrible moment, isn't it? The names have families as well as records, and human motives to explain the sad little dossiers and their make-believe sins. When that happens I am sorry for you." She paused for a moment, then continued:

"It's like the State and the People. The State is a dream too, a symbol of nothing at all, an emptiness, a mind without a body, a game played with clouds in the sky. But States make war, don't they, and imprison people? To dream in doctrines —how tidy! My husband and I have both been tidied now, haven't we?" She was looking at him steadily. Her accent was more noticeable now.

"You call yourself the State, Mr. Smiley; you have no place among real people. You dropped a bomb from the sky: don't come down here and look at the blood, or hear the scream."

She had not raised her voice, she looked above him now, and beyond.

"You seem shocked. I should be weeping, I suppose, but I've no more tears, Mr. Smiley—I'm barren; the children of my grief are dead. Thank you for coming, Mr. Smiley; you can go back, now—there's nothing you can do here."

He sat forward in his chair, his podgy hands nursing one another on his knees. He looked worried and sanctimonious, like a grocer reading the lesson. The skin of his face was white and glistened at the temples and on the upper lip. Only under his eyes was there any colour : mauve half-moons bisected by the heavy frame of his spectacles.

"Look, Mrs. Fennan; that interview was almost a formality. I think your husband enjoyed it, I think it even made him happy to get it over."

"How *can* you say that, how can you, now this. . . ."

"But I tell you it's true : why, we didn't even hold the thing in a Government office—when I got there I found Fennan's office was a sort of right of way between two other rooms, so we walked out into the park and finished up at a café—scarcely an inquisition, you see. I even told him not to worry—I told him that. I just don't understand the letter—it doesn't . . ."

"It's not the letter, Mr. Smiley, that I'm thinking of. It's what he said to me."

"How do you mean?"

"He was deeply upset by the interview, he told me so. When he came back on Monday night he was desperate, almost incoherent. He collapsed in a chair and I persuaded him to go to bed. I gave him a sedative which lasted him half the night. He was still talking about it the next morning. It occupied his whole mind until his death."

The telephone was ringing upstairs. Smiley got up.

"Excuse me—that will be my office. Do you mind?"

"It's in the front bedroom, directly above us."

Smiley walked slowly upstairs in a state of complete bewilderment. What on earth should he say to Maston now?

He lifted the receiver, glancing mechanically at the number on the apparatus.

"Walliston 2944."

"Exchange here. Good morning. Your eight-thirty call."

"Oh—Oh yes, thank you very much."

He rang off, grateful for the temporary respite. He glanced briefly round the bedroom. It was the Fennans' own bedroom, austere but comfortable. There were two armchairs in front of the gas fire. Smiley remembered now that Elsa Fennan had been bedridden for three years after the war. It was probably a survival from those years that they still sat in the bedroom in the evenings. The alcoves on either side of the fireplace were full of books. In the furthest corner, a typewriter on a desk. There was something intimate and touching about the arrangement, and perhaps for the first time Smiley was filled with an immediate sense of the tragedy of Fennan's death. He returned to the drawing-room.

"It was for you. Your eight-thirty call from the exchange."

He was aware of a pause and glanced incuriously towards her. But she had turned away from him and was standing looking out of the window, her slender back very straight and still, her stiff, short hair dark against the morning light.

Suddenly he stared at her. Something had occurred to him which he should have realised upstairs in the bedroom, something so improbable that for a moment his brain was unable to grasp it. Mechanically he went on talking; he must get out of there, get away from the telephone and Maston's hysterical questions, get away from Elsa Fennan and her dark, restless house. Get away and think.

"I have intruded too much already, Mrs. Fennan, and I must now take your advice and return to Whitehall."

Again the cold, frail hand, the mumbled expressions of sympathy. He collected his coat from the hall and stepped out into the early sunlight. The winter sun had just appeared for a moment after the rain, and it repainted in pale, wet colours the trees and houses of Merridale Lane. The sky was still dark grey, and the world beneath it strangely luminous, giving back the sunlight it had stolen from nowhere.

He walked slowly down the gravel path, fearful of being called back.

He returned to the police station, full of disturbing thoughts. To begin with it was not Elsa Fennan who had asked the exchange for an eight-thirty call that morning.

CHAPTER IV

COFFEE AT THE FOUNTAIN

THE C.I.D. SUPERINTENDENT at Walliston was a large, genial soul who measured professional competence in years of service and saw no fault in the habit. Sparrow's Inspector Mendel on the other hand was a thin, weasel-faced gentleman who spoke very rapidly out of the corner of his mouth. Smiley secretly likened him to a gamekeeper—a man who knew his territory and disliked intruders.

"I have a message from your Department, sir. You're to ring the Adviser at once." The Superintendent indicated his telephone with an enormous hand and walked out through the open door of his office. Mendel remained. Smiley looked at him owlishly for a moment, guessing his man.

"Shut the door." Mendel moved to the door and pulled it quietly to.

"I want to make an enquiry of the Walliston telephone exchange. Who's the most likely contact?"

"Assistant Supervisor normally. Supervisor's always in the clouds; Assistant Supervisor does the work."

"Someone at 15 Merridale Lane asked to be called by the exchange at 8.30 this morning. I want to know what time the request was made and who by. I want to know whether there's a standing request for a morning call, and if so let's have the details."

"Know the number?"

"Walliston 2944. Subscriber Samuel Fennan, I should think."

Mendel moved to the telephone and dialled o. While he waited for a reply he said to Smiley : "You don't want any-one to know about this, do you?"

"No one. Not even you. There's probably nothing in it. If we start bleating about murder we'll . . ."

Mendel was through to the exchange, asking for the Assistant Supervisor.

"Walliston C.I.D. here, Superintendent's office. We have an enquiry . . . yes, of course . . . ring me back then . . . C.I.D. outside line, Walliston 2421."

He replaced the receiver and waited for the exchange to ring him. "Sensible girl," he muttered, without looking at Smiley. The telephone rang and he began speaking at once.

"We're investigating a burglary in Merridale Lane. Number 18. Just possible they used No. 15 as an observation point for a job on the opposite house. Have you got any way of finding out whether calls were originated or received on Walliston 2944 in the last twenty-four hours?"

There was a pause. Mendel put his hand over the mouth-piece and turned to Smiley with a very slight grin. Smiley suddenly liked him a good deal.

"She's asking the girls," said Mendel; "and she'll look at the dockets." He turned back to the telephone and began jotting down figures on the Superintendent's pad. He stiffened abruptly and leaned forward on the desk.

"Oh yes." His voice was casual, in contrast to his attitude; "I wonder when she asked for that?" Another pause . . . "19.55 hours . . . a man, eh? The girl's sure of that, is she? . . . Oh, I see, oh, well, that fixes that. Thanks very much indeed all the same. Well, at least we know where we stand . . . not at all, you've been very helpful . . . just a theory, that's all . . . have to think again, won't we? Well, thanks very much. Very kind, keep it under your hat . . . Cheerio." He rang off, tore the page from the pad and put it in his pocket.

Smiley spoke quickly : "There's a beastly café down the

road. I need some breakfast. Come and have a cup of coffee."
The telephone was ringing; Smiley could almost feel Maston
the other end. Mendel looked at him for a moment and
seemed to understand. They left it ringing and walked quickly
out of the police station towards the High Street.

The Fountain Café (Proprietor Miss Gloria Adam) was all
Tudor and horse brasses and local honey at sixpence more
than anywhere else. Miss Adam herself dispensed the nastiest
coffee south of Manchester and spoke of her customers as "My
Friends". Miss Adam did not do business with friends, but
simply robbed them, which somehow added to the illusion
of genteel amateurism which Miss Adam was so anxious to
preserve. Her origin was obscure, but she often spoke of her
late father as "The Colonel". It was rumoured among those of
Miss Adam's friends who had paid particularly dearly for their
friendship that the colonelcy in question had been granted by
the Salvation Army.

Mendel and Smiley sat at a corner table near the fire,
waiting for their order. Mendel looked at Smiley oddly : "The
girl remembers the call clearly; it came right at the end of
her shift—five to eight last night. A request for an 8.30 call
this morning. It was made by Fennan himself—the girl is
positive of that."

"How?"

"Apparently this Fennan had rung the exchange on Christmas Day and the same girl was on duty. Wanted to wish them
all a Happy Christmas. She was rather bucked. They had
quite a chat. She's sure it was the same voice yesterday, asking
for the call. 'Very cultured gentleman,' she said."

"But it doesn't make sense. He wrote a suicide letter at
10.30. What happened between 8 and 10.30?"

Mendel picked up a battered old briefcase. It had no lock
—more like a music case, thought Smiley. He took from it a
plain buff folder and handed it to Smiley. "Facsimile of the
letter. Super said to give you a copy. They're sending the
original to the F.O. and another copy straight to Marlene
Dietrich."

"Who the devil's she?"

"Sorry sir. What we call your Adviser, sir. Pretty general in the Branch, sir. Very sorry, sir."

How beautiful, thought Smiley, how absolutely beautiful. He opened the folder and looked at the facsimile. Mendel went on talking : "First suicide letter I've ever seen that was typed. First one I've seen with the time on it, for that matter. Signature looks O.K., though. Checked it at the station against a receipt he once signed for lost property. Right as rain."

The letter was typed, probably a portable. Like the anonymous denunciation; that was a portable too. This one was signed with Fennan's neat, legible signature. Beneath the printed address at the head of the page was typed the date, and beneath that the time : 10.30 p.m. :

> "Dear Sir David,
>
> After some hesitation I have decided to take my life. I cannot spend my remaining years under a cloud of disloyalty and suspicion. I realise that my career is ruined, that I am the victim of paid informers.
>
> Yours sincerely,
Samuel Fennan."

Smiley read it through several times, his mouth pursed in concentration, his eyebrows raised a little as if in surprise. Mendel was asking him something :

"How d'you get on to it?"

"On to what?"

"This early call business."

"Oh, I took the call. Thought it was for me. It wasn't—it was the exchange with this thing. Even then the penny didn't drop. I assumed it was for her, you see. Went down and told her."

"Down?"

"Yes. They keep the telephone in the bedroom. It's a sort of bed-sitter, really . . . she used to be an invalid, you know, and they've left the room as it was then, I suppose. It's like a study, one end; books, typewriter, desk and so forth."

"Typewriter?"

"Yes. A portable. I imagine he did this letter on it. But

* *

you see when I took that call I'd forgotten it couldn't possibly be Mrs. Fennan who'd asked for it."

"Why not?"

"She's an insomniac—she told me. Made a sort of joke of it. I told her to get some rest and she just said : 'My body and I must put up with one another twenty hours a day. We have lived longer than most people already.' There was more of it—something about not enjoying the luxury of sleep. So why should she want a call at 8.30?"

"Why should her husband—why should anyone? It's damn nearly lunch time. God help the Civil Service."

"Exactly. That puzzles me too. The Foreign Office admittedly starts late—ten o'clock, I think. But even then Fennan would be pushed to dress, shave, breakfast and catch the train on time if he didn't wake till 8.30. Besides, his wife could call him."

"She might have been shooting a line about not sleeping," said Mendel. "Women do, about insomnia and migraine and stuff. Makes people think they're nervous and temperamental. Cock, most of it."

Smiley shook his head : "No, she couldn't have made the call, could she? She wasn't home till 10.45. But even supposing she made a mistake about the time she got back, she couldn't have gone to the telephone without seeing her husband's body first. And you're not going to tell me that her reaction on finding her husband dead was to go upstairs and ask for an early call?"

They drank their coffee in silence for a while.

"Another thing," said Mendel.

"Yes?"

"His wife got back from the theatre at quarter to eleven, right?"

"That's what she says."

"Did she go alone?"

"No idea."

"Bet she didn't. I'll bet she *had* to tell the truth there, and timed the letter to give herself an alibi."

Smiley's mind went back to Elsa Fennan, her anger, her

submission. It seemed ridiculous to talk about her in this way. No : not Elsa Fennan. No.

"Where was the body found?" Smiled asked.

"Bottom of the stairs."

"Bottom of the stairs?"

"True. Sprawled across the hall floor. Revolver underneath him."

"And the note. Where was that?"

"Beside him on the floor."

"Anything else?"

"Yes. A mug of cocoa in the drawing-room."

"I see. Fennan decides to commit suicide. He asks the exchange to ring him at 8.30. He makes himself some cocoa and puts it in the drawing-room. He goes upstairs and types his last letter. He comes down again to shoot himself, leaving the cocoa undrunk. It all hangs together nicely."

"Yes, doesn't it. Incidentally, hadn't you better ring your office?"

He looked at Mendel equivocally. "That's the end of a beautiful friendship," he said. As he walked towards the coin box beside a door marked "Private" he heard Mendel saying : "I bet you say that to all the boys." He was actually smiling as he asked for Maston's number.

Maston wanted to see him at once.

He went back to their table. Mendel was stirring another cup of coffee as if it required all his concentration. He was eating a very large bun.

Smiley stood beside him. "I've got to go back to London."

"Well, this will put the cat among the pigeons." The weasel face turned abruptly towards him; "or will it?" He spoke with the front of his mouth while the back of it continued to deal with the bun.

"If Fennan was murdered, no power on earth can prevent the Press from getting hold of the story," and to himself added : "I don't think Maston would like that. He'd prefer suicide."

"Still, we've got to face that, haven't we?"

Smiley paused, frowning earnestly. Already he could hear

34

Maston deriding his suspicions, laughing them impatiently away. "I don't know," he said. "I really don't know."

Back to London, he thought, back to Maston's Ideal Home, back to the rat-race of blame. And back to the unreality of containing a human tragedy in a three-page report.

It was raining again, a warm incessant rain now, and in the short distance between the Fountain Café and the police station he got very wet. He took off his coat and threw it into the back of the car. It was a relief to be leaving Walliston—even for London. As he turned on to the main road he saw out of the corner of his eye the figure of Mendel stoically trudging along the pavement towards the station, his grey trilby shapeless and blackened by the rain. It hadn't occurred to Smiley that he might want a lift to London, and he felt ungracious. Mendel, untroubled by the niceties of the situation, opened the passenger door and got in.

"Bit of luck," he observed. "Hate trains. Cambridge Circus you going to? You can drop me Westminster way, can't you?"

They set off and Mendel produced a shabby green tobacco tin and rolled himself a cigarette. He directed it towards his mouth, changed his mind and offered it to Smiley, lighting it for him with an extraordinary lighter that threw a two-inch blue flame. "You look worried sick," said Mendel.

"I am."

There was a pause, Mendel said : "It's the devil you don't know that gets you."

They had driven another four or five miles when Smiley drew the car into the side of the road. He turned to Mendel.

"Would you mind awfully if we drove back to Walliston?"

"Good idea. Go and ask her."

He turned the car and drove slowly back into Walliston, back to Merridale Lane. He left Mendel in the car and walked down the familiar gravel path.

She opened the door and showed him into the drawing room without a word. She was wearing the same dress, and Smiley wondered how she had passed the time since he had left her that morning.

Had she been walking about the house or sitting motionless

in the drawing-room? Or upstairs in the bedroom with the leather chairs? How did she see herself in her new widowhood? Could she take it seriously yet, was she still in that secretly elevated state which immediately follows bereavement? Still looking at herself in mirrors, trying to discern the change, the horror in her own face, and weeping when she could not?

Neither of them sat down—both instinctively avoided a repetition of that morning's meeting.

"There was one thing I felt I must ask you, Mrs. Fennan. I'm very sorry to have to bother you again."

"About the call, I expect; the early morning call from the exchange.

"Yes."

"I thought that might puzzle you. An insomniac asks for an early morning call." She was trying to speak brightly.

"Yes. It did seem odd. Do you often go to the theatre?"

"Yes. Once a fortnight. I'm a member of the Weybridge Repertory Club you know. I try and go to everything they do. I have a seat reserved for me automatically on the first Tuesday of each run. My husband worked late on Tuesdays. He never came; he'd only go to classical theatre."

"But he liked Brecht didn't he? He seemed very thrilled with the 'Berliner Ensemble' performances in London."

She looked at him for a moment, and then smiled suddenly—the first time he had seen her do so. It was an enchanting smile; her whole face lit up like a child's.

Smiley had a fleeting vision of Elsa Fennan as a child— a spindly, agile tomboy like George Sand's 'Petite Fadette'— half woman, half glib, lying girl. He saw her as a wheedling *Backfisch,* fighting like a cat for herself alone, and he saw her too, starved and shrunken in prison camp, ruthless in her fight for self-preservation. It was pathetic to witness in that smile the light of her early innocence, and a steeled weapon in her fight for survival.

"I'm afraid the explanation of that call is very silly," she said. "I suffer from a terrible memory—really awful. Go shopping and forget what I've come to buy, make an appointment on the telephone and forget it the moment I replace the receiver. I ask people to stay the week-end and we are out when they arrive. Occasionally, when there is something I simply have to remember, I ring the exchange and ask for a call a few minutes before the appointed time. It's like a knot in one's handkerchief, but a knot can't ring a bell at you can it?"

Smiley peered at her. His throat felt rather dry, and he had to swallow before he spoke.

"And what was the call for this time, Mrs. Fennan?"

Again the enchanting smile: "There you are. I completely forget."

CHAPTER V

MASTON AND CANDLELIGHT

As he drove slowly back towards London Smiley ceased to be conscious of Mendel's presence.

There had been a time when the mere business of driving a car was a relief to him; when he had found in the unreality of a long, solitary journey a palliative to his troubled brain, when the fatigue of several hours' driving had allowed him to forget more sombre cares.

It was one of the subtler landmarks of middle age, perhaps, that he could no longer thus subdue his mind. It needed sterner measures now: he even tried on occasion to plan in his head a walk through a European city—to record the shops and buildings he would pass, for instance, in Bern on a walk from the Münster to the University. But despite such energetic mental exercise, the ghosts of time present would intrude and drive his dreams away. It was Ann who had robbed him of his peace, Ann who had once made the present so important and taught him the habit of reality, and when she went there was nothing.

He could not believe that Elsa Fennan had killed her husband. Her instinct was to defend, to hoard the treasures of her life, to build about herself the symbols of normal existence. There was no aggression in her, no will but the will to preserve.

But who could tell? What did Hesse write? "Strange to wander in the mist, each is alone. No tree knows his neighbour. Each is alone." We know nothing of one another, nothing, Smiley mused. However closely we live together, at whatever time of day or night we sound the deepest thoughts in one another, we know nothing. How am I judging Elsa Fennan? I think I understand her suffering and her frightened lies, but what do I know of her? Nothing.

Mendel was pointing at a sign-post.

". . . That's where I live. Mitcham. Not a bad spot really Got sick of bachelor quarters. Bought a decent little semi-detached down here. For my retirement."

"Retirement? That's a long way off."

"Yes. Three days. That's why I got this job. Nothing to it; no complications. Give it to old Mendel, he'll muck it up."

"Well, well. I expect we shall both be out of a job by Monday."

He drove Mendel to Scotland Yard and went on to Cambridge Circus.

He realised as he walked into the building that everyone knew. It was the way they looked; some shade of difference in their glance, their attitude. He made straight for Maston's room. Maston's secretary was at her desk and she looked up quickly as he entered.

"Adviser in?"

"Yes. He's expecting you. He's alone. I should knock and go in." But Maston had opened the door and was already calling him. He was wearing a black coat and pinstripe trousers. Here goes the cabaret, thought Smiley.

"I've been trying to get in touch with you. Did you not receive my message?" said Maston.

"I did, but I couldn't possibly have spoken to you."

"I don't quite follow?"

"Well, I don't believe Fennan committed suicide—I think he was murdered. I couldn't say that on the telephone."

Maston took off his spectacles and looked at Smiley in blank astonishment.

"Murdered. Why?"

"Well, Fennan wrote his letter at 10.30 last night, if we are to accept the time on his letter as correct."

"Well?"

"Well, at 7.55 he rang up the exchange and asked to be called at 8.30 the next morning."

"How on earth do you know that?"

"I was there this morning when the exchange rang. I took the call thinking it might be from the Department."

"How can you possibly say that it was Fennan who ordered the call?"

"I had enquiries made. The girl at the exchange knew Fennan's voice well; she was sure it was he, and that he rang at five to eight last night."

"Fennan and the girl knew each other, did they?"

"Good heavens no. They just exchanged pleasantries occasionally."

"And how do you conclude from this that he was murdered?"

"Well I asked his wife about this call . . ."

"And?"

"She lied. Said she ordered it herself. She claimed to be frightfully absent-minded—she gets the exchange to ring her occasionally, like tying a knot in a handkerchief, when she has an important appointment. And another thing—just before shooting himself he made some cocoa. He never drank it."

Maston listened in silence. At last he smiled and got up.

"We seem to be at cross purposes," he said. "I send you down to discover why Fennan shot himself. You come back and say he didn't. We're not policemen, Smiley."

"No. I sometimes wonder what we are."

"Did you hear of anything that affects our position here—anything that explains his action at all? Anything to substantiate the suicide letter?"

Smiley hesitated before replying. He had seen it coming.

"Yes. I understood from Mrs. Fennan that her husband was very upset after the interview." He might as well hear the whole story. "It obsessed him, he couldn't sleep after it. She had to give him a sedative. Her account of Fennan's reaction to my interview entirely substantiates the letter." He was silent for a minute, blinking rather stupidly before him. "What I am trying to say is that I don't believe her. I don't believe Fennan wrote that letter, or that he had any intention of trying." He turned to Maston. "We simply cannot dismiss the inconsistencies. Another thing," he plunged on, "I haven't had an expert comparison made but there's a similarity between the anonymous letter and Fennan's suicide note. The type looks identical. It's ridiculous I know but there it is. We must bring the police in—give them the facts."

"Facts?" said Maston. "What facts? Suppose she did lie—she's an odd woman by all accounts, foreign, Jewish. Heaven knows the tributaries of her mind. I'm told she suffered in the war, persecuted and so forth. She may see in you the oppressor, the inquisitor. She spots you're on to something, panics and tells you the first lie that comes into her head. Does that make her a murderess?"

"Then why did Fennan make the call? Why make himself a nightcap?"

"Who can tell?" Maston's voice was richer now, more persuasive. "If you or I, Smiley, were ever driven to that dreadful point where we were determined to destroy ourselves, who can tell what our last thoughts on earth would be? And what of Fennan? He sees his career in ruins, his life has no meaning. Is it not conceivable that he should wish, in a moment of weakness or irresolution, to hear another human voice, feel again the warmth of human contact before he dies? Fanciful, sentimental, perhaps; but not improbable in a man so overwrought, so obsessed that he takes his own life."

Smiley had to give him credit—it was a good performance and he was no match for Maston when it came to this. Abruptly he felt inside himself the rising panic of frustration beyond endurance. With panic came an uncontrollable fury with this posturing sycophant, this obscene cissy with his greying hair and his reasonable smile. Panic and fury welled up in a sudden tide, flooding his breast, suffusing his whole body. His face felt hot and red, his spectacles blurred, and tears sprang to his eyes, adding to his humiliation.

Maston went on, mercifully unaware : "You cannot expect me to suggest to the Home Secretary on this evidence that the police have reached a false conclusion; you know how tenuous our police liaison is. On the one hand we have your suspicions : that in short Fennan's behaviour last night was not consistent with the intent to die. His wife has apparently lied to you. Against that we have the opinion of trained detectives, who found nothing disturbing in the circumstances of death, and we have Mrs. Fennan's statement that her husband was upset by his interview. I'm sorry, Smiley, but there it is."

There was complete silence. Smiley was slowly recovering himself, and the process left him dull and inarticulate. He peered myopically before him, his pouchy, lined face still pink, his mouth slack and stupid. Maston was waiting for him to speak, but he was tired and suddenly utterly disinterested. Without a glance at Maston he got up and walked out.

He reached his own room and sat down at the desk. Mechanically he looked through his work. His in-tray contained little—some office circulars and a personal letter addressed to G. Smiley Esq., Ministry of Defence. The handwriting was unfamiliar; he opened the envelope and read the letter.

"Dear Smiley,

It is essential that I should lunch with you tomorrow at the Compleat Angler at Marlow. Please do your best to meet me there at one o'clock. There is something I have to tell you.

Yours,
Samuel Fennan."

The letter was handwritten and dated the previous day, Tuesday, 3rd January. It had been postmarked in Whitehall at 6.0 p.m.

He looked at it stodgily for several minutes, holding it stiffly before him and inclining his head to the left. Then he put the letter down, opened a drawer of the desk and took out a single clean sheet of paper. He wrote a brief letter of resignation to Maston, and attached Fennan's invitation with a pin. He pressed the bell for a secretary, left the letter in his out-tray and made for the lift. As usual it was stuck in the basement with the registry's tea trolley, and after a short wait he began walking downstairs. Halfway down he remembered that he had left his mackintosh and a few bits and pieces in his room. Never mind, he thought, they'll send them on.

He sat in his car in the car park, staring through the drenched windscreen.

He didn't care, he just damn well didn't care. He was surprised certainly. Surprised that he had so nearly lost control. Interviews had played a great part in Smiley's life, and he had long ago come to consider himself proof against them all : disciplinary, scholastic, medical and religious. His secretive nature detested the purpose of all interviews, their oppressive intimacy, their inescapable reality. He remembered one deliriously happpy dinner with Ann at Quaglinos when he had described to her the Chameleon-Armadillo system for beating the interviewer.

They had dined by candlelight; white skin and pearls—they were drinking brandy—Ann's eyes wide and moist, only for him; Smiley playing the lover and doing it wonderfully well; Ann loving him and thrilled by their harmony.

". . . and so I learned first to be a chameleon."

"You mean you sat there burping, you rude toad?"

"No, it's a matter of colour. Chameleons change colour."

"Of course they change colour. They sit on green leaves and go green. Did you go green, toad?"

His fingers ran lightly over the tips of hers. "Listen, minx, while I explain the Smiley Chameleon-Armadillo technique for the impertinent interviewer." Her face was very close to his and she adored him with her eyes.

"The technique is based on the theory that the interviewer, loving no one so well as himself, will be attracted by his own image. You therefore assume the exact social, temperamental, political and intellectual colour of your inquisitor."

"Pompous toad. But intelligent lover."

"Silence. Sometimes this method founders against the idiocy or ill-disposition of the inquisitor. If so, become an armadillo."

"And wear linear belts, toad?"

"No, place him in a position so incongruous that you are superior to him. I was prepared for confirmation by a retired bishop. I was his whole flock, and received on one half holiday sufficient guidance for a diocese. But by contemplating the bishop's face, and imagining that under my gaze it became covered in thick fur, I maintained the ascendancy. From then on the skill grew. I could turn him into an ape, get him stuck in sash windows, send him naked to Masonic banquets, condemn him, like the serpent, to go about on his belly. . ."

"*Wicked* lover-toad."

And so it had been. But in his recent interviews with Maston the power of detachment had left him; he was getting too involved. When Maston made the first moves, Smiley had been too tired and disgusted to compete. He supposed Elsa Fennan had killed her husband, that she had some good reason and it just did not bother him any more. The problem no longer existed; suspicion, experience, perception, common sense—for Maston these were not the organs of fact. Paper was fact, Ministers were fact, Home Secretaries were hard fact. The Department did not concern itself with the vague impressions of a single officer when they conflicted with policy.

Smiley was tired, deeply, heavily tired. He drove slowly homewards. Dinner out tonight. Something rather special. It was only lunch-time now—he would spend the afternoon pursuing Olearius across the Russian continent on his Hansa voyage. Then dinner at Quaglinos, and a solitary toast to the successful murderer, to Elsa perhaps, in gratitude for ending the career of George Smiley with the life of Sam Fennan.

He remembered to collect his laundry in Sloane Street, and finally turned into Bywater Street, finding a parking space about three houses down from his own. He got out carrying the brown paper parcel of laundry, locked the car laboriously, and walked all round it from habit, testing the handles. A thin rain was still falling. It annoyed him that someone had parked outside his house again. Thank goodness Mrs. Chapel had closed his bedroom window, otherwise the rain would have . . .

He was suddenly alert. Something had moved in the drawing-room. A light, a shadow, a human form; something, he was certain. Was it sight or instinct? Was it the latent skill of his own tradecraft which informed him? Some fine sense or nerve, some remote faculty of perception warned him now and he heeded the warning.

Without a moment's thought he dropped his keys back into his overcoat pocket, walked up the steps to his own front door and rang the bell.

It echoed shrilly through the house. There was a moment's silence, then came to Smiley's ears the distinct sound of footsteps approaching the door, firm and confident. A scratch of the chain, a click of the Ingersoll latch and the door was opened, swiftly, cleanly.

Smiley had never seen him before. Tall, fair, handsome, thirty-five odd. A light grey suit, white shirt and silver tie——habillé en diplomate. German or Swede. His left hand remained nonchalantly in his jacket pocket.

Smiley peered at him apologetically :

"Good afternoon. Is Mr. Smiley in, please?"

The door was opened to its fullest extent. A tiny pause.

"Yes. Won't you come in?"

For a fraction of a second he hesitated. "No thanks. Would you please give him this?" He handed him the parcel of laundry, walked down the steps again, to his car. He knew he was still being watched. He started the car, turned and drove into Sloane Square without a glance in the direction of his house. He found a parking place in Sloane Street, pulled in and rapidly wrote in his diary seven sets of numbers. They belonged to the seven cars parked along Bywater Street.

What should he do? Stop a policeman? Whoever he was, he was probably gone by now. Besides there were other considerations. He locked the car again and crossed the road to a telephone kiosk. He rang Scotland Yard, got through to Special Branch and asked for Inspector Mendel. But it appeared that the Inspector, having reported back to the Superintendent, had discreetly anticipated the pleasures of retirement and left for Mitcham. Smiley got his address after a good deal of prevarication, and set off once more in his car, covering three sides of a square and emerging at Albert Bridge. He had a sandwich and a large whisky at a new pub overlooking the river and a quarter of an hour later was crossing the bridge on the way to Mitcham, the rain still beating down on his inconspicuous little car. He was worried, very worried indeed.

CHAPTER VI

TEA AND SYMPATHY

It was still raining as he arrived. Mendel was in his garden wearing the most extraordinary hat Smiley had ever seen. It had begun life as an Anzac hat but its enormous brim hung low all the way round, so that he resembled nothing so much as a very tall mushroom. He was brooding over a tree stump, a wicked looking pick-axe poised obediently in his sinewy right hand.

He looked at Smiley sharply for a moment, then a grin slowly crossed his thin face as he extended his hand.

"Trouble," said Mendel.

"Trouble."

Smiley followed him up the path and into the house. Suburban and comfortable.

"There's no fire in the living-room—only just got back. How about a cup of tea in the kitchen?"

They went into the kitchen. Smiley was amused to notice the extreme tidiness, the almost feminine neatness of everything about him. Only the police calendar on the wall spoilt the illusion. While Mendel put a kettle on and busied himself with cups and saucers, Smiley related dispassionately what had happened in Bywater Street. When he had finished Mendel looked at him for a long time in silence.

"But why did he ask you in?"

Smiley blinked and coloured a little. "That's what I wondered. It put me off my balance for a moment. It was lucky I had the parcel."

He took a drink of tea. "Though I don't believe he was taken in by the parcel. He may have been, but I doubt it. I doubt it very much."

"Not taken in?"

"Well, I wouldn't have been. Little man in a Ford delivering parcels of linen. Who could I have been? Besides, I asked for Smiley and then didn't want to see him—he must have thought that was pretty queer."

"But what was he after? What would he have done with you? Who did he think you were?"

"That's just the point, that's just it, you see. I think it was me he was waiting for, but of course he didn't expect me to ring the bell. I put him off balance. I think he wanted to kill me. That's why he asked me in : he recognised me but only just, probably from a photograph."

Mendel looked at him in silence for a while.

"Christ," he said.

"Suppose I'm right," Smiley continued, "all the way. Suppose Fennan *was* murdered last night and I *did* nearly follow him this morning. Well, unlike your trade, mine doesn't normally run to a murder a day."

"Meaning what?"

"I don't know. I just don't know. Perhaps before we go much further you'd check on these cars for me. They were parked in Bywater Street this morning."

"Why not do it yourself?"

Smiley looked at him, puzzled, for a second. Then it dawned on him that he hadn't mentioned his resignation.

"Sorry. I didn't tell you, did I? I resigned this morning. Just managed to get it in before I was sacked. So I'm free as air. And about as employable."

Mendel took the list of numbers from him and went into the hall to telephone. He returned a couple of minutes later.

"They'll ring back in an hour," he said. "Come on. I'll show you round the estate. Know anything about bees, do you?"

"Well, a very little, yes. I got bitten with the natural history bug at Oxford." He was going to tell Mendel how he had wrestled with Goethe's metamorphoses of plants and animals in the hope of discovering, like Faust, "what sustains the world at its inmost point". He wanted to explain why it was impossible to understand nineteenth-century Europe without a working knowledge of the naturalistic sciences, he felt earnest and full of important thoughts, and knew secretly that this was because his brain was wrestling with the day's events, that he was in a state of nervous excitement. The palms of his hands were moist.

Mendel led him out of the back door: three neat beehives stood against the low brick wall which ran along the end of the garden. Mendel spoke as they stood in the fine rain:

"Always wanted to keep them, see what it's all about. Been reading it all up—frightens me stiff, I can tell you. Odd little beggars." He nodded a couple of times in support of this statement, and Smiley looked at him again with interest. His face was thin but muscular, its expression entirely uncommunicative; his iron grey hair was cut very short and spiky. He seemed quite indifferent to the weather, and the weather to him. Smiley knew exactly the life that lay behind Mendel, had seen in policemen all over the world the same leathern skin, the same reserves of patience, bitterness and anger. He could guess the long, fruitless hours of surveillance in every kind of weather, waiting for someone who might never come ... or come and go too quickly. And he knew how much Mendel and the rest of them were at the mercy of personalities—capricious and bullying, nervous and changeful, occasionally wise and sympathetic. He knew how intelligent men could be broken by the stupidity of their superiors, how weeks of patient work night and day could be cast aside by such a man.

Mendel led him up the precarious path laid with broken stone to the beehives and, still oblivious of the rain, began taking one to pieces, demonstrating and explaining. He spoke in jerks, with quite long pauses between phrases, indicating precisely and slowly with his slim fingers.

At last they went indoors again, and Mendel showed him the two downstairs rooms. The drawing-room was all flowers : flowered curtains and carpet, flowered covers on the furniture. In a small cabinet in one corner were some Toby jugs and a pair of very handsome pistols beside a cup for target shooting.

Smiley followed him upstairs. There was a smell of paraffin from the stove on the landing, and a surly bubbling from the cistern in the lavatory.

Mendel showed him his own bedroom.

"Bridal chamber. Bought the bed at a sale for a quid. Box spring mattress. Amazing what you can pick up. Carpets are ex-Queen Elizabeth. They change them every year. Bought them at a store in Watford."

Smiley stood in the doorway, somehow rather embarrassed. Mendel turned back and passed him to open the other bedroom door.

"And that's your room. If you want it." He turned to Smiley. "I wouldn't stay at your place tonight if I were you. You never know, do you? Besides, you'll sleep better here. Air's better."

Smiley began to protest.

"Up to you. You do what you like." Mendel grew surly and embarrassed. "Don't understand your job, to be honest, any more than you know police work. You do what you like. From what I've seen of you, you can look after yourself."

They went downstairs again. Mendel had lit the gas fire in the drawing-room.

"Well, at least you must let me give you dinner tonight," said Smiley.

The telephone rang in the hall. It was Mendel's secretary about the car numbers.

Mendel came back. He handed Smiley a list of seven names and addresses. Four of the seven could be discounted; the registered addresses were in Bywater Street. Three remained : a hired car from the firm of Adam Scarr and Sons of Battersea, a trade van belonging to the Severn Tile Company, Eastbourne; and the third was listed specially as the property of the Panamanian Ambassador.

"I've got a man on the Panamanian job now. There'll be no difficulty there—they've only got three cars on the Embassy strength.

"Battersea's not far," Mendel continued. "We could pop over there together. In your car."

"By all means, by all means," Smiley said quickly; "and we can go in to Kensington for dinner. I'll book a table at the 'Entrechat'."

It was four o'clock. They sat for a while talking in a rather desultory way about bees and house-keeping, Mendel quite at ease and Smiley still bothered and awkward, trying to find a way of talking, trying not to be clever. He could guess what Ann would have said about Mendel. She would have loved him, made a person of him, had a special voice and face for imitating him, would have made a story of him until he fitted into their lives and wasn't a mystery any more : "Darling, who'd have thought he could be so *cosy*! The last man I'd ever thought would tell me where to buy cheap fish. And what a darling little house—*no bother*—he must know Toby jugs are hell and he just doesn't care. I think he's a pet. Toad, do ask him to dinner. You must. Not to giggle at but to *like*."

He wouldn't have asked him, of course, but Ann would be content—she'd found a way to like him. And having done so, forgotten him.

That was what Smiley wanted, really—a way to like Mendel. He was not as quick as Ann at finding one. But Ann was Ann—she practically murdered an Etonian nephew once for drinking claret with fish, but if Mendel had lit a pipe over her *crêpe suzette*, she probably would not have noticed.

Mendel made more tea and they drank it. At about a quarter past five they set off for Battersea in Smiley's car. On the way Mendel bought an evening paper. He read it with difficulty, catching the light from the street lamps. After a few minutes he spoke with sudden venom :

"Krauts. *Bloody* Krauts. God, I hate them !"

"Krauts?"

"Krauts. Huns, Jerries. Bloody Germans. Wouldn't give you sixpence for the lot of them. Carnivorous ruddy sheep. Kicking Jews about again. Us all over. Knock 'em down, set 'em up. Forgive and forget. *Why* bloody well forget, I'd like to know? Why forget theft, murder and rape just because millions committed it? Christ, one poor little sod of a bank clerk pinches ten bob and the whole of the Metropolitan's on to him. But Krupp and all that mob—oh no. Christ, if I was a Jew in Germany I'd . . ."

Smiley was suddenly wide awake : "What would you do? What would you do, Mendel?"

"Oh, I suppose I'd sit down under it. It's statistics now, politics. It isn't sense to give them H-bombs so it's politics. And there's the Yanks—millions of ruddy Jews in America. What do they do? Damn all : give the Krauts more bombs. All chums together—blow each other up."

Mendel was trembling with rage, and Smiley was silent for a while, thinking of Elsa Fennan.

"What's the answer?" he asked, just for something to say.

"Christ knows," said Mendel savagely.

They turned into Battersea Bridge Road and drew up beside a constable standing on the pavement. Mendel showed his Police card.

"Scarr's garage? Well it isn't hardly a garage, sir, just a yard. Scrap metal he handles mostly, and second-hand cars. If they won't do for one they'll do for the other, that's what Adam says. You want to go down Prince of Wales Drive till you come to the hospital. It's tucked in there between a couple of pre-fabs. Bomb site it is really. Old Adam straightened it out with some cinders and no one's ever moved him."

"You seem to know a lot about him," said Mendel.

"I should do, I've run him in a few times. There's not much in the book that Adam hasn't been up to. He's one of our hardy perennials, Scarr is."

"Well, well. Anything on him at present?"

"Couldn't say, sir. But you can have him any time for illegal betting. And Adam's practically under the Act already."

They drove towards Battersea Hospital. The park on their right looked black and hostile behind the street lamps.

"What's under the Act?" asked Smiley.

"Oh, he's only joking. It means your record's so long you're eligible for Preventive Detention—years of it. He sounds like my type," Mendel continued. "Leave him to me."

They found the yard as the constable had described, between two dilapidated pre-fabs in an uncertain row of hutments erected on the bomb site. Rubble, clinker and refuse lay everywhere. Bits of asbestos, timber and old iron, presumably acquired by Mr. Scarr for resale or adaptation, were piled in a corner, dimly lit by the pale glow which came from the farther pre-fab. The two men looked round them in silence for a moment. Then Mendel shrugged, put two fingers in his mouth and whistled shrilly.

"Scarr!" he called. Silence. The outside light on the far pre-fab went on, and three or four pre-war cars in various stages of dilapidation became dimly discernible.

The door opened slowly and a girl of about twelve stood on the threshold.

"Your dad in, dear?" asked Mendel.

"Nope. Gone to the Prod, I 'spect."

"Righto, dear. Thanks."

They walked back to the road.

"What on earth's the Prod, or daren't I ask?" said Smiley.

"Prodigal's Calf. Pub round the corner. We can walk it—only a hundred yards. Leave the car here."

It was only just after opening time. The public bar was empty, and as they waited for the landlord to appear the door swung open and a very fat man in a black suit came in. He walked straight to the bar and hammered on it with a half-crown.

"Wilf," he shouted; "Take your finger out, you got customers, you lucky boy." He turned to Smiley; "Good evening, friend."

From the rear of the pub a voice replied: "Tell 'em to leave their money on the counter and come back later."

The fat man looked at Mendel and Smiley blankly for a moment, then suddenly let out a peal of laughter: "Not them, Wilf—they're busies!" The joke appealed to him so much that he was finally compelled to sit on the bench that ran along the side of the room, with his hands on his knees, his huge shoulders heaving with laughter, the tears running down his cheeks. Occasionally he said "Oh dear, oh dear," as he caught his breath before another outburst.

Smiley looked at him with interest. He wore a very dirty stiff white collar with rounded edges, a flowered red tie carefully pinned outside the black waistcoat, army boots and a shiny black suit, very threadbare and without a vestige of a crease in the trousers. His shirt cuffs were black with sweat, grime and motor oil and held in place by paper-clips twisted into a knot.

The landlord appeared and took their orders. The stranger bought a large whisky and ginger wine and took it at once to the saloon bar, where there was a coal fire. The landlord watched with disapproval.

"That's him all over, mean sod. Won't pay saloon prices, but likes the fire."

"Who is he?" asked Mendel.

"Him? Scarr his name is. Adam Scarr. Christ knows why Adam. See him in the Garden of Eden : bloody grotesque, that's what it is. They say round here that if Eve gave him an apple he'd eat the ruddy core." The landlord sucked his teeth and shook his head. Then he shouted to Scarr : "Still, you're good for business, aren't you, Adam? They come bloody miles to see you, don't they? Teenage monster from outer space, that's what you are. Come and see. Adam Scarr : one look and you'll sign the pledge."

More hilarious laughter. Mendel leant over to Smiley. "You go and wait in the car—you're better out of this. Got a fiver?"

Smiley gave him five pounds from his wallet, nodded his agreement and walked out. He could imagine nothing more frightful than dealing with Scarr.

"You Scarr?" said Mendel.

"Friend, you are correct."

"TRX 0891. That your car?"

Mr. Scarr frowned at his whisky and ginger. The question seemed to sadden him.

"Well?" said Mendel.

"She was, squire, she was."

"What the hell do you mean?"

Scarr raised his right hand a few inches then let it gently fall. "Dark waters, squire, murky waters."

"Listen, I've got bigger fish to fry than ever you dreamed of. I'm not made of glass, see? I couldn't care bloody less about your racket. Where's that car?"

Scarr appeared to consider this speech on its merits. "I see the light, friend. You wish, for information."

"Of course I bloody well do."

"These are hard times, squire. The cost of living, dear boy, is a rising star. Information is an item, a saleable item, is it not?"

"You tell me who hired that car and you won't starve."

"I don't starve now, friend. I want to eat better."

53

"A fiver."

Scarr finished his drink and replaced his glass noisily on the table. Mendel got up and bought him another.

"It was pinched," said Scarr. "I had it a few years for self-drive, see. For the deepo."

"The *what*?"

"The deepo—the deposit. Bloke wants a car for a day. You take twenty quid deposit in notes, right? When he comes back he owes you forty bob, see? You give him a cheque for thirty-eight quid, show it on your books as a loss and the job's worth a tenner. Got it?"

Mendel nodded.

"Well, three weeks ago a bloke come in. Tall Scotsman. Well-to-do, he was. Carried a stick. He paid the deepo, took the car, and I never see him nor the car again. Robbery."

"Why not report it to the police?"

Scarr paused and drank from his glass. He looked at Mendel sadly.

"Many factors would argue against, squire."

"Meaning you'd pinched it yourself?"

Scarr looked shocked. "I have since heard distressing rumours about the party from which I obtained the vehicle. I will say no more," he added piously.

"When you rented him the car he filled in forms, didn't he? Insurance, receipt and so on? Where are they?"

"False, all false. He gave me an address in Ealing. I went there and it didn't exist. I have no doubt the name was also fictitious."

Mendel screwed the money into a roll in his pocket, and handed it across the table to Scarr. Scarr unfolded it and, quite unselfconscious, counted it in full view of anyone who cared to look.

"I know where to find you," said Mendel; "and I know a few things about you. If that's a load of cock you've sold me I'll break your bloody neck."

It was raining again and Smiley wished he had brought a

hat. He crossed the road, entered the side street which accommodated Mr. Scarr's establishment and walked towards the car. There was no one in the street, and it was oddly quiet. Two hundred yards down the road Battersea General Hospital, small and neat, shed multiple beams of light from its uncurtained windows. The pavement was very wet and the echo of his own footsteps was crisp and startling.

He drew level with the first of the two pre-fabs which bordered Scarr's yard. A car was parked in the yard with its sidelights on. Curious, Smiley turned off the street and walked towards it. It was an old MG saloon, green probably, or that brown they went in for before the war. The number-plate was barely lit, and caked in mud. He stooped to read it, tracing the letters with his forefinger : TRX 0891. Of course—that was one of the numbers he had written down this morning.

He heard a footstep behind him and stood up, half turning. He had begun to raise his arm as the blow fell.

It was a terrible blow—it seemed to split his skull in two. As he fell he could feel the warm blood running freely over his left ear. "Not again, oh Christ, not again," thought Smiley. But he hardly felt the rest—just a vision of his own body, far away, being slowly broken like rock; cracked and split into fragments, then nothing. Nothing but the warmth of his own blood as it ran over his face into the cinders, and far away the beating of the stonebreakers. But not here. Far away.

CHAPTER VII

MR. SCARR'S STORY

MENDEL LOOKED AT him and wondered whether he was dead. He emptied the pockets of his own overcoat and laid it gently over Smiley's shoulders, then he ran, ran like a madman towards the hospital, crashed through the swing-doors of the out-patients' department into the bright, twenty-four hour interior of the hospital. A young coloured doctor was on duty. Mendel showed him his card, shouted something to him, took him by the arm, tried to lead him down the road. The doctor smiled patiently, shook his head and telephoned for an ambulance.

Mendel ran back down the road and waited. A few minutes later the ambulance arrived and skilful men gathered Smiley up and took him away.

"Bury him," thought Mendel; "I'll make the bastard pay."

He stood there for a moment, staring down at the wet patch of mud and cinders where Smiley had fallen; the red glow of the car's rear lights showed him nothing. The ground had been hopelessly churned by the feet of the ambulance men and a few inhabitants from the pre-fabs who had come and gone like shadowy vultures. Trouble was about. They didn't like trouble.

"Bastard," Mendel hissed, and walked slowly back towards the pub.

The saloon bar was filling up. Scarr was ordering another drink. Mendel took him by the arm. Scarr turned and said:

"Hello, friend, back again. Have a little of what killed Auntie."

"Shut up," said Mendel; "I want another word with you. Come outside."

Mr. Scarr shook his head and sucked his teeth sympathetically.

"Can't be done, friend, can't be done. Company." He indicated with his head an eighteen-year-old blonde with off-white lipstick and an improbable bosom, who sat quite motionless at a corner table. Her painted eyes had a permanently startled look.

"Listen," whispered Mendel; "in just two seconds I'll tear your bloody ears off, you lying sod."

Scarr consigned his drinks to the care of the landlord and made a slow, dignified exit. He didn't look at the girl.

Mendel led him across the street towards the pre-fabs. The side lights of Smiley's car shone towards them eighty yards down the road.

They turned into the yard. The MG was still there. Mendel had Scarr firmly by the arm, ready if necessary to force the forearm back and upwards, breaking or dislocating the shoulder joint.

"Well, well," cried Scarr with apparent delight; "she's returned to the bosom of her ancestors."

"Stolen, was it?" said Mendel. "Stolen by a tall Scotsman with a walking stick and an address in Ealing. Decent of him to bring it back, wasn't it. Friendly gesture, after all this time. You've mistaken your bloody market, Scarr." Mendel was shaking with anger. "And why are the side lights on? Open the door."

Scarr turned to Mendel in the dark, his free hand slapping his pockets in search of keys. He extracted a bunch of three or four, felt through them and finally unlocked the car door. Mendel got in, found the passenger light in the roof and switched it on. He began methodically to search the inside of the car. Scarr stood outside and waited.

He searched quickly but thoroughly. Glove tray, seats, floor, rear window-ledge: nothing. He slipped his hand inside the map pocket on the passenger door, and drew out a map and an envelope. The envelope was long and flat, grey-blue in colour with a linen finish. Continental, thought Mendel. There was no writing on it. He tore it open. There were ten used five-pound notes inside and a piece of plain postcard. Mendel held it to the light and read the message printed on it with a ball-point pen:

"FINISHED NOW. SELL IT."

There was no signature.

He got out of the car, and seized Scarr by the elbows. Scarr stepped back quickly. "What's your problem, friend?" he asked.

Mendel spoke softly. "It's not my problem, Scarr, it's yours. The biggest bloody problem you ever had. Conspiracy to murder, attempted murder, offences under the Official Secrets Act. And you can add to that contravention of the Road Traffic Act, conspiracy to defraud the Inland Revenue and about fifteen other charges that will occur to me while you nurse your problem on a cell bed."

"Just a minute, copper, let's not go over the moon. What's the story? Who the hell's talking about murder?"

"Listen, Scarr, you're a little man, come in on the fringe of the big spenders, aren't you. Well now you're the big spender. I reckon it'll cost you fifteen years."

"Look, shut up, will you."

"No I won't, little man. You're caught between two big ones, see, and you're the mug. And what will I do? I'll bloody well laugh myself sick while you rot in the Scrubs and contemplate your fat belly. See that hospital, do you? There's a bloke dying there, murdered by your tall Scotsman. They found him half an hour ago bleeding like a pig in your yard. There's another one dead in Surrey, and for all I know there's one in every bloody home county. So it's your problem, you poor sod, not mine. Another thing—you're the only one who knows who he is, aren't you? He might want to tidy that up a bit, mightn't he?"

Scarr walked slowly round to the other side of the car. "Get in, copper," he said.

Mendel sat in the driving seat and unlocked the passenger door from the inside. Scarr sat himself beside him. They didn't put the light on.

"I'm in a nice way of business round here," said Scarr quietly, "and the pickings is small but regular. Or was till this bloke come along."

"What bloke?"

"Bit by bit, copper. don't rush me. That was four years ago. I didn't believe in Father Christmas till I met him. Dutch, he said he was, in the diamond business. I'm not pretending I thought he was straight, see, because you're not barmy and nor am I. I never asked what he done and he never told me, but I guessed it was smuggling. Money to burn he had, came off him like leaves in autumn. 'Scarr,' he said; 'you're a man of business. I don't like publicity, never did, and I hear we're birds of a feather. I want a car. Not to keep, but to borrow.' He didn't put it quite like that because of the lingo, but that's the sense of it. 'What's your proposition?' I says. 'Let's have a proposition.'

" 'Well,' he says; 'I'm shy. I want a car that no one can ever get on to, supposing I had an accident. Buy a car for me, Scarr, a nice old car with something under the bonnet. Buy it in your own name,' he says, 'and keep it wrapped up for me. There's five hundred quid for a start, and twenty quid a month for garaging. And there's a bonus, Scarr, for every day I take it out. But I'm shy, see, and you don't know me. That's what the money's for,' he says. 'It's for not knowing me.'

"I'll never forget that day. Raining cats and dogs it was, and me bent over an old taxi I'd got off a bloke in Wandsworth. I owed a bookie forty quid, and the coppers were sensitive about a car I'd bought on the never never and flogged in Clapham."

Mr. Scarr drew breath, and let it out again with an air of comic resignation.

"And there he was, standing over me like my own conscience, showering old singles on me like used tote tickets."

"What did he look like?" asked Mendel.

"Quite young he was. Tall, fair chap. But cool—cool as charity. I never saw him after that day. He sent me letters posted in London and typed on plain paper. Just 'Be ready

Monday night', 'Be ready Thursday night', and so on. We had it all arranged. I left the car out in the yard, full of petrol and teed up. He never said when he'd be back. Just ran it in about closing time or later, leaving the lights on and the doors locked. He'd put a couple of quid in the map pocket for each day he'd been away."

"What happened if anything went wrong, if you got pinched for something else?"

"We had a telephone number. He told me to ring and ask for a name."

"What name?"

"He told me to choose one. I chose Blondie. He didn't think that was very funny but we stuck to it. Primrose 0098."

"Did you ever use it?"

"Yes, a couple of years ago I took a bint to Margate for ten days. I thought I'd better let him know. A girl answered the 'phone—Dutch too, by the sound of her. She said Blondie was in Holland, and she'd take a message. But after that I didn't bother."

"Why not?"

"I began to notice, see. He came regular once a fortnight, the first and third Tuesdays except January and February. This was the first January he come. He brought the car back Thursday usually. Odd him coming back tonight. But this is the end of him, isn't it?" Scarr held in his enormous hand the piece of postcard he had taken from Mendel.

"Did he miss at all? Away long periods?"

"Winters he kept away more. January he never come, nor February. Like I said."

Mendel still had the £50 in his hand. He tossed them into Scarr's lap.

"Don't think you're lucky. I wouldn't be in your shoes for ten times that lot. I'll be back."

Mr. Scarr seemed worried.

"I wouldn't have peached," he said; "but I don't want to be mixed up in nothing, see. Not if the old country's going to suffer, eh, squire?"

"Oh, shut up," said Mendel. He was tired. He took the postcard back, got out of the car and walked away towards the hospital.

There was no news at the hospital. Smiley was still unconscious. The C.I.D. had been informed. Mendel would do better to leave his name and address and go home. The hospital would telephone as soon as they had any news. After a good deal of argument Mendel obtained from the sister the key to Smiley's car.

Mitcham, he decided, was a lousy place to live.

CHAPTER VIII

REFLECTIONS IN A HOSPITAL WARD

He hated the bed as a drowning man hates the sea. He hated the sheets that imprisoned him so that he could move neither hand nor foot.

And he hated the room because it frightened him. There was a trolley by the door with instruments on it, scissors, bandages and bottles, strange objects that carried the terror of the unknown, swathed in white linen for the last Communion. There were jugs, tall ones half covered with napkins, standing like white eagles waiting to tear at his entrails, little glass ones with rubber tubing coiled inside them like snakes. He hated everything, and he was afraid. He was hot and the sweat ran off him, he was cold and the sweat held him, trickling over his ribs like cold blood. Night and day alternated without recognition from Smiley. He fought a relentless battle against sleep, for when he closed his eyes they seemed to turn inwards on the chaos of his brain; and when sometimes by sheer weight his eyelids drew themselves together he would summon all his strength to tear them apart and stare again at the pale light wavering somewhere above him.

Then came a blessed day when someone must have drawn the blinds and let in the grey winter light. He heard the sound of traffic outside and knew at last that he would live.

So the problem of dying once more became an academic one—a debt he would postpone until he was rich and could pay in his own way. It was a luxurious feeling, almost of purity. His mind was wonderfully lucid, ranging like Prometheus over his whole world; where had he heard that : "the mind becomes separated from the body, rules a paper kingdom . . ."? He was bored by the light above him, and wished there was more to look at. He was bored by the grapes, the smell of honeycomb and flowers, the chocolates. He wanted books, and literary journals; how could he keep up with his reading if they gave him no books? There was so little research done on his period as it was, so little creative criticism on the seventeenth century.

It was three weeks before Mendel was allowed to see him. He walked in holding a new hat and carrying a book about bees. He put his hat on the end of the bed and the book on the bedside table. He was grinning.

"I bought you a book," he said; "about bees. They're clever little beggars. Might interest you."

He sat on the edge of the bed. "I got a new hat. Daft really. Celebrate my retirement."

"Oh yes, I forgot. You're on the shelf too." They both laughed, and were silent again.

Smiley blinked. "I'm afraid you're not very distinct at the moment. I'm not allowed to wear my old glasses. They're getting me some new ones." He paused. "You don't know who did this to me, do you?"

"May do. Depends. Got a lead, I think. I don't know enough, that's the trouble. About your job, I mean. Does the East German Steel Mission mean anything to you?"

"Yes, I think so. It came here four years ago to try and get a foot in the Board of Trade."

Mendel gave an account of his transactions with Mr. Scarr. "... Said he was Dutch. The only way Scarr had of getting in touch with him was by ringing a Primrose telephone number. I checked the subscriber. Listed as the East German Steel Mission, in Belsize Park. I sent a bloke to sniff round. They've cleared out. Nothing there at all, no furniture, nothing. Just the telephone, and that's been ripped out of its socket."

"When did they go?"

"3rd January. Same day as Fennan was murdered." He looked at Smiley quizzically. Smiley thought for a minute and said :

"Get hold of Peter Guillam at the Ministry of Defence and bring him here tomorrow. By the scruff of the neck."

Mendel picked up his hat and walked to the door.

"Goodbye," said Smiley; "thank you for the book."

"See you tomorrow," said Mendel, and left.

Smiley lay back in bed. His head was aching. Damn, he thought, I never thanked him for the honey. It had come from Fortnums, too.

Why the early morning call? That was what puzzled him more than anything. It was silly, really, Smiley supposed, but of all the unaccountables in the case, that worried him most.

Elsa Fennan's explanation had been so stupid, so noticeably unlikely. Ann, yes; she would make the exchange stand on its head if she'd felt like it, but not Elsa Fennan. There was nothing in that alert, intelligent little face, nothing in her total independence to support the ludicrous claim to absent-mindedness. She could have said the exchange had made a mistake, had called the wrong day, anything. Fennan, yes; he had been absent-minded. It was one of the odd inconsistencies about Fennan's character which had emerged in the enquiries before the interview. A voracious reader of Westerns and a passionate chess player, a musician and a spare time philosopher, a deep thinking man—but absent-minded. There had been a frightful row once about him taking some secret papers out of the Foreign Office, and it turned out that he had put them in his despatch case with his *Times* and the evening paper before going home to Walliston.

Had Elsa Fennan, in her panic, taken upon herself the mantle of her husband? Or the *motive* of her husband? Had Fennan asked for the call to remind *him* of something, and had Elsa borrowed the motive? Then what did Fennan need to be reminded of—and what did his wife so strenuously wish to conceal?

Samuel Fennan. The new world and the old met in him. The eternal Jew, cultured, cosmopolitan, self-determinate, industrious and perceptive : to Smiley, immensely attractive. The child of his century; persecuted, like Elsa, and driven from his adopted Germany to University in England. By the sheer weight of his ability he had pushed aside disadvantage and prejudice, finally to enter the Foreign Office. It had been a remarkable achievement, owed to nothing but his own brilliance. And if he was a little conceited, a little disinclined to bide the decision of minds more pedestrian than his own, who could blame him? There had been some embarrassment when Fennan pronounced himself in favour of a divided Germany, but it had all blown over, he had been transferred to an Asian desk, and the affair was forgotten. For the rest, he had been generous to a fault, and popular both in Whitehall and in Surrey, where he devoted several hours each week-end to charity work. His great love was skiing. Every year he took all his leave at once and spent six weeks in Switzerland or Austria. He had visited Germany only once, Smiley remembered—with his wife about four years ago.

It had been natural enough that Fennan should join the Left at Oxford. It was the great honeymoon period of University communism, and its causes, heaven knows, lay close enough to his heart. The rise of Fascism in Germany and Italy, the Japanese invasion of Manchuria, the Franco rebellion in Spain, the slump in America, and above all the wave of anti-Semitism that was sweeping across Europe : it was inevitable that Fennan should seek an outlet for his anger and revulsion. Besides, the Party was respectable then; the failure of the Labour Party and the Coalition Government had convinced many intellectuals that the Communists alone could provide an effective alternative to Capitalism and Fascism. There was the excitement, an air of conspiracy and comradeship which must have appealed to the flamboyance in Fennan's character and given him comfort in his loneliness. There was talk of going to Spain; some *had* gone, like Cornford from Cambridge, never to return.

Smiley could imagine Fennan in those days—volatile and earnest, no doubt bringing to his companions the experience of real suffering, a veteran among cadets. His parents had died—his father had been a banker with the foresight to keep a small account in Switzerland. There had not been much, but enough to see him through Oxford, and protect him from the cold wind of poverty.

Smiley remembered so well that interview with Fennan; one among many, yet different. Different because of the language. Fennan was so articulate, so quick, so sure. "Their greatest day," he had said, "was when the miners came. They came from the Rhondda, you know, and to the comrades it seemed the spirit of Freedom had come down with them from the hills. It was a hunger march. It never seemed to occur to the Group that the marchers might actually *be* hungry, but it occurred to me. We hired a truck and the girls made stew —tons of it. We got the meat cheap from a sympathetic butcher in the market. We drove the truck out to meet them. They ate the stew and marched on. They didn't like us really you know, didn't trust us." He laughed. "They were so small —that's what I remember best—small and dark like elves. We hoped they'd sing and they did. But not for us—for themselves. That was the first time I had met Welshmen.

"It made me understand my own race better, I think— I'm a Jew, you know."

Smiley had nodded.

"They didn't know what to do when the Welshmen had gone. What do you do when a dream has come true? They realised then why the Party didn't much care about intellectuals. I think they felt cheap, mostly, and ashamed. Ashamed of their beds and their rooms, their full bellies and their clever essays. Ashamed of their talents and their humour. They were always saying how Keir Hardie taught himself shorthand with a piece of chalk on the coal face, you know. They were ashamed of having pencils and paper. But it's no good just throwing them away, is it? That's what I learnt in the end. That's why I left the Party, I suppose."

Smiley wanted to ask him how Fennan himself had felt, but Fennan was talking again. He had shared nothing with them, he had come to realise that. They were not men, but children, who dreamed of freedom-fires, gipsy music and one world tomorrow, who rode on white horses across the Bay of Biscay or with a child's pleasure bought beer for starving elves from Wales; children who had no power to resist the Eastern sun, and obediently turned their tousled heads towards it. They loved each other and believed they loved mankind, they fought each other and believed they fought the world.

Soon he found them comic and touching. To him, they might as well have knitted socks for soldiers. The disproportion between the dream and reality drove him to a close examination of both; he put all his energy into philosophical and historical reading, and found, to his surprise, comfort and peace in the intellectual purity of Marxism. He feasted on its intellectual ruthlessness, was thrilled by its fearlessness, its academic reversal of traditional values. In the end it was this and not the Party that gave him strength in his solitude, a philosophy which exacted total sacrifice to an unassailable formula, which humiliated and inspired him; and when he finally found success, prosperity and integration, he turned his back sadly upon it as a treasure he had outgrown and must leave at Oxford with the days of his youth.

This was how Fennan had described it and Smiley had understood. It was scarcely the story of anger and resentment that Smiley had come to expect in such interviews, but (perhaps because of that) it seemed more real. There was another thing about that interview : Smiley's conviction that Fennan had left something important unsaid.

Was there any *factual* connection between the incident in Bywater Street and Fennan's death? Smiley reproached himself for being carried away. Seen in perspective, there was nothing but the sequence of events to suggest that Fennan and Smiley were part of a single problem.

The sequence of events, that is, and the weight of Smiley's intuition, experience or what you will—the extra sense that had told him to ring the bell and not use his key, the sense that did not, however, warn him that a murderer stood in the night with a piece of lead piping.

The interview had been informal, that was true. The walk in the park reminded him more of Oxford than of Whitehall. The walk in the park, the café in Millbank—yes, there had been a procedural difference too, but what did it amount to? An official of the Foreign Office walking in the park, talking earnestly with an anonymous little man . . . Unless the little man was *not* anonymous!

Smiley took a paper-back book and began to write in pencil on the fly-leaf:

"Let us assume what is by no means proven: that the murder of Fennan and the attempted murder of Smiley *are* related. What circumstances connected Smiley with Fennan *before* Fennan's death?

1. Before the interview on Monday, 2nd January, I had never met Fennan. I read his file at the Department and I had certain preliminary enquiries made.
2. On 2nd January I went alone to the Foreign Office by taxi. The F.O. arranged the interview, but did not, repeat not, know in advance who would conduct it. Fennan therefore had no prior knowledge of my identity, nor had anyone else outside the Department.
3. The interview fell into two parts; the first at the F.O., when people wandered through the room and took no notice of us at all, the second outside when anyone could have seen us."

What followed? Nothing, unless . .

Yes, that was the only possible conclusion : unless whoever saw them together recognised not only Fennan but Smiley as well, and was violently opposed to their association.

Why? In what way was Smiley dangerous? His eyes suddenly opened very wide. Of course—in one way, in one way only—*as a security officer*.

He put down his pencil.

And so whoever killed Sam Fennan was anxious that he should not talk to a security officer. Someone in the Foreign Office, perhaps, But essentially someone who knew Smiley too. Someone Fennan had known at Oxford, known as a communist, someone who feared exposure, who thought that Fennan would talk, had talked already, perhaps? And if he had talked already then of course Smiley would have to be killed—killed quickly before he could put in his report.

That would explain the murder of Fennan and the assault on Smiley. It made some sense, but not much. He had built a card-house as high as it would go, and he still had cards in his hand. What about Elsa, her lies, her complicity, her fear? What about the car and the 8.30 call? What about the anonymous letter? If the murderer was frightened of contact between Smiley and Fennan, he would scarcely call attention to Fennan by denouncing him. Who then? Who?

He lay back and closed his eyes. His head was throbbing again. Perhaps Peter Guillam could help. He was the only hope. His head was going round. It hurt terribly.

CHAPTER IX

TIDYING UP

Mᴇɴᴅᴇʟ sʜᴏᴡᴇᴅ Pᴇᴛᴇʀ Gᴜɪʟʟᴀᴍ into the ward, grinning hugely.

"Got him," he said.

The conversation was awkward; strained for Guillam at least, by the recollection of Smiley's abrupt resignation and the incongruity of meeting in a hospital ward. Smiley was wearing a blue bedjacket, his hair was spiky and untidy above the bandages and he still had the trace of a heavy bruise on his left temple.

After a particularly awkward pause, Smiley said: "Look, Peter, Mendel's told you what happened to me. You're the expert—what do we know about the East German Steel Mission?"

"Pure as the driven snow, dear boy, except for their sudden departure. Only about three men and a dog in the thing. They hung out in Hampstead somewhere. No one quite knew why they were here when they first came but they've done quite a decent job in the last four years."

"What are their terms of reference?"

"God knows. I think they thought when they arrived that they were going to persuade the Board of Trade to break the European steel rings, but they got the cold shoulder. Then they went in for consular stuff with the accent on machine tools and finished products, exchange of industrial and technical information and so on. Nothing to do with what they came for but rather more acceptable, I gather."

"Who were they?"

"Oh—couple of technicians—Professor Doktor someone and Doktor someone else—couple of girls and a general dogsbody."

"Who was the dogsbody?"

"Don't know. Some young diplomat to iron out the wrinkles.

We have them recorded at the Department. I can send you details, I suppose."

"If you don't mind."

"No, of course not."

There was another awkward pause. Smiley said : "Photographs would be a help, Peter. Could you manage that?"

"Yes, yes, of course." Guillam looked away from Smiley in some embarrassment. "We don't know much about the East Germans really, you know. We get odd bits here and there, but on the whole they're something of a mystery. If they operate at all they don't do it under Trade or Diplomatic cover—that's why, if you're right about this chap, it's so odd him coming from the Steel Mission."

"Oh," said Smiley, flatly.

"How do they operate?" asked Mendel.

"It's hard to generalise from the very few isolated cases we do know of. My impression is that they run their agents direct from Germany with no contact between controller and agent in the operational zone."

"But that must limit them terribly," cried Smiley. "You may have to wait months before your agent can travel to a meeting place outside his own country. He may not have the necessary cover to make the journey at all."

"Well, obviously it does limit him, but their targets seem to be so insignificant. They prefer to run foreign nationals—Swedes, expatriate Poles and what not, on short-term missions, where the limitations of their technique don't matter. In exceptional cases where they have an agent resident in the target country, they work on a courier system, which corresponds to the Soviet pattern."

Smiley was listening now.

"As a matter of fact," Guillam went on, "the Americans intercepted a courier quite recently, which is where we learnt the little we do know about G.D.R. technique."

"Such as what?"

"Oh, well, never waiting at a rendezvous, never meeting at the stated time but twenty minutes before; recognition signals —all the usual conjuring tricks that give a gloss to low grade information. They muck about with names, too. A courier may have to contact three or four agents—a controller may run as many as fifteen. They never invent cover names for themselves."

"What do you mean? Surely they must."

"They get the agent to do it for them. The agent chooses a name, any name he likes, and the controller adopts it. A gimmick really—" he stopped, looking at Mendel in surprise.

Mendel had leapt to his feet.

Guillam sat back in his chair and wondered if he were allowed to smoke. He decided reluctantly that he wasn't. He could have done with a cigarette.

"Well?" said Smiley. Mendel had described to Guillam his interview with Mr. Scarr.

"It fits," said Guillam. "Obviously it fits with what we know. But then we don't know all that much. If Blondie was a courier, it is exceptional—in my experience at least—that he should use a trade delegation as a staging post."

"You said the Mission had been here four years," said Mendel. "Blondie first came to Scarr four years ago."

No one spoke for a moment. Then Smiley said earnestly: "Peter, it is possible, isn't it? I mean they might under certain operational conditions need to have a station over here as well as couriers."

"Well, of course, if they were on to something really big they might."

"Meaning if they had a highly placed resident agent in play?"

"Yes, roughly."

"And assuming they had such an agent, a Maclean or Fuchs, it is conceivable that they would establish a station here under trade cover with no operation function except to hold the agent's hand?"

"Yes, it's conceivable. But it's a tall order, George. What you're suggesting is that the agent is run from abroad, serviced by courier and the courier is serviced by the Mission, which

71

is also the agent's personal guardian angel. He'd have to be some agent."

"I'm not suggesting quite that—but near enough. And I accept that the system demands a high-grade agent. Don't forget we only have Blondie's word for it that he came from abroad."

Mendel chipped in: "This agent—would he be in touch with the Mission direct?"

"Good lord, no," said Guillam. "He'd probably have an emergency procedure for getting in touch with them—a telephone code or something of the sort."

"How does that work?" asked Mendel.

"Varies. Might be on the wrong number system. You dial the number from a call box and ask to speak to George Brown. You're told George Brown doesn't live there so you apologise and ring off. The time and the rendezvous are prearranged—the emergency signal is contained in the name you ask for. Someone will be there."

"What else would the Mission do?" asked Smiley.

"Hard to say. Pay him probably. Arrange a collecting place for reports. The controller would make all those arrangements for the agent, of course, and tell him his part of it by courier. They work on the Soviet principle a good deal, as I told you —even the smallest details are arranged by control. The people in the field are allowed very little independence."

There was another silence. Smiley looked at Guillam and then at Mendel, then blinked and said:

"Blondie didn't come to Scarr in January and February, did he?"

"No," said Mendel; "this was the first year."

"Fennan always went skiing in January and February. This was the first time in four years he'd missed."

"I wonder," said Smiley; "whether I ought to go and see Maston again."

Guillam stretched luxuriously and smiled: "You can always try. He'll be thrilled to hear you've been brained. I've a sneaking feeling he'll think Battersea's on the coast, but not to worry. Tell him you were attacked while wandering about in someone's private yard—he'll understand. Tell him about your assailant, too, George. You've never seen him, mind, and you don't know his name, but he's a courier of the East German Intelligence Service. Maston will back you up; he always does. Specially when he's got to report to the Minister."

Smiley looked at Guillam and said nothing.

"After your bang on the head, too," Guillam added; "he'll understand."

"But, Peter—"

"I know, George, I know."

"Well, let me tell you another thing. Blondie collected his car on the first Tuesday of each month."

"So?"

"Those were the nights Elsa Fennan went to the Weybridge Rep. Fennan worked late on Tuesdays, she said."

Guillam got up. "Let me dig about, George. Cheerio. Mendel, I'll probably give you a ring tonight. I don't see what we can do now, anyway, but it would be nice to know, wouldn't it?" He reached the door. "Incidentally, where are Fennan's possessions—wallet, diary and so forth? Stuff they found on the body?"

"Probably still at the Station," said Mendel; "until after the inquest."

Guillam stood looking at Smiley for a moment, wondering what to say.

"Anything you want, George?"

"No thanks—Oh, there is one thing."

"Yes,"

"Could you get the C.I.D. off my back? They've visited me three times now and of course they've got nowhere locally. Could you make this an Intelligence matter for the time being? Be mysterious and soothing?"

"Yes, I should think so."

"I know it's difficult, Peter, because I'm not—"

"Oh another thing just to cheer you up. I had that comparison made between Fennan's suicide note and the anonymous letter. They were done by different people on the same machine. Different pressures and spacing but identical type face. So long, old dear. Tuck into the grapes."

Guillam closed the door behind him. They heard his footsteps echoing crisply down the bare corridor.

Mendel rolled himself a cigarette.

"Lord," said Smiley; "does nothing frighten you? Haven't you seen the Sister here?"

Mendel grinned and shook his head.

"You can only die once," he said, putting the cigarette between his thin lips. Smiley watched him light it. He produced his lighter, took the hood off it and rotated the wheel with his stained thumb, swiftly cupping both hands around it and nursing the flame towards the cigarette. There might have been a hurricane blowing.

"Well, you're the crime expert," said Smiley. "How are we doing?"

"Messy," said Mendel. "Untidy."

"Why?"

"Loose ends everywhere. No police work. Nothing checked. Like algebra."

"What's algebra got to do with it?"

"You've got to prove what *can* be proved, first. Find the constants. Did she really go to the theatre? Was she alone? Did the neighbours hear her come back? If so, what time? Was Fennan really late Tuesdays? Did his Missus go to the theatre regular *every* fortnight like she said?"

"And the 8.30 call. Can you tidy that for me?"

"You've got that call on the brain, haven't you?"

"Yes. Of all the loose ends, that's the loosest. I brood over it, you know, and there just isn't any sense in it. I've been through his train timetable. He was a punctual man— often got to the F.O. before anyone else, unlocked his own cupboard. He would have caught the 8.54, the 9.8 or at worst the 9.14. The 8.54 got him in at 9.38—he liked to be at his office by a quarter to ten. He couldn't possibly want to be woken at 8.30."

"Perhaps he just liked bells," said Mendel, getting up.

"And the letters," Smiley continued. "Different typists but the same machine. Discounting the murderer two people had access to that machine : Fennan and his wife. If we accept that Fennan typed the suicide note—and he certainly signed it—we must accept that it was Elsa who typed the denunciation. Why did she do that?"

Smiley was tired out, relieved that Mendel was going.

"Off to tidy up. Find the constants."

"You'll need money," said Smiley, and offered him some from the wallet beside his bed. Mendel took it without ceremony, and left.

Smiley lay back. His head was throbbing madly, burning hot. He thought of calling the nurse and cowardice prevented him. Gradually the throbbing eased. He heard from outside the ringing of an ambulance bell as it turned off Prince of Wales drive into the hospital yard. "Perhaps he just liked bells," he muttered and fell asleep.

He was woken by the sound of argument in the corridor— he heard the Sister's voice raised in protest; he heard footsteps and Mendel's voice, urgent in contradiction. The door opened suddenly and someone put the light on. He blinked and sat up, glancing at his watch. It was a quarter to six. Mendel was talking to him, almost shouting. What was he trying to say? Something about Battersea Bridge . . . the river police . . . missing since yesterday. . . . He was wide awake. Adam Scarr was dead.

CHAPTER X

THE VIRGIN'S STORY

MENDEL DROVE VERY well, with a kind of schoolma'am-ish pedantry that Smiley would have found comic. The Weybridge road was packed with traffic as usual. Mendel hated motorists. Give a man a car of his own and he leaves humility and common sense behind him in the garage. He didn't care who it was—he'd seen bishops in purple doing seventy in a built-up area, frightening pedestrians out of their wits. He liked Smiley's car. He liked the fussy way it had been maintained, the sensible extras, wing mirrors and reversing light. It was a decent little car.

He liked people who looked after things, who finished what they began. He liked thoroughness and precision. No skimping. Like this murderer. What had Scarr said? "Young, mind, but cool. Cool as charity." He knew that look, and Scarr had known it too . . . the look of complete negation that reposes in the eyes of a young killer. Not the look of a wild beast, not the grinning savagery of a maniac, but the look born of supreme efficiency, tried and proven. It was a stage beyond the experience of war. The witnessing of death in war brings a sophistication of its own; but beyond that, far beyond, is the conviction of supremacy in the heart of the professional killer. Yes, Mendel had seen it before : the one that stood apart from the gang, pale eyed, expressionless, the one the girls went after, spoke of without smiling. Yes, he was a cool one all right.

Scarr's death had frightened Mendel. He made Smiley promise not to go back to Bywater Street when he was released from hospital. With any luck they'd think he was dead, anyway. Scarr's death proved one thing, of course : the murderer was still in England, still anxious to tidy up. "When I get up," Smiley had said last night, "we must get him out of his hole again. Put out bits of cheese." Mendel knew who the cheese would be : Smiley. Of course if they were right about the motive there would be other cheese too : Fennan's wife. In fact, Mendel thought grimly, it doesn't say much for her that she hasn't been murdered. He felt ashamed of himself and turned his mind to other things. Such as Smiley again.

Odd little beggar, Smiley was. Reminded Mendel of a fat boy he'd played football with at school. Couldn't run, couldn't kick, blind as a bat but played like hell, never satisfied till he'd got himself torn to bits. Used to box, too. Came in wide open swinging his arms about : got himself half killed before the referee stopped it. Clever bloke, too.

Mendel stopped at a roadside café for a cup of tea and a bun, then drove into Weybridge. The Repertory Theatre was in a one way street leading off the High Street where parking was impossible. Finally he left the car at the railway station and walked back into the town.

The front doors of the theatre were locked. Mendel walked round to the side of the building under a brick archway. A green door was propped open. It had push bars on the inside and the words "stage door" scribbled in chalk. There was no bell; a faint smell of coffee issued from the dark green corridor within. Mendel stepped through the doorway and walked down the corridor, at the end of which he found a stone staircase with a metal handrail leading upwards to another green door. The smell of coffee was stronger, and he heard the sound of voices.

"Oh rot, darling, frankly. If the culture vultures of blissful Surrey want Barrie three months running let them have it, say I. It's either Barrie or 'A Cuckoo in the Nest' for the third year running and for me Barrie gets it by a short head"—this from a middle-aged female voice.

A querulous male replied : "Well, Ludo can always do Peter Pan, can't you Ludo?"

"Bitchie, bitchie," said a third voice, also male, and Mendel opened the door.

He was standing in the wings of the stage. On his left was a piece of thick hardboard with about a dozen switches mounted on a wooden panel. An absurd rococo chair in gilt and embroidery stood beneath it for the prompter and factotum.

In the middle of the stage two men and a woman sat on barrels smoking and drinking coffee. The décor represented the deck of a ship. A mast with rigging and rope ladder occupied the centre of the stage, and a large cardboard cannon pointed disconsolately towards a backcloth of sea and sky.

The conversation stopped abruptly as Mendel appeared on the stage. Someone murmured: "My dear, the ghost at the feast," and they all looked at him and giggled.

The woman spoke first: "Are you looking for someone, dear?"

"Sorry to butt in. Wanted to talk about becoming a subscriber to the theatre. Join the club."

"Why yes, of course. How nice," she said, getting up and walking over to him; "How *very* nice." She took his left hand in both her own and squeezed it, stepping back at the same time and extending her arms to their full length. It was her chatelaine gesture—Lady Macbeth receives Duncan. She put her head on one side and smiled girlishly, retained his hand and led him across the stage to the opposite wing. A door led into a tiny office littered with old programmes and posters, greasepaint, false hair and tawdry pieces of nautical costume.

"Have you seen our panto this year? 'Treasure Island.' Such a *gratifying* success. And so much more *social content*, don't you think, than those vulgar nursery tales?"

Mendel said. "Yes, wasn't it," without the least idea of what she was talking about, when his eye caught a pile of bills rather neatly assembled and held together by a bull-dog clip. The top one was made out to Mrs. Ludo Oriel and was four months overdue.

She was looking at him shrewdly through her glasses. She was small and dark, with lines on her neck and a great deal of make-up. The lines under her eyes had been levelled off with greasepaint but the effect had not lasted. She was wearing slacks and a chunky pullover liberally splashed with distemper. She smoked incessantly. Her mouth was very long, and as she held her cigarette in the middle of it in a direct line beneath her nose, her lips formed an exaggerated convex curve, distorting the lower half of her face and giving her an ill-tempered and impatient look. Mendel thought she would probably be difficult and clever. It was a relief to think she couldn't pay her bills.

"You *do* want to join the club, don't you?"

"No."

She suddenly flew into a rage: "If you're another bloody tradesman you can get out. I've said I'll pay and I will, just don't pester me. If you let people think I'm finished I *will* be and you'll be the losers, not me."

"I'm not a creditor, Mrs. Oriel. I've come to offer you money."

She was waiting.

"I'm a divorce agent. Rich client. Like to ask you a few questions. We're prepared to pay for your time."

"Christ," she said with relief. "Why didn't you say so in the first place?" They both laughed. Mendel put five pounds on top of the bills, counting them down.

"Now," said Mendel; "how do you keep your club subscription list? What are the benefits of joining?"

"Well, we have watery coffee on stage every morning at eleven sharp. Members of the club can mix with the cast during the break between rehearsals from 11.0 to 11.45. They pay for whatever they have, of course, but entry is strictly limited to club members."

"Quite."

"That's probably the part that interests you. We seem to get nothing but pansies and nymphos in the morning."

"It may be. What else goes on?"

"We put on a different show each fortnight. Members can reserve seats for a particular day of each run—the second Wednesday of each run, and so on. We always begin a run on the first and third Mondays of the month. The show begins at 7.30 and we hold the club reservations until 7.20. The girl at the box office has the seating plan and strikes off each seat as it's sold. Club reservations are marked in red and aren't sold off till last."

"I see. So if one of your members doesn't take his usual seat, it will be marked off on the seating plan."

"Only if it's sold."

"Of course."

"We're not often full after the first week. We're trying to do a show a week, you see, but it's not easy to get the—er—facilities. There isn't the support for two-week runs really."

"No, no, quite. Do you keep old seating plans?"

"Sometimes, for the accounts."

"How about Tuesday the third of January?"

She opened a cupboard and took out a sheaf of printed seating plans. "This is the second fortnight of our pantomime, of course. Tradition."

"Quite," said Mendel.

"Now who is it you're so interested in?" asked Mrs. Oriel, picking up a ledger from the desk.

"Small blonde party, aged about forty-two or three. Name of Fennan, Elsa Fennan."

Mrs. Oriel opened her ledger. Mendel quite shamelessly looked over her shoulder. The names of club members were entered neatly in the left-hand column. A red tick on the extreme left of the page indicated that the member had paid his subscription. On the right-hand side of the page were notes of standing reservations made for the year. There were about eighty members.

"Name doesn't ring a bell. Where does she sit?"

"No idea."

"Oh, yes, here we are. Merridale Lane, Walliston. Merridale!—I *ask* you. Let's look. A rear stall at the end of a row Very odd choice, don't you think? Seat number R2. But God knows whether she took it on 3rd January. I shouldn't think we've got the plan any more, though I've never thrown anything away in my life. Things just evaporate, don't they?" She looked at him out of the corner of her eye, wondering whether she'd earned her five pounds. "Tell you what, we'll ask the Virgin." She got up and walked to the door; "Fennan ... Fennan. ..." she said. "Half a sec, that does ring a bell. I wonder why. Well I'm damned—of course—the music case." She opened the door "Where's the Virgin?" she said, talking to someone on the stage.

"God knows."

"Helpful pig," said Mrs. Oriel, and closed the door again. She turned to Mendel : "The Virgin's our white hope. English rose, local solicitor's stage-struck daughter, all lisle stockings and get-me-if-you-can. We loathe her. She gets a part occasionally because her father pays tuition fees. She does seating in the evenings sometimes when there's a rush—she and Mrs. Torr, the cleaner, who does cloaks. When things are quiet, Mrs. Torr does the whole thing and the Virgin mopes about in the wings hoping the female lead will drop dead." She paused. "I'm damned sure I remember 'Fennan'. Damn sure I do. I wonder where that cow *is*." She disappeared for a couple of minutes and returned with a tall and rather pretty girl with fuzzy blonde hair and pink cheeks—good at tennis and swimming.

"This is Elizabeth Pidgeon. She may be able to help. Darling, we want to find out a Mrs. Fennan, a club member. Didn't you tell me something about her?"

"Oh, *yes,* Ludo." She must have thought she sounded sweet. She smiled vapidly at Mendel, put her head on one side and twined her fingers together. Mendel jerked his head towards her.

"Do you know her?" asked Mrs. Oriel.

"Oh *yes,* Ludo. She's madly musical; at least I think she must be because she always brings her music. She's madly thin and odd. She's foreign, isn't she, Ludo?"

"Why odd?" asked Mendel.

"Oh, well, last time she came she got in a frightful pet about the seat next to her. It was a club reservation you see and simply hours after twenty past. We'd just started the panto season and there were millions of people wanting seats so I let it go. She kept on saying she was sure the person would come because he always did."

"Did he?" asked Mendel.

"No. I let the seat go. She must have been in an awful pet because she left after the second act, and forgot to collect her music case."

"This person she was so sure would turn up," said Mendel; "is he friendly with Mrs. Fennan?"

Ludo Oriel gave Mendel a suggestive wink.

"Well, gosh, I should think *so*, he's her husband, isn't he?"

Mendel looked at her for a minute and then smiled: "Couldn't we find a chair for Elizabeth?" he said.

"Gosh, thanks," said the Virgin, and sat on the edge of an old gilt chair like the prompter's chair in the wings. She put her red, fat hands on her knees and leaned forward, smiling all the time, thrilled to be the centre of so much interest. Mrs. Oriel looked at her venomously.

"What makes you think he was her husband, Elizabeth?" There was an edge to his voice which had not been there before.

"Well, I know they arrive separately, but I thought that as they had seats apart from the rest of the club reservations, they must be husband and wife. And of course he always brings a music case too."

"I see. What else can you remember about that evening Elizabeth?"

"Oh, well, lots really because you see I felt awful about her leaving in such a pet and then later that night she rang up. Mrs. Fennan did, I mean. She said her name and said she'd left early and forgotten her music case. She'd lost the ticket for it, too, and was in a frightful state. It sounded as if she was crying. I heard someone's voice in the background, and then she said someone would drop in and get it if that would be all right without the ticket. I said of course, and half an hour later the man came. He's rather super. Tall and fair."

"I see," said Mendel; "thank you very much, Elizabeth, you've been very helpful."

"Gosh, that's O.K." She got up.

"Incidentally," said Mendel. "This man who collected her music case—he wasn't by any chance the same man who sits beside her in the theatre, was he?"

"Rather. Gosh, sorry, I should have said that."

"Did you talk to him?"

"Well, just to say here you are, sort of thing."

"What kind of voice had he?"

"Oh, foreign, like Mrs. Fennan's—she *is* foreign, isn't she? That's what I put it down to—all her fuss and state—foreign temperament."

She smiled at Mendel, waited a moment then walked out like Alice.

"Cow," said Mrs. Oriel, looking at the closed door. Her eyes turned to Mendel. " Well, I hope you've got your five quids' worth."

"I think so," said Mendel.

CHAPTER XI

THE UNRESPECTABLE CLUB

Mendel found Smiley sitting in an armchair fully dressed, Peter Guillam was stretched luxuriously on the bed, a pale green folder held casually in his hand. Outside, the sky was black and menacing.

"Enter the third murderer," said Guillam as Mendel walked in. Mendel sat down at the end of the bed and nodded happily to Smiley, who looked pale and depressed.

"Congratulations. Nice to see you on your feet."

"Thank you. I'm afraid if you did see me on my feet you wouldn't congratulate me. I feel as weak as a kitten."

"When are they letting you go?"

"I don't know when they expect me to go—"

"Haven't you asked?"

"No."

"Well you'd better. I've got news for you. I don't know what it means but it means something."

"Well, well," said Guillam; "everyone's got news for every-one else. Isn't that exciting. George has been looking at my family snaps"—he raised the green folder a fraction of an inch —"and recognises all his old chums."

Mendel felt baffled and rather left out of things. Smiley intervened : "I'll tell you all about it over dinner tomorrow evening. I'm getting out of here in the morning, whatever they say. I think we've found the murderer and a lot more besides. Now let's have your news." There was no triumph in his eyes. Only anxiety.

Membership of the club to which Smiley belonged is not quoted among the respectable acquisitions of those who adorn the pages of "Who's Who". It was formed by a young rene-gade of the Junior Carlton named Steed-Asprey, who had been warned off by the Secretary for blaspheming within the hearing of a South African bishop. He persuaded his former Oxford landlady to leave her quiet house in Hollywell and take over two rooms and a cellar in Manchester Square which a monied relative put at his disposal. It had once had forty members who each paid fifty guineas a year. There were thirty-one left. There were no women and no rules, no secre-tary and no bishops. You could take sandwiches and buy a bottle of beer, you could take sandwiches and buy nothing at all. As long as you were reasonably sober and minded your own business, no one gave tuppence what you wore, did, or said, or whom you brought with you. Mrs. Sturgeon no longer devilled at the bar, or brought you your chop in front of the fire in the cellar, but presided in genial comfort over the min-istrations of two retired sergeants from a small border regi-ment.

Naturally enough, most of the members were approximate contemporaries of Smiley at Oxford. It had always been agreed that the club was to serve one generation only, that it would grow old and die with its members. The war had taken its toll of Jebedee and others, but no one had ever suggested they should elect new members. Besides, the premises were now their own, Mrs. Sturgeon's future had been taken care of and the club was solvent.

It was a Saturday evening and only half a dozen people were there. Smiley had ordered their meal, and a table was set for them in the cellar, where a bright coal fire burned in a brick hearth. They were alone, there was sirloin and claret; outside the rain fell continuously. For all three of them the world seemed an untroubled and decent place that night, despite the strange business that brought them together.

"To make sense of what I have to tell you," began Smiley at last, addressing himself principally to Mendel, "I shall have to talk at length about myself. I'm an intelligence officer by trade as you know—I've been in the Service since the Flood, long before we were mixed up in power politics with Whitehall. In those days we were understaffed and underpaid. After the usual training and probation in South America and Central Europe, I took a job lecturing at a German University, talent spotting for young Germans with an agent potential." He paused, smiled at Mendel and said : "Forgive the jargon." Mendel nodded solemnly and Smiley went on. He knew he was being pompous, and didn't know how to prevent himself.

"It was shortly before the last war, a terrible time in Germany then, intolerance run mad. I would have been a lunatic to approach anyone myself. My only chance was to be as nondescript as I could, politically and socially colourless, and to put forward candidates for recruitment by someone else. I tried to bring some back to England for short periods on students' tours. I made a point of having no contact at all with the Department when I came over because we hadn't any idea in those days of the efficiency of German Counter Intelligence. I never knew who was approached, and of course it was much better that way. In case I was blown, I mean.

"My story really begins in 1938. I was alone in my rooms one summer evening. It had been a beautiful day, warm and peaceful. Fascism might never have been heard of. I was working in my shirt sleeves at a desk by my window, not working very hard because it was such a wonderful evening."

He paused, embarrassed for some reason, and fussed a little with the port. Two pink spots appeared high on his cheeks. He felt slightly drunk though he had had very little wine.

"To resume," he said, and felt an ass: "I'm sorry, I feel a little inarticulate . . . Anyway, as I sat there, there was a knock on the door and a young student came in. He was nineteen, in fact, but he looked younger. His name was Dieter Frey. He was a pupil of mine, an intelligent boy and remarkable to look at." Smiley paused again, staring before him. Perhaps it was his illness, his weakness, which brought the memory so vividly before him.

"Dieter was a very handsome boy, with a high forehead and a lot of unruly black hair. The lower part of his body was deformed, I think by infantile paralysis. He carried a stick and leaned heavily upon it when he walked. Naturally he cut a rather romantic figure at a small university; they thought him Byronic and so on. In fact I could never find him romantic myself. The Germans have a passion for discovering young genius, you know, from Herder to Stefan George—somebody lionised them practically from the cradle. But you couldn't lionise Dieter. There was a fierce independence, a ruthlessness about him which scared off the most determined patron. This defensiveness in Dieter derived not only from his deformity, but his race, which was Jewish. How on earth he kept his place at University I could never understand. It was possible that they didn't know he was a Jew—his beauty might have been southern, I suppose, Italian, but I don't really see how. To me he was obviously Jewish.

"Dieter was a socialist. He made no secret of his views even in those days. I once considered him for recruitment, but it seemed futile to take on anyone who was so obviously earmarked for concentration camp. Besides he was too volatile, too swift to react, too brightly painted, too vain. He led all the societies at the University—debating, political, poetry and so on. In all the athletic guilds he held honorary positions. He had the nerve not to drink in a University where you proved your manhood by being drunk most of your first year.

"That was Dieter, then: a tall, handsome, commanding

cripple, the idol of his generation; a Jew. And that was the man who came to see me that hot summer evening.

"I sat him down and offered him a drink, which he refused. I made some coffee, I think, on a gas ring. We spoke in a desultory way about my last lecture on Keats. I had complained about the application of German critical methods to English poetry, and this had led to some discussion—as usual —on the Nazi interpretation of 'decadence' in art. Dieter dragged it all up again and became more and more outspoken in his condemnation of modern Germany and finally of Nazism itself. Naturally, I was guarded—I think I was less of a fool in those days than I am now. In the end he asked me point blank what I thought of the Nazis. I replied rather pointedly that I was disinclined to criticise my hosts, and that anyway I didn't think politics were much fun. I shall never forget his reply. He was furious, struggled to his feet and shouted at me : *'Von Freude ist nicht die Rede!'*—'We're not talking about fun!'" Smiley broke off and looked across the table to Guillam : "I'm sorry, Peter. I'm being rather long-winded."

"Nonsense, old dear. You tell the story in your own way." Mendel grunted his approval; he was sitting rather stiffly with both hands on the table before him. There was no light in the room now except the bright glow of the fire, which threw tall shadows on the rough-cast wall behind him. The port decanter was three parts empty; Smiley gave himself a little and passed it on.

"He raved at me. He simply did not understand how I could apply an independent standard of criticism to art and remain so insensitive to politics, how I could bleat about artistic freedom when a third of Europe was in chains. Did it mean nothing to me that contemporary civilisation was being bled to death? What was so sacred about the eighteenth century that I could throw the twentieth away? He had come to me because he enjoyed my seminars and thought me an enlightened man, but he now realised that I was worse than all of them.

"I let him go. What else could I do? On paper he was

87

suspect anyway—a rebellious Jew with a University place still mysteriously free. But I watched him. The term was nearly over and the long vacation soon to begin. In the closing debate of the term three days later he was dreadfully outspoken. He really frightened people, you know, and they grew silent and apprehensive. The end of the term came and Dieter departed without a word of farewell to me. I never expected to see him again.

"It was about six months before I did. I had been visiting friends near Dresden, Dieter's home town, and I arrived half an hour early at the station. Rather than hang around on the platform I decided to go for a stroll. A couple of hundred metres from the station was a tall, rather grim seventeenth-century house. There was a small courtyard in front of it with tall iron railings and a wrought-iron gate. It had apparently been converted into a temporary prison : a group of shaven prisoners, men and women, were being exercised in the yard, walking round the perimeter. Two guards stood in the centre with tommy guns. As I watched I caught sight of a familiar figure, taller than the rest, limping, struggling to keep up with them. It was Dieter. They had taken his stick away.

"When I thought about it afterwards, of course, I realised that the Gestapo would scarcely arrest the most popular member of the University while he was still up. I forgot about my train, went back into the town and looked for his parents in the telephone book. I knew his father had been a doctor so it wasn't difficult. I went to the address and only his mother was there. The father had died already in a concentration camp. She wasn't inclined to talk about Dieter, but it appeared that he had not gone to a Jewish prison but to a general one, and ostensibly for 'a period of correction' only. She expected him back in about three months. I left him a message to say I still had some books of his and would be pleased to return them if he would call on me.

"I'm afraid the events of 1939 must have got the better of me, because I don't believe I gave Dieter another thought that year. Soon after I returned from Dresden my Department ordered me back to England. I packed and left within forty-eight hours, to find London in a turmoil. I was given a new assignment which required intensive preparation, briefing and training. I was to go back to Europe at once and activate almost untried agents in Germany who had been recruited against such an emergency. I began to memorise the dozen odd names and addresses. You can imagine my reaction when I discovered Dieter Frey among them.

"When I read his file I found he had more or less recruited himself by bursting in on the consulate in Dresden and demanding to know why no one lifted a finger to stop the persecution of the Jews." Smiley paused and laughed to himself; "Dieter was a great one for getting people to do things." He glanced quickly at Mendel and Guillam. Both had their eyes fixed on him.

"I suppose my first reaction was pique. The boy had been right under my nose and I hadn't considered him suitable—what was some ass in Dresden up to? And then I was alarmed to have this firebrand on my hands, whose impulsive temperament could cost me and others our lives. Despite the slight changes in my appearance and the new cover under which I was operating, I should obviously have to declare myself to Dieter as plain George Smiley from the University, so he could blow me sky high. It seemed a most unfortunate beginning, and I was half resolved to set up my network without Dieter. In the event I was wrong. He was a magnificent agent.

"He didn't curb his flamboyance, but used it skilfully as a kind of double bluff. His deformity kept him out of the Services and he found himself a clerical job on the railways. In no time he worked his way to a position of real responsibility and the quantity of information he obtained was fantastic. Details of troop and ammunition transports, their destination and date of transit. Later he reported on the effectiveness of our bombing, pinpointed key targets. He was a brilliant organiser and I think that was what saved him. He did a wonderful job on the railways, made himself indispensable, worked all hours of the night and day; became almost inviolate. They even gave him a civilian decoration for exceptional merit and I suppose the Gestapo conveniently lost his file.

"Dieter had a theory that was pure Faust. Thought alone was valueless. You must act for thought to become effective. He used to say that the greatest mistake man ever made was to distinguish between the mind and the body : an order does not exist if it is not obeyed. He used to quote Kleist a great deal : 'if all eyes were made of green glass, and if all that seems white was really green, who would be the wiser?' Something like that.

"As I say, Dieter was a magnificent agent. He even went so far as to arrange for certain freights to be transported on good flying nights for the convenience of our bombers. He had tricks all his own—a natural genius for the nuts and bolts of espionage. It seemed absurd to suppose it could last, but the effect of our bombing was often so widespread that it would have been childish to attribute it to one person's betrayal—let alone to a man so notoriously outspoken as Dieter.

"Where he was concerned my job was easy. Dieter put in a lot of travelling as it was—he had a special pass to get him around. Communication was child's play by comparison with some agents. Occasionally we would actually meet and talk in a café, or he would pick me up in a Ministry car and drive me sixty or seventy miles along a main road, as if he were giving me a lift. But more often we would take a journey in the same train and swap briefcases in the corridor or go to the theatre with parcels and exchange cloakroom tickets. He seldom gave me actual reports but just carbon copies of transit orders. He got his secretary to do a lot—he made her keep a special float which he 'destroyed' every three months by emptying it into his brief case in the lunch hour.

"Well, in 1943 I was recalled. My trade cover was rather thin by then I think, and I was getting a bit shop-soiled." He stopped and took a cigarette from Guillam's case.

"But don't let's get Dieter out of perspective," he said : "he was my best agent, but he wasn't my only one. I had a lot of headaches of my own—running him was a picnic by comparison with some. When the war was over I tried to find out from my successor what had become of Dieter and the rest of them. Some were resettled in Australia and Canada, some just drifted away to what was left of their home towns. Dieter hesitated, I gather. The Russians were in Dresden, of course, and he may have had doubts. In the end he went—he had to really, because of his mother. He hated the Americans, anyway. And of course he was a socialist.

"I heard later that he had made his career there. The administrative experience he had picked up during the war got him some Government job in the new republic. I suppose that his reputation as a rebel and the suffering of his family cleared the way for him. He must have done pretty well for himself."

"Why?" asked Mendel.

"He was over here until a month ago running the Steel Mission."

"That's not all," said Guillam quickly. "In case you think your cup is full, Mendel, I spared you another visit to Weybridge this morning and called on Elizabeth Pidgeon. It was George's idea." He turned to Smiley : "She is a sort of Moby Dick isn't she—big white man-eating whale."

"Well?" said Mendel.

"I showed her a picture of that young diplomat by the name of Mundt they kept in tow there to pick up the bits. Elizabeth recognised him at once as the nice man who collected Elsa Fennan's music case. Isn't that jolly?"

"But—"

"I know what you're going to ask, you clever youth. You want to know whether George recognised him too. Well, George did. It's the same nasty fellow who tried to lure him into his own house in Bywater Street. Doesn't he get around?"

Mendel drove to Mitcham. Smiley was dead tired. It was raining again and cold. Smiley hugged his greatcoat round him and, despite his tiredness, watched with quiet pleasure the busy London night go by. He had always loved travelling. Even now, if he had the choice, he would cross France by train rather than fly. He could still respond to the magic noises of a night journey across Europe, the oddly cacophonous chimes and the French voices suddenly waking him from English dreams. Ann had loved it too and they had twice travelled

91

overland to share the dubious joys of that uncomfortable journey.

When they got back Smiley went straight to bed while Mendel made some tea. They drank it in Smiley's bedroom.

"What do we do now?" asked Mendel.

"I thought I might go to Walliston tomorrow."

"You ought to spend the day in bed. What do you want to do there?"

"See Elsa Fennan."

"You're not safe on your own. You'd better let me come. I'll sit in the car while you do the talking. She's a Yid, isn't she?"

Smiley nodded.

"My dad was Yid. He never made such a bloody fuss about it."

CHAPTER XII

DREAM FOR SALE

SHE OPENED THE door and stood looking at him for a moment in silence.

"You could have let me know you were coming," she said.

"I thought it safer not to."

She was silent again. Finally she said: "I don't know what you mean." It seemed to cost her a good deal.

"May I come in?" said Smiley. "We haven't much time."

She looked old and tired, less resilient perhaps. She led him into the drawing-room and with something like resignation indicated a chair.

Smiley offered her a cigarette and took one himself. She was standing by the window. As he looked at her, watched her quick breathing, her feverish eyes, he realised that she had almost lost the power of self-defence.

When he spoke, his voice was gentle, concessive. To Elsa Fennan it must have seemed like a voice she had longed for, irresistible, offering all strength, comfort, compassion and safety. She gradually moved away from the window and her right hand, which had been pressed against the sill, trailed wistfully along it, then fell to her side in a gesture of submission. She sat opposite him, her eyes upon him in complete dependence, like the eyes of a lover.

"You must have been terribly lonely," he said; "no one can stand it for ever. It takes courage, too, and it's so hard to be brave alone. They never understand that, do they? They never know what it costs—the sordid tricks of lying and deceiving, the isolation from ordinary people. They think you can run on their kind of fuel—the flag waving and the music. But you need a different kind of fuel, don't you, when you're alone? You've got to hate, and it needs strength to hate all the time. And what you must love is so remote, so vague when you're not part of it." He paused. Soon, he thought, soon you'll break. He prayed desperately that she would accept him, accept his comfort. He looked at her. Soon she would break.

"I said we hadn't much time. Do you know what I mean?"

She had folded her hands on her lap and was looking down at them. He saw the dark roots of her yellow hair and wondered why on earth she dyed it. She showed no sign of having heard his question.

"When I left you that morning a month ago I drove to my home in London. A man tried to kill me. That night he nearly succeeded—he hit me on the head three or four times. I've just come out of hospital. As it happens I was lucky. Then there was the garage man he hired the car from. The river police recovered his body from the Thames not long ago. There were no signs of violence—he was just full of whisky. They can't understand it—he hadn't been near the river for years. But then we're dealing with a competent man, aren't we? A trained killer. It seems he's trying to remove anyone who can connect him with Samuel Fennan. Or his wife, of course. Then there's that young blonde girl at the Repertory Theatre . . ."

"What are you saying?" she whispered; "What are you trying to tell me?"

Smiley suddenly wanted to hurt her, to break the last of her will, to remove her utterly as an enemy. For so long she had haunted him as he had lain helpless, had been a mystery and a power.

"What games did you think you were playing, you two? Do you think you can flirt with power like theirs, give a little and not give all? Do you think that *you* can stop the dance— control the strength you give them? What dreams did you cherish, Mrs. Fennan, that had so little of the world in them?"

She buried her face in her hands and he watched the tears run between her fingers. Her body shook with great sobs and her words came slowly, wrung from her.

"No, no dreams. I had no dream but him. He had one dream, yes . . . one great dream." She went on crying, helpless, and Smiley, half in triumph, half in shame, waited for her to speak again. Suddenly she raised her head and looked at him, the tears still running down her cheeks. "Look at me," she said; "what dream did they leave me? I dreamed of long golden hair and they shaved my head, I dreamed of a beautiful body and they broke it with hunger. I have seen what human beings are, how could I believe in a formula for human beings? I said to him, oh I said to him a thousand times; 'only make no laws, no fine theories, no judgements, and the people may love, but give them one theory, let them invent one slogan, and the game begins again.' I told him that. We talked whole nights away. But no, that little boy must have his dream, and if a new world was to be built, Samuel Fennan must build it. I said to him, 'Listen,' I said; 'they have given you all you have, a home, money and trust. Why do you do it to them?' And he said to me: 'I do it *for* them. I am the surgeon and one day they will understand.' He was a child, Mr. Smiley, they led him like a child."

He dared not speak, dared put nothing to the test.

"Five years ago he met that Dieter. In a ski hut near Garmisch. Freitag told us later that Dieter had planned it that way—Dieter couldn't ski anyway because of his legs. Nothing seemed real then; Freitag wasn't a real name. Fennan christened him Freitag like Man Friday in Robinson Crusoe. Dieter found that so funny and afterwards we never talked of Dieter but always of Mr. Robinson and Freitag." She broke off now and looked at him with a very faint smile: "I'm sorry," she said; "I'm not very coherent."

"I understand," said Smiley.

"That girl—what did you say about that girl?"

"She's alive. Don't worry, Go on."

"Fennan liked you, you know. Freitag tried to kill you . . . why?"

"Because I came back, I suppose, and asked you about the 8.30 call. You told Freitag that, didn't you?"

"Oh, God," she said, her fingers at her mouth.

"You rang him up, didn't you? As soon as I'd gone?"

"Yes, yes. I was frightened. I wanted to warn him to go, him and Dieter, to go away and never come back, because I knew you'd find out. If not today then one day, but I knew you'd find out in the end. Why would they never leave me alone? They were frightened of me because they knew I had no dreams that I only wanted Samuel, wanted him safe to love and care for. They relied on that."

Smiley felt his head throbbing erratically. "So you rang him straight away," he said. "You tried the Primrose number first and couldn't get through."

"Yes," she said vaguely. "Yes, that's right. But they're both Primrose numbers."

"So you rang the *other* number, the alternative . . ."

She drifted back to the window, suddenly exhausted and limp; she seemed happier now—the storm had left her reflective and, in a way, content.

"Yes. Freitag was a great one for alternative plans."

"What was the other number?" Smiley insisted. He watched her anxiously as she stared out of the window into the dark garden.

"Why do you want to know?"

He came and stood beside her at the window, watching her profile. His voice was suddenly harsh and energetic.

"I said the girl was all right. You and I are alive, too. But don't think that's going to last."

She turned to him with fear in her eyes, looked at him for a moment, then nodded. Smiley took her by the arm and guided her to a chair. He ought to make her a hot drink or something. She sat down quite mechanically, almost with the detachment of insipient madness.

"The other number was 9747."

"Any address—did you have an address?"

"No, no address. Only the telephone. Tricks on the telephone. No address," she repeated, with unnatural emphasis, so that Smiley looked at her and wondered. A thought suddenly struck him—a memory of Dieter's skill in communication.

"Freitag didn't meet you the night Fennan died, did he? He didn't come to the theatre?"

"No."

"That was the first time he had missed, wasn't it? You panicked and left early."

"No . . . yes, yes, I panicked."

"No you didn't! You left early because you had to, it was the arrangement. *Why* did you leave early? Why?"

Her hands hid her face.

"Are you still mad?" Smiley shouted. "Do you still think you can control what you have made? Freitag will kill you, kill the girl, kill, kill, kill. Who are you trying to protect, a girl or a murderer?"

She wept and said nothing. Smiley crouched beside her, still shouting.

"I'll tell you why you left early, shall I? I'll tell you what I think. It was to catch the last post that night from Weybridge. He hadn't come, you hadn't exchanged cloakroom tickets, had you, so you obeyed the instructions, you posted your ticket to him and you *have* got an address, not written down but remembered, remembered for ever: 'if there is a crisis, if I do not come, this is the address': is that what he said? An address never to be used or spoken of, an address forgotten and remembered for ever? Is that right? Tell me!"

She stood up, her head turned away, went to the desk and found a piece of paper and a pencil. The tears still ran freely over her face. With agonising slowness she wrote the address, her hand faltering and almost stopping between the words.

He took the paper from her, folded it carefully across the middle and put it in his wallet.

Now he would make her some tea.

She looked like a child rescued from the sea. She sat on the edge of the sofa holding the cup tightly in her frail hands, nursing it against her body. Her thin shoulders were hunched forward, her feet and ankles pressed tightly together. Smiley, looking at her, felt he had broken something he should never have touched because it was so fragile. He felt an obscene, coarse bully, his offerings of tea a futile recompense for his clumsiness.

He could think of nothing to say. After a while, she said: "He liked you, you know. He really liked you . . . he said you were a clever little man. It was quite a surprise when Samuel called anyone clever." She shook her head slowly. Perhaps it was the reaction that made her smile: "He used to say there were two forces in the world, the positive and the negative. 'What shall I do then?' he would ask me: 'let them ruin their harvest because they give me bread? Creation, progress, power, the whole future of mankind waits at their door: shall I not let them in?' And I said to him: 'But, Samuel, maybe the people are happy without these things?' But you know he didn't think of people like that.

"But I couldn't stop him. You know the strangest thing about Fennan? For all that thinking and talking, he had made up his mind long ago what he would do. All the rest was poetry. He wasn't co-ordinated, that's what I used to tell him . . ."

". . . and yet you helped him," said Smiley.

"Yes, I helped him. He wanted help so I gave it him. He was my life."

"I see."

"That was a mistake. He was a little boy, you know. He forgot things just like a child. And so vain. He had made up his mind to do it and he did it so badly. He didn't think of it as you do, or I do. He simply didn't think of it like that. It was his work and that was all.

"It began so simply. He brought home a draft telegram one night and showed it to me. He said; 'I think Dieter ought to see that'—that was all. I couldn't believe it to begin with—that he was a spy, I mean. Because he was, wasn't he? And gradually, I realised. They began to ask for special things. The music case I got back from Freitag began to contain orders, and sometimes money. I said to him: 'Look at what they are sending you—do you want this?' We didn't know what to do with the money. In the end we gave it away mostly, I don't know why. Dieter was very angry that winter, when I told him."

"What winter was that?" asked Smiley.

"The second winter with Dieter—1956 in Mürren. We met him first in January, 1955. That was when it began. And shall I tell you something? Hungary made no difference to Samuel, not a tiny bit of difference. Dieter was frightened about him then, I know, because Freitag told me. When Fennan gave me the things to take to Weybridge that November I nearly went mad. I shouted at him: 'Can't you see it's the same? The same guns, the same children dying in the streets? Only the dream has changed, the blood is the same colour. Is this what you want?' I asked him: 'Would you do this for Germans, too? It's me who lies in the gutter, will you let them do it to *me*?' But he just said: 'No, Elsa, this is different.' And I went on taking the music case. Do you understand?"

"I don't know. I just don't know. I think perhaps I do."

"He was all I had. He was my life. I protected myself, I suppose. And gradually I became a part of it, and then it was too late to stop. . . . And then you know," she said, in a whisper; "there were times when I was glad, times when the world seemed to applaud what Samuel was doing. It was not a pretty sight for us, the new Germany. Old names had come back, names that had frightened us as children. The dreadful, plump pride returned, you could see it even in the photographs in the papers, they marched with the old rhythm. Fennan felt that too, but then thank God he hadn't seen what I saw.

"We were in a camp outside Dresden, where we used to live. My father was paralysed. He missed tobacco more than anything and I used to roll cigarettes from any rubbish I could find in the camp—just to pretend with. One day a guard saw him smoking and began laughing. Some others came and they laughed too. My father was holding the cigarette in his paralysed hand and it was burning his fingers. He didn't know, you see.

"Yes, when they gave guns to the Germans again, gave them money and uniforms, then sometimes—just for a little while—I was pleased with what Samuel had done. We are Jews, you know, and so . . ."

"Yes, I know, I understand," said Smiley: "I saw it too, a little of it."

"Dieter said you had."

"Dieter said that?"

"Yes. To Freitag. He told Freitag you were a very clever man. You once deceived Dieter before the war, and it was only long afterwards that he found out, that's what Freitag said. He said you were the best he'd ever met."

"When did Freitag tell you that?"

She looked at him for a long time. He had never seen in any face such hopeless misery. He remembered how she had said to him before; "The children of my grief are dead." He understood that now, and heard it in her voice when at last she spoke :

"Why isn't it obvious? The night he murdered Samuel. That's the great joke, Mr. Smiley. At the very moment when Samuel could have done so much for them—not just a piece here and a piece there, but all the time—so many music cases—at that moment their own fear destroyed them, turned them into animals and made them kill what they had made.

"Samuel always said; 'they will win because they *know* and the others will perish because they do not : men who work for

99

a dream will work for ever'—that's what he said. But I knew their dream, I knew it would destroy us. What has not destroyed? Even the dream of Christ."

"It was Dieter then, who saw me in the park with Fennan?"

"Yes."

"And thought—"

"Yes. Thought that Samuel had betrayed him. Told Freitag to kill Samuel."

"And the anonymous letter?"

"I don't know. I don't know who wrote it. Someone who knew Samuel I suppose, someone from the office who watched him and knew. Or from Oxford, from the Party. I don't know. Samuel didn't know either."

"But the suicide letter—"

She looked at him, and her face crumpled. She was almost weeping again. She bowed her head :

"I wrote it. Freitag brought the paper, and I wrote it. The signature was already there. Samuel's signature."

Smiley went over to her, sat beside her on the sofa and took her hand. She turned on him in a fury and began screaming at him :

"Take your hands off me! Do you think I'm yours because I don't belong to them? Go away! Go away and kill Freitag and Dieter, keep the game alive, Mr. Smiley. But don't think I'm on *your* side, d'you hear? Because I'm the wandering Jewess, the no-man's land, the battlefield for your toy soldiers. You can kick me and trample on me, see, but never, never touch me, never tell me you're sorry, d'you hear? Now get out! Go away and kill."

She sat there, shivering as if from cold. As he reached the door he looked back. There were no tears in her eyes.

Mendel was waiting for him in the car.

CHAPTER XIII

THE INEFFICIENCY OF SAMUEL FENNAN

They arrived at Mitcham at lunch time. Peter Guillam was waiting for them patiently in his car.

"Well, children; what's the news?"

Smiley handed him the piece of paper from his wallet. "There was an emergency number, too—Primrose 9747. You'd better check it but I'm not hopeful of that either."

Peter disappeared into the hall and began telephoning. Mendel busied himself in the kitchen and returned ten minutes later with beer, bread and cheese on a tray. Guillam came back and sat down without saying anything. He looked worried. "Well," he said at last; "what did she say, George?"

Mendel cleared away as Smiley finished the account of his interview that morning.

"I see," said Guillam. "How very worrying. Well, that's it, George, I shall have to put this on paper today, and I'll have to go to Maston at once. Catching dead spies is a poor game really—and causes a lot of unhappiness."

"What access did he have at the F.O.?" asked Smiley.

"Recently a lot. That's why they felt he should be interviewed, as you know."

"What kind of stuff, mainly?"

"I don't know yet. He was on an Asian desk until a few months ago but his new job was different."

"American, I seem to remember," said Smiley. "Peter?"

"Yes."

"Peter, have you thought at all *why* they wanted to kill Fennan so much. I mean, supposing he *had* betrayed them, as they thought, why kill him? They had nothing to gain."

"No; no, I suppose they hadn't. That does need some explaining, come to think of it . . . or does it? Suppose Fuchs or

Maclean had betrayed them, I wonder what would have happened. Suppose they had reason to fear a chain reaction—not just here but in America—all over the world? Wouldn't they kill him to prevent that? There's so much we shall just never know."

"Like the 8.30 call?" said Smiley.

"Cheerio. Hang on here till I ring you, will you? Maston's bound to want to see you. They'll be running down the corridors when I tell them the glad news. I shall have to wear that special grin I reserve for bearing really disastrous tidings."

Mendel saw him out and then returned to the drawing-room. "Best thing you can do is put your feet up," he said. "You look a ruddy mess, you do."

"Either Mundt's here or he's not," thought Smiley as he lay on the bed in his waistcoat, his hands linked under his head. "If he's not, we're finished. It will be for Maston to decide what to do with Elsa Fennan, and my guess is he'll do nothing.

"If Mundt *is* here, it's for one of three reasons : A, because Dieter told him to stay and watch the dust settle; B, because he's in bad odour and afraid to go back; C, because he has unfinished business.

"A is improbable because it's not like Dieter to take needless risks. Anyway, it's a woolly idea.

"B is unlikely because, while Mundt may be afraid of Dieter he must also, presumably, be frightened of a murder charge here. His wisest plan would be to go to another country.

"C is more likely. If I was in Dieter's shoes I'd be worried sick about Elsa Fennan. The Pidgeon girl is immaterial—without Elsa to fill in the gaps she presents no serious danger. She was not a conspirator and there is no reason why she should particularly remember Elsa's friend at the theatre. No, Elsa constitutes the real danger."

There was, of course, a final possibility, which Smiley was quite unable to judge : the possibility that Dieter had other agents to control here through Mundt. On the whole he was inclined to discount this, but the thought had no doubt crossed Peter's mind.

No . . . it still didn't make sense—it wasn't tidy. He decided to begin again.

What do we know? He sat up to look for pencil and paper and at once his head began throbbing. Obstinately he got off the bed and took a pencil from the inside pocket of his jacket. There was a writing pad in his suitcase. He returned to the bed, shaped the pillows to his satisfaction, took four aspirins from the bottle on the table and propped himself against the pillows, his short legs stretched before him. He began writing. First he wrote the heading in a neat, scholarly hand, and underlined it.

"What do we know?"

Then he began, stage by stage, to recount as dispassionately as possible the sequence of events hitherto :

"On Monday 2nd January Dieter Frey saw me in the park talking to his agent and concluded . . ." Yes, what *did* Dieter conclude? That Fennan had confessed, was going to confess? That Fennan was *my* agent? ". . . and concluded that Fennan was dangerous, for reasons still unknown. The following evening, the first Tuesday in the month, Elsa Fennan took her husband's reports in a music case to the Weybridge Repertory Theatre, in the agreed way, and left the case in the cloakroom in exchange for a ticket. Mundt was to bring his own music case and do the same thing. Elsa and Mundt would then exchange tickets during the performance. Mundt did not appear. Accordingly she followed the emergency procedure and posted the ticket to a prearranged address, having left the theatre early to catch the last post from Weybridge. She then drove home to be met by Mundt, who had, by then, murdered Fennan, probably on Dieter's orders. He had shot him at point blank range as soon as he met him in the hall. Knowing Dieter, I suspect that he had long ago taken the precaution of keeping in London a few sheets of blank writing paper signed with samples, forged or authentic, of Sam Fennan's signature, in case it was ever necessary to compromise or blackmail him. Assuming this to be so, Mundt brought a sheet with him in order to type the suicide letter over the signature on Fennan's own typewriter. In the ghastly scene which must have followed Elsa's arrival, Mundt realised that Dieter had wrongly interpreted Fennan's encounter with Smiley, but relied on Elsa to preserve her dead husband's reputation—not to mention her own complicity. Mundt was therefore reasonably safe. Mundt made Elsa type the letter, perhaps because he did not trust his English. (Note : But who the devil typed the *first* letter, the denunciation?)

"Mundt then, presumably, demanded the music case he had failed to collect, and Elsa told him that she had obeyed standing instructions and posted the cloakroom ticket to the Hampstead address, leaving the music case at the theatre. Mundt reacted significantly : he forced her to telephone the theatre and to arrange for him to collect the case that night on his way back to London. Therefore either the address to which the ticket was posted was no longer valid, or Mundt intended at that stage to return home early the next morning without having time to collect the ticket and the case.

"Smiley visits Walliston early on the morning of Wednesday 4th January and during the *first* interview takes an 8.30 call from the exchange which (beyond reasonable doubt) Fennan requested at 7.55 the previous evening. WHY?

"Later that morning S. returns to Elsa Fennan to ask about the 8.30 call—which she knew (on her own admission) would 'worry me' (no doubt Mundt's flattering description of my powers had had its effect). Having told S. a futile story about her bad memory she panics and rings Mundt.

"Mundt, presumably equipped with a photograph or a description from Dieter, decides to liquidate S. (on Dieter's authority?) and later that day nearly succeeds. (Note : Mundt did not return the car to Scarr's garage till the night of the 4th. This does not necessarily prove that Mundt had no plans for flying earlier in the day. If he had originally meant to fly in the morning he might well have left the car at Scarr's earlier and gone to the airport by bus.)

"It does seem pretty likely that Mundt changed his plans after Elsa's telephone call. It is not clear that he changed them *because* of her call." Would Mundt really be panicked by Elsa? Panicked into staying, panicked into murdering Adam Scarr, he wondered.

The telephone was ringing in the hall . . .

"George, it's Peter. No joy with the address or the telephone number. Dead end."

"What do you mean?"

"The telephone number and the address both led to the same place—furnished apartment in Highgate village."

"Well?"

"Rented by a pilot in Lufteuropa. He paid his two months' rent on 5th January and hasn't come back since."

"Damn."

"The landlady remembers Mundt quite well. The pilot's friend. A nice polite gentleman he was, for a German, very open handed. He used to sleep on the sofa quite often."

"Oh God."

"I went through the room with a toothcomb. There was a desk in the corner. All the drawers were empty except one, which contained a cloakroom ticket. I wonder where that came from . . . Well, if you want a laugh, come round to the Circus. The whole of Olympus is seething with activity. Oh, incidentally—"

"Yes?"

"I dug around at Dieter's flat. Another lemon. He left on 4th January. Didn't tell the milkman."

"What about his mail?"

"He never received any, apart from bills. I also had a look at Comrade Mundt's little nest : couple of rooms over the Steel Mission. The furniture went out with the rest of the stuff. Sorry."

"I see."

"I'll tell you an odd thing though, George. You remember

I thought I might get on to Fennan's personal possessions—wallet, note-book and so on? From the police."

"Yes."

"Well, I did. His diary's got Dieter's full name entered in the address section with the Mission telephone number against it. Bloody cheek."

"It's more than that. It's lunacy. Good Lord."

"Then for the fourth of January the entry is 'Smiley C.A. Ring 8.30.' That was corroborated by an entry for the third, which ran 'request call for Wed. morning.' There's your mysterious call."

"Still unexplained." A pause.

"George, I sent Felix Taverner round to the F.O. to do some ferreting. It's worse than we feared in one way, but better in another."

"Why?"

"Well, Taverner got his hands on the registry schedules for the last two years. He was able to work out what files have been marked to Fennan's section. Where a file was particularly requested by that section they still have a requisition form."

"I'm listening."

"Felix found that three or four files were usually marked in to Fennan on a Friday afternoon and marked out again on Monday morning; the inference is that he took the stuff home at week-ends."

"Oh my Lord!"

"But the odd thing is, George, that during the last six months, since his posting in fact, he tended to take home *unclassified* stuff which wouldn't have been of interest to anyone."

"But it was during the last months that he began dealing mainly with secret files," said Smiley. "He could take home anything he wanted."

"I know, but he didn't. In fact you'd almost say it was deliberate. He took home very low-grade stuff barely related to his daily work. His colleagues can't understand it now they think about it—he even took back some files handling subjects outside the scope of his section."

"And unclassified."

"Yes—of no conceivable intelligence value."

"How about earlier, before he came into his new job? What kind of stuff went home then?"

"Much more what you'd expect—files he'd used during the day, policy and so on."

"Secret?"

"Some were, some weren't. As they came."

"But nothing unexpected—no particularly delicate stuff that didn't concern him?"

"No. Nothing. He had opportunity galore quite frankly and didn't use it. Windy, I suppose."

"So he ought to be if he puts his controller's name in his diary."

"And make what you like of this : he'd arranged at the F.O. to take a day off on the fourth—the day after he died. Rather an event apparently—he was a glutton for work, they say."

"What's Maston doing about all this?" asked Smiley, after a pause.

"Going through the files at the moment and rushing in to see me with bloody fool questions every two minutes. I think he gets lonely in there with hard facts."

"Oh, he'll beat them down, Peter, don't worry."

"He's already saying that the whole case against Fennan rests on the evidence of a neurotic woman."

"Thanks for ringing, Peter."

"Be seeing you, dear boy. Keep your head down."

Smiley replaced the receiver and wondered where Mendel was. There was an evening paper on the hall table, and he glanced vaguely at the headline "Lynching : World Jewry Protests" and beneath it the account of the lynching of a Jewish shopkeeper in Dusseldorf. He opened the drawing-room door—Mendel was not there. Then he caught sight of him through the window wearing his gardening hat, hacking savagely with a pick-axe at a tree stump in the front garden.

Smiley watched him for a moment, then went upstairs again to rest. As he reached the top of the stairs the telephone began ringing again.

"George—sorry to bother you again. It's about Mundt."

"Yes?"

"Flew to Berlin last night by B.E.A. Travelled under another name but was easily identified by the air hostess. That seems to be that. Hard luck, chum."

Smiley pressed down the cradle with his hand for a moment, then dialled Walliston 2944. He heard the number ringing the other end. Suddenly the dialling tone stopped and instead he heard Elsa Fennan's voice:

"Hullo ... Hullo ... *Hullo*?"

Slowly he replaced the receiver. She was alive.

Why on earth *now*? Why should Mundt go home *now*, five weeks after murdering Fennan, three weeks after murdering Scarr; why had he eliminated the lesser danger—Scarr—and left Elsa Fennan unharmed, neurotic and embittered, liable at any moment to throw aside her own safety and tell the whole story? What effect might that terrible night not have had upon her? How could Dieter trust a woman now so lightly bound to him? Her husband's good name could no longer be preserved might she not, in God knows what mood of vengeance or repentance, blurt out the whole truth? Obviously, a little time must elapse between the murder of Fennan and the murder of his wife, but what event, what information, what danger, had decided Mundt to return last night? A ruthless and elaborate plan to preserve the secrecy of Fennan's treason had now apparently been thrown aside unfinished. What had happened yesterday that Mundt could know of? Or was the timing of his departure a coincidence? Smiley refused to believe it was. If Mundt had remained in England after the two murders and the assault on Smiley, he had done so unwillingly, waiting upon some opportunity or event that would release him. He would not stay a moment longer than he need. Yet what had he done since Scarr's death? Hidden in some lonely room, locked away from light and news. Then why did he now fly home so suddenly?

And Fennan—what spy was this who selected innocuous information for his masters when he had such gems at his fingertips? A change of heart, perhaps? A weakening of purpose? Then why did he not tell his wife, for whom his crime was a constant nightmare, who would have rejoiced at his conversion? It seemed now that Fennan had never shown any preference for secret papers—he had simply taken home whatever files currently might occupy him. But certainly a weakening of purpose would explain the strange summons to Marlow and Dieter's conviction that Fennan was betraying him. And who wrote the anonymous letter?

Nothing made sense, nothing. Fennan himself—brilliant, fluent and attractive—had deceived so naturally, so expertly. Smiley had really liked him. Why then had this practised deceiver made the incredible blunder of putting Dieter's name in his diary—and shown so little judgement or interest in the selection of intelligence?

Smiley went upstairs to pack the few possessions which Mendel had collected for him from Bywater Street. It was all over.

CHAPTER XIV

THE DRESDEN GROUP

HE STOOD ON the doorstep and put down his suitcase, fumbling for his latchkey. As he opened the door he recalled how Mundt had stood there looking at him, those very pale blue eyes calculating and steady. It was odd to think of Mundt as Dieter's pupil. Mundt had proceeded with the inflexibility of a trained mercenary—efficient, purposeful, narrow. There had been nothing original in his technique : in everything he had been a shadow of his master. It was as if Dieter's brilliant and imaginative tricks had been compressed into a manual which Mundt had learnt by heart, adding only the salt of his own brutality.

Smiley had deliberately left no forwarding address and a heap of mail lay on the door mat. He picked it up, put it on the hall table and began opening doors and peering about him, a puzzled, lost expression on his face. The house was strange to him, cold and musty. As he moved slowly from one room to another he began for the first time to realise how empty his life had become.

He looked for matches to light the gas fire, but there were none. He sat in an armchair in the living-room and his eyes wandered over the bookshelves and the odds and ends he had collected on his travels. When Ann had left him he had begun by rigorously excluding all trace of her. He had even got rid of her books. But gradually he had allowed the few remaining symbols that linked his life with hers to reassert themselves : wedding presents from close friends which had meant too much to be given away. There was a Watteau sketch from Peter Guillam, a Dresden group from Steed-Asprey.

He got up from his chair and went over to the corner cupboard where the group stood. He loved to admire the beauty of those figures, the tiny rococo courtesan in shepherd's costume, her hands outstretched to one adoring lover, her little face bestowing glances on another. He felt inadequate before that fragile perfection, as he had felt before Ann when he first began the conquest which had amazed society. Somehow those little figures comforted him : it was as useless to expect fidelity of Ann as of this tiny shepherdess in her glass case. Steed-Asprey had bought the group in Dresden before the war, it had been the prize of his collection and he had given it to them. Perhaps he had guessed that one day Smiley might have need of the simple philosophy it propounded.

Dresden : of all German cities, Smiley's favourite. He had loved its architecture, its odd jumble of mediaeval and classical buildings, sometimes reminiscent of Oxford, its cupolas, towers and spires, its copper-green roofs shimmering under a hot sun. Its name meant "town of the forest-dwellers" and it was there that Wenceslas of Bohemia had favoured the minstrel poets with gifts and privilege. Smiley remembered the last time he had been there, visiting a University acquaintance, a Professor of Philology he had met in England. It was on that visit that he had caught sight of Dieter Frey, struggling round the prison courtyard. He could see him still, tall and angry, monstrously altered by his shaven head, somehow too big for that little prison. Dresden, he remembered, had been Elsa's birthplace. He remembered glancing through her personal particulars at the Ministry : Elsa *née* Freimann, born 1917 in Dresden, Germany, of German parents; educated Dresden : imprisoned 1938-45. He tried to place her against the background of her home, the patrician Jewish family living out its life amid insult and persecution. "I dreamed of long golden hair and they shaved my head." He realised with sickening accuracy why she dyed her hair. She might have been like this shepherdess, round-bosomed and pretty. But the body had been broken with hunger so that it was frail and ugly, like the carcass of a tiny bird.

He could picture her on the terrible night when she found her husband's murderer standing by his body : hear her breathless, sobbing explanation of why Fennan had been in the park with Smiley : and Mundt unmoved, explaining and reasoning, compelling her finally to conspire once more against her will in this most dreadful and needless of crimes, dragging her to the telephone and forcing her to ring the theatre, leaving her finally tortured and exhausted to cope with the enquiries that were bound to follow, even to type that futile suicide letter over Fennan's signature. It was inhuman beyond belief and, he added to himself, for Mundt a fantastic risk.

She had, of course, proved herself a reliable enough accomplice in the past, cool-headed and, ironically, more skilful than Fennan in the techniques of espionage. And, heaven knows, for a woman who had been through such a night as that, her performance at their first meeting had been a marvel.

As he stood gazing at the little shepherdess, poised eternally between her two admirers, he realised dispassionately that there was another quite different solution to the case of Samuel Fennan, a solution which matched every detail of circumstance, reconciled the nagging inconsistencies apparent in Fennan's character. The realisation began as an academic exercise without reference to personalities; Smiley manoeuvred the characters like pieces in a puzzle, twisting them this way and that to fit the complex framework of established facts—and then, in a moment, the pattern had suddenly re-formed with such assurance that it was a game no more.

His heart beat faster, as with growing astonishment Smiley retold to himself the whole story, reconstructed scenes and incidents in the light of his discovery. Now he knew why Mundt had left England that day, why Fennan chose so little that was of value to Dieter, had asked for the 8.30 call, and why his wife had escaped the systematic savagery of Mundt. Now at last he knew who had written the anonymous letter. He saw how he had been the fool of his own sentiment, had played false with the power of his mind.

He went to the telephone and dialled Mendel's number. As soon as he had finished speaking to him he rang Peter Guillam. Then he put on his hat and coat and walked round the corner to Sloane Square. At a small newsagent's beside Peter Jones he bought a picture postcard of Westminster Abbey. He made his way to the underground station and travelled north to Hampstead, where he got out. At the main post office he bought a stamp and addressed the postcard in stiff, continental capitals to Elsa Fennan. In the panel for correspondence he wrote in spiky longhand : "Wish you were here." He posted the card and noted the time, after which he returned to Sloane Square. There was nothing more he could do.

He slept soundly that night, rose early the following morning, a Saturday, and walked round the corner to buy croissants and coffee beans. He made a lot of coffee and sat in the kitchen reading *The Times* and eating his breakfast. He felt curiously calm and when the telephone rang at last he folded his paper carefully together before going upstairs to answer it.

"George, it's Peter"—the voice was urgent, almost triumphant : "George, she's bitten, I swear she has!"

"What happened?"

"The post arrived at exactly 8.35. By 9.30 she was walking briskly down the drive, booted and spurred. She made straight for the railway station and caught the 9.52 to Victoria. I put Mendel on the train and hared up by car, but I was too late to meet the train this end."

"How will you make contact with Mendel again?"

"I gave him the number of the Grosvenor Hotel and I'm there now. He's going to ring me as soon as he gets a chance and I'll join him wherever he is."

"Peter, you're taking this gently, aren't you?"

"Gentle as the wind, dear boy. I think she's losing her head. Moving like a greyhound."

Smiley rang off. He picked up his *Times* and began studying the theatre column. He must be right . . . he must be.

After that the morning passed with agonising slowness. Sometimes he would stand at the window, his hands in his pockets, watching leggy Kensington girls going shopping with beautiful young men in pale blue pullovers, or the car-cleaning brigade toiling happily in front of their houses, then drifting away to talk motoring shop and finally setting off purposefully down the road for the first pint of the week-end.

At last, after what seemed an interminable delay, the front-door bell rang and Mendel and Guillam came in, grinning cheerfully, ravenously hungry.

"Hook, line and sinker," said Guillam. "But let Mendel tell you—he did most of the dirty work. I just got in for the kill."

Mendel recounted his story precisely and accurately, looking at the ground a few feet in front of him, his thin head slightly on one side.

"She caught the 9.52 to Victoria. I kept well clear of her on the train and picked her up as she went through the barrier. Then she took a taxi to Hammersmith."

"A taxi?" Smiley interjected. "She must be out of her mind."

"She's rattled. She walks fast for a woman anyway, mind,

but she damn nearly ran going down the platform. Got out at the Broadway and walked to the Sheridan Theatre. Tried the doors to the box office but they were locked. She hesitated a moment then turned back and went to a café a hundred yards down the road. Ordered coffee and paid for it at once. About forty minutes later she went back to the Sheridan. The box office was open and I ducked in behind her and joined the queue. She bought two rear stalls for next Thursday, Row T, 27 and 28. When she got outside the theatre she put one ticket in an envelope and sealed it up. Then she posted it. I couldn't see the address but there was a sixpenny stamp on the envelope."

Smiley sat very still. "I wonder," he said; "I wonder if he'll come."

"I caught up with Mendel at the Sheridan," said Guillam. "He saw her into the café and then rang me. After that he went in after her."

"Felt like a coffee myself," Mendel went on. "Mr. Guillam joined me. I left him there when I joined the ticket queue, and he drifted out of the café a bit later. It was a decent job and no worries. She's rattled, I'm sure. But not suspicious."

"What did she do after that?" asked Smiley.

"Went straight back to Victoria. We left her to it."

They were silent for a moment, then Mendel said:

"What do we do now?"

Smiley blinked and gazed earnestly into Mendel's grey face.

"Book tickets for Thursday's performance at the Sheridan."

They were gone and he was alone. He still had not begun to cope with the quantity of mail which had accumulated in his absence. Circulars, catalogues from Blackwells, bills and the usual collection of soap vouchers, frozen pea coupons, football pool forms and a few private letters still lay unopened on the hall table. He took them into the drawing-room, settled in an armchair and began opening the personal letters first. There was one from Maston, and he read it with something approaching embarrassment.

"My dear George,

I was so sorry to hear from Guillam about your accident, and I do hope that by now you have made a full recovery.

You may recall that in the heat of the moment you wrote me a letter of resignation before your misfortune, and I just wanted to let you know that I am not, of course, taking this seriously. Sometimes when events crowd in upon us our sense of perspective suffers. But old campaigners like ourselves, George, are not so easily put off the scent. I look forward to seeing you with us again as soon as you are strong enough, and in the meantime we continue to regard you as an old and loyal member of the staff."

Smiley put this on one side and turned to the next letter. Just for a moment he did not recognise the handwriting; just for a moment he looked bleakly at the Swiss stamp and the expensive hotel writing paper. Suddenly he felt slightly sick, his vision blurred and there was scarcely strength enough in his fingers to tear open the envelope. What did she want? If money, she could have all he possessed. The money was his own, to spend as he wished; if it gave him pleasure to squander it on Ann, he would do so. There was nothing else he had to give her—she had taken it long ago. Taken his courage, his love, his compassion, carried them jauntily away in her little jewel case to fondle occasionally on odd afternoons when the time hung heavy in the Cuban sun, to dangle them perhaps before the eyes of her newest lover, to compare them even with similar trinkets which others before or since had brought her.

"My darling George,

I want to make you an offer which no gentleman could accept. I want to come back to you.

I'm staying at the Baur-au-Lac at Zurich till the end of the month. Let me know.

Ann."

Smiley picked up the envelope and looked at the back of it: "Madame Juan Alvida." No, no gentleman could accept that offer. No dream could survive the daylight of Ann's departure with her saccharine Latin and his orange-peel grin. Smiley had once seen a news film of Alvida winning some race in Monte Carlo. The most repellent thing about him, he remembered, had been the hair on his arms. With his goggles and the motor oil and that ludicrous laurel-wreath he had looked exactly like an anthropoid ape fallen from a tree. He was wearing a white tennis shirt with short sleeves, which had somehow remained spotlessly clean throughout the race, setting off those black monkey arms with repulsive clarity.

That was Ann: Let me know. Redeem your life, see whether it can be lived again and let me know. I have wearied my lover, my lover has wearied me, let me shatter your world again : my own bores me. I want to come back to you ... I want, I want ...

Smiley got up, the letter still in his hand and stood again before the porcelain group. He remained there several minutes, gazing at the little shepherdess. She was so beautiful.

CHAPTER XV

THE LAST ACT

THE SHERIDAN'S THREE-ACT production of "Edward II" was playing to a full house. Guillam and Mendel sat in adjacent seats at the extreme end of the circle, which formed a wide U facing the stage. The left-hand end of the circle afforded a view of the rear stalls, which were otherwise concealed. An empty seat separated Guillam from a party of young students buzzing with anticipation.

They looked down thoughtfully on a restless sea of bobbing heads and fluttering programmes, stirring in sudden waves as later arrivals took their places. The scene reminded Guillam of an Oriental dance, where the tiny gestures of hand and foot animate a motionless body. Occasionally he would glance towards the rear stalls, but there was still no sign of Elsa Fennan or her guest.

Just as the recorded overture was ending he looked again briefly towards the two empty stalls in the back row and his heart gave a sudden leap as he saw the slight figure of Elsa Fennan sitting straight and motionless, staring fixedly down the auditorium like a child learning deportment. The seat on her right, nearest the gangway, was still empty.

Outside in the street taxis were drawing up hastily at the theatre entrance and an agreeable selection of the established and the disestablished hurriedly over-tipped their cabmen and spent five minutes looking for their tickets. Smiley's taxi took him past the theatre and deposited him at the Clarendon Hotel, where he went straight downstairs to the dining-room and bar.

"I'm expecting a call any moment," he said. "My name's Savage. You'll let me know, won't you?"

The barman turned to the telephone behind him and spoke to the receptionist.

"And a small whisky and soda, please; will you have one yourself?"

"Thank you sir, I never touch it."

The curtain rose on a dimly lit stage and Guillam, peering towards the back of the auditorium, tried at first without success to penetrate the sudden darkness. Gradually his eyes accustomed themselves to the faint glow cast by the emergency lamps, until he could just discern Elsa in the half light; and still the empty seat beside her.

Only a low partition separated the rear stalls from the gangway which ran along the back of the auditorium, and behind it were several doors leading to the foyer, bar and cloak rooms. For a brief moment one of these opened and an oblique shaft of light was cast as if by design upon Elsa Fennan, illuminating with a thin line one side of her face, making its hollows black by contrast. She inclined her head slightly, as if listening to something behind her, half rose in her seat, then sat down again, deceived, and resumed her former attitude.

Guillam felt Mendel's hand on his arm, turned, and saw his lean face thrust forward, looking past him. Following Mendel's gaze, he peered down into the well of the theatre, where a tall figure was slowly making his way towards the back of the stalls; he was an impressive sight, erect and handsome, a lock of black hair tumbling over his brow. It was he whom Mendel watched with such fascination, this elegant giant limping up the gangway. There was something different about him, something arresting and disturbing. Through his glasses Guillam watched his slow and deliberate progress, admired the grace and measure of his uneven walk. He was a man apart, a man you remember, a man who strikes a chord deep in your experience, a man with the gift of universal familiarity : to Guillam he was a living component of all our romantic dreams, he stood at the mast with Conrad, sought the lost Greece with Byron and with Goethe visited the shades of classical and mediaeval hells.

As he walked, thrusting his good leg forward, there was a defiance, a command, that could not go unheeded. Guillam noticed how heads turned in the audience, and eyes followed him obediently.

Pushing past Mendel, Guillam stepped quickly through the emergency exit into the corridor behind. He followed the corridor down some steps and arrived at last at the foyer. The box office had closed down, but the girl was still poring hopelessly over a page of laboriously compiled figures, covered with alterations and erasions.

"Excuse me," said Guillam; "but I must use your telephone —it's urgent, do you mind?"

"Ssh!" She waved a pencil at him impatiently, without looking up. Her hair was mousy, her oily skin glistened from the fatigue of late nights and a diet of chipped potatoes. Guillam waited a moment, wondering how long it would be before she found a solution to that tangle of spidery numerals which would match the pile of notes and silver in the open cash box beside her.

"Listen," he urged; "I'm a police officer—there's a couple of heroes upstairs who are after your cash. Now will you let me use that telephone?"

"Oh Lord," she said in a tired voice, and looked at him for the first time. She wore glasses and was very plain. She was neither alarmed nor impressed; "I wish they'd perishing well take the money. It sends me up the wall." Pushing her accounts to one side she opened a door beside the little kiosk and Guillam squeezed in.

"Hardly decent, is it?" the girl said with a grin. Her voice was nearly cultured—probably a London undergraduate earning pin-money, thought Guillam. He rang the Clarendon and asked for Mr. Savage. Almost immediately he heard Smiley's voice.

"He's here," said Guillam, "been here all the time. Must have bought an extra ticket; he was sitting in the front stalls. Mendel suddenly spotted him limping up the aisle."

"Limping?"

"Yes, it's not Mundt. It's the other one. Dieter."

Smiley did not reply and after a moment Guillam said: "George—are you there?"

"We've had it I'm afraid, Peter. We've got nothing against Frey. Call the men off, they won't find Mundt tonight. Is the first act over yet?"

"Must be just coming up for the interval."

"I'll be round in twenty minutes. Hang on to Elsa like grim death—if they leave and separate Mendel's to stick to Dieter. You stay in the foyer for the last act in case they leave early."

Guillam replaced the receiver and turned to the girl. "Thanks," he said, and put four pennies on her desk. She hastily gathered them together and pressed them firmly into his hand.

"For God's sake," she said; "don't add to my troubles."

He went outside into the street and spoke to a plain clothes man loitering on the pavement. Then he hurried back and rejoined Mendel as the curtain fell on the first act.

Elsa and Dieter were sitting side by side. They were talking happily together, Dieter laughing, Elsa animated and articulate like a puppet brought to life by her master. Mendel watched them in fascination. She laughed at something Dieter said, leant forward and put her hand on his arm. He saw her thin fingers against his dinner jacket, saw Dieter incline his head and whisper something to her, so that she laughed again. As Mendel watched, the theatre lights dimmed and the noise of conversation subsided as the audience quickly prepared for the second act.

Smiley left the Clarendon and walked slowly along the pavement towards the theatre. Thinking about it now, he realised that it was logical enough that Dieter should come, that it would have been madness to send Mundt. He wondered how long it could be before Elsa and Dieter discovered that it was not Dieter who had summoned her, not Dieter who had sent the postcard by a trusted courier. That, he reflected, should be an interesting moment. All he prayed for now was the opportunity of one more interview with Elsa Fennan.

A few minutes later he slipped quietly into the empty seat beside Guillam. It was a long time since he had seen Dieter.

He had not changed. He was the same improbable romantic with the magic of a charlatan; the same unforgettable figure which had struggled over the ruins of Germany, implacable of purpose, satanic in fulfilment, dark and swift like the Gods of the North. Smiley had lied to them that night in his club; Dieter *was* out of proportion, his cunning, his conceit, his strength and his dream—all were larger than life, undiminished by the moderating influence of experience. He was a man who thought and acted in absolute terms, without patience or compromise.

Memories returned to Smiley that night as he sat in the dark theatre and watched Dieter across a mass of motionless faces, memories of dangers shared, of mutual trust when each had held in his hand the life of the other.... Just for a second Smiley wondered whether Dieter had seen him, had the feeling that Dieter's eyes were upon him, watching him in the dim half light.

Smiley got up as the second act drew to a close; as the curtain fell he made quickly for the side exit and waited discreetly in the corridor until the bell rang for the last act. Mendel joined him shortly before the end of the interval, and Guillam slipped past them to take up his post in the foyer.

"There's trouble," Mendel said. "They're arguing. She looks frightened. She keeps on saying something and he just shakes his head. She's panicking I think, and Dieter looks worried. He's started looking round the theatre as if he was trapped, getting the measure of the place, making plans. He glanced up to where you'd been sitting."

"He won't let her leave alone," said Smiley. "He'll wait and get out with the crowd. They won't leave before the end. He probably reckons he's surrounded : he'll bargain on flustering us by parting from her suddenly in the middle of a crowd—just losing her."

"What's our game? Why can't we go down there and get them?"

"We just wait; I don't know what for. We've no proof. No proof of murder and none of espionage until Maston decides to do something. But remember this : Dieter doesn't know that. If Elsa's jumpy and Dieter's worried, they'll do some-thing—that's certain. So long as they think the game is up, we've a chance. Let them bolt, panic, anything. So long as they do something...."

It was dark in the theatre again, but out of the corner of his eye Smiley saw Dieter leaning over Elsa whispering to her. His left hand held her arm, his whole attitude was one of urgent persuasion and reassurance.

The play dragged on, the shouts of soldiers and the screams of the demented king filled the theatre, until the dreadful climax of his foul death, when an audible sigh rose from the stalls beneath them. Dieter had his arm round Elsa's shoulders now, he had gathered the folds of her thin wrap about her neck and protected her as if she were a sleeping child. They remained like this until the final curtain. Neither applauded, Dieter looked about for Elsa's handbag, said something reassuring to her and put it on her lap. She nodded very slightly. A warning roll of the drums brought the audience to its feet for the national anthem—Smiley rose instinctively and noticed to his surprise that Mendel had vanished. Dieter slowly stood up and as he did so Smiley realised that something had happened. Elsa was still sitting and though Dieter gently prevailed on her to rise, she made no answering sign. There was something oddly dislocated in the way she sat, in the way her head lolled forward on her shoulders. . . .

The last line of the anthem was beginning as Smiley rushed to the door, ran down the corridor, down the stone stairs to the foyer. He was just too late—he was met by the first crowd of anxious theatre-goers hastening towards the street in search of taxis. He looked wildly among the crowd for Dieter and knew it was hopeless—that Dieter had done what he himself would have done, had chosen one of the dozen emergency exits which led to the street and safety. He pushed his bulky frame gradually through the middle of the crowd towards the entrance to the stalls. As he twisted this way and that, forcing himself between oncoming bodies, he caught sight of Guillam at the edge of the stream searching hopelessly for Dieter and Elsa. He shouted to him, and Guillam turned quickly.

Struggling on, Smiley at last found himself against the low partition and he could see Elsa Fennan sitting motionless as all around her men stood up and women felt for their coats and handbags. Then he heard the scream. It was sudden, short and utterly expresive of horror and disgust. A girl was standing in the gangway looking at Elsa. She was young and very pretty, the fingers of her right hand were raised to her mouth, her face was deathly white. Her father, a tall cadaverous man, stood behind her. He grasped her shoulders quickly and drew her back as he caught sight of the dreadful thing before him.

Elsa's wrap had slipped from her shoulders and her head was lolling on to her chest.

Smiley had been right. "Let them bolt, panic, anything . . . so long as they do *something* . . ." And this was what they had done : this broken, wretched body was witness to their panic.

"You'd better get the police, Peter. I'm going home. Keep me out of it, if you can. You know where to find me." He nodded, as if to himself; "I'm going home."

It was foggy, and a fine rain was falling as Mendel quickly darted across the Fulham Palace Road in pursuit of Dieter. The headlights of cars came suddenly out of the wet mist twenty yards from him; the noise of traffic was high-pitched and nervous as it groped its uncertain way.

He had no choice but to keep close on Dieter's heels, never more than a dozen paces behind him. The pubs and cinemas had closed but the coffee bars and dance halls still attracted noisy groups crowding the pavements. As Dieter limped ahead of him Mendel staged his progression by the street lamps, watching his silhouette suddenly clarify each time it entered the next cone of light.

Dieter was walking swiftly despite his limp. As his stride lengthened his limp became more pronounced, so that he seemed to swing his left leg forward by a sudden effort of his broad shoulders.

There was a curious expression on Mendel's face, not of hatred or iron purpose but of frank distaste. To Mendel, the frills of Dieter's profession meant nothing. He saw in his quarry only the squalor of a criminal, the cowardice of a man who paid others to do his killing. When Dieter had gently disengaged himself from the audience and moved towards the side exit, Mendel saw what he had been waiting for : the stealthy act of a common criminal. It was something he expected and understood. To Mendel there was only one criminal class, from pickpocket and sneakthief to the big operator tampering with company law; they were outside the law and it was his distasteful but necessary vocation to remove them to safe keeping. This one happened to be German.

The fog grew thick and yellow. Neither of them wore a coat. Mendel wondered what Mrs. Fennan would do now. Guillam would take care of her. She hadn't even looked at Dieter when he slinked off. She was an odd one that, all skin and bones and good works by the look of her. Lived on dry toast and Bovril.

Dieter turned abruptly down a side street to the right then another to the left. They had been walking for nearly an hour and he showed no sign of slowing down. The street seemed empty : certainly Mendel could hear no other footsteps but their own, crisp and short, the echo corrupted by the fog. They were in a narrow street of Victorian houses with hastily contrived Regency style façades, heavy porches and sash windows. Mendel guessed they were somewhere near Fulham Broadway, perhaps beyond it, nearer the King's Road. Still Dieter's pace did not flag, still the crooked shadow thrust forward into the fog, confident of its path, urgent in its purpose.

As they approached a main road Mendel heard again the plaintive whine of traffic, brought almost to a standstill by the fog. Then from somewhere above them a yellow street light shed a pale glow, its outline clearly drawn like the aura of a winter sun. Dieter hesitated a moment on the kerb, then, chancing the ghostly traffic that nosed its way past them from nowhere, he crossed the road and plunged at once into one of the innumerable side streets that led, Mendel was certain, towards the river.

Mendel's clothes were soaking wet, and the thin rain ran over his face. They must be near the river now; he thought he could detect the smell of tar and coke, feel the insidious cold of the black water. Just for a moment he thought Dieter had vanished. He move forward quickly, nearly tripped on a kerb, went forward again and saw the railings of the Embankment in front of him. Steps led upwards to an iron gate in the railings and this was slightly open. He stood at the gate and peered beyond, down into the water. There was a stout wooden gangway and Mendel heard the uneven echo as Dieter, hidden by the fog, followed his strange course to the water's edge. Mendel waited, then, wary and silent, he made his way down the gangway. It was a permanent affair with heavy pine handrails on either side. Mendel reckoned it had been there some time. The low end of the gangway was joined to a long raft made of duckboard and oil-drums. Three dilapidated houseboats loomed in the fog, rocking gently on their moorings.

Noiselessly Mendel crept on to the raft, examining each of the houseboats in turn. Two were close together, connected by a plank. The third was moored some fifteen feet away, and a light was burning in her forward cabin. Mendel returned to the Embankment, closing the iron gate carefully behind him.

He walked slowly down the road, still uncertain of his bearings. After about five minutes the pavement took him suddenly to the right and the ground rose gradually. He guessed he was on a bridge. He lit his cigarette lighter, and its long flame cast a glow over the stone wall on his right. He moved the lighter back and forth, and finally came upon a wet and dirty metal plate bearing the words "Battersea Bridge." He made his way back to the iron gate and stood for a moment, orientating himself exactly in the light of his knowledge.

Somewhere above him and to his right the four massive chimneys of Fulham Power Station stood hidden in the fog. To his left was Cheyne Walk with its row of smart little boats reaching to Battersea Bridge. The place where he now stood marked the dividing line between the smart and the squalid, where Cheyne Walk meets Lots Road, one of the ugliest streets in London. The southern side of this road consists of vast warehouses, wharves and mills, and the northern side presents an unbroken line of dingy houses typical of the side streets of Fulham.

It was in the shadow of the four chimneys, perhaps sixty

feet from the Cheyne Walk moorings, that Dieter Frey had found a sanctuary. Yes, Mendel knew the spot well. It was only a couple of hundred yards up river from where the earthly remains of Mr. Adam Scarr had been recovered from the unyielding arms of the Thames.

CHAPTER XVI

ECHOES IN THE FOG

It was long after midnight when Smiley's telephone rang. He got up from the armchair in front of the gas fire and plodded upstairs to his bedroom, his right hand gripping the banisters tightly as he went. It was Peter, no doubt, or the police, and he would have to make a statement. Or even the Press. The murder had taken place just in time to catch today's papers and mercifully too late for last night's news broadcast. What would this be? "Maniac killer in theatre?" "Death-lock murder—woman named"? He hated the Press as he hated advertising and television, he hated mass-media, the relentless persuasion of the twentieth century. Everything he admired or loved had been the product of intense individualism. That was why he hated Dieter now, hated what he stood for more strongly than ever before : it was the fabulous impertinence of renouncing the individual in favour of the mass. When had mass philosophies ever brought benefit or wisdom? Dieter cared nothing for human life : dreamed only of armies of faceless men bound by their lowest common denominators; he wanted to shape the world as if it were a tree, cutting off what did not fit the regular image; for this he fashioned blank, soulless automatons like Mundt. Mundt was faceless like Dieter's army, a trained killer born of the finest killer breed.

He picked up the telephone and gave his number. It was Mendel.

"Where are you?"

"Near Chelsea Embankment. Pub called the Balloon, in Lots Road. Landlord's a chum of mine. I knocked him up. . . . Listen, Elsa's boy friend is lying up in a houseboat by Chelsea flour mill. Bloody miracle in the fog, he is. Must have found his way by Braille."

"Who?"

"Her boy friend, her escort at the theatre. Wake up, Mr. Smiley; what's eating you?"

"You followed Dieter?"

"Of course I did. That was what you told Mr. Guillam, wasn't it? He was to stick to the woman and me the man. . . . How did Mr. Guillam get on by the way? Where did Elsa get to?"

"She didn't get anywhere. She was dead when Dieter left. Mendel, are you there? Look, for God's sake, how do I find you? Where is this place, will the police know it?"

"They'll know. Tell them he's in a converted landing craft called 'Sunset Haven'. She's lying against the eastern side of Sennen Wharf, between the flour mills and Fulham Power Station. They'll know . . . but the fog's thick, mind, very thick."

"Where can I meet you?"

"Cut straight down to the river. I'll meet you where Battersea Bridge joins the north bank."

"I'll come at once, as soon as I've rung Guillam."

He had a gun somewhere, and for a moment he thought of looking for it. Then, somehow, it seemed pointless. Besides, he reflected grimly, there'd be the most frightful row if he used it. He rang Guillam at his flat and gave him Mendel's message : "And, Peter, they must cover all ports and airfields; order a special watch on river traffic and seabound craft. They'll know the form."

He put on an old mackintosh and a pair of thick leather gloves and slipped quickly out into the fog.

Mendel was waiting for him by the bridge. They nodded

to one another and Mendel led him quickly along the Embankment, keeping close to the river wall to avoid the trees that grew along the road. Suddenly Mendel stopped, seizing Smiley by the arm in warning. They stood motionless, listening. Then Smiley heard it too, the hollow ring of footsteps on a wooden floor, irregular like the footsteps of a limping man. They heard the creak of an iron gate, the clang as it was closed, then the footsteps again, firm now upon the pavement, growing louder, coming towards them. Neither moved. Louder, nearer, then they faltered, stopped. Smiley held his breath, trying desperately at the same time to see an extra yard into the fog, to glimpse at the waiting figure, he knew was there.

Then suddenly he came, rushing like a massive wild beast, bursting through them, knocking them apart like children and running on, lost again, the uneven echo fading in the distance. They turned and chased after him, Mendel in front and Smiley following as best he could, the image vivid in his mind of Dieter, gun in hand, bursting on them out of the night fog. Ahead, the shadow of Mendel turned abruptly to the right, and Smiley followed blindly. Then suddenly the rhythm had changed to the scuffle of fighting. Smiley ran forward, heard the unmistakable sound of a heavy weapon striking a human skull, and then he was upon them : saw Mendel on the ground, and Dieter stooping over him, raising his arm to hit him again with the heavy butt of an automatic pistol.

Smiley was out of breath. His chest was burning from the bitter, rank fog, his mouth hot and dry, filled with a taste like blood. Somehow he summoned breath and he shouted desperately :

"Dieter !"

Frey looked at him, nodded and said :

"*Servus*, George," and hit Mendel a hard, brutal blow with the pistol. He got up slowly, holding the pistol downwards and using both hands to cock it.

Smiley ran at him blindly, forgetting what little skill he had ever possessed, swinging with his short arms, striking with his open hands. His head was against Dieter's chest and he pushed forward, punching Dieter's back and sides. He was mad and, discovering in himself the energy of madness, pressed Dieter back still further towards the railing of the bridge, while Dieter, off balance and hindered by his weak leg, gave way. Smiley knew Dieter was hitting him, but the decisive blow never came. He was shouting at Dieter; "Swine, swine!" and as Dieter receded still further Smiley found his arms free and once more struck at his face with clumsy, childish blows. Dieter was leaning back and Smiley saw the clean curve of his throat and chin, as with all his strength he thrust his open hand upwards. This fingers closed over Dieter's jaw and mouth and he pushed further and further. Dieter's hands were at Smiley's throat, then suddenly they were clutching at his collar to save himself as he sank slowly backwards. Smiley beat frantically at his arms, and then he was held no more and Dieter was falling, falling into the swirling fog beneath the bridge, and there was silence. No shout, no splash. He was gone; offered like a human sacrifice to the London fog and the foul black river lying beneath it.

Smiley leant over the bridge, his head throbbing wildly, blood pouring from his nose, the fingers of his right hand feeling broken and useless. His gloves were gone. He looked down into the fog and could see nothing.

"Dieter!" he cried in anguish; "Dieter!"

He shouted again, but his voice choked and tears sprang to his eyes. "Oh dear God what have I done, Oh Christ, Dieter, why didn't you stop me, why didn't you hit me with the gun, why didn't you shoot?" He pressed his clenched hands to his face tasting the salt blood in the palms mixed with the salt of his tears. He leant against the parapet and cried like a child. Somewhere beneath him a cripple dragged himself through the filthy water, lost and exhausted, yielding at last to the stenching blackness till it held him and drew him down.

He woke to find Peter Guillam sitting on the end of his bed pouring out tea.

"Ah, George. Welcome home. It's two in the afternoon."

"And this morning—?"

"This morning, dear boy, you were carolling on Battersea Bridge with Comrade Mendel."

"How is he . . . Mendel, I mean?"

"Suitably ashamed of himself. Recovering fast."

"And Dieter—"

"Dead."

Guillam handed him a cup of tea and some ratafia biscuits from Fortnums.

"How long have you been here, Peter?"

"Well, we came here in a series of tactical bounds, as it were. The first was to Chelsea Hospital where they licked your wounds and gave you a fairly substantial tranquilliser. Then we came back here and I put you to bed. That was disgusting. Then I did a spot of telephoning and, so to speak, went round with a pointed stick tidying up the mess. I looked in on you now and again. Cupid and Psyche. You were either snoring like a saddleback or reciting Webster."

"God."

"Duchess of Malfi, I think it was. 'I bad thee, when I was distracted of my wits, go kill my dearest friend, and thou hast done it!' Dreadful nonsense, George, I'm afraid."

"How did the police find us—Mendel and me?"

"George, you may not know it but you were bellowing pejoratives at Dieter as if—"

"Yes, of course. You heard."

"We heard."

"What about Maston? What does Maston say about all this?"

"I think he wants to see you. I have a message from him asking you to drop in as soon as you feel well enough. I don't know what he thinks about it. Nothing at all I should imagine."

"What do you mean?"

Guillam poured out more tea.

"Use your loaf, George. All three principals in this little fairy tale have now been eaten by bears. No secret information has been compromised for the last six months. Do you really think Maston wants to dwell on the details? Do you really think he is bursting to tell the Foreign Office the good tidings—and admit that we only catch spies when we trip over their dead bodies?"

The front-door bell rang and Guillam went downstairs to answer it. In some alarm Smiley heard him admit the visitor to the hall, then the subdued sound of voices, footsteps coming up the stairs. There was a knock on the door and Maston came in. He was carrying an absurdly large bunch of flowers and looked as though he had just been to a garden party. Smiley remembered it was Friday: no doubt he was going to Henley this week-end. He was grinning. He must have been grinning all the way up the stairs.

"Well, George, in the wars again!"

"Yes, I'm afraid so. Another accident."

He sat on the edge of the bed, leaning across it, one arm supporting him the other side of Smiley's legs.

There was a pause and then he said :

"You got my note, George?"

"Yes."

Another pause.

"There has been talk of a new section in the Department, George. We (your Department, that is) feel we should devote more energy to technique research, with particular application to satellite espionage. That is also the Home Office view, I'm pleased to say. Guillam has agreed to advise on terms of reference. I wondered if you'd take it on for us. Running it I mean, with the necessary promotion of course and the option of extending your service after the statutory retirement age. Our personnel people are right behind me on this."

"Thank you . . . perhaps I could think about it, may I?"

"Of course . . . of course," Maston looked slightly put out. "When will you let me know? It may be necessary to take on some new men and the question of space arises. . . . Have the week-end to think about it will you and let me know on Monday. The Secretary was quite willing for you to—"

"Yes, I'll let you know. It's very good of you."

"Not at all. Besides I am only the Adviser you know, George. This is really an internal decision. I'm just the bringer of good news, George; my usual function of errand boy."

Maston looked at Smiley hard for a moment, hesitated and then said : "I've put the Ministers in the picture . . . as far as is necessary. We discussed what action should be taken. The Home Secretary was also present."

"When was this?"

"This morning. Some very grave issues were raised. We considered a protest to the East Germans and an extradition order for this man Mundt."

"But we don't recognise East Germany."

"Precisely. That was the difficulty. It is however possible to lodge a protest with an intermediary."

"Such as Russia?"

"Such as Russia. In the event, however, certain factors militated against this. It was felt that publicity, whatever form it took, would ultimately rebound against the nation's interests. There is already considerable popular hostility in this country to the rearmament of Western Germany. It was felt that any evidence of German intrigue in Britain—whether inspired by the Russians or not—might encourage this hostility. There is, you see, no positive evidence that Frey was operating for the Russians. It might well be represented to the public that he was operating on his own account or on behalf of a united Germany."

"I see."

"So far very few people indeed are aware of the facts at all. That is most fortunate. On behalf of the police the Home Secretary has tentatively agreed that they will do their part in playing the affair down as far as possible. . . . Now this man Mendel, what's he like. Is he trustworthy?"

Smiley hated Maston for that.

"Yes," he said.

Maston got up. "Good," he said, "good. Well I must get along. Anything you want at all, anything I can do?"

"No, thank you. Guillam is looking after me admirably."

Maston reached the door. "Well good luck, George. Take the job if you can." He said this quickly in a subdued voice with a pretty, sidelong smile as if it meant rather a lot to him.

"Thank you for the flowers," said Smiley.

Dieter was dead, and he had killed him. The broken fingers of his right hand, the stiffness of his body and the sickening headache, the nausea of guilt, all testified to this. And Dieter had let him do it, had not fired the gun, had remembered their friendship when Smiley had not. They had fought in a cloud, in the rising stream of the river, in a clearing in a timeless forest : they had met, two friends rejoined, and fought like beasts. Dieter had remembered and Smiley had not. They had come from different hemispheres of the night, from different worlds of thought and conduct. Dieter, mercurial, absolute, had fought to build a civilisation. Smiley, rationalistic, protective, had fought to prevent him. "Oh God," said Smiley aloud, "who was then the gentleman . . .?"

Laboriously he got out of bed and began to dress. He felt better standing up.

CHAPTER XVII

DEAR ADVISER

DEAR ADVISER,

I am at last able to reply to Personnel's offer of a higher appointment in the Department. I am sorry that I have taken so long to do this, but as you know, I have not been well recently, and have also had to contend with a number of personal problems outside the scope of the Department.

As I am not entirely free of my indisposition, I feel it

would be unwise for me to accept their offer. Kindly convey this decision to Personnel.

I am sure you will understand.

Yours,
George Smiley."

"Dear Peter,

I enclose a note on the Fennan case. This is the only copy. Please pass it to Maston when you have read it. I thought it would be valuable to record the events—even if they did not take place.

Ever,
George."

"The Fennan Case

"On Monday, 2nd January, I interviewed Samuel Arthur Fennan, a senior member of the Foreign Office, in order to clarify certain allegations made against him in an anonymous letter. The interview was arranged in accordance with the customary procedure, that is to say with the consent of the F.O. We knew of nothing adverse to Fennan beyond communist sympathy while at Oxford in the thirties, to which little significance was attached. The interview was therefore in a sense a strictly routine affair.

"Fennan's room at the Foreign Office was found to be unsuitable and we agreed to continue our discussion in St. James's Park, availing ourselves of the good weather.

"It has subsequently transpired that we were recognised and observed in this by an agent of the East German Intelligence Service, who had co-operated with me during the war. It is not certain whether he had placed Fennan under some kind of surveillance, or whether his presence in the park was coincidental.

"On the night of 3rd January it was reported by Surrey police that Fennan had committed suicide. A typewritten suicide note signed by Fennan claimed that he had been victimised by the security authorities.

"The following facts, however, emerged during investigation, and suggested foul play :

"1. At 7.55 p.m. on the night of his death Fennan had asked the Walliston exchange to call him at 8.30 the following morning.

"2. Fennan had made himself a cup of cocoa shortly before his death, and had not drunk it.

"3. He had supposedly shot himself in the hall, at the bottom of the stairs. The note was beside the body

"4. It seemed inconsistent that he should type his last letter, as he seldom used a typewriter, and even more remarkable that he should come downstairs to the hall to shoot himself.

"5. On the day of his death he posted a letter inviting me in urgent terms to lunch with him at Marlow the following day.

"6. Later it also transpired that Fennan had requested a day's leave for Wednesday, 4th January. He did not apparently mention this to his wife.

"7. It was also noted that the suicide letter had been typed on Fennan's own machine—and that it contained certain peculiarities in the typescript similar to those in the anonymous letter. The laboratory report concluded, however, that the two letters had not been typed by the same hand, though originating from the same machine.

"Mrs. Fennan, who had been to the theatre on the night her husband died, was invited to explain the 8.30 call from the exchange and falsely claimed to have requested it herself. The exchange was positive that this was not the case. Mrs. Fennan claimed that her husband had been nervous and depressed since his security interview, which corroborated the evidence of his final letter.

"On the afternoon of 4th January, having left Mrs. Fennan earlier in the day, I returned to my house in Kensington. Briefly observing somebody at the window, I rang the front-door bell. A man opened the door who has since been identified as a member of the East German Intelligence Service.

He invited me into the house but I declined his offer and returned to my car, noting at the same time the numbers of cars parked nearby.

That evening I visited a small garage in Battersea to enquire into the origin of one of these cars which was registered in the name of the proprietor of the garage. I was attacked by an unknown assailant and beaten senseless. Three weeks later the proprietor himself, Adam Scarr, was found dead in the Thames near Battersea Bridge. He had been drunk at the time of drowning. There were no signs of violence and he was known as a heavy drinker.

"It is relevant that Scarr had for the last four years provided an anonymous foreigner with the use of a car, and had received generous rewards for doing so. Their arrangements were designed to conceal the identity of the borrower even from Scarr himself, who only knew his client by the nickname 'Blondie' and could only reach him through a telephone number. The telephone number is of importance : it was that of the East German Steel Mission.

"Meanwhile, Mrs. Fennan's alibi for the evening of the murder had been investigated and significant information came to light :

"1. Mrs. Fennan attended the Weybridge Repertory Theatre twice a month, on the first and third Tuesdays. (*N.B.* Adam Scarr's client had collected his car on the first and third Tuesday's of each month.)

"2. She always brought a music case and left it in the cloakroom.

"3. When visiting the theatre she was always joined by a man whose description corresponded with that of my assailant and Scarr's client. It was even mistakenly assumed by a member of the theatre staff that this man was Mrs. Fennan's husband. He too brought a music case and left it in the cloakroom.

"4. On the evening of the murder Mrs. Fennan had left the theatre early after her friend had failed to arrive and had forgotten to reclaim her music case. Late that night she telephoned the theatre to ask if the case could be called for at once. She had lost her cloakroom ticket. The case was collected—by Mrs. Fennan's usual friend.

"At this point the stranger was identified as an employee of the East German Steel Mission named Mundt. The principal of the Mission was Herr Dieter Frey, a war-time collaborator of our Service, with extensive operational experience. After the war he had entered Government service in the Soviet zone of Germany. I should mention that Frey had operated with me during the war in enemy territory and had shown himself to be a brilliant and resourceful agent.

"I now decided to conduct a third interview with Mrs. Fennan. She broke down and confessed to having acted as an intelligence courier for her husband, who had been recruited by Frey on a skiing holiday five years ago. She herself had co-operated unwillingly, partly in loyalty to her husband and partly to protect him from his own carelessness in performing his espionage role. Frey had seen Fennan talking to me in the park. Assuming I was still operationally employed, he had concluded that Fennan was either under suspicion or a double agent. He instructed Mundt to liquidate Fennan, and his wife had been compelled into silence by her own complicity. She had even typed the text of the suicide letter on Fennan's typewriter over a specimen of her husband's signature.

"The means whereby she passed to Mundt the intelligence procured by her husband is relevant. She placed notes and copied documents in a music case, which she took to the theatre. Mundt brought a similar case containing money and instructions and, like Mrs. Fennan, left it in the cloakroom. They had only to exchange cloakroom tickets. When Mundt failed to appear at the theatre on the night in question, Mrs. Fennan obeyed standing instructions and posted the ticket to an address in Highgate. She left the theatre early in order to catch the last post from Weybridge. When later that night Mundt demanded the music case she told him what she had done. Mundt insisted on collecting the case that night, for he did not wish to make another journey to Weybridge.

"When I had interviewed Mrs. Fennan the following morning, one of my questions (about the 8.30 call) alarmed her so much that she telephoned Mundt. This accounts for the assault upon me later that day.

"Mrs. Fennan provided me with the address and telephone number she used when contacting Mundt—whom she knew by the cover name of Freitag. Both led to the apartment of a 'Lufteuropa' pilot who often entertained Mundt and provided accommodation for him when he required it. The pilot (presumably a courier of the East German Intelligence Service) has not returned to this country since 5th January.

"This, then, was the sum of Mrs. Fennan's revelations, and in a sense they led nowhere. The spy was dead, his murderers had vanished. It only remained to assess the extent of the damage. An official approach was now made to the Foreign Office and Mr. Felix Taverner was instructed to calculate from Foreign Office schedules what information had been compromised. This involved listing all files to which Fennan had had access since his recruitment by Frey. Remarkably, this revealed no systematic acquisition of secret files. Fennan had drawn no secret files except those which directly concerned him in his duties. During the last six months, when his access to sensitive papers was substantially increased, he had actually taken home *no* files of secret classification. The files he took home over this period were of universally low grade, and some treated subjects actually outside the scope of his section. This was not consistent with Fennan's role as a spy. It was, however, possible that he had lost heart for his work, and that his luncheon invitation to me was a first step to confession. With this in mind he might also have written the anonymous letter which could have been designed to put him in touch with the Department.

"Two further facts should be mentioned at this point. Under an assumed name and with a false passport, Mundt left the country by air on the day after Mrs. Fennan made her confession. He evaded the notice of the airport authorities, but was retrospectively identified by the air hostess. Secondly, Fennan's diary contained the full name and official telephone number of Dieter Frey—a flagrant breach of the most elementary rule of espionage.

"It was hard to understand why Mundt had waited three weeks in England after murdering Scarr, and even harder to reconcile Fennan's activities as described by his wife with the obviously unplanned and unproductive selection of files. Re-examination of the facts led repeatedly to this conclusion: the only evidence that Fennan was a spy came from his wife. If the facts were as she described them, why had she been allowed to survive the determination of Mundt and Frey to eliminate those in possession of dangerous knowledge?

"On the other hand, might she not herself be the spy?

"This would explain the date of Mundt's departure: he left as soon as he had been reassured by Mrs. Fennan that I had accepted her ingenious confession. It would explain the entry in Fennan's diary: Frey was a chance skiiing acquaintance and an occasional visitor to Walliston. It would make sense of Fennan's choice of files—if Fennan deliberately chose unclassified papers at a time when his work was mainly secret there could be only one explanation: he had come to suspect his wife. Hence the invitation to Marlow, following naturally upon our encounter the previous day. Fennan had decided to tell me of his apprehensions and had taken a day's leave to do so—a fact of which his wife was not apparently aware. This would also explain why Fennan denounced himself in an anonymous letter: he wished to put himself in touch with us *as a preliminary to denouncing his wife*.

"Continuing the supposition it was remarkable that in matters of tradecraft Mrs. Fennan alone was efficient and conscientious. The technique used by herself and Mundt recalled that of Frey during the war. The secondary arrangement to post the cloakroom ticket if no meeting took place was typical of his scrupulous planning. Mrs. Fennan, it seemed, had acted with a precision scarcely compatible with her claim to be an unwilling party to her husband's treachery.

"While logically, Mrs. Fennan now came under suspicion as a spy, there was no reason to believe that her account of what happened on the night of Fennan's murder was necessarily untrue. Had she known of Mundt's intention to murder her husband she would not have taken the music case to the theatre, and would not have posted the cloakroom ticket.

"There seemed no way of proving the case against her unless it was possible to reactivate the relationship between Mrs. Fennan and her controller. During the war Frey had devised an ingenious code for emergency communication by the use of snapshots and picture postcards. The actual subject of the photograph contained the message. A religious subject such as a painting of a Madonna or a church conveyed a request for an early meeting. The recipient would send in reply an entirely unrelated letter, making sure to date it. A meeting would take place at a prearranged time and place exactly five days after the date on the letter.

"It was just possible that Frey, whose tradecraft had evidently altered so little since the war, might have clung to this system—which, after all, would only seldom be needed. Relying on this I therefore posted to Elsa Fennan a picture postcard depicting a church. The card was posted from Highgate. I hoped somewhat forlornly that she would assume it had come to her through the agency of Frey. She reacted at once by sending to an unknown address abroad a ticket for a London theatre performance five days ahead. Mrs. Fennan's communication reached Frey, who accepted it as an *urgent summons*. Knowing that Mundt had been compromised by Mrs. Fennan's 'confession' he decided to come himself.

"They therefore met at the Sheridan Theatre, Hammersmith, on Thursday, 15th February.

"At first each assumed that the other had initiated the meeting, but when Frey realised they had been brought together by a deception he took drastic action. It may be that he suspected Mrs. Fennan of luring him into a trap, that he realised he was under surveillance. We shall never know. In any event, he murdered her. His method of doing this is best described in the coroner's report at the inquest: 'a single degree of pressure had been applied on the larynx, in particular to the horns of the thyroid cartilage, causing almost immediate death. It would appear that Mrs. Fennan's assailant was no layman in these matters.'

"Frey was pursued to a houseboat moored near Cheyne Walk, and while violently resisting arrest he fell into the river, from which his body has now been recovered."

CHAPTER XVIII

BETWEEN TWO WORLDS

Smiley's unrespectable club was usually empty on Sundays, but Mrs. Sturgeon left the door unlocked in case any of her gentlemen chose to call in. She adopted the same stern, possessive attitude towards her gentlemen as she had done in her landlady days at Oxford, when she had commanded from her fortunate boarders more respect than the entire assembly of dons and proctors. She forgave everything but somehow managed to suggest on each occasion that her forgiveness was unique, and would never, never happen again. She had once made Steed-Asprey put ten shillings in the poor box for bringing seven guests without warning, and afterwards provided the dinner of a lifetime.

They sat at the same table as before. Mendel looked a shade sallower, a shade older. He scarcely spoke during the meal, handling his knife and fork with the same careful precision which he applied to any task. Guillam supplied most of the conversation, for Smiley, too, was less talkative than usual. They were at ease in their companionship and no one felt unduly the need to speak.

"Why did she do it?" Mendel asked suddenly.

Smiley shook his head slowly : "I think I know, but we can only guess. I think she dreamed of a world without conflict, ordered and preserved by the new doctrine. I once angered her, you see, and she shouted at me: 'I'm the wandering Jewess,' she said; 'the no-man's land, the battlefield of your toy soldiers.' As she saw the new Germany rebuilt in the image of the old, saw the plump pride return, as she put it, I think it was just too much for her; I think she looked at the futility of her suffering and the prosperity of her persecutors and rebelled. Five years ago, she told me, they met Dieter on a skiing holiday in Germany. By that time the re-establishment of Germany as a prominent western power was well under way."

"Was she a communist?"

"I don't think she liked labels. I think she wanted to help build one society which could live without conflict. Peace is a dirty word now, isn't it? I think she wanted peace."

"And Dieter?" asked Guillam.

"God knows what Dieter wanted. Honour, I think, and a socialist world." Smiley shrugged. "They dreamed of peace and freedom. Now they're murderers and spies."

"Christ Almighty," said Mendel.

Smiley was silent again, looking into his glass, At last he said: "I can't expect you to understand. You only saw the end of Dieter. I saw the beginning. He went the full circle. I don't think he ever got over being a traitor in the war. He had to put it right. He was one of those world-builders who seem to do nothing but destroy: that's all."

Guillam gracefully intervened: "What about the 8.30 call?"

"I think it's pretty obvious. Fennan wanted to see me at Marlow and he'd taken a day's leave. He can't have told Elsa he was having a day off or she'd have tried to explain it away to me. He staged a phone call to give himself an excuse for going to Marlow. That's my guess, anyway."

The fire crackled in the wide hearth.

He caught the midnight plane to Zurich. It was a beautiful night, and through the small window beside him he watched the grey wing, motionless against the starlit sky, a glimpse of eternity between two worlds. The vision soothed him, calmed his fears and his doubts, made him fatalistic towards the inscrutable purpose of the universe. It all seemed to matter so little—the pathetic quest for love, or the return to solitude.

Soon the lights of the French coast came in sight. As he watched, he began to sense vicariously the static life beneath him; the rank smell of Gaulloises Bleues, garlic and good food, the raised voices in the bistro. Maston was a million miles off, locked away with his arid paper and his shiny politicians.

Smiley presented an odd figure to his fellow passengers— a little, fat man, rather gloomy, suddenly smiling, ordering a drink. The young, fair-haired man beside him examined him closely out of the corner of his eye. He knew the type well—the tired executive out for a bit of fun. He found it rather disgusting.

A MURDER OF QUALITY

To Ann

FOREWORD

THERE ARE PROBABLY a dozen great schools of whom it will be confidently asserted that Carne is their deliberate image. But he who looks among their common rooms for the D'Arcys, Fieldings and Hechts will search in vain.

JOHN LE CARRE

CONTENTS

CHAPTER I

BLACK CANDLES

THE GREATNESS OF Carne School has been ascribed by common consent to Edward VI, whose educational zeal is ascribed by history to the Duke of Somerset. But Carne prefers the respectability of the monarch to the questionable politics of his adviser, drawing strength from the conviction that Great Schools, like Tudor Kings, were ordained in Heaven.

And indeed its greatness is little short of miraculous. Founded by obscure monks, endowed by a sickly boy king, and dragged from oblivion by a Victorian bully, Carne had straightened its collar, scrubbed its rustic hands and face and presented itself shining to the courts of the twentieth century. And in the twinkling of an eye, the Dorset bumpkin was London's darling : Dick Whittington had arrived. Carne had parchments in Latin, seals in wax and Lammas Land behind the Abbey. Carne had property, cloisters and woodworm, a whipping block and a line in the Doomsday Book—then what more did it need to instruct the sons of the rich?

And they came; each Half they came (for terms are not elegant things), so that throughout a whole afternoon the trains would unload sad groups of black-coated boys on to the station platform. They came in great cars that shone with mournful purity. They came to bury poor King Edward, trundling handcarts over the cobbled streets or carrying tuck boxes like little coffins. Some wore gowns, and when they walked they looked like crows, or black angels come for the burying. Some followed singly like undertakers' mutes, and you could hear the clip of their boots as they went. They were always in mourning at Carne; the small boys because they must stay and the big boys because they must leave, the masters because mourning was respectable and the wives because respectability was underpaid; and now, as the Lent Half (as the Easter term was called) drew to its end, the cloud of gloom was as firmly settled as ever over the grey towers of Carne.

Gloom and the cold. The cold was crisp and sharp as flint. It cut the faces of the boys as they moved slowly from the deserted playing fields after the school match. It pierced their black topcoats and turned their stiff, pointed collars into icy rings round their necks. Frozen, they plodded from the field to the long walled road which led to the main tuck shop and the town, the line gradually dwindling into groups, and the groups into pairs. Two boys who looked even colder than the rest crossed the road and made their way along a narrow path which led towards a distant but less populated tuck shop.

"I think I shall die if ever I have to watch one of those beastly rugger games again. The noise is fantastic," said one. He was tall with fair hair, and his name was Caley.

"People only shout because the dons are watching from the pavilion," the other rejoined; "that's why each house has to stand together. So that the house dons can swank about how loud their houses shout."

"What about Rode?" asked Caley. "Why does he stand with us and make us shout, then? He's not a house don, just a bloody usher."

"He's sucking up to house dons all the time. You can see him in the quad between lessons buzzing round the big men. All the junior masters do." Caley's companion was a cynical red-haired boy called Perkins, Captain of Fielding's house.

"I've been to tea with Rode," said Caley.

"Rode's hell. He wears brown boots. What was tea like?"

"Bleak. Funny how tea gives them away. Mrs. Rode's quite decent, though—homely in a plebby sort of way: doyleys and china birds. Food's good: Women's Institute, but good."

"Rode's doing Corps next Half. That'll put the lid on it. He's so *keen,* bouncing about all the time. You can tell he's not a gentleman. You know where he went to school?"

"No."

"Branxome Grammar. Fielding told my Mama, when she came over from Singapore last Half."

"God. Where's Branxome?"

"On the coast. Near Bournemouth. I haven't been to tea with anyone except Fielding." Perkins added after a slight pause. "You get roast chestnuts and crumpets. You're never allowed to thank him, you know. He says emotionalism is only for the lower classes. That's typical of Fielding. He's not like a don at all. I think boys bore him. The whole house goes to tea with him once a half, he has us in turn, four at a time, and that's about the only time he talks to most men."

They walked on in silence for a while until Perkins said : "Fielding's giving another dinner party tonight."

"He's pushing the boat out these days," Caley replied, with disapproval. "Suppose the food in your house is worse than ever?"

"It's his last Half before he retires. He's entertaining every don and all the wives separately by the end of the Half. Black candles every evening. For mourning. Hells extravagant."

"Yes. I suppose it's a sort of gesture."

"My Pater says he's a queer."

They crossed the road and disappeared into the tuck shop, where they continued to discuss the weighty affairs of Mr. Terence Fielding, until Perkins drew their meeting reluctantly to a close. Being a poor hand at science, he was unfortunately obliged to take extra tuition in the subject.

The dinner party to which Perkins had alluded that afternoon was now drawing to a close. Mr. Terence Fielding, senior housemaster of Carne, gave himself some more port and pushed the decanter wearily to his left. It was his port, the best he had. There was enough of the best to last the Half—and after that, be damned. He felt a little tired after watching the match, and a little drunk, and a little bored with Shane Hecht and her husband. Shane was so hideous. Massive and enveloping, like a faded Valkyrie. All that black hair. He should have asked someone else. The Snows for instance, but he was too clever. Or Felix D'Arcy, but D'Arcy interrupted. Ah well, a little later he would annoy Charles Hecht, and Hecht would get in a pet and leave early.

Hecht was fidgeting, wanting to light his pipe, but Fielding damn well wouldn't have it. Hecht could have a cigar if he wanted to smoke. But his pipe could stay in his dinner-jacket pocket, where it belonged, or didn't belong, and his athletic profile could remain unadorned.

"Cigar, Hecht?"

"No thanks, Fielding. I say, do you mind if I . . ."

"I can recommend the cigars. Young Havelake sent them from Havana. His father's ambassador there, you know."

"Yes, dear," said Shane tolerantly; "Vivian Havelake was in Charles' troop when Charles was commandant of the Cadets."

"Good boy, Havelake," Hecht observed, and pressed his lips together to show he was a strict judge.

"It's amusing how things have changed." Shane Hecht said this rapidly with a rather wooden smile, as if it weren't really amusing. "Such a grey world we live in, now.

"I remember before the war when Charles inspected the Corps on a white horse. We don't do that kind of thing now, do we? I've got nothing against Mr. Iredale as commandant, nothing at all. What *was* his regiment, Terence, do you know? I'm sure he does it very nicely, whatever they do now in the Corps—he gets on so well with the boys, doesn't he? His wife's such a nice person. . . . I wonder why they can never keep their servants. I hear Mr. Rode will be helping out with the Corps next Half."

"Poor little Rode," said Fielding slowly; "running about like a puppy, trying to earn his biscuits. He tries so hard; have you seen him cheering at school matches? He'd never seen a game of rugger before he came here, you know. They don't play rugger at grammar schools—it's all soccer. Do you remember when he first came, Charles? It was fascinating. He lay very low at first, drinking us in : the games, the vocabulary, the manners. Then, one day it was as if he had been given the power of speech, and he spoke in our language. It was amazing, like plastic surgery. It was Felix D'Arcy's work of course—I've never seen anything quite like it before."

"Dear Mrs. Rode," said Shane Hecht in that voice of abstract vagueness which she reserved for her most venomous pronouncements : "So sweet . . . and such simple taste, don't you think? I mean, whoever would have dreamed of putting those china ducks on the wall? Big ones at the front and little ones at the back. Charming, don't you think? Like one of those teashops. I wonder where she bought them. I must ask her. I'm told her father lives near Bournemouth. It must be so lonely for him, don't you think? Such a vulgar place; no one to talk to."

Fielding sat back and surveyed his own table. The silver was good. The best in Carne, he had heard it said, and he inclined to agree. This Half he had nothing but black candles. It was the sort of thing people remembered when you'd gone : "Dear old Terence—marvellous host. He dined every member of the staff during his last Half, you know, wives too. Black candles, rather touching. It broke his heart giving up his house." But he must annoy Charles Hecht. Shane would like that. Shane would egg him on because she hated Charles, because within her great ugly body she was as cunning as a snake.

Fielding looked at Hecht and then at Hecht's wife, and she smiled back at him, the slow rotten smile of a whore. For a moment Fielding thought of Hecht pasturing in that thick body : it was a scene redolent of Lautrec . . . yes, that was it! Charles pompous and top-hatted, seated stiffly upon the plush coverlet; she massive, pendulous and bored. The image pleased him : so perverse to consign that fool Hecht from the Spartan cleanliness of Carne to the brothels of nineteenth-century Paris. . . .

Fielding began talking, pontificating rather, with an air of friendly objectivity which he knew Hecht would resent.

"When I look back on my thirty years at Carne, I realise I have achived rather less than a road sweeper." They were watching him now—"I used to regard a road sweeper as a person inferior to myself. Now, I rather doubt it. Something is dirty, he makes it clean, and the state of the world is advanced. But I—what have *I* done. Entrenched a ruling class which is distinguished by neither talent, culture nor wit; kept alive for one more generation the distinctions of a dead age."

Charles Hecht, who had never perfected the art of not listening to Fielding, grew red and fussed at the other end of the table.

"Don't we teach them, Fielding? What about our successes, our scholarships?"

"I have never taught a boy in my life, Charles. Usually the boy wasn't clever enough; occasionally, I wasn't. In most boys you see, perception dies with puberty. In a few it persists, though where we find it we take good care at Carne to kill it. If it survives our efforts the boy wins a scholarship. . . . Bear with me, Shane; it's my last Half."

"Last Half or not, you're talking through your hat, Fielding," said Hecht, angrily.

"That is traditional at Carne. These successes, as you call them, are the failures, the rare boys who have not learned the lessons of Carne. They have ignored the cult of mediocrity. We can do nothing for them. But for the rest, for the puzzled little clerics and the blind little soldiers, for them the truth of Carne is written on the wall, and they hate us."

Hecht laughed rather heavily.

"Why do so many come back, then, if they hate us so much? Why do they remember us and come and see us?"

"Because we, dear Charles, are the writing on the wall! The one lesson of Carne they never forget. They come back to read *us*, don't you see? It was from us they learnt the secret of life : that we grow old without growing wise. They realised that nothing happened when we grew up : no blinding light on the road to Damascus, no sudden feeling of maturity." Fielding put his head back and gazed at the clumsy Victorian moulding on the ceiling, and the halo of dirt round the light rose.

"We just got a little older. We made the same jokes, thought the same thoughts, wanted the same things. Year in, year out, Hecht, we were the same people, not wiser, not better; we haven't had an original thought between us for the last fifty years of our lives. They saw what a trick it all was, Carne and us; our academic dress, our schoolroom jokes, our wise little offerings of guidance. And that's why they come back year after year of their puzzled barren lives to gaze fascinated at you and me, Hecht, like children at a grave, searching for the secret of life and death. Oh yes, they have learned *that* from us."

Hecht looked at Fielding in silence for a moment.

"Decanter, Hecht?" said Fielding, in a slightly conciliatory way, but Hecht's eyes were still upon him.

"If that's a joke . . ." he began, and his wife observed with satisfaction that he was very angry indeed.

"I wish I knew, Charles," Fielding replied with apparent earnestness. "I really wish I knew. I used to think it was clever to confuse comedy with tragedy. Now I wish I could distinguish them." He rather liked that.

They had coffee in the drawing-room, where Fielding resorted to gossip, but Hecht was not to be drawn. Fielding rather wished he had let him light his pipe. Then he recalled his vision of the Hechts in Paris, and it restored him. He had been rather good this evening. There were moments when he convinced himself.

While Shane fetched her coat, the two men stood together in the hall, but neither spoke. Shane returned, an ermine stole, yellow with age, draped over her great white shoulders. She inclined her head to the right, smiled and held out her hand to Fielding, the fingers down.

"Terence, darling," she said, as Fielding kissed her fat knuckles; "so kind. And in your last Half. You must dine with us before you go. So sad. So few of us left." She smiled again, half closing her eyes to indicate emotional disturbance, then followed her husband into the street. It was still bitterly cold and snow was in the air.

Fielding closed and carefully bolted the door behind them —perhaps a fraction earlier than courtesy required—and returned to the dining-room. Hecht's port glass was still about half full. Fielding picked it up and carefully poured the contents back into the decanter. He hoped Hecht wasn't too upset; he hated people to dislike him. He snuffed the black candles and damped their wicks between his forefinger and thumb. Switching on the light, he took from the sideboard a sixpenny notebook, and opened it. It contained his list of dining guests for the remainder of the Half. With his fountain pen he placed a neat tick against the name Hecht. They were done. On Wednesday he would have the Rodes. The husband was quite good value, but she, of course, was hell. . . . it was not always the way with married couples. The wives as a rule were so much more sympathetic.

He opened the sideboard and took from it a bottle of brandy and a tumbler. Holding them both in the same hand, he shuffled wearily back to the drawing-room, resting his other hand on the wall as he went. God! He felt old, suddenly; that thin line of pain across the chest, that heaviness in the legs and feet. Such an effort being with people—on stage all the time. He hated to be alone, but people bored him. Being alone was like being tired, but unable to sleep. Some German poet had said that; he'd quoted it once, "You may sleep but I must dance." Something like that.

"That's how I am," thought Fielding. "That's how Carne is, too; an old satyr dancing to the music." The music grew faster and their bodies older, but they must dance on—there were young men waiting in the wings. It had been funny once dancing the old dances in a new world. He poured himself some more brandy. He'd be pleased to leave in a way, even though he'd have to go on teaching somewhere else.

But it had its beauty, Carne. . . . The Abbey Close in

spring . . . the flamingo figures of boys waiting for the ritual of worship . . . the ebb and flow of children, like the seasons of the year, and the old men dying among them. He wished he could paint; he would paint the pageant of Carne in the fallow browns of autumn. . . . What a shame, thought Fielding, that a mind so perceptive of beauty had no talent for creation.

He looked at his watch. Quarter to twelve. Nearly time to go out . . . to dance, and not to sleep.

CHAPTER II

THE THURSDAY FEELING

I⊤ was Thursday evening and the *Christian Voice* had just been put to bed. This was scarcely an historic event in Fleet Street. The pimply boy from Despatch who took away the ragged pile of page-proofs showed no more ceremony than was strictly demanded by the eventual prospect of his Christmas bonus. And even in this respect he had learned that the secular journals of Unipress were more provident of material charity than the *Christian Voice*; charity being in strict relation to circulation.

Miss Brimley, the journal's editor, adjusted the air cushion beneath her and lit a cigarette. Her secretary and sub-editor—the appointment carried both responsibilities—yawned, dropped the aspirin bottle into her handbag, combed out her ginger hair and bade Miss Brimley good night, leaving behind her as usual the smell of strongly scented powder and an empty paper-tissue box. Miss Brimley listened contentedly to the clipping echo of her footsteps as it faded down the corridor. It pleased her to be alone at last, tasting the anticlimax. She never failed to wonder at herself, how every Thursday morning brought the same slight uneasiness as she entered the vast Unipress building and stood a little absurdly on one escalator after the other, like a drab parcel on a luxury liner. Heaven knows, she had run the *Voice* for fourteen years, and there were those who said its layout was the best thing Unipress did. Yet the Thursday feeling never left her, the wakeful anxiety that one day, perhaps today, they wouldn't be ready when the despatch boy came. She often wondered what would happen then. She had heard of failures elsewhere in that vast combine, of features disapproved and staff rebuked. It was a mystery to her why they kept the *Voice* at all, with its expensive room on the seventh floor and a circulation which, if Miss Brimley knew anything, hardly paid for the paper-clips.

The *Voice* had been founded at the turn of the century by old Lord Landsbury, together with a Nonconformist daily newspaper and the *Temperance Gazette*. But the *Gazette* and the daily were long since dead, and Landsbury's son had woken one morning not long ago to find his whole business and every man and woman of it, every stick of furniture, ink, paperclips, and galley-pins, bought by the hidden gold of Unipress.

That was three years ago and every day she had waited for her dismissal. But it never came; no directive, no question, no word. And so, being a sensible woman, she continued exactly as before and ceased to wonder.

And she was glad. It was easy to sneer at the *Voice*. Every week it offered humbly and without fanfares evidence of the Lord's intervention in the world's affairs, retold in simple and somewhat unscientific terms the early history of the Jews, and provided over a fictitious signature motherly advice to whomever should write and ask for it. The *Voice* scarcely concerned itself with the fifty-odd millions of the population who had never heard of it. It was a family affair, and rather than abuse those who were not members, it did its best for those who were. For them it was kind, optimistic, and informative. If a million children were dying of the plague in

India, you may be sure that the weekly editorial described the miraculous escape from fire of a Methodist family in Kent. The *Voice* did not advise you how to disguise the encroaching wrinkles round your eyes, or control your spreading figure; did not dismay you, if you were old, by its own eternal youth. It was itself middle-aged and middle class, counselled caution to girls and charity to all. Nonconformity is the most conservative of habits and families which took the *Voice* in 1903 continued to take it in 1960.

Miss Brimley was not quite the image of her journal. The fortunes of war and the caprice of Intelligence work had thrown her into partnership with the younger Lord Landsbury, and for the six years of war they had worked together efficiently and inconspicuously in an unnamed building in Knightsbridge. The fortunes of peace rendered both unemployed, but Landsbury had the good sense, as well as the generosity, to offer Miss Brimley a job. The *Voice* had ceased publication during the war, and no one seemed anxious to renew it. At first Miss Brimley had felt a little ashamed at reviving and editing a journal which in no way expressed her own vague deism, but quite soon, as the touching letters came in and the circulation recovered, she developed an affection for her job—and for her readers—which outweighed her earlier misgivings. The *Voice* was her life, and its readers her preoccupation. She struggled to answer their odd, troubled questions, sought advice of others where she could not provide it herself, and in time, under a handful of pseudonyms, became if not their philosopher, their guide, friend and universal aunt.

Miss Brimley put out her cigarette, absently tidied the pins, paper-clips, scissors and paste into the top right-hand drawer of her desk, and gathered together the afternoon mail from her in-tray which, because it was Thursday, she had left untouched. There were several letters addressed to Barbara Fellowship, under which name the *Voice* had, since its foundation, answered both privately and through its published columns the many problems of its correspondents. They could wait until tomorrow. She rather enjoyed the "problem post", but Friday morning was when she read it. She opened the little filing cabinet at her elbow and dropped the letters into a box file at the front of the compartment. As she did so, one of them fell on its back and she noticed with surprise that the sealed flap was embossed with an elegant blue dolphin. She picked the envelope out of the cabinet and looked at it curiously, turning it over several times. It was of pale grey paper, very faintly lined. Expensive—perhaps hand-made. Beneath the dolphin was a tiny scroll on which she could just discern the legend, *Regem defendere diem videre*. The postmark was Carne, Dorset. That must be the school crest. But why was Carne familiar to her? Miss Brimley was proud of her memory, which was excellent, and she was vexed when it failed her. As a last resort she opened the envelope with her faded ivory paper knife and read the letter.

Dear Miss Fellowship,

I don't know if you are a real person but it doesn't matter, because you always give such good, kind answers. It was me who wrote last June about the pastry mix. I am not mad and I know my husband is trying to kill me. Could I please come and see you as soon as it's convenient? I'm sure you'll believe me, and understand that I am normal. Could it be *as soon as possible* please, I am so afraid of the long nights. I don't know who else to turn to. I could try Mr. Cardew at the Tabernacle but he wouldn't believe me and Dad's too sensible. I might as well be dead. There's something not quite right about him. At night when he thinks I'm asleep he just lies watching the darkness. I know it's wrong to think such wicked things and have fear in our hearts, but I can't help it.

I hope you don't get many letters like this.

Yours faithfully,

Stella Rode (Mrs.)

née Glaston.

She sat quite still at her desk for a moment, looking at the address in handsome blue engraving at the top of the page : "North Fields, Carne School, Dorset." In that moment of shock and astonishment one phrase forced itself upon her mind. "The value of intelligence depends on its breeding." That was John Landsbury's favourite dictum. Until you know the pedigree of the information you cannot evaluate a report. Yes, that was what he used to say: "We are not democratic. We close the door on intelligence without parentage." And she used to reply: "Yes, John, but even the best families had to begin somewhere."

But Stella Rode *had* parentage. It all came back to her now. She was the Glaston girl. The girl whose marriage was reported in the editorial, the girl who won the summer competition; Samuel Glaston's daughter from Branxome. She had a card in Miss Brimley's index.

Abruptly she stood up, the letter still in her hand, and walked to the uncurtained window. Just in front of her was a contemporary window-box of woven white metal. It was odd, she reflected, how she could never get anything to grow in that window-box. She looked down into the street, a slight sensible figure leaning forward a little and framed by the incandescent fog outside; fog made yellow from the stolen light of London's streets. She could just distinguish the street lamps far below, pale and sullen. She suddenly felt the need for fresh air, and on an impulse quite alien to her usual calm, she opened the window wide. The quick cold and the angry surge of noise burst in on her, and the insidious fog followed. The sound of traffic was constant, so that for a moment she thought it was the turning of some great machine. Then above its steady growl she heard the newsboys. Their cries were like the cries of gulls against a gathering storm. She could see them now, sentinels among the hastening shadows.

It might be true. That had always been the difficulty. Right through the war it was the same restless search. It might be true. It was no use relating reports to probability when there was no quantum of knowledge from which to start. She remembered the first intelligence from France on flying bombs, wild talk of concrete runways in the depths of a forest. You had to resist the dramatic, you had to hold out against it. Yet it might be true. Tomorrow, the day after, those newsboys down there might be shouting it, and Stella Rode *née* Glaston might be dead. And if that was so, if there was the remotest chance that this man was plotting to kill this woman, then she, Ailsa Brimley, must do what she could to prevent it. Besides, Stella Glaston had a claim on her assistance if anyone did : both her father and her grandfather had taken the *Voice*, and when Stella married five years ago Miss Brimley had put a couple of lines about it in the editorial. The Glastons sent her a Christmas card every year. They were one of the original families to subscribe. . . .

It was cold at the window, but she remained there, still fascinated by the half hidden shadows joining and parting beneath her, and the useless street lights burning painfully among them. She began to imagine him as one of those shadows, pressing and jostling, his murderer's eyes turned to sockets of dark. And suddenly she was frightened and needed help.

But not the police, not yet. If Stella Rode had wanted that she would have gone herself. Why hadn't she? For love? For fear of looking a fool? Because instinct was not evidence? They wanted fact. But the fact of murder was death. Must they wait for that?

Who would help? She thought at once of Landsbury, but he was farming in Rhodesia. Who else had been with them in the war? Fielding and Jebedee were dead, Steed, Asprey vanished. Smiley—where was he? George Smiley, the cleverest and perhaps the oddest of them all. Of course, Miss Brimley remembered now. He made that improbable marriage and went back to research at Oxford. But he hadn't stayed there. . . . The marriage had broken up. . . . What *had* he done after that?

She returned to her desk and picked up the S-Z directory. Ten minutes later she was sitting in a taxi, heading for Sloane Square. In her neatly gloved hand she held a cardboard folder containing Stella Rode's card from the index and the correspondence which had passed between them at the time of the Summer Competition. She was nearly at

Piccadilly when she remembered she'd left the office window open. It didn't seem to matter much.

"With other people it's Persian cats or golf. With me it's the *Voice* and my readers. I'm a ridiculous spinster, I know, but there it is. I won't go to the police until I've tried *something*, George."

"And you thought you'd try me?"

"Yes."

She was sitting in the study of George Smiley's house in Bywater Street; the only light came from the complicated lamp on his desk, a black spider of a thing shining brightly on to the manuscript notes which covered the desk.

"So you've left the Service?" she said.

"Yes, yes, I have." He nodded his round head vigorously, as if reassuring himself that a distasteful experience was really over, and mixed Miss Brimley a whisky and soda. "I had another spell there after ... Oxford. It's all very different in peacetime, you know," he continued.

Miss Brimley nodded.

"I can imagine it. More time to be bitchy." Smiley said nothing, just lit a cigarette and sat down opposite her.

"And the people have changed. Fielding, Steed, Jebedee. All gone." She said this in a matter-of-fact way as she took from her large sensible handbag Stella Rode's letter. "This is the letter, George."

When he had read it, he held it briefly towards the lamp, his round face caught by the light in a moment of almost comic earnestness. Watching him, Miss Brimley wondered what impression he made on those who did not know him well. She used to think of him as the most forgettable man she had ever met; short and plump, with heavy spectacles and thinning hair, he was at first sight the very prototype of an unsuccessful middle-aged bachelor in a sedentary occupation. His natural diffidence in most practical matters was reflected in his clothes, which were costly and unsuitable, for he was clay in the hands of his tailor, who robbed him.

He had put down the letter on the small marquetry table beside him, and was looking at her owlishly.

"This other letter she sent you, Brim. Where is it?"

She handed him the folder. He opened it and after a moment read aloud Stella Rode's other letter:

Dear Miss Fellowship,

I would like to submit the following suggestion for your "Kitchen Hints" competition.

Make your basic batch of cake mixture once a month. Cream equal quantities of fat and sugar and add one egg for every six ounces of the mixture. For puddings and cakes, add flour to the required quantity of basic mixture.

This will keep well for a month.

I enclose stamped addressed envelope.

Yours sincerely,

Stella Rode (*née* Glaston).

PS.—Incidentally, you can prevent wire wool from rusting by keeping it in a jar of soapy water. Are we allowed two suggestions? If so, please can this be my second?"

"She won the competition," Miss Brimley observed, "but that's not the point. This is what I want to tell you George. She's a Glaston, and the Glastons have been reading the *Voice* since it started. Stella's grandfather was old Rufus Glaston, a Lancashire pottery king; he and John Landsbury's father built chapels and tabernacles in practically every village in the Midlands. When Rufus died the *Voice* put out a memorial edition and old Landsbury himself wrote the obituary. Samuel Glaston took on his father's business, but had to move south because of his health. He ended up near Bournemouth, a widower with one daughter, Stella. She's the last of all that family. The whole lot are as down to earth as you could wish, Stella included, I should think. I don't think any of them is likely to be suffering from delusions of persecution."

Smiley was looking at her in astonishment.

"My dear Brim, I can't possibly take that in. How on earth do you know all this?"

Miss Brimley smiled apologetically.

"The Glastons are easy—they're almost part of the magazine. They send us Christmas cards, and boxes of chocolates on the anniversary of our foundation. We've got about five hundred families who form what I call our Establishment. They were in on the *Voice* from the start and they've kept up ever since. They write to us, George; if they're worried they write and say so; if they're getting married, moving house, retiring from work, if they're ill, depressed, or angry, they write. Not often, Heaven knows; but enough."

"How do you remember it all?"

"I don't. I keep a card index. I always write back you see . . . only . . ."

"Yes?"

Miss Brimley looked at him earnestly.

"This is the first time anyone has written because she's frightened."

"What do you want me to do?"

"I've only had one bright idea so far. I seem to remember Adrian Fielding had a brother who taught at Carne. . . ."

"He's a housemaster there, if he hasn't retired."

"No, he retires this Half—it was in *The Times* some weeks ago, in that little bit on the Court page where Carne always announces itself. It said : 'Carne School reassembles today for the Lent Half. Mr. T. R. Fielding will retire at the end of the Half, having completed his statutory fifteen years as a housemaster.' "

Smiley laughed.

"Really, Brim, your memory is absurd!"

"It was the mention of Fielding . . . Anyway, I thought you could ring him up. You must know him."

"Yes, yes. I know him. At least, I met him once at Magdalen High Table. But—" Smiley coloured a little.

"But what, George?"

"Well he's not quite the man his brother was, you know."

"How could he be?" Miss Brimley rejoined a little sharply. "But he can tell you something about Stella Rode. And her husband."

"I don't think I could do that on the telephone. I think I'd rather go and see him. But what's to stop you ringing up Stella Rode?"

"Well, I can't tonight, can I? Her husband will be in. I thought I'd put a letter in the post to her tonight telling her she can come to see me any time. But," she continued, making a slight, impatient movement with her foot, "I want to do something *now*, George."

Smiley nodded and went to the telephone. He rang directory enquiries and asked for Terence Fielding's number. After a long delay he was told to ring Carne School central exchange, who would connect him with whomever he required. Miss Brimley, watching him, wished she knew a little more about George Smiley, how much of that diffidence was assumed, how vulnerable he was.

"The best," Adrian had said. "The strongest and the best."

But so many men learnt strength during the war, learnt terrible things, and put aside their knowledge with a shudder when it ended.

The number was ringing now. She heard the dialling tone and for a moment was filled with apprehension. For the first time she was afraid of making a fool of herself, afraid of becoming involved in unlikely explanations with angular, suspicious people.

"Mr. Terence Fielding, please...." A pause.

"Fielding, good evening. My name is George Smiley; I knew your brother well in the war. We have in fact met.... Yes, yes, quite right—Magdalen, was it not, the summer before last? Look, I wonder if I might come and see you on a personal matter ... it's a little difficult to discuss on the telephone. A friend of mine has received a rather disturbing letter from the wife of a Carne master.... Well, I—Rode, Stella Rode; her husband ..."

He suddenly stiffened, and Miss Brimley, her eyes fixed upon him, saw with alarm how his chubby face broke into an expression of pain and disgust. She no longer heard what he was saying. She could only watch the dreadful transformation of his face, the whitening knuckles of his hand clutching the receiver. He was looking at her now, saying something ... it was too late. Stella Rode was dead. She had been murdered late on Wednesday night. They'd actually been dining with Fielding the night it happened.

CHAPTER III

THE NIGHT OF THE MURDER

THE SEVEN-FIVE FROM Waterloo to Yeovil is not a popular train, though it provides an excellent breakfast. Smiley had no difficulty in finding a first-class compartment to himself. It was a bitterly cold day, dark and the sky heavy with snow. He sat huddled in a voluminous travelling coat of Continental origin, holding in his gloved hands a bundle of the day's papers. Because he was a precise man and did not care to be hurried, he had arrived thirty minutes before the train was due to depart. Still tired after the stresses of the previous night, when he had sat up talking with Ailsa Brimley until Heaven knew what hour, he was disinclined to read. Looking out of the window on to an almost empty station, he caught sight, to his great surprise, of Miss Brimley herself making her way along the platform, peering in at the windows, a carrier bag in her hand. He lowered the window and called to her.

"My dear Brim, what are you doing here at this dreadful hour? You should be in bed."

She sat down opposite him and began unpacking her bag and handing him its contents: thermos, sandwiches and chocolate.

"I didn't know whether there was a breakfast car," she explained; "and besides, I wanted to come and see you off. You're such a dear, George, and I wish I could come with you, but Unipress would go mad if I did. The only time they notice you is when you're not there."

"Have you seen the papers?" he asked.

"Just briefly, on the way here. They seem to think it wasn't him, but some madman. . . ."

"I know, Brim. That's what Fielding said, wasn't it?" There was a moment's awkward silence.

"George, am I being an awful ass, letting you go off like this? I was so sure last night, but now I wonder . . ."

"After you left I rang Ben Sparrow of Special Branch. You remember him, don't you? He was with us in the war. I told him the whole story."

"George! At three in the morning?"

"Yes. He's ringing the Divisional Superintendent at Carne. He'll tell him about the letter, and that I'm coming down. Ben had an idea that a man named Rigby would be handling the case. Rigby and Ben were at police college together." He looked at her kindly for a moment. "Besides, I'm a man of leisure, Brim. I shall enjoy the change."

"Bless you, George," said Miss Brimley, woman enough to believe him. She got up to go, and Smiley said to her :

"Brim, if you should need any more help or anything and can't get hold of me, there's a man called Mendel who lives in Mitcham, a retired police inspector. He's in the book. If you get hold of him and mention me, he'll do what he can for you. I've booked a room at the Sawley Arms."

Alone again, Smiley surveyed uneasily the assortment of food and drink which Miss Brimley had provided. He had promised himself the luxury of breakfast in the restaurant car. He would keep the sandwiches and coffee for later, that would be the best thing; for lunch, perhaps. And he would breakfast properly.

In the restaurant car Smiley read first the less sensational reports on the death of Stella Rode. It appeared that on Wednesday evening Mr. and Mrs. Rode had been guests at dinner of Mr. Terence Fielding, the senior housemaster at Carne and brother of the late Adrian Fielding, the celebrated French scholar who had vanished during the war while specially employed by the War Office. They had left Mr. Fielding's house together at about ten to eleven and walked the half mile from the centre of Carne to their house, which stood alone at the edge of the famous Carne playing fields. As they reached their house Mr. Rode remembered that he had left at Mr. Fielding's house some examination papers which urgently required correction that night. (At this point Smiley remembered that he had failed to pack his dinner jacket, and that Fielding would almost certainly ask him to dine.) Rode determined to walk back to Fielding's house and collect the papers, therefore, starting back at about five past eleven. It appears that Mrs. Rode made herself a cup of tea and sat down in the drawing-room to await his return.

Adjoining the back of the house is a conservatory, the inner door of which leads to the drawing-room. It was there that Rode eventually found his wife when he returned. There were signs of a struggle, and certain inexpensive articles of jewellery were missing from the body. The confusion in the conservatory was terrible. Fortunately there had been a fresh fall of snow on Wednesday afternoon, and detectives from Dorchester were examining the footprints and other traces early on Thursday morning. Mr. Rode had been treated for shock at Dorchester Central Hospital. The police wished to interview a woman from the adjacent village of Pylle who was locally known as "Mad Janie" on account of her eccentric and solitary habits. Mrs. Rode who was well known in Carne for her energetic work on behalf of the International Refugee Year, had apparently shown a charitable interest in her welfare, and she had vanished without trace since the night of the murder. The police were currently of the opinion that the murderer had caught sight of Mrs. Rode through the drawing-room window (she had not drawn the curtains) and that Mrs. Rode had admitted the murderer at the front door in the belief that it was her husband returning from Mr. Fielding's house. The Home Office pathologist had been asked to conduct a post-mortem examination.

The other reports were not so restrained: "Murder most foul has desecrated the hallowed playing fields of Carne" one article began, and another, "Science teacher discovers murdered wife in blood-spattered conservatory". A third screamed, "Mad woman sought in Carne murder". With an expression of distaste, Smiley screwed up all the newspapers except the *Guardian* and *The Times* and tossed them on to the luggage rack.

He changed at Yeovil for a local line to Sturminster, Okeford and Carne. It was something after eleven o'clock when he finally arrived at Carne station.

He telephoned the hotel from the station and sent his luggage ahead by taxi. The Sawley Arms was only full at Commemoration and on St. Andrew's Day. Most of the year it was empty; sitting like a prim Victorian lady, its slate roof in the mauve of half mourning, on ill tended lawns midway between the station and Carne Abbey.

Snow still lay on the ground, but the day was fine and dry, and Smiley decided to walk into the town and arrange to meet the police officer conducting the investigation of the murder. He left the station, with its foretaste of Victorian austerity, and walked along the avenue of bare trees which led towards the great Abbey tower, flat and black against the colourless winter sky. He crossed the Abbey Close, a serene and beautiful square of mediaeval houses, the roofs snow-covered, the white lawns shaded with pin strokes of grass. As he passed the west door of the Abbey, the soft snow creaking where he trod, the clock high above him struck the half-hour, and two knights on horseback rode out from their little castle over the door, and slowly raised their lances to each other in salute. Then, as if it were all part of the same clockwork mechanism, other doors all round the Close opened too, releasing swarms of black-coated boys who stampeded across the snow towards the Abbey. One boy passed so close that his gown brushed against Smiley's sleeve. Smiley called to him as he ran past:

"What's going on?"

"Sext," shouted the boy in reply, and was gone.

He passed the main entrance to the school and came at once upon the municipal part of the town, a lugubrious nineteenth-century fairyland in local stone, stitched together by a complexity of Gothic chimneys and crenel windows. Here was the town hall, and beside it, with the flag of St. George floating at its masthead, the Carne Constabulary Headquarters, built ninety years ago to withstand the onslaughts of archery and battering rams.

He gave his name to the Duty Sergeant, and asked to see the officer investigating the death of Mrs. Rode. The Sergeant, an elderly, inscrutable man, addressed himself to the telephone with a certain formality, as if he were about to perform a difficult conjuring trick. To Smiley's surprise, he was told that Inspector Rigby would be pleased to see him at once, and a police cadet was summoned to show him the way. He was led at a spanking pace up the wide staircase in the centre of the hall, and in a matter of moments found himself before the Inspector.

He was a very short man, and very broad. He could have been a Celt from the tin-mines of Cornwall or the collieries of Wales. His dark grey hair was cut very close; it came to a point in the centre of his brow like a devil's cap. His hands were large and powerful, he had the trunk and stance of a wrestler, but he spoke slowly, with a Dorset burr to his soft voice. Smiley quickly noticed that he had one quality rare among small men: the quality of openness. Though his eyes were dark and bright and the movements of his body swift, he imparted a feeling of honesty and straight dealing.

"Ben Sparrow rang me this morning, sir. I'm very pleased you've come. I believe you've got a letter for me."

Rigby looked at Smiley thoughtfully over his desk, and decided that he liked what he saw. He had got around in the war and had heard a little, just a very little, of the work of George Smiley's service. If Ben said Smiley was all right, that

173

was good enough for him—or almost. But Ben had said more than that.

"Looks like a frog, dresses like a bookie, and has a brain I'd give my eyes for. Had a very nasty war. Very nasty indeed."

Well, he looked like a frog, right enough. Short and stubby, round spectacles with thick lenses that made his eyes big. And his clothes *were* odd. Expensive, mind, you could see that. But his jacket seemed to drape where there wasn't any room for drape. What did surprise Rigby was his shyness. Rigby had expected someone a little brash, a little too smooth for Carne, whereas Smiley had an earnest formality of manner which appealed to Rigby's conservative taste.

Smiley took the letter from his wallet and put it on the desk, while Rigby extracted an old pair of gold-rimmed spectacles from a battered metal case and adjusted the ends carefully over his ears.

"I don't know if Ben explained," said Smiley, "but this letter was sent to the correspondence section of a small Nonconformist journal to which Mrs. Rode subscribed."

"And Miss Fellowship is the lady who brought you the letter?"

"No; her name is Brimley. She is the editor of the magazine. Fellowship is just a pen-name for the correspondence column."

The brown eyes rested on him for a moment.

"When did she receive this letter?"

"Yesterday, the seventeenth. Thursday's the day they go to press, their busy day. The afternoon mail doesn't get opened till the evening, usually. This was opened about six o'clock, I suppose."

"And she brought it straight to you?"

"Yes."

"Why?"

"She worked for me during the war, in my department. She was reluctant to go straight to the police—I was the only person she could think of who wasn't a policeman," he added stupidly. "Who could help, I mean."

"May I ask what you yourself, sir, do for a living?"

"Nothing much. A little private research on seventeenth-century Germany." It seemed a very silly answer.

Rigby didn't seem bothered.

"What's this earlier letter she talks about?"

Smiley offered him the second envelope, and again the big, square hand received it.

"It appears she won this competition," Smiley explained. "That was her winning entry. I gather she comes from a family which has subscribed to the magazine since its foundation. That's why Miss Brimley was less inclined to regard the letter as nonsense. Not that it follows."

"Not that what follows?"

"I meant that the fact that her family had subscribed to a journal for fifty years does not logically affect the possibility that she was unbalanced."

Rigby nodded, as if he saw the point, but Smiley had an uncomfortable feeling that he did not.

"Ah," said Rigby, with a slow smile. "Women, eh?"

Smiley, completely bewildered, gave a little laugh. Rigby was looking at him thoughtfully.

"Know any of the staff, here, do you, sir?"

"Only Mr. Terence Fielding. We met at an Oxford dinner some time ago. I thought I'd call round and see him. I knew his brother pretty well."

Rigby appeared to stiffen slightly at the mention of Fielding, but he said nothing, and Smiley went on:

"It was Fielding I rang when Miss Brimley brought me the letter. He told me the news. That was last night."

"I see."

They looked at one another again in silence. Smiley discomfited and slightly comic. Rigby appraising him, wondering how much to say.

"How long are you staying?" he said at last.

"I don't know," Smiley replied. "Miss Brimley wanted to come herself, but she has her paper to run. She attached great importance, you see, to doing all she could for Mrs. Rode, even though she was dead. Because she was a subscriber, I mean. I promised to see that the letter arrived quickly in the right hands. I don't imagine there's much else I can do. I shall probably stay on for a day or two just to have a word with Fielding . . . go to the funeral, I suppose. I've booked in at the Sawley Arms."

"Fine hotel, that."

Rigby put his spectacles carefully back into their case and dropped the case into a drawer.

"Funny place, Carne. There's a big gap between the Town and Gown, as we say; neither side knows nor likes the other. It's fear that does it, fear and ignorance. It makes it hard in a case like this. Oh, I can call on Mr. Fielding and Mr. D'Arcy and they say, 'Good day, Sergeant,' and give me a cup of tea in the kitchen, but I can't get among them. They've got their own community, see, and no one outside it can get in. No gossip in the pubs, no contacts, nothing . . . just cups of tea and bits of seed cake, and being called Sergeant." Rigby laughed suddenly, and Smiley laughed with him in relief. "There's a lot I'd like to ask them, a lot of things; who liked the Rodes and who didn't, whether Mr. Rode's a good teacher and whether his wife fitted in with the others. I've got all the facts I want, but I've got no clothes to hang on them." He looked at Smiley expectantly. There was a very long silence.

"If you want me to help, I'd be delighted," said Smiley at last. "But give me the facts first."

"Stella Rode was murdered between about ten past eleven and quarter to twelve on the night of Wednesday the sixteenth. She must have been struck fifteen to twenty times with a cosh or bit of piping or something. It was a terrible murder . . . terrible. There are marks all over her body. At a guess I would say she came fom the drawing-room to the front door to answer the bell or something, when she opened the door she was struck down and dragged to the conservatory. The conservatory door was unlocked, see?"

"I see. . . . It's odd that he should have known that, isn't it?"

"The murderer may have been hiding there already : we can't tell from the prints just there. He was wearing boots—wellington boots, size 10½. We would guess from the spacing of the footprints in the garden that he was about six foot tall. When he had got her to the conservatory he must have hit her again and again—mainly on the head. There's a lot of what we call travelled blood in the conservatory, that's to say, blood spurted from an open artery. There's no sign of that anywhere else."

"And no sign of it on her husband?"

"I'll come to that later, but the short answer is, no." He paused a moment and continued :

"Now, I said there were footprints, and so there were. The murderer came through the back garden. Where he came from and went to, Heaven alone knows. You see, there are no tracks leading away—not wellingtons. None at all. Of course, it's possible the outgoing tracks followed the path to the front gate and got lost in all the to-ing and fro-ing later that night. But I don't think we'd have lost them even then." He glanced at Smiley, then went on :

"He left one thing behind him in the conservatory—an old cloth belt, navy blue, from a cheap overcoat by the look of it. We're working on that now."

"Was she . . . robbed or anything?"

"No sign of interference. She was wearing a string of green beads round her neck, and they've gone, and it looks as though he tried to get the rings off her finger, but they were too tight." He paused.

"I need hardly tell you that we've had reports from every corner of the country about tall men in blue overcoats and gumboots. But none of them had wings as far as I know. Or seven-league boots for jumping from the conservatory to the road."

They paused, while a police cadet brought in tea on a tray. He put it on the desk, looked at Smiley out of the corner of his eye and decided to let the Inspector pour out. He guided the teapot round so that the handle was towards Rigby and withdrew. Smiley was amused by the immaculate condition of the tray cloth, by the matching china and the tea-strainer, laid before them by the enormous hands of the cadet. Rigby poured out the tea and they drank for a moment in silence. There was, Smiley reflected, something devastatingly competent about Rigby. The very ordinariness of the man and his room identified him with the society he protected. The non-descript furniture, the wooden filing cupboards, the bare walls the archaic telephone with its separate earpiece, the brown frieze round the wall and the brown paint on the door, the glistening linoleum and the faint smell of carbolic, the burbling gas-fire and the calendar from the Prudential—these were the evidence of rectitude and moderation; their austerity gave comfort and reassurance. Rigby continued :

"Rode went back to Fielding's house for the examination papers. Fielding confirms that, of course. He arrived at Fielding's house at about 11.35, near as Fielding can say. He hardly spent any time there at all—just collected his papers at the door—they were in a small writing-case he uses for carrying exercise books. He doesn't remember whether he saw anyone on the road. He thinks a bicycle overtook him, but he can't be sure. If we take Rode's word for it, he walked straight home. When he got there he rang the bell. He was wearing a dinner jacket and so he hadn't got his key with him. His wife was expecting him to ring the bell, you see. That's the devil of it. It was a moonlit night, mind, and snow on the ground, so you could see a mighty long way. He called her, but she didn't answer. Then he saw the footprints going round to the side of the house. Not just footprints, but blood marks and the snow all churned up where the body had been dragged to the conservatory. But he didn't know it was blood in the moonlight, it just showed up dark, and Rode said afterwards he thought it was the dirty water from the gutters running over on to the path.

"He followed the prints round until he came to the conservatory. It was darker in there and he fumbled for the light switch, but it didn't work."

"Did he light a match?"

"No, he didn't have any. He's a non-smoker. His wife didn't approve of smoking. He moved forward from the door. The conservatory walls are mainly glass except for the bottom three feet, but the roof is tiled. The moon was high that night, and not much light got in at all, except through the partition window between the drawing-room and the conservatory—but she'd only had the little table light on in the drawing-room. So he groped his way forward, talking all the time, calling Stella, his wife. As he went, he tripped over something and nearly fell. He knelt down and felt with his hands, up and down her body. He realised that his hands were covered in blood. He doesn't remember much after that, but there's a senior master living a hundred yards up the road—Mr. D'Arcy his name is, lives with his sister, and he heard him screaming on the road. D'Arcy went out to him. Rode had blood all over his hands and face and seemed to be out of his mind. D'Arcy rang for the police and I got there at about one o'clock that morning. I've seen some nasty things in my time, but this is the worst. Blood everywhere. Whoever killed her must have been covered in it. There's an outside tap against the conservatory wall. The tap had been turned on, probably by the murderer to rinse his hands. The boffins have found traces of blood in the snow underneath it. The tap was lagged recently by Rode I gather. . . ."

"And fingerprints?" Smiley asked. "What about them?"

"Mr. Rode's were everywhere. On the floor, the walls and windows, on the body itself. But there were other prints; smudges of blood, little more, made with a gloved hand probably."

"And they were the murderer's?"

"They had been made *before* Rode made his. In some cases Rode's prints were partly superimposed on the glove prints."

Smiley was silent for a moment.

"These examination papers he went back for. Were they as important as all that?"

"Yes. I gather they were. Up to a point anyway? The marks had to be handed in to Mr. D'Arcy by midday on Friday."

"But why did he take them to Fielding's in the first place?"

"He didn't. He'd been invigilating exams all afternoon and the papers were handed in to him at six o'clock. He put them in his little case and had them taken to Fielding's by a boy—head boy in Mr. Fielding's house, name of Perkins. Rode was on Chapel duty last week, so he didn't have time to return home before dinner."

"Where did he change then?"

"In the Tutors' Robing Room, next to the Common Room. There are facilities there, mainly for games tutors who live some distance from Carne."

"The boy who brought this case to Fielding's house—who was he?"

"I can't tell you much more than I've said. His name is Perkins; he's head of Mr. Fielding's house. Fielding has spoken to him and confirmed Rode's statement. . . . House tutors are very possessive about their boys, you know . . . don't like them to be spoken to by rough policemen." Rigby seemed to be slightly upset.

"I see," Smiley said at last, helplessly, and then : "But how do you explain the letter?"

"It isn't only the letter we've got to explain."

Smiley looked at him sharply.

"What do you mean?"

"I mean," said Rigby slowly, "that Mrs. Rode did several pretty queer things in the last few weeks."

CHAPTER IV

TOWN AND GOWN

"Mrs. Rode was Chapel, of course," Rigby continued "and we've quite a community in Carne. Truth to tell," he added with a slow smile, "my wife belongs to it.

"A couple of weeks ago our Minister called round to see me. It was in the evening, about half past six, I suppose. I was just thinking of going home, see. He walked in here and sat himself down where you're sitting now. He's a big fellow, the Minister, a fine man; comes from up North, where Mrs. Rode came from. Cardew, his name is."

"The Mr. Cardew in the letter?"

"That's him. He knew all about Mrs. Rode's family before the Rodes ever came here. Glaston's quite a name up North, and Mr. Cardew was very pleased when he heard that Stella Rode was Mr. Glaston's daughter; very pleased indeed. Mrs. Rode came to the Tabernacle regular as clockwork—you can imagine, and they like to see that round here. My wife was pleased as Punch, I can tell you. It was the first time, I suppose, that anyone from the School had done that. Most of the Chapel people here are tradespeople—what we call the locals." Rigby smiled again. "It isn't often that town and gown come together so to speak. Not here."

"How about her husband? Was he Chapel too?"

"Well, he had been, so she told Mr. Cardew. Mr. Rode was born and bred in Branxome, and all his family were Chapel people. That's how Mr. and Mrs. Rode first met, I gather—at Branxome Tabernacle. Ever been there, have you? A fine church Branxome, right up on the hill there, overlooking the sea."

Smiley shook his head and Rigby's wide brown eyes rested on him thoughtfully for a moment.

"You should," he said, "you should go and see that. It seems," he continued, "that Mr. Rode turned Church of

England when he came to Carne. Even tried to persuade his wife to do the same. They're very strong at the School. I heard that from my wife, as a matter of fact. I never let her gossip as a rule, being a policeman's wife and that, but Mr. Cardew told her that himself."

"I see," said Smiley.

"Well now, Cardew came and saw me. He was all worried and bothered with himself. He didn't know what he should make of it, but he wanted to talk to me as a friend and not as a policeman." Rigby looked sour, "When people say that to me, I always know that they want to talk to me as a policeman. Then he told me his story. Mrs. Rode had called to see him that afternoon. He'd been out visiting a farmer's wife over in Okeford and didn't come home until half past five or thereabouts, so Mrs. Cardew had had to talk to her and hold the fort until the Minister came home. Mrs. Rode was white as a sheet, sitting very still by the fire. As soon as the Minister arrived, Mrs. Cardew left them alone and Stella Rode started talking about her husband."

He paused. "She said Mr. Rode was going to kill her. In the long nights. She seemed to have a kind of fixation about being murdered in the long nights. Cardew didn't take it too seriously at first, but thinking about it afterwards, he decided to let me know."

Smiley looked at him sharply.

"He couldn't make out what she meant. He thought she was out of her mind. He's a down-to-earth man, see, although he's a Minister. I think he was probably a bit too firm with her. He asked her what put this dreadful thought into her head, and she began to weep. Not hysterical, apparently, but just crying quietly to herself. He tried to calm her down, promised to help her any way he could, and asked her again what had given her this idea. She just shook her head, then got up, walked over to the door, still shaking her head in despair. She turned to him, and he thought she was going to say something, but she didn't. She just left."

"How very curious," said Smiley, "that she lied about that

in her letter. She went out of her way to say she *hadn't* told Cardew."

Rigby shrugged his great shoulders.

"If you'll pardon me," he said, "I'm in a darned awkward position. The Chief Constable would sooner cut his throat than call in Scotland Yard. He wants an arrest and he wants one quick. We've got enough clues to cover a Christmas tree; footprints, time of the murder, indication of murderer's clothing and even the weapon itself."

Smiley looked at him in surprise.

"You've *found* the weapon, then?"

Rigby hesitated. "Yes, we've found it. There's hardly a soul knows this, sir, and I'll trouble you to remember that. We found it the morning after the murder, four miles north of Carne on the Okeford road, tossed into a ditch. Eighteen inches of what they call coaxial cable. Know what that is, do you? It comes in all sizes, but this piece is about two inches in diameter. It has a copper rod running down the middle and plastic insulation between the rod and the outer cover. There was blood on it : Stella Rode's blood group, and hairs from her head, stuck to the blood. We're keeping that very dark indeed. By the Grace of God, it was found by one of our own men. It pinpoints the line of the murderer's departure."

"There's no doubt, I suppose, that it *is* the weapon?" Smiley asked lamely.

"We found particles of copper in the wounds on the body."

"It's odd, isn't it," Smiley suggested reflectively, "that the murderer should have carried the weapon so far before getting rid of it? Specially if he was walking. You'd think he'd want to get rid of it as soon as he could."

"It is odd. Very odd. The Okeford road runs beside the canal for half of those four miles; he could have pitched the cable into the canal anywhere along there. We'd never have been the wiser."

"Was the cable old?"

"Not particularly. Just standard type. It could have come

from almost anywhere." Rigby hesitated a minute, then burst out :

"Look, sir, this is what I am trying to say. The circumstances of this case demand a certain type of investigation : wide-scale search, detailed laboratory work, mass enquiry. That's what the Chief wants, and he's right. We've no case against the husband at all, and to be frank he's precious little use to us. He seems a bit lost, a bit vague, contradicting himself on little things that don't matter, like the date of his marriage or the name of his doctor. It's a shock, of course, I've seen it before. I know all about your letter, sir, and it's damned odd, but if you can tell me how he could have produced wellington boots out of a hat and got rid of them afterwards, battered his wife to death without leaving more than a few smudges of blood on himself, and got the weapon four miles from the scene of the crime, all within ten minutes of being at Fielding's house, I'll be grateful to you. We're looking for a stranger, six foot tall, wearing newish Dunlop Wellington boots size $10\frac{1}{2}$, leather gloves and an old blue overcoat stained with blood. A man who travels on foot who was in the area of North Fields between 11.10 and 11.45 on the night of the murder, who left in the direction of Okeford, taking with him one and a half feet of coaxial cable, a string of green beads and an imitation diamond clip, valued at twenty-three and six. We're looking for a maniac, a man who kills for pleasure or the price of a meal." Rigby paused, smiled wistfully and added, "Who can fly fifty feet through the air. But with information like this how else should we spend our time? What else can we look for? I can't put men on to chasing shadows when there's work like that to be done."

"I understand that."

"But I'm an old policeman, Mr. Smiley, and I like to know what I'm about. I don't like looking for people I can't believe in, and I don't like being cut off from witnesses. I like to meet people and talk to them, nose about here and there, get to know the country. But I can't do that, not at the school. Do you follow me? So we've got to rely on laboratories, tracker dogs and nation-wide searches, but somehow in my bones I don't think it's altogether one of those cases."

"I read in the paper about a woman, a Mad Janie . . ."

"I'm coming to that. Mrs. Rode was a kindly woman, easy to talk to. I always found her so, anyway. Some of the women at Chapel took against her, but you know what women are. It seems she got friendly with this Janie creature. Janie came begging, selling herbs and charms at the back door; you know the kind of thing. She's queer, talks to birds and all that. She lives in a disused Norman chapel over to Pylle. Stella Rode used to give her food and clothes—the poor soul was often as not half-starved. Now Janie's disappeared. She was seen early Wednesday night on the lane towards North Fields and hasn't been seen since. That don't mean a thing. These people come and go in their own way. They'll be all over the neighbourhood for years, then one day they're gone like snow in the fire. They've died in a ditch, maybe, or they've took ill and crept away like a cat. Janie's not the only queer one round here. There's a lot of excitement because we found a spare set of footprints running along the fringe of trees at the far end of the garden. They were a woman's prints by the look of them, and at one point they come quite close to the conservatory. Could be a gypsy or a beggar woman. Could be anything, but I expect it's Janie right enough. I hope to Heaven it was, sir; we could do with an eye-witness, even a mad one."

Smiley stood up. As they shook hands, Rigby said, "Good-bye, sir. Ring me any time, any time at all." He scribbled a telephone number on the pad in front of him, tore off the sheet and gave it to Smiley. "That's my home number." He showed Smiley to the door, seemed to hesitate, then he said, "You're not a Carnian yourself by any chance, are you, sir?"

"Good heavens, no."

Again Rigby hesitated. "Our Chief's a Carnian. Ex-Indian Army. Brigadier Havelock. This is his last year. He's very interested in this case. Doesn't like me messing around the school. Won't have it."

"I see."

"He wants an arrest quickly."

"And outside Carne, I suppose?"

"Goodbye, Mr. Smiley. Don't forget to ring me. Oh, another thing I should have mentioned. That bit of cable . . ."

"Yes?"

"Mr. Rode used a length of the same stuff in a demonstration lecture on elementary electronics. Mislaid it about three weeks ago."

Smiley walked slowly back to his hotel.

My Dear Brim,

As soon as I arrived I handed your letter over to the C.I.D. man in charge of the case—it was Rigby, as Ben had supposed: he looks like a mixture of Humpty-Dumpty and a Cornish elf—very short and broad—and I don't think he's anyone's fool.

To begin at the middle—our letter didn't have quite the effect we expected; Stella Rode evidently told Cardew, the local Baptist Minister, two weeks ago, that her husband was trying to kill her in the long nights, whatever they are. As for the circumstances of the murder—the account in the *Guardian* is substantially correct.

In fact, the more Rigby told me, the less likely it became that she was killed by her husband. Almost everything pointed away from him. Quite apart from motive, there is the location of the weapon, the footprints in the snow (which indicate a tall man in wellingtons), the presence of unidentified glove-prints in the conservatory. Add to that the strongest argument of all : whoever killed her must have been covered in blood—the conservatory was a dreadful sight, Rigby tells me. Of course, there *was* blood on Rode when he was picked up by his colleague in the lane, but only smears which could have resulted from stumbling over the body in the dark. Incidentally, the footprints only go into the garden and not out.

As things stand at the moment, there is, as Rigby points out, only one interpretation—the murderer was a stranger, a tramp, a madman perhaps, who killed her for pleasure or for her jewellery (which was worthless) and made off along the Okeford road, throwing the weapon into a ditch. (But why carry it four miles—and why not throw it into the canal the other side of the ditch? The Okeford road crosses Okemoor, which is all cross-dyked to prevent flooding.) If this interpretation is correct, then I suppose we attribute Stella's letter and her interview with Cardew to a persecuted mind, or the premonition of death, depending on whether we're superstitious. If that is so, it is the most monstrous coincidence I have ever heard of. Which brings me to my final point.

I rather gathered from what Rigby *didn't* say that his Chief Constable was treading on his tail, urging him to scour the country for tramps in bloodstained blue overcoats (you remember the belt). Rigby, of course, has no alternative but to follow the signs and do as his Chief expects—but he is clearly uneasy about something—either something he hasn't told me, or something he just feels in his bones. I think he was sincere when he asked me to tell him anything I found out about the *School* end—the Rodes themselves, the way they fitted in, and so on. Carne's monastery walls are still pretty high, he feels. . . .

So I'll just sniff around a bit, I think, and see what goes on. I rang Fielding when I got back from the police station and he's asked me to supper tonight. I'll write again as soon as I have anything to tell you.

George.

Having carefully sealed the envelope, pressing down the corners with his thumbs, Smiley locked his door and made his way down the wide marble staircase, treading carefully on the meagre coconut matting that ran down the centre. There was a red wooden letter box in the hall for the use of residents, but Smiley, being a cautious man, avoided it. He walked to the pillar box at the corner of the road, posted his letter and wondered what to do about lunch. There were, of course, the sandwiches and coffee provided by Miss Brimley.

Reluctantly he returned to the hotel. It was full of journal-ists, and Smiley hated journalists. It was also cold, and he hated the cold. And there was something very familiar about sandwiches in a hotel bedroom.

CHAPTER V

CAT AND DOG

It was just after seven o'clock that evening when George Smiley climbed the steps which led up to the front door of Mr. Terence Fielding's house. He rang, and was admitted to the hall by a little plump woman in her middle fifties. To his right a log fire burned warmly on a pile of wood ash and above him he was vaguely aware of a minstrel gallery and a mahogany staircase, which rose in a spiral to the top of the house. Most of the light seemed to come from the fire, and Smiley could see that the walls around him were hung with a great number of paintings of various styles and periods, and the chimney-piece was laden with all manner of *objets d'art*. With an involuntary shudder, he noticed that neither the fire nor the pictures quite succeeded in banishing the faint smell of school—of polish bought wholesale, of cocoa and community cooking. Corridors led from the hall, and Smiley observed that the lower part of each wall was painted a dark brown or green according to the inflexible rule of school decorators. From one of these corridors the enormous figure of Mr. Terence Fielding emerged.

He advanced on Smiley, massive and genial, with his splendid mane of grey hair falling anyhow across his forehead, and his gown billowing behind him.

"Smiley? Ah! You've met True, have you—Miss True-body, my housekeeper? Marvellous this snow, isn't it? Pure

Breughel! Seen the boys skating by the Eyot? Marvellous sight! Black suits, coloured scarves, pale sun; all there, isn't it, all there! Breughel to the life. Marvellous!" He took Smiley's coat and flung it on to a decrepit deal chair with a rush seat which stood in the corner of the hall.

"You like that chair—you recognise it?"

"I don't think I do," Smiley replied in some confusion.

"Ah, you should, you know, you should! Had it made in Provence before the war. Little carpenter I knew. Place it now? Facsimile of Van Gogh's yellow chair; some people recognise it." He led the way down a corridor and into a large comfortable study adorned with Dutch tiles, small pieces of Renaissance sculpture, mysterious bronzes, china dogs and unglazed vases; and Fielding himself towering magnificent among them.

As senior housemaster of Carne, Fielding wore, in place of the customary academic dress, a wonderful confection of heavy black skirts and legal bib, like a monk in evening dress. All this imparted a suggestion of clerical austerity in noted contrast to the studied flamboyance of his personality. Evidently conscious of this, he sought to punctuate the solemnity of his uniform and gave to it a little of his own temperament, by adorning it with flowers carefully chosen from his garden. He had scandalised the tailors of Carne, whose frosted windows carried the insignia of royal households, by having buttonholes let into his gown. These he would fill according to his mood with anything from hibernia to bluebells. This evening he wore a rose, and from its freshness Smiley deduced that he had this minute put it into place, having ordered it specially.

"Sherry wine or Madeira?"

"Thank you; a glass of sherry."

"Tart's drink, Madeira," Fielding called, as he poured from a decanter, "but boys like it. Perhaps that's why. They're frightful flirts." He handed Smiley a glass and added, with a dramatic modification of his voice:

"We're all rather subdued at the moment by this dreadful

business. We've never had anything quite like it, you know. Have you seen the evening papers?"

"No, I'm afraid I haven't. But the Sawley Arms is packed with journalists of course."

"They've really gone to town. They've got the Army out in Hampshire, playing about with mine-detectors. God knows what they expect to find."

"How have the boys taken it?"

"They adore it! My own house has been particularly fortunate, of course, because the Rodes were dining here that night. Some oaf from the police even wanted to question one of my boys."

"Indeed," said Smiley innocently. "What on earth about?"

"Oh, God knows," Fielding replied abruptly, and then, changing the subject, he asked, "You knew my brother well, didn't you? He talked about you, you know."

"Yes, I knew Adrian very well. We were close friends."

"In the war, too?"

"Yes."

"Were you in his crowd, then?"

"What crowd?"

"Steed-Asprey, Jebedee. All those people."

"Yes."

"I never really heard how he died. Did you?"

"No."

"We didn't see much of one another in later years, Adrian and I. Being a fraud, I can't afford to be seen beside the genuine article," Fielding declared, with something of his earlier panache. Smiley was spared the embarrassment of a reply by a quiet knock at the door, and a tall red-haired boy came timidly into the room.

"I've called the Adsum, sir, if you're ready, sir."

"Damn," said Fielding, emptying his glass. "Prayers." He turned to Smiley.

"Meet Perkins, my head prefect. Musical genius, but a problem in the schoolroom. That right, Tim? Stay here or come as you like. It only lasts ten minutes."

"Rather less tonight, sir," said Perkins. "It's the Nunc Dimittis."

"Thank God for small mercies," Fielding declared, tugging briefly at his bib, as he led Smiley at a spanking pace out into the corridor and across the hall, with Perkins stalking along behind them. Fielding was speaking all the time without bothering to turn his head:

"I'm glad you've chosen this evening to come. I never entertain on Saturdays as a rule because everyone else does, though none of us quite knows what to do about entertaining at the moment. Felix D'Arcy will be coming tonight, but that's hardly entertaining. D'Arcy's a professional. Incidentally, we normally dress in the evening, but it doesn't matter."

Smiley's heart sank. They turned a corner and entered another corridor.

"We have prayers at all hours here. The Master's revived the seven Day Hours for the Offices: Prime, Terce, Sext and so on. A surfeit during the Half, abstinence during the holidays, that's the system, like games. Useful in the house for roll-calls, too." He led the way down yet another corridor, flung open a double door at the end of it and marched straight into the dining-room, his gown filling gracefully behind him. The boys were waiting for him.

"More sherry? What did you think of prayers? They sing quite nicely, don't they? One or two good tenors. We tried some plainsong last Half; quite good, really quite good. D'Arcy will be here soon. He's a frightful toad. Looks like a Sickert model fifty years after—all trousers and collar. However, you're lucky his sister isn't accompanying him. She's worse!"

"What's his subject?" They were back in Fielding's study.

"Subject! I'm afraid we don't have subjects here. None of us has read a word on any subject since we left University." He lowered his voice and added darkly, "That's if we *went* to University. D'Arcy teaches French. D'Arcy is senior tutor by election, bachelor by profession, sublimated pansy by inclination . . . " he was standing quite still now, his head thrown back and his right hand stretched out towards Smiley, ". . . and his subject is other people's shortcomings. He is principally, however, self-appointed majordomo of Carne protocol. If you wear a gown on a bicycle, reply incorrectly to an invitation, make a fault in the *placement* of your dinner guests or speak of a colleague as 'Mister', D'Arcy will find you out and admonish you."

"What are the duties of Senior Tutor, then?" Smiley asked, just for something to say.

"He's the referee between the classics and the scientists; arranges the timetable and vets the exam. results. But principally, poor man, he must reconcile the Arts with the Sciences." He shook his head sagely. "And it takes a better man than D'Arcy to do that. Not, mind you," he added wearily, "that it makes the least difference who wins the extra hour on Friday evenings. Who cares? Not the boys, poor dears, that's certain."

Fielding talked on, at random and always in superlatives, sometimes groping in the air with his hand as if to catch the more elusive metaphors; now of his colleagues with caustic derision, now of boys with compassion if not with understanding; now of the Arts with fervour—and the studied bewilderment of a lonely disciple.

"Carne isn't a school. It's a sanatorium for intellectual lepers. The symptoms began when we came down from University; a gradual putrification of our intellectual extremities. From day to day our minds die, our spirits atrophy and rot. We watch the process in one another, hoping to forget it in ourselves." He paused, and looked reflectively at his hands.

"In me the process is complete. You see before you a dead soul, and Carne is the body I live in." Much pleased by this confession, Fielding held out his great arms so that the sleeves of his gown resembled the wings of a giant bat, "the Vampire of Carne", he declared, bowing deeply. "Alcoholique et poète!" A bellow of laughter followed this display.

Smiley was fascinated by Fielding, by his size, his voice, the wanton inconstancy of his temperament, by his whole big-screen style; he found himself attracted and repelled by this succession of contradictory poses; he wondered whether he was supposed to take part in the performance, but Fielding seemed so dazzled by the footlights that he was indifferent to the audience behind them. The more Smiley watched, the more elusive seemed the character he was trying to comprehend : changeful but sterile, daring but fugitive; colourful unbounded, ingenuous, yet deceitful and perverse. Smiley began to wish he could acquire the material facts of Fielding —his means, his ambitions and disappointments.

His reverie was interrupted by Miss Truebody. Felix D'Arcy had arrived.

No candles, and a cold supper admirably done by Miss Truebody. Not claret, but hock, passed round like port. And at last, at long last, Fielding mentioned Stella Rode.

They had been talking rather dutifully of the Arts and the Sciences. This would have been dull (for it was uninformed) had not D'Arcy constantly been goaded by Fielding, who seemed anxious to exhibit D'Arcy in his worst light. D'Arcy's judgements of people and problems were largely coloured by what he considered "seemly" (a favourite word) and by an effeminate malice towards his colleagues. After a while Fielding asked who was replacing Rode during his absence, to which D'Arcy said, "No one," and added unctuously :

"It was a terrible shock to the community, this affair."

"Nonsense," Fielding retorted. "Boys love disaster. The further we are from death the more attractive it seems. They find the whole affair most exhilarating."

"The publicity has been most unseemly," said D'Arcy, "most. I think that has been prominent in the minds of many of us in the Common Room." He turned to Smiley :

"The press, you know, is a constant worry here. In the past it could never have happened. Formerly our great families and institutions were not subjected to this intrusion. No, indeed not. But today all that is changed. Many of us are compelled to subscribe to the cheaper newspapers for this very reason. One Sunday newspaper mentioned no fewer than four of Hecht's old boys in one edition. All of them in an unseemly context, I may say. And of course such papers never fail to mention that the boy is a Carnian. You know, I suppose, that we have the young prince here. (I myself have the honour to supervise his French studies). The young Sawley is also at Carne. The activity of the press during his parents' divorce suit was deplorable. Quite deplorable. The Master wrote to the Press Council, you know. I drafted the letter myself. But on this tragic occasion they have excelled themselves. We even had the press at Compline last night, you know, waiting for the Special Prayer. They occupied the whole of the two rear pews on the west side. Hecht was doing Chapel Duty and tried to have them removed." He paused, raised his eyebrows in gentle reproach and smiled. "He had no business to, of course, but that never stopped the good Hecht." He turned to Smiley, "One of our *athletic* brethren," he explained.

"Stella was too common for you, Felix, wasn't she?"

"Not at all," said D'Arcy quickly. "I would not have you say that of me, Terence. I am by no means discriminatory in the matter of class; merely of manners. I grant you, in that particular field, I found her wanting."

"In many ways she was just what we needed," Fielding continued, addressing Smiley and ignoring D'Arcy. "She was everything we're forced to ignore—she was red-brick, council estates, new towns, the very antithesis of Carne!" He turned suddenly to D'Arcy and said, "But to you, Felix, she was just bad form."

"Not at all; merely unsuitable."

Fielding turned to Smiley in despair.

"Look," he said. "We talk academic here, you know, wear academic dress and hold high table dinners in the Common Room; we have long graces in Latin that none of us can translate. We go to the Abbey and the wives sit in the hencoop in their awful hats. But it's a charade. It means nothing."

D'Arcy smiled wanly.

"I cannot believe, my dear Terence, that anyone who keeps such an excellent table as yourself can have so low an opinion of the refinements of social conduct." He looked to Smiley for support and Smiley dutifully echoed the compliment. "Besides, we know Terence of old at Carne. I am afraid we are accustomed to his roar."

"I know why you disliked that woman, Felix. She was honest, and Carne has no defence against that kind of honesty."

D'Arcy suddenly became very angry indeed.

"Terence, I will not have you say this. I simply will not have it. I feel I have a certain duty at Carne, as indeed we all have, to restore and maintain those standards of behaviour which suffered so sadly in the war. I am sensible that this determination has made me on more than one occasion unpopular. But such comment or advice as I offer is never—I beg you to notice this—is *never* directed against personalities, only against behaviour, against unseemly lapses in conduct. I will acknowledge that more than once I was compelled to address Rode on the subject of his wife's conduct. That is a matter quite divorced from personalities, Terence. I will not have it said that I disliked Mrs. Rode. Such a suggestion would be disagreeable at all times, but under the present tragic circumstances it is deplorable. Mrs. Rode's own . . . background and education did not naturally prepare her for our ways; that is quite a different matter. It does, however, illustrate the point that I wish to emphasise, Terence : it was a question of enlightenment, not of criticism. Do I make myself clear?"

"Abundantly," Fielding answered dryly.

"Did the other wives like her?" Smiley ventured.

"Not entirely," D'Arcy replied crisply.

"The wives ! My God !" Fielding groaned, putting his hand to his brow. There was a pause.

"Her clothes, I believe, were a source of distress to some of them. She also frequented the public laundry. This, too, would not make a favourable impression. I should add that she did not attend our church. . . ."

"Did she have any close friends among the wives?" Smiley persisted.

"I believe young Mrs. Snow took to her."

"And you say she was dining here the night she was murdered?"

"Yes," said Fielding quietly, "Wednesday. And it was Felix and his sister who took in poor Rode afterwards. . . ." He glanced at D'Arcy.

"Yes, indeed," said D'Arcy abruptly. His eyes were on Fielding, and it seemed to Smiley that something had passed between them. "We shall never forget, never. . . . Terence, if I may talk shop for just one moment, Perkins' construe is abysmal; I declare I have never seen work like it. Is he unwell? His mother is a most cultured woman, a cousin of the Samfords, I am told."

Smiley looked at him and wondered. His dinner jacket was faded, green with age. Smiley could almost hear him saying it had belonged to his grandfather. The skin of his face was so unlined that he somehow suggested fatness without being fat. His voice was pitched on one insinuating note, and he smiled all the time, whether he was speaking or not. The smile never left his smooth face, it was worked into the malleable fabric of his flesh, stretching his lips across his perfect teeth and opening the corners of his red mouth, so that it seemed to be held in place by the invisible fingers of his dentist. Yet D'Arcy's face was far from unexpressive; every mark showed. The smallest movement of his mouth or nose, the quickest glance or frown, were there to read and interpret. And he wanted to change the subject. Not away from Stella Rode (for he returned to discussing her himself a moment later), but away from the particular evening on which she died, away from the precise narration of events. And what was more, there was not a doubt in Smiley's mind that Fielding had seen it too, that in that look which passed between them was a pact of fear, a warning perhaps, so that from that moment Fielding's manner changed, he grew sullen

and preoccupied, in a way that puzzled Smiley long afterwards.

D'Arcy turned to Smiley and addressed him with cloying
intimacy.

"*Do* forgive my deplorable descent into Carne gossip. You
find us a little cut off here, do you not? We are often held
to be cut off, I know. Carne is a 'Snob School', that is the
cry. You may read it every day in the gutter press. And yet,
despite the claims of the *avant-garde*," he said, glancing slyly
at Fielding, "I may say that *no one* could be less of a snob
than Felix D'Arcy." Smiley noticed his hair. It was very
fine and ginger, growing from the top and leaving his pink
neck bare.

"Take poor Rode, for instance. I certainly don't hold
Rode's background against him in any way, poor fellow. The
Grammar Schools do a splendid job, I am sure. Besides, he
settled down here very well. I told the Master so. I said to
him that Rode had settled down well; he does Chapel duty
quite admirably—that was the very point I made. I hope I
have played my part, what is more, in helping him to fit in.
With careful instruction, such people can, as I said to the
Master, learn our customs and even our manners; and the
Master agreed."

Smiley's glass was empty and D'Arcy without consulting
Fielding, filled it for him from the decanter. His hands were
polished and hairless, like the hands of a girl.

"But," he continued, "I must be honest. Mrs. Rode did not
adapt herself so willingly to our ways." Still smiling, he sip-
ped delicately from his glass. He wants to put the record
straight, thought Smiley.

"She would never really have fitted in at Carne; that is
my opinion—though I am sure I never voiced it while she was
alive. Her background was against her. The fault was not
hers—it was her background which, as I say, was unfortunate. Indeed, if we may speak frankly and in confidence, I
have reason to believe it was her past that brought about her
death."

"Why do you say that?" asked Smiley quickly, and D'Arcy replied with a glance at Fielding, "It appears she was expecting to be attacked."

"My sister is devoted to dogs," D'Arcy continued. "You may know that already perhaps. King Charles spaniels are her *forte*. She took a first at the North Dorset last year and was commended at Cruft's shortly afterwards for her 'Queen of Carne'. She sells to America, you know. I dare say there are few people in the country with Dorothy's knowledge of the breed. The Master's wife found occasion to say the very same thing a week ago. Well, the Rodes were our neighbours, as you know, and Dorothy is not a person to neglect her neighbourly duties. Where duty is concerned, you will not find her discriminatory, I assure you. The Rodes also had a dog, a large mongrel, quite an intelligent animal, which they brought with them. (I have little idea where they came from, but that is another matter.) They appeared quite devoted to the dog, and I have no doubt they were. Rode took it with him to watch the football until I had occasion to advise him against it. The practice was giving rise to unseemly humour among the boys. I have found the same thing myself when exercising Dorothy's spaniels.

"I shall come to the point presently. Dorothy uses a vet called Harriman, a superior type of person who lives over toward Sturminster. A fortnight ago she sent for him. 'Queen of Carne' was coughing badly and Dorothy asked Harriman to come over. A bitch of her quality is not to be taken lightly, I assure you."

Fielding groaned, and D'Arcy continued, oblivious:

"I happened to be at home, and Harriman stayed for a cup of coffee. He is, as I say, a superior type of person. Harriman made some reference to the Rodes' dog and then the truth came out; Mrs. Rode had had the dog destroyed the previous day. She said it had bitten the postman. Some long and confused story; the Post Office would sue, the police had been round and I don't know what else. And, anyway, she said, the dog couldn't really protect, it could only warn. She had said so to Harriman, 'It wouldn't do any good.' "

"Wasn't she upset about losing the dog?" asked Smiley.

"Oh, indeed, yes. Harriman said she was in tears when she arrived. Mrs. Harriman had to give her a cup of tea. They suggested she should give the dog another chance, put it in kennels for a while, but she was adamant, quite adamant. Harriman was most perplexed. So was his wife. When they discussed it afterwards they agreed that Mrs. Rode's behaviour had not been quite normal. Not normal at all, in fact. Another curious fact was the condition of the dog : it had been maltreated, seriously so. Its back was marked as if from beatings."

"Did Harriman follow up this remark she made? About not doing any good? What did Harriman make of it?" Smiley was watching D'Arcy intently.

"She repeated it to Mrs. Harriman, but she wouldn't explain it. However, I think the explanation is obvious enough."

"Oh?" said Fielding.

D'Arcy put his head on one side and plucked coyly at the lobe of his ear.

"We all have a little of the detective in us," he said. "Dorothy and I talked it over after the—death. We decided that Stella Rode had formed some unsavoury association before coming to Carne, which had recently been revived . . . possibly against her will. Some violent ruffian—an old admirer —who would resent the improvement in her station."

"How badly was the postman bitten by the dog?" Smiley asked.

D'Arcy turned to him again.

"That is the extraordinary thing. That is the very crux of the story, my dear fellow : the postman hadn't been bitten at all. Dorothy enquired. Her whole story was an absolute string of lies from beginning to end."

They rose from the table and made their way to Fielding's study, where Miss Truebody had put the coffee. The conversation continued to wander back and forth over Wednesday's tragedy. D'Arcy was obsessed with the indelicacy of it all—the persistence of journalists, the insensitivity of the police, the uncertainty of Mrs. Rode's origin, the misfortune of her husband. Fielding was still oddly silent, sunk in his own thoughts, from which he occasionally emerged to glance at D'Arcy with a look of hostility. At exactly a quarter to eleven D'Arcy pronounced himself tired, and the three of them went into the great hall, where Miss Truebody produced a coat for Smiley and a coat and muffler and cap for D'Arcy. Fielding accepted D'Arcy's thanks with a sullen nod. He turned to Smiley :

"That business you rang me about. What was it exactly?"

"Oh—a letter from Mrs. Rode just before she was murdered," said Smiley vaguely, "the police are handling it now, but they do not regard it as . . . significant. Not significant at all. She seems to have had a sort of"—he gave an embarrassed grin—"persecution complex. Is that the expression? However, we might discuss it some time. You must dine with me at the Sawley before I go back. Do you come to London at all? We might meet in London perhaps, at the end of the Half."

D'Arcy was standing in the doorway, looking at the new fall of snow which lay white and perfect on the pavement before him.

"Ah," he said, with a little knowing laugh, "the long nights, eh, Terence, the long nights."

CHAPTER VI

HOLLY FOR THE DEVIL

"What are the long nights?" Smiley asked, as he and D'Arcy walked briskly away from Fielding's house through the new snow towards the Abbey Close.

"We have a proverb that it always snows at Carne in the long nights. That is the traditional term here for the nights of Lent," D'Arcy replied. "Before the Reformation the monks of the Abbey kept a vigil during Lent between the Offices of Compline and Lauds. You may know that already perhaps. As there is no longer a religious order attached to the Abbey, the custom has fallen into disuse. We continue to observe it, however, by the saying of Compline during Lent. Compline was the last of the Canonical Day Hours and was said before retiring for the night. The Master, who has a great respect for traditions of this kind, has reintroduced the old words for our devotions. Prime was the dawn Office, as you are no doubt aware. Terce was at the third hour of daylight—that is to say at 9.0 a.m. Thus we no longer refer to Morning Prayer, but to Terce. I find it delightful. Similarly, during Advent and Lent we say Sext at midday in the Abbey."

"Are all these services compulsory?"

"Of course. Otherwise it would be necessary to make arrangements for those boys who did not attend. That is not desirable. Besides, you forget that Carne is a religious foundation."

It was a beautiful night. As they crossed the Close, Smiley looked up at the tower. It seemed smaller and more peaceful in the moonlight. The whiteness of the new snow lit the very sky itself; the whole Abbey was so sharply visible against it that even the mutilated images of saints were clear in every sad detail of their defacement, wretched figures, their purpose lost, with no eyes to see the changing world.

They reached the cross-roads to the south of the Abbey

"The parting of the ways, I fear," said D'Arcy, extending his hand.

"It's a beautiful night," Smiley replied quickly, "let me come with you as far as your house."

"Gladly," said D'Arcy dryly.

They turned down North Fields Lane. A high stone wall ran along one side; and on the other the great expanse of playing fields, twenty or more rugby pitches, bordered the road for over half a mile. They walked this distance in silence, until D'Arcy stopped and pointed with his stick past Smiley towards a small house on the edge of the playing fields.

"That's North Fields, the Rodes' house. It used to belong to the head groundsman, but the school added a wing a few years ago, and now it's a staff house. My own house is rather larger, and lies further up the road. Happily, I am fond of walking."

"Was it along here that you found Stanley Rode that night?"

There was a pause, then D'Arcy said: "It was nearer to my house, about a quarter of a mile further on. He was in a terrible condition, poor fellow, terrible. I am myself unable to bear the sight of blood. If I had known how he would look when I brought him into the house, I do not think I could have done it. Mercifully, my sister Dorothy is a most competent woman."

They walked on in silence, until Smiley said: "From what you were saying at dinner, the Rodes were a very ill-assorted couple."

"Precisely. If her death had happened any other way, I would describe it as providential: a blessed release for Rode. She was a thoroughly mischievous woman, Smiley, who made it her business to hold her husband up to ridicule. I believe it was intentional. Others do not. I do, and I have my reasons. She took pleasure in deriding her husband."

"And Carne too, no doubt."

"Just so. This is a critical moment in Carne's development. Many Public Schools have conceded to the vulgar clamour for change—change at any price. Carne, I am pleased to say, has not joined these Gadarene swine. That makes it more important than ever that we protect ourselves from within as well as from without." He spoke with surprising vehemence.

"But was she really such a problem? Surely her husband could have spoken to her?"

"I never encouraged him to do so, I assure you. It is not my practice to interfere between man and wife."

They reached D'Arcy's house. A high laurel hedge entirely concealed the house from the road, except for two multiple chimney-stacks which were visible over the top of it, confirming Smiley's impression that the house was large and Victorian.

"I am not ashamed of the Victorian taste," said D'Arcy as he slowly opened the gate; "but then, I am afraid we are not close to the modern idiom at Carne. This house used to be the rectory for North Fields Church, but the church is now served by a priest-in-charge from the Abbey. The vicarage is still within the school's gift, and I was fortunate enough to receive it. Good night. You must come for sherry before you go. Do you stay long?"

"I doubt it," Smiley replied, "but I am sure you have enough worries at the moment."

"What do you mean?" D'Arcy said sharply.

"The press, the police and all the attendant fuss."

"Ah yes, just so. Quite so. Nevertheless, our community life must continue. We always have a small party in the middle of the Half, and I feel it is particularly important that we should do so on this occasion. I will send a note to the Sawley tomorrow. My sister would be charmed. Good night." He clanged the gate to, and the sound was greeted by the frantic barking of dogs from somewhere behind the house. A window opened and a harsh female voice called :

"Is that you, Felix?"

"Yes, Dorothy."

"Why do you have to make such a bloody noise? You've woken those dogs again." The window closed with a significant thud, and D'Arcy, without so much as a glance in

Smiley's direction, disappeared quickly into the shadow of the house.

Smiley set off along the road again, back towards the town. After walking for about ten minutes he stopped and looked again towards the Rodes' house a hundred yards across the playing fields. It lay in the shadow of a small coppice of fir trees, dark and secret against the white fields. A narrow lane led towards the house; there was a brick pillar-box on one corner and a small oak sign-post, quite new, pointed along the lane, which must, he decided, lead to the village of Pylle. The legend upon the sign was obscured by a film of snow, and Smiley brushed it away with his hand, so that he could read the words "North Fields", done in a contrived Gothic script which must have caused D'Arcy considerable discomfort. The snow in the lane was untrodden; obviously more had fallen recently. There could not be much traffic between Pylle and Carne. Glancing quickly up and down the main road he began making his way along the lane. The hedge rose high on either side, and soon Smiley could see nothing but the pale sky above him, and the straggling willow wands reaching towards it. Once he thought he heard the sound of a footstep close behind him, but when he stopped he heard nothing but the furtive rustle of the laden hedges. He grew more conscious of the cold : it seemed to hang in the still damp of the sunken road, to clutch and hold him like the chill air of an empty house. Soon the hedge on his left gave way to a sparse line of trees, which Smiley judged to belong to the coppice he had seen from the road. The snow beneath the trees was patchy, and the bare ground looked suddenly ugly and torn. The lane took him in a gradual curve to the left and, quite suddenly the house stood before him, gaunt and craggy in the moonlight. The walls were brick and flint, half obscured by the mass of ivy which grew in profusion across them, tumbling over the porch in a tangled mane.

He glanced towards the garden. The coppice which bordered the lane encroached almost as far as the corner of the house, and extended to the far end of the lawn, screening the house from the playing fields. The murderer had reached the house by a path which led across the lawn and through the trees to the lane at the farthest end of the garden. Looking carefully at the snow on the lawn, he was able to discern the course of the path. The white glazed door to the left of the house must lead to the conservatory . . . And suddenly he knew he was afraid—afraid of the house, afraid of the sprawling dark garden. The knowledge came to him like an awareness of pain. The ivy walls seemed to reach forward and hold him, like an old woman cosseting an unwilling child. The house was large, yet dingy, holding to itself unearthly shapes, black and oily in the sudden contrasts of moonlight. Fascinated despite his fear, he moved towards it. The shadows broke and reformed, darting swiftly and becoming still, hiding in the abundant ivy, or merging with the black windows.

He observed in alarm the first involuntary movement of panic. He was afraid, then suddenly the senses joined in one concerted cry of terror, where sight and sound and touch could no longer be distinguished in the frenzy of his brain. He turned round and ran back to the gate. As he did so, he looked over his shoulder towards the house.

A woman was standing in the path, looking at him, and behind her the conservatory door swung slowly on its hinges.

For a second she stood quite still, then turned and ran back towards the conservatory. Forgetting his fear, Smiley followed. As he reached the corner of the house he saw to his astonishment that she was standing at the door, rocking it gently back and forth in a thoughtful, leisurely way, like a child. She had her back to Smiley, until suddenly she turned to him and spoke, with a soft Dorset drawl, and the childish lilt of a simpleton :

"I thought you was the Devil, Mister, but you'm got no wings."

Smiley hesitated. If he moved forward, she might take fright again and run. He looked at her across the snow, trying to make her out. She seemed to be wearing a bonnet or shawl over her head, and a dark cape over her shoulders. In her hand she held a sprig of leaves, and these she gently waved back and forth as she spoke to him.

"But you'm carn't do nothin', Mister, 'cos I got the holly fer to hold yer. So you do bide there, Mister, for little Jane can hold yer." She shook the leaves vehemently towards him and began laughing softly. She still had one hand upon the door, and as she spoke her head lolled to one side.

"You bide away from little Jane, Mister, however pretty she'm do be."

"Yes, Jane," said Smiley softly, "you're a very pretty girl I can see that; and that's a pretty cape you're wearing, Jane."

Evidently pleased with this, she clutched the lapels of her cape and turned slowly round, in a child's parody of a fine lady.

As she turned, Smiley saw the two empty sleeves of an overcoat swinging at her sides.

"There's some do laugh at Janie," she said, a note of petulance in her voice, "but there's not many seen the Devil fly, Mister. But Janie seed 'im, Janie seed 'im. Silver wings like fishes, 'e done 'ad, Janie saw."

"Where did you find that coat, Janie?"

She put her hands together and shook her head slowly from side to side.

"He'm a bad one. Ooh, he'm a bad one, Mister," and she laughed softly. "I seed 'im flying, riding' on the wind," she laughed again, "and the moon be'ind 'im, lightin' up the way! They'm close as sisters, moon and Devil."

On an impulse Smiley seized a handful of ivy from the side of the house and held it out to her, moving slowly forward as he did so.

"Do you like flowers, Janie? Here are flowers for Janie; pretty flowers for pretty Janie." He had nearly reached her when with remarkable speed she ran across the lawn, disappeared into the trees and ran off down the lane. Smiley let her go. He was drenched in sweat.

As soon as he reached the hotel he telephoned Detective Inspector Rigby.

CHAPTER VII

KING ARTHUR'S CHURCH

THE COFFEE LOUNGE of the Sawley Arms resembles nothing so much as the Tropical Plants Pavilion at Kew Gardens. Built in an age when cactus was the most fashionable of plants and bamboo its indispensable companion, the lounge was conceived as the architectural image of a jungle clearing. Steel pillars, fashioned in segments like the trunk of a palm tree, supported a high glass roof whose regal dome replaced the African sky. Enormous urns of bronze or green-glazed earthenware contained all that was elegant and prolific in the cactus world, and between them very old residents could relax on sofas of spindly bamboo, sipping warm coffee and re-living the discomforts of safari.

Smiley's efforts to obtain a bottle of whisky and a syphon of soda at half past eleven at night were not immediately rewarded. It seemed that, like carrion from the carcase, the journalists had gone. The only sign of life in the hotel was the night porter, who treated his request with remote disapproval and advised him to go to bed. Smiley, by no means naturally persistent, discovered a half-crown in his overcoat pocket and thrust it a little irritably into the old man's hand. The result, though not magical, was effective, and by the time Rigby had made his way to the hotel, Smiley was seated in front of a bright gas fire in the coffee lounge with glasses and a whisky bottle before him.

Smiley retold his experiences of the evening with careful accuracy.

"It was the coat that caught my eye. It was a heavy over-coat like a man's," he concluded. "I remembered the blue belt and . . ." He left the sentence unfinished. Rigby nodded, got up and walked briskly across the lounge and through the swing doors to the porter's desk. Ten minutes later, he returned.

"I think we'd better go and pull her in," he said simply. "I've sent for a car."

"We?" asked Smiley.

"Yes, if you wouldn't mind. What's the matter? Are you frightened?"

"Yes," he replied, "Yes, I am."

The village of Pylle lies to the south of North Fields, upon a high spur which rises steeply from the flat, damp pastures of the Carne valley. It consists of a handful of stone cottages and a small inn where you may drink beer in the landlord's parlour. Seen from Carne playing fields, the village could easily be mistaken for an outcrop of rock upon a tor, for the hill on which it stands appears conical from the northern side. Local historians claim that Pylle is the oldest settlement in Dorset, that its name is Anglo-Saxon for harbour, and that it served the Romans as a port when all the lowlands around were covered by the sea. They will tell you, too, that King Arthur rested there after seven months at sea, and paid homage to Saint Andrew, the patron saint of sailors, on the site of Pylle Church, where he burned a candle for each month he had spent afloat; and that in the church, built to commemorate his visit and standing to this day lonely and untended on the hillside, there is a bronze coin as witness to his visit—the very one King Arthur gave to the verger before he set sail again for the Isle of Avalon.

Inspector William Rigby, himself a keen local historian, gave Smiley a somewhat terse précis of Pylle's legendary past as he drove cautiously along the snow-covered lanes.

"These small, out-of-the-way villages are pretty strange places," he concluded. "Often only three or four families, all so inbred you can no more sort them out than a barnful of cats. That's where your village idiots come from. They call it the Devil's Mark; I call it incest. They hate to have them in the village, you know—they'll drive them away at any price, like trying to wash away their shame, if you follow me."

"I follow you."

"This Jane's the religious sort. There's one or two of them turn that way. The villagers at Pylle are all Chapel now, see, so there's been no use for King Arthur's Church since Wesley. It's empty, falling to bits. There's a few from the valley go up to see it, for its history, like, but no one cares for it, or didn't not till Janie moved in."

"Moved in?"

"Yes. She's taken to cleaning the church out night and day, bringing in wild flowers and such. That's why they say she's a witch."

They passed Rode's house in silence and after turning a sharp bend began climbing the long steep hill that led to Pylle village. The snow in the lane was untouched and apart from occasional skidding they progressed without difficulty. The lower slopes of the hill were wooded, and the lane dark, until suddenly they emerged to find themselves on a smooth plateau, where a savage wind blew the fine snow like smoke across the fields, whipping it against the car. The snow had risen in drifts to one side of the lane, and the going became increasingly difficult.

Finally Rigby stopped the car and said :

"We'll walk from here, sir, if you don't mind."

"How far is it?"

"Short and sour, I'd say. That's the village straight ahead."

Through the windscreen, Smiley could discern behind the drifting veils of blown snow two low buildings about a quarter of a mile away. As he looked, a tall, muffled figure advanced towards them along the lane.

"That's Ted Mundy," said Rigby with satisfaction, "I told him to be here. He's the sergeant from Okeford." He leaned out of the car window and called merrily :

"Hullo, Ted there, you old buzzard, how be?" Rigby opened the back door of the car and the sergeant climbed in. Smiley and Mundy were briefly introduced.

"There's a light in the church," said Mundy, "but I don't know whether Janie's there. I can't ask no one in the village, see, or I'd have the whole lot round me. They thought she'd gone for good."

"Does she sleep there then, Ted? She got a bed there or something?" Rigby asked, and Smiley noticed with pleasure that his Dorset accent was more pronounced when he spoke to Mundy.

"So they say, Bill. I couldn't find no bed when I looked in there Saturday. But I tell you an odd thing, Bill. It seems Mrs. Rode used to come up here sometimes, to the chapel, to see Janie."

"I heard about that," said Rigby shortly. "Now which way's the church, Ted?"

"Over the hill," said Mundy. "Outside the village, in a paddock." He turned to Smiley. "That's quite common round here, sir, as I expect you know." Mundy spoke very slowly, choosing his words. "You see, when they had the plague they left their dead in the villages and moved away; not far though, on account of their land and the church. Terrible it was, terrible." Somehow Mundy managed to imply that the Black Death was a fairly recent disaster in those parts, if not actually within living memory.

They got out of the car, forcing the doors against the strong wind, and made their way towards the village, Mundy leading and Smiley in third place. The driven snow, fine and hard, stung their faces. It was an unearthly walk, high on that white hill on such a night. The curve of the bleak hill's crest and the moaning of the wind, the snow cloud which sped across the moon, the dismal, unlit cottages so cautiously passed, belonged to another corner of the world.

Mundy led them sharply to the left, and Smiley guessed that by avoiding the centre of the village he hoped to escape the notice of its inhabitants. After about twenty minutes' walking, often through deep snow, they found themselves following a low hedge between two fields. In the furthest corner of the right hand field they saw a pale light glimmering across the snow, so pale that at first Smiley had to look away from it, then run his eyes back along the line of that distant hedge to make sure he was not deceived. Rigby stopped, beckoning to the others.

"I'll take over now," he said. He turned to Smiley. "I'd be obliged, sir, if you'd stand off a little. If there's any trouble we don't want you mixed up in it, do we?"

"Of course."

"Ted Mundy, you come up by me."

They followed the hedge until they came to a stile. Through the gap in the hedge they saw the church clearly now, a low building more like a tithe barn than a church. At one end a pale glow, like the uncertain light of a candle, shone dimly through the leaded windows.

"She's there," said Mundy, under his breath, as he and Rigby moved forward. Smiley following some distance behind.

They were crossing the field now, Rigby leading, and the church drawing ever closer. New sounds disturbed the moaning of the storm; the parched creak of a door, the mutter of a crumbling roof, the incessant sigh of wind upon a dying house. The two men in front of Smiley had stopped, almost in the shadow of the church wall, and were whispering together. Then Mundy walked quietly away, disappearing round the corner of the church. Rigby waited a moment, then approached the narrow entrance in the rear wall, and pushed the door.

It opened slowly, creaking painfully on its hinges. Then he disappeared into the church. Smiley was waiting outside when suddenly above all the sounds of night he heard a scream, so taut and shrill and clear that it seemed to have no source, but to ride everywhere upon the wind, to mount the ravaged sky on wings; and Smiley had a vision of Mad Janie as he had seen her earlier that night, and he heard again in her demented cry the dreadful note of madness. For a moment he waited. The echo died. Then slowly, terrified, he walked through the snow to the open doorway.

Two candles and an oil lamp on the bare altar shed a dim light over the tiny chapel. In front of the altar, on the sanctuary step, sat Jane, looking vaguely towards them. Her vacuous face was daubed with stains of green and blue, her filthy clothes were threaded with sprigs of evergreen and all about her on the floor were the bodies of small animals and birds.

The pews were similarly decorated with dead creatures of all kinds; and on the altar, broken twigs and little heaps of holly leaves. Between the candles stood a crudely-fashioned cross. Stepping forward past Rigby, Smiley walked quickly down the aisle, past the lolling figure of Jane, until he stood before the altar. For a moment he hesitated, then turned and called softly to Rigby.

On the cross, draped over its three ends like a crude diadem, was a string of green beads.

CHAPTER VIII

FLOWERS FOR STELLA

He woke with the echo of her scream in his ears. He had meant to sleep late, but his watch said half-past seven. He put on his bedside lamp, for it was still half-dark, and peered owlishly round the room. There were his trousers, flung over the chair, the legs still sodden from the snow. There were his shoes; he'd have to buy another pair. And there beside him were the notes he had made early that morning before going to sleep, transcriptions from memory of some of Mad Jane's monologue on the journey back to Carne, a journey he would never forget. Mundy had sat with her in the back. She spoke to herself as a child does, asking questions and then in the patient tones of an adult for whom the reply is self-evident, providing the answer.

One obsession seemed to fill her mind: she had seen the devil. She had seen him flying on the wind, his silver wings stretched out behind him. Sometimes the recollection amused her, sometimes inflated her with a sense of her own importance or beauty, and sometimes it terrified her, so that she moaned and wept and begged him to go away. Then Mundy would speak kindly to her, and try to calm her. Smiley wondered whether policemen grew accustomed to the squalor of such things, to clothes that were no more than stinking rags wound round wretched limbs, to puling imbeciles who clutched and screamed and wept. She must have been living on the run for nights on end, finding her food in the fields and dustbins since the night of the murder. . . . What had she done that night? What had she seen? Had she killed Stella Rode? Had she seen the murderer, and fancied *him* to be the devil flying on the wind? Why should she think that? If Janie did not kill Stella Rode, what had she seen that so frightened her that for three long winter nights she prowled in terror like an animal in the forest? Had the devil within taken hold of Janie and given power to her arm as she struck down Stella? Was that the devil who rode upon the wind?

But the beads and the coat and the footprints which were not hers—what of them? He lay there thinking, and achieving nothing. At last it was time to get up: it was the morning of the funeral.

As he was getting out of bed the telephone rang. It was Rigby. His voice sounded strained and urgent. "I want to see you," he said. "Can you call round?"

"Before or after the funeral?"

"Before, if possible. What about now?"

"I'll be there in ten minutes."

Rigby looked, for the first time since Smiley had met him, tired and worried.

"It's Mad Janie," he said. "The Chief thinks we should charge her."

"What for?"

"Murder," Rigby replied crisply, pushing a thin file across the table. "The old fool's made a statement . . . a sort of confession."

They sat in silence while Smiley read the extraordinary statement. It was signed with Mad Janie's mark—J. L.—drawn in a childish hand in letters an inch high. The constable who had taken it down had begun by trying to condense and simplify her account, but by the end of the first page he had obviously despaired. At last Smiley came to the description of the murder:

"So I tells my darling, I tells her: 'You are a naughty creature to go with the devil,' but her did not hearken, see, and I took angry with her, but she paid no call. I can't abide them as go with devils in the night, and I told her. She ought to have had holly, mister, there's the truth. I told her, mister, but she never would hearken, and that's all Janie's saying, but she drove the devil off, Janie did, and there's one will thank me, that's my darling and I took her jewels for the saints I did, to pretty out the church, and a coat for to keep me warm."

Rigby watched him as he slowly replaced the statement on the desk.

"Well, what do you think of it?"

Smiley hesitated; "It's pretty good nonsense as it stands," he replied at last.

"Of course it is," said Rigby, with something like contempt. "She saw something, Lord knows what, when she was out on the prowl; stealing, I shouldn't wonder. She may have robbed the body, or else she picked up the beads where the murderer dropped them. We've traced the coat. Belonged to a Mr. Jardine, a baker in Carne East. Mrs. Jardine gave it to Stella Rode last Wednesday morning for the refugees. Janie must have pinched it from the conservatory. That's what she meant by 'a coat for to keep me warm'. But she no more killed Stella Rode than you or I did. What about the footprints, the glovemarks in the conservatory? Besides, she's not strong enough, Janie isn't, to heave that poor woman forty feet through the snow. This is a man's work, as anyone can see."

"Then what exactly ...?"

"We've called off the search, and I'm to prepare a case against one Jane Lyn of the village of Pylle for the wilful murder of Stella Rode. I wanted to tell you myself before you read it all over the papers. So that you'd know how it was."

"Thanks."

"In the meantime, if there's any help I can give you, we're still willing." He hesitated, seemed about to say something, then to change his mind.

As he made his way down the wide staircase Smiley felt useless and very angry, which was scarcely the right frame of mind in which to attend a funeral.

It was an admirably conducted affair. Neither the flowers nor the congregation exceeded what was fitting to the occasion. She was not buried at the Abbey, out of deference perhaps to her simplicity of taste, but in the parish churchyard not far from Northfields. The Master was detained that day, as he was on most days, and had sent instead his wife, a small, very vague woman who had spent a long time in India. D'Arcy was much in evidence, fluttering here and there before the ceremony like an anxious beadle; and Mr. Cardew had come to guide poor Stella through the unfamiliarities of High Anglican procedure. The Hechts were there, Charles all in black, scrubbed and shining, and Shane in dramatic weeds, and a hat with a very broad brim.

Smiley, who, like the others, had arrived early in anticipation of the unwholesome public interest which the ceremony might arouse, found himself a seat near the entrance of the church. He watched each new arrival with interest, waiting for his first sight of Stanley Rode.

Several tradesmen arrived, pressed into bulging serge and black ties, and formed a small group south of the aisle, away from the staff and their wives. Soon they were joined by other members of the town community, women who had known Mrs. Rode at the Tabernacle; and then by Rigby, who looked straight at Smiley and gave no sign. Then on the stroke of three a tall old man walked slowly through the doorway, looking straight before him, neither knowing nor seeing anyone. Beside him was Stanley Rode.

It was a face which at first sight meant nothing to Smiley, seeming to have neither the imprint of temperament nor the components of character; it was a shallow, ordinary face, inclining to plumpness, and lacking quality. It matched his short, ordinary body and his black, ordinary hair; it was suitably compressed into an expression of sorrow. As Smiley watched him turn into the centre aisle and take his place among the principal mourners, it occurred to him that Rode's very walk and bearing successfully conveyed something entirely alien to Carne. If it is vulgar to wear a pen in the breast pocket of your jacket, to favour Fair Isle pullovers and brown ties, to bob a little and turn your feet out as you walk, then Rode beyond a shadow of doubt was vulgar, for though he did not now commit these sins, his manner implied them all.

They followed the coffin into the churchyard and gathered round the open grave. D'Arcy and Fielding were standing together, seemingly intent upon the service. The tall, elderly figure who had entered the church with Rode was now visibly moved, and Smiley guessed that he was Stella's father, Samuel Glaston. As the service ended, the old man walked quickly away from the crowd, nodding briefly to Rode, and disappeared into the church. He seemed to struggle as he went, like a man walking against a strong wind.

The little group moved slowly away from the graveside, until only Rode remained, an oddly stiff figure, taut and constrained, his eyes wide but somehow sightless, his mouth set in a strict, pedagogic line. Then, as Smiley watched, Rode seemed to wake from a dream; his body suddenly relaxed and he too walked slowly but quite confidently away from the grave towards the small group which by now had reassembled at the churchyard gate. As he did so, Fielding, at the edge of the group, caught sight of him approaching and, to Smiley's astonishment, walked deliberately and quite quickly away with an expression of strong distaste. It was not the calculated act of a man wishing to insult another, for it attracted the notice neither of Rode nor of anyone else standing by. Terence Fielding, for once, appeared to be in the grip of a genuine emotion, and indifferent to the impression he created.

Reluctantly Smiley approached the group. Rode was rather to one side, the D'Arcys were there, and three or four members of the staff. No one was talking much.

"Mr. Rode?" he enquired.

"That's right, yes." He spoke slowly, a trace of an accent carefully avoided.

"I'm representing Miss Brimley of the *Christian Voice*."

"Oh, yes."

"She was most anxious that the journal should be represented. I thought you would like to know that."

"I saw your wreath; very kind, I am sure."

"Your wife was one of our most loyal supporters," Smiley continued. "We regarded her almost as one of the family."

"Yes, she was very keen on the *Voice*." Smiley wondered whether Rode was always as impassive as this, or whether bereavement had made him listless.

"When did you come?" Rode asked suddenly.

"On Friday."

"Making a week-end of it, eh?"

Smiley was so astonished that for a moment he could think of nothing to say. Rode was still looking at him, waiting for an answer.

"I have one or two friends here . . . Mr. Fielding. . . ."

"Oh, Terence." Smiley was convinced that Rode was not on Christian-name terms with Fielding.

"I would like, if I may," Smiley ventured, "to write a small obituary for Miss Brimley. Would you have any objection?"

"Stella would have liked that."

"If you are not too upset, perhaps I could call round to-morrow for one or two details?"

"Certainly."

"Eleven o'clock?"

"It will be a pleasure," Rode replied, almost pertly, and they walked together to the churchyard gate.

CHAPTER IX

THE MOURNERS

IT WAS A CHEAP trick to play on a man who had suddenly lost his wife. Smiley knew that. As he gently unlatched the gate and entered the drive, where two nights ago he had conducted his strange conversation with Jane Lyn, he acknowledged that in calling on Rode under any pretext at such a time he was committing a thoroughly unprincipled act. It was a peculiarity of Smiley's character that throughout the whole of his clandestine work he had never managed to reconcile the means to the end. A stringent critic of his own motives, he had discovered after long observation that he tended to be less a creature of intellect than his tastes and habits might suggest; once in the war he had been described by his superiors as possessing the cunning of Satan and the conscience of a virgin, which seemed to him not wholly unjust.

He pressed the bell and waited.

Stanley Rode opened the door. He was very neatly dressed, very scrubbed.

"Oh hullo," he said, as if they were old friends. "I say, you haven't got a car, have you?"

"I'm afraid I left it in London."

"Never mind." Rode sounded disappointed. "Thought

we might have gone out for a drive, had a chat as we went. I get a bit fed-up, kicking around here on my own. Miss D'Arcy asked me to stay over at their place. Very good people they are, very good indeed; but somehow I didn't wish it, not yet."

"I understand."

"Do you?" They were in the hall now, Smiley was getting out of his overcoat, Rode waiting to receive it. "I don't think many do—the loneliness I mean. Do you know what they've done, the Master and Mr. D'Arcy? They meant it well, I know. They've farmed out all my correcting—my exam. correcting, you understand. What am I supposed to do here, all on my own? I've no teaching, nothing; they've all taken a hand. You'd think they wanted to get rid of me."

Smiley nodded vaguely. They moved towards the drawing-room, Rode leading the way.

"I know they did it for the best, as I said. But after all, I've got to spend the time somehow. Simon Snow got some of my division to correct. Have you met him by any chance? Sixty-one per cent. he gave one boy—sixty-one. The boy's an absolute fool; I told Fielding at the beginning of the Half that he wouldn't possibly get his Remove. Perkins his name is, a nice enough boy; head of Fielding's house. He'd have been lucky to get thirty per cent. . . . sixty-one, Snow gave him. I haven't seen the papers yet, of course, but it's impossible, quite impossible."

They sat down.

"Not that I don't want the boy to get on. He's a nice enough boy, nothing special, but well-mannered. Mrs. Rode and I meant to have him here to tea this Half. We would have done, in fact, if it hadn't been for . . ." There was a moment's silence. Smiley was going to speak when Rode stood up and said:

"I've a kettle on the stove, Mr. . . ."

"Smiley."

"I've a kettle on the stove, Mr. Smiley. May I make you a cup of coffee?" That little stiff voice with the corners carefully defined, like a hired morning suit, thought Smiley.

Rode returned a few minutes later with a tray and measured their coffee in precise quantities, according to their taste.

Smiley found himself continually irritated by Rode's social assumptions, and his constant struggle to conceal his origin. You could tell all the time, from every word and gesture, what he was; from the angle of his elbow as he drank his coffee, from the swift, expert pluck at the knee of his trouser leg as he sat down.

"I wonder," Smiley began, "whether perhaps I might now ..."

"Go ahead, Mr. Smiley."

"We are, of course, largely interested in Mrs. Rode's association with ... our Church."

"Quite."

"You were married at Branxome, I believe."

"Branxome Hill Tabernacle; fine church." D'Arcy wouldn't have liked the way he said that; cocksure lad on a motor-bike. Pencils in the outside pocket.

"When was that?"

"September, fifty-one."

"Did Mrs. Rode engage in charitable work in Branxome? I know she was very active here."

"No, not at Branxome, but a lot here. She had to look after her father at Branxome, you see. It was refugee relief she was keen on here. That didn't get going much until late 1956—the Hungarians began it, and then this last year. ..."

Smiley peered thoughtfully at Rode from behind his spectacles, forgot himself, blinked, and looked away.

"Did she take a large part in the social activities of Carne? Does the staff have its own Women's Institute and so on?" he asked innocently.

"She did a bit, yes. But, being Chapel, she kept mainly with the Chapel people from the town ... you should ask Mr. Cardew about that; he's the Minister."

"But may I say, Mr. Rode, that she took an active part in school affairs as well?"

Rode hesitated.

"Yes, of course," he said.

"Thank you."

There was a moment's silence, then Smiley continued: "Our readers will, of course, remember Mrs. Rode as the winner of our Kitchen Hints competition. Was she a good cook, Mr. Rode?"

"Very good, for plain things, not fancy."

"Is there any little fact that you would specially like us to include, anything she herself would like to be remembered by?"

Rode looked at him with expressionless eyes. Then he shrugged.

"No, not really. I can't think of anything. Oh, you could say her father was a magistrate up North. She was proud of that."

Smiley finished his coffee and stood up.

"You've been very patient with me, Mr. Rode. We're most grateful, I assure you. I'll take care to send you an advance copy of our notice...."

"Thanks. I did it for her, you see. She liked the *Voice*; always did. Grew up with it."

They shook hands.

"By the way, do you know where I can find old Mr. Glaston? Is he staying in Carne or has he returned to Branxome?"

"He was up here yesterday. He's going back to Branxome this afternoon. The police wanted to see him before he left."

"I see."

"He's staying at the Sawley."

"Thank you. I might try and see him before I go."

"When do you leave, then?"

"Quite soon, I expect. Goodbye, then, Mr. Rode. Incidentally—" Smiley began.

"Yes?"

"If ever you're in London and at a loose end, if ever you want a chat ... and a cup of tea, we're always pleased to see you at the *Voice*, you know. Always."

"Thanks. Thanks very much Mr.—"

"Smiley."

"Thanks, that's very decent. No one's said that to me for a long time. I'll take you up on that one day. Very good of you."

"Goodbye." Again they shook hands; Rode's was dry and cool. Smooth.

He returned to the Sawley Arms, sat himself at a desk in the empty residents' lounge and wrote a note to Mr. Glaston:

Dear Mr. Glaston,

I am here on behalf of Miss Brimley of the *Christian Voice*. I have some letters from Stella which I think you would like to see. Forgive me for bothering you at this sad moment; I understand you are leaving Carne this afternoon and wondered if I might see you before you left.

He carefully sealed the envelope and took it to the reception desk. There was no one there, so he rang the bell and waited. At last a porter came, an old turnkey with a grey, bristly face, and after examining the envelope critically for a long time, he agreed, against an excessive fee, to convey it to Mr. Glaston's room. Smiley stayed at the desk, waiting for his answer.

Smiley himself was one of those solitaries who seem to have come into the world fully educated at the age of eighteen. Obscurity was his nature, as well as his profession. The byways of espionage are not populated by the brash and colourful adventurers of fiction. A man who, like Smiley, has lived and worked for years among his country's enemies learns only one prayer : that he may never, never be noticed. Assimilation is his highest aim, he learns to love the crowds who pass him in the street without a glance; he clings to them for his anonymity and his safety. His fear makes him servile—he could embrace the shoppers who jostle him in their impatience, and force him from the pavement. He could adore the officials, the police, the bus conductors, for the terse indifference of their attitudes.

But this fear, this servility, this dependence, had developed in Smiley a perception for the colour of human beings: a swift, feminine sensitivity to their characters and motives. He knew mankind as a huntsman knows his cover, as a fox the wood. For a spy must hunt while he is hunted, and the crowd is his estate. He could collect their gestures and their words, record the interplay of glance and movement, as a huntsman can record the twisted bracken and the broken twig, or as a fox detects the signs of danger.

Thus, while he waited patiently for Glaston's reply and recalled the crowded events of the last forty-eight hours, he was able to order and assess them with detachment. What was the cause of D'Arcy's attitude to Fielding, as if they were unwilling partners to a shabby secret? Staring across the neglected hotel gardens towards Carne Abbey, he was able to glimpse behind the lead roof of the Abbey the familiar battlements of the school: keeping the new world out and the old world secure. In his mind's eye he saw the Great Court now, as the boys came out of Chapel: the black-coated groups in the leisured attitudes of eighteenth-century England. And he remembered the other school beside the police station: Carne High School; a little tawdry place like a porter's lodge in an empty graveyard, as detached from the tones of Carne as its brick and flint from the saffron battlements of School Hall.

Yes, he reflected, Stanley Rode had made a long, long journey from the Grammar School at Branxome. And if he killed his wife, then the motive, Smiley was sure, and even the means, were to be found in that hard road to Carne.

"It was kind of you to come," said Glaston; "kind of Miss Brimley to send you. They're good people at the *Voice*; always were." He said this as if "good" were an absolute quality with which he was familiar.

"You'd better read the letters, Mr. Glaston. The second one will shock you, I'm afraid, but I'm sure you'll agree that it would be wrong of me not to show it to you." They were sitting in the lounge, the mammoth plants like sentinels beside them.

He handed Glaston the two letters, and the old man took them firmly and read them. He held them a good way from him to read, thrusting his strong head back, his eyes half closed, the crisp line of his mouth turned down at the corners. At last he said:

"You were with Miss Brimley in the war, were you?"

"I worked with John Landsbury, yes."

"I see. That's why she came to you?"

"Yes."

"Are you Chapel?"

"No."

He was silent for a while, his hands folded on his lap, the letters before him on the table.

"Stanley was Chapel when they married. Then he went over. Did you know that?"

"Yes."

"Where I come from in the North, we don't do that. Chapel was something we'd stood up for and won. Almost like the vote."

"I know."

His back was as straight as a soldier's. He looked stern rather than sad. Quite suddenly, his eyes turned towards Smiley, and he looked at him long and carefully.

"Are you a schoolmaster?" he asked, and it occurred to Smiley that in his day Samuel Glaston had been a very shrewd man of business.

"No. . . . I'm more or less retired."

"Married?"

"I was."

Again the old man fell silent, and Smiley wished he had left him alone.

"She was a great one for chatter," he said at last.

Smiley said nothing.

"Have you told the police?"

"Yes, but they knew already. That is, they knew that Stella thought her husband was going to murder her. She'd tried to tell Mr. Cardew. . . ."

"The Minister?"

"Yes. He thought she was overwrought and . . . deluded."

"Do you think she wasn't?"

"I don't know. I just don't know. But from what I have heard of your daughter I don't believe she was unbalanced. *Something* roused her suspicions, something frightened her very much. I don't believe we can just disregard that. I don't believe it was a coincidence that she was frightened before she died. And therefore I don't believe that the beggar-woman murdered her."

Samuel Glaston nodded slowly. It seemed to Smiley that the old man was trying to show interest, partly to be polite, and partly because if he did not it would be a confession that he had lost interest in life itself.

Then, after a long silence, he carefully folded up the letters and gave them back. Smiley waited for him to speak, but he said nothing.

After a few moments Smiley got up and walked quietly from the room.

CHAPTER X

LITTLE WOMEN

SHANE HECHT SMILED, and drank some more sherry. "You must be dreadfully important," she said to Smiley, "for D'Arcy to serve decent sherry. What are you, *Almanach de Gotha*?"

"I'm afraid not. D'Arcy and I were both dining at Terence Fielding's on Saturday night and D'Arcy asked me for sherry."

"Terence is *wicked*, isn't he? Charles loathes him. I'm afraid they see Sparta in quite different ways. . . . Poor Terence. It's his last Half, you know."

"I know."

"So sweet of you to come to the funeral yesterday. I hate funerals, don't you? Black is so insanitary. I always remember King George V's funeral. Lord Sawley was at Court in those days, and gave Charles two tickets. So kind. I always think it's *spoilt* us for ordinary funerals in a way. Although I'm never quite *sure* about funerals, are you? I have a suspicion that they are largely a lower-class recreation; cherry brandy and seed cake in the parlour. I think the tendency of people like ourselves is for a *quiet* funeral these days; no flowers, just a short obituary and a memorial service later." Her small eyes were bright with pleasure. She finished her sherry and held out her empty glass to Smiley.

"Would you mind, dear. I hate sherry, but Felix is so mean."

Smiley filled her glass from the decanter on the table.

"Dreadful about the murder, wasn't it? That beggar-woman must be mad. Stella Rode was such a nice person, I always thought . . . and so *unusual*. She did such clever things with the same dress. . . . But she had such curious friends. All for Hans the woodcutter and Pedro the fisherman, if you know what I mean."

"Was she popular at Carne?"

Shane Hecht laughed gently : "No one is popular at Carne . . . but she wasn't easy to like. . . . She would wear black crêpe on Sundays. . . . Forgive me, but do the lower classes always do that? The townspeople liked her, I believe. They adore anyone who betrays Carne. But then she was a Christian Scientist or something."

"Baptist, I understand," said Smiley unthinkingly.

She looked at him for a moment with unfeigned curiosity. "How sweet," she murmured. "Tell me, what *are* you?"

Smiley made some facetious reply about being unemployed, and realised that it was only by a hair's-breadth that he had avoided explaining himself to Shane Hecht like a small boy. Her very ugliness, her size and voice, coupled with the sophisticated malice of her conversation, gave her the dangerous quality of command. Smiley was tempted to compare her with Fielding, but for Fielding other people scarcely existed. For Shane Hecht they did exist : they were there to be found wanting in the minute tests of social behaviour, to be ridiculed, cut off and destroyed.

"I read in the paper that her father was quite well off. From the North. Second generation. Remarkable really how *unspoilt* she was . . . so natural. . . . You wouldn't think she *needed* to go to the launderette or to make friends with beggars. . . . Though, of course, the Midlands are different, aren't they? Only about three good families between Ipswich and Newcastle. Where did you say you came from, dear?"

"London."

"How nice. I went to tea with Stella once. Milk in first and Indian. So different," and she looked at Smiley suddenly and said "I'll tell you something. She almost aroused an admiration in me, I found her so insufferable. She was one of those tiresome little snobs who think that only the humble are virtuous." Then she smiled and added, "I even agreed with Charles about Stella Rode, and that's saying something. If you're a student of mankind, do go and have a look at him, the contrast is riveting." But at the moment they were joined by D'Arcy's sister, a bony, virile woman with untidy grey hair and an arrogant, hunting mouth.

"Dorothy darling," Shane murmured; "such a lovely party. So *kind*. And so *exciting* to meet somebody from London, don't you think? We were talking about poor Mrs. Rode's funeral."

"Stella Rode may have been damn' bad form, Shane, but she did a lot for my refugees."

"Refugees?" asked Smiley innocently.

"Hungarians. Collecting for them. Clothes, furniture, money. One of the few wives who *did* anything." She looked sharply at Shane Hecht, who was smiling benignly past her towards her husband : "Busy little creature, she was; didn't mind rolling her sleeves up, going from door to door. Got her little women on to it at the Baptist chapel and brought in a mass of stuff. You've got to hand it to them, you know. They've got *spirit*. Felix, more sherry!"

There were about twenty in the two rooms, but Smiley, who had arrived a little late, found himself attached to a group of about eight who stood nearest the door: D'Arcy and his sister; Charles and Shane Hecht; a young mathematician called Snow and his wife; a curate from the Abbey and Smiley himself, bewildered and mole-like behind his spectacles. Smiley looked quickly round the room, but could see no sign of Fielding.

"...Yes," Dorothy D'Arcy continued, "she was a good little worker, very ... right to the end. I went over there on Friday with that parson man from the tin tabernacle—Cardew—to see if there was any refugee stuff to tidy up. There wasn't a thing out of place—every bit of clothing she had was all packed up and addressed; we just had to send it off. She was a damn' good little worker, I will say. Did a splendid job at the bazaar, you know."

"Yes, darling," said Shane Hecht sweetly. "I remember it well. It was the day I presented her to Lady Sawley. She wore such a *nice* little hat—the one she wore on Sundays, you know. And *so* respectful. She called her 'my lady'." She turned to Smiley and breathed: "Rather feudal, don't you think, dear? I always like that: so few of us left."

The mathematician and his wife were talking to Charles Hecht in a corner and a few minutes later Smiley managed to extricate himself from the group and join them.

Ann Snow was a pretty girl with a rather square face and a turned-up nose. Her husband was tall and thin, with an agreeable stoop. He held his sherry glass between straight, slender fingers as if it were a chemical retort and when he spoke he seemed to address the sherry rather than his listener; Smiley remembered them from the funeral. Hecht was looking pink and rather cross, sucking at his pipe. They talked in a desultory way, their conversation dwarfed by the exchanges of the adjoining group. Hecht eventually drifted away from

228

them, still frowning and withdrawn, and stood ostentatiously alone near the door.

"Poor Stella," said Ann Snow after a moment's silence. "Sorry," she added. "I can't get her out of my mind yet. It seems mad, just mad. I mean why should she *do* it, that Janie woman?"

"Did you like Stella?" Smiley asked.

"Of course we did. She was sweet. We've been here four Halves now, but she was the only person here who's ever been *kind* to us." Her husband said nothing, just nodded at his sherry. "Simon wasn't a boy at Carne, you see—most of the staff were—so we didn't know anyone and no one was really interested. They all pretended to be terribly pleased with us, of course, but it was Stella who really . . ."

Dorothy D'Arcy was descending on them. "Mrs. Snow," she said crisply, "I've been meaning to talk to you. I want you to take over Stella Rode's job on the refugees." She cast an appraising look in Simon's direction : "The Master's very keen on refugees."

"Oh, my goodness !" Ann Snow replied, aghast. "I couldn't possibly, Miss D'Arcy, I . . ."

"Couldn't? Why couldn't you? You helped Mrs. Rode with her stall at the bazaar, didn't you?"

"So that's where she got her clothes from," breathed Shane Hecht behind them. Ann was fumbling on :

"But . . . well I haven't quite got Stella's nerve, if you under-stand what I mean; and besides, she was a Baptist : all the locals helped her and gave her things, and they all liked her. With me it would be different."

"Lot of damn' nonsense," declared Miss D'Arcy, who spoke to all her juniors as if they were grooms or erring children; and Shane Hecht beside her said : "Baptists are the people who don't like private pews, aren't they? I do so agree—one feels that if one's paid one simply has to go."

The curate who had been talking cricket in a corner, was startled into mild protest : "Oh, come, Mrs. Hecht, the private pew had many advantages . . ." and embarked on a diffuse apologia for ancient custom, to which Shane listened with every sign of the most assiduous interest. When at last he finished she said : "Thank you, William dear, so sweet," turned her back on him and added to Smiley in a stage whisper : "William Trumper—one of Charles' old pupils—such a triumph when he passed his Certificate."

Smiley, anxious to dissociate himself from Shane Hecht's vengeance on the curate, turned to Ann Snow, but she was still at the mercy of Miss D'Arcy's charitable intentions, and Shane was still talking to him :

"The only Smiley I ever heard of married Lady Ann Sercombe at the end of the war. She left him soon afterwards, of course. A very curious match. I understand he was quite unsuitable. She was Lord Sawley's cousin, you know. The Sawleys have been connected with Carne for four hundred years. The present heir is a pupil of Charles; we often dine at the Castle. I never did hear what became of Ann Sercombe . . . she went to Africa, you know . . . or was it India? No it was America. So tragic. One doesn't talk about it at the Castle." For a moment the noise in the room stopped. For a moment, no more, he could discern nothing but the steady gaze of Shane Hecht upon him, and knew she was waiting for an answer. And then she released him as if to say : "I could crush you, you see. But I won't, I'll let you live," and she turned and walked away.

He contrived to take his leave at the same time as Ann and Simon Snow. They had an old car and insisted on running Smiley back to his hotel. On the way there, he said :

"If you have nothing better to do, I would be happy to give you both dinner at my hotel. I imagine the food is dreadful."

The Snows protested and accepted, and a quarter of an hour later they were all three seated in a corner of the enormous dining-room of the Sawley Arms, to the great despondency of three waiters and a dozen generations of Lord Sawley's forbears, puffy men in crumbling pigment.

"We really got to know her our second Half," Ann Snow ran on. "Stella didn't do much mixing with the other wives—

she'd learnt her lesson by then. She didn't go to coffee parties and things, so it was really luck that we did meet. When we first came there wasn't a staff house available for us : we had to spend the first Half in a hotel. We moved in to a little house in Bread Street at the end of our second Half. Moving was chaos—Simon was examining for the scholarships and we were terribly broke, so we had to do everything we possibly could for ourselves. It was a wet Thursday morning when we moved. The rain was simply teeming down; but none of our good pieces would get in through the front door, and in the end Mulligan's just dumped me on the doorstep and let me sort it out." She laughed, and Smiley thought what an agreeable child she was. "They were absolutely foul. They would have just driven off, I think, but they wanted a cheque as soon as they'd done the delivery, and the bill was pounds more than the estimate. I hadn't got the cheque-book, of course, Simon had gone off with it. Mulligan's even threatened to take all the stuff away again. It was monstrous. I think I was nearly in tears." She nearly is now, thought Smiley. "Then out of the blue Stella turned up. I can't think how she even knew we were moving—I'm sure no one else did. She'd brought an overall and an old pair of shoes and she'd come to help. When she saw what was going on she didn't bother with the men at all, just went to a phone and rang Mr. Mulligan himself. I don't know what she said to him, but she made the foreman talk to him afterwards and there was no more trouble after that. She was terribly happy —happy to *help*. She was that sort of person. They took the door right out and managed to get everything in. She was marvellous at helping without managing. The rest of the wives," she added bitterly, "are awfully good at managing, but don't help at all."

Smiley nodded, and discreetly filled their glasses.

"Simon's leaving," Ann said, suddenly confidential. "He's got a grant and we're going back to Oxford. He's going to do a D.Phil. and get a University job."

They drank to his success, and the conversation turned to

other things until Smiley asked: "What's Rode himself like to work with?"

"He's a good schoolmaster," said Simon, slowly, "but tiring as a colleague."

"Oh, he was *quite* different from Stella," said Ann; "Terribly Carne-minded. D'Arcy adopted him and he got the bug. Simon says all the grammar school people go that way —it's the fury of the convert. It's sickening. He even changed his religion when he got to Carne. Stella didn't, though; she wouldn't dream of it."

"The Established Church has much to offer at Carne," Simon observed, and Smiley enjoyed the dry precision of his delivery.

"Stella can't exactly have hit it off with Shane Hecht," Smiley probed gently.

"Of *course* she didn't!" Ann declared angrily. "Shane was horrid to her, always sneering at her because she was honest and simple about the things she liked. Shane hated Stella— I think it was because Stella didn't *want* to be a lady of quality. She was quite happy to be herself. That's what really worried Shane. Shane likes people to compete so that she can make fools of them."

"So does Carne," said Simon, quietly.

"She was awfully good at helping out with the refugees. That was how she got into real trouble." Ann Snow's slim hands gently rocked her brandy glass.

"Trouble?"

"Just before she died. Hasn't anyone told you? About her frightful row with D'Arcy's sister?"

"No."

"Of course, they wouldn't have done. Stella never gossiped."

"Let me tell you," said Simon. "It's a good story. When the Refugee Year business started, Dorothy D'Arcy was fired with charitable enthusiasm. So was the Master. Dorothy's enthusiasms always seem to correspond with his. She started collecting clothes and money and packing them off to London. All very laudable, but there was a perfectly good town appeal going, launched by the Mayor. That wasn't good enough for Dorothy, though: the school must have its own appeal; you can't mix your charity. I think Felix was largely behind it. Anyway, after the thing had been going for a few months the refugee centre in London apparently wrote to Dorothy and asked whether anyone would be prepared to accommodate a refugee couple. Instead of publicising the letter, Dorothy wrote straight back and said she would put them up herself. So far so good. The couple turned up, Dorothy and Felix pointed a proud finger at them and the local press wrote it all up as an example of British humanity.

"About six weeks later, one afternoon, these two turned up on Stella's doorstep. The Rodes and the D'Arcys are neighbours, you see, and anyway Stella had tried to take an interest in Dorothy's refugees. The woman was in floods of tears and the husband was shouting blue murder, but that didn't worry Stella. She had them straight into the drawing-room and gave them a cup of tea. Finally, they managed to explain in basic English that they had run away from the D'Arcys because of the treatment they received. The girl was expected to work from morning till night in the kitchen, and the husband was acting as unpaid kennel-boy for those beastly spaniels that Dorothy breeds. The ones without noses."

"King Charles," Ann prompted.

"It was about as awful as it could be. The girl was pregnant and he was a fully qualified engineer, so neither of them were exactly suited to domestic service. They told Stella that Dorothy was away till the evening—she'd gone to a dog show. Stella advised them to stay with her for the time being, and that evening she went round and told Dorothy what had happened. She had quite a nerve, you see. Although it wasn't nerve really. She just did the simple thing. Dorothy was furious, and demanded that Stella should return 'her refugees' immediately. Stella replied that she was sure that they wouldn't come, and went home. When Stella got home she rang up the refugee people in London and asked their advice. They sent a woman down to see Dorothy and the couple, and the result was that they returned to London the following day.... You can imagine what Shane Hecht would have made of that story."

"Didn't she ever find out?"

"Stella never told anyone except us, and we didn't pass it on. Dorothy just let it be known that the refugees had gone to some job in London, and that was that."

"How long ago did this happen?"

"They left exactly three weeks ago," said Ann to her husband. "Stella told me about it when she came to supper the night you were in Oxford for your interview. That was three weeks ago tonight." She turned to Smiley:

"Poor Simon's been having an awful time. Felix D'Arcy unloaded all Rode's exam. correcting on to him. It's bad enough doing one person's correction—two is frantic."

"Yes," replied Simon reflectively. "It's been a bad week. And rather humiliating in a way. Several of the boys who were up to me for science last Half are now in Rode's forms. I'd regarded one or two of them as practically unteachable, but Rode seems to have brought them on marvellously. I corrected one boy's paper—Perkins—sixty-one per cent for elementary science. Last Half he got fifteen per cent in a much easier paper. He only got his remove because Fielding raised hell. He was in Fielding's house."

"Oh I know—a red-haired boy, a prefect."

"Good Lord," cried Simon. "Don't say you know him?"

"Oh, Fielding introduced us," said Smiley vaguely. "Incidentally—no one else ever mentioned that incident to you about Miss D'Arcy's refugees, did they? Confirmed it, as it were?"

Ann Snow looked at him oddly. "No. Stella told us about it, but of course Dorothy D'Arcy never referred to it at all. She must have *hated* Stella, though."

He saw them to their car, and waited despite their protests while Simon cranked it. At last they drove off, the car bellowing down the silent street. Smiley stood for a moment on the pavement, an odd, lonely figure peering down the empty road.

CHAPTER XI

A COAT TO KEEP HER WARM

A DOG THAT HAD not bitten the postman; a devil that rode upon the wind; a woman who knew that she would die; a little, worried man in an overcoat standing in the snow outside his hotel and the laborious chime of the Abbey clock telling him to go to bed.

Smiley hesitated, then with a shrug crossed the road to the hotel entrance, mounted the step and entered the cheap, yellow light of the residents' hall. He walked slowly up the stairs.

He detested the Sawley Arms. That muted light in the hall was typical : inefficient, antiquated and smug. Like the waiters in the dining-room and the lowered voices in the residents' lounge, like his own hateful bedroom with its blue and gilt urns, and the framed tapestry of a Buckinghamshire garden.

His room was bitterly cold; the maid must have opened the window. He put a shilling in the meter and lit the gas. The fire bubbled grumpily and went out. Muttering, Smiley looked around for some paper to write on, and discovered some, much to his surprise, in the drawer of the writing desk. He changed into his pyjamas and dressing gown and crawled miserably into bed. After sitting there uncomfortably for some minutes he got up, fetched his overcoat and spread it over the eiderdown. A coat for to keep her warm. . . .

How did her statement read? "There's one will thank me, that's my darling and I took her jewels for the saints I did, and a coat for to keep me warm. . . ." The coat had been given to Stella last Wednesday for the refugees. It seemed reasonable to assume from the way the statement read that Janie had taken the coat from the outhouse at the same time as she took the beads from Stella's body. But Dorothy D'Arcy had been round there on Friday morning—of course she had, with Mr. Cardew—she was talking about it at her party that very evening : "There wasn't a thing out of place—every bit of clothing she had was all packed up and addressed—a damn' good little worker, I will say. . . ." Then why hadn't Stella packed the overcoat? If she packed everything else, why not the overcoat too?

Or had Janie stolen the coat earlier in the day, before Stella made her parcel? If that was so, it went some way to weakening the case against her. But it was not so. It was not so because it was utterly improbable that Janie should steal a coat in the afternoon and return to the house the same evening.

"Start at the beginning," Smiley muttered, a little sententiously to the crested paper on his lap. "Janie stole the coat at the same time as she stole the beads—that is, after Stella was dead. Therefore either the coat was not packed with the other clothes, or . . ."

Or what? *Or somebody else, somebody who was not Stella Rode, packed up the clothes after Stella had died and before Dorothy D'Arcy and Mr. Cardew went round to North Fields on Friday morning. And why the devil, thought Smiley, should anyone do that?*

It had been one of Smiley's cardinal principles in research, whether among the incunabula of an obscure poet or the laboriously gathered fragments of intelligence, not to proceed beyond the evidence. A fact, once logically arrived at, should not be extended beyond its natural significance. Accordingly he did not speculate with the remarkable discovery he had made, but turned his mind to the most obscure problem of all : motive for murder.

He began writing :

"Dorothy D'Arcy—resentment after refugee fiasco. As a motive for murder—definitely thin." Yet why did she seem to go out of her way to sing Stella's praises?

"Felix D'Arcy—resented Stella Rode for not observing Carne's standards. As a motive for murder—ludicrous.

"Shane Hecht—hatred.

"Terence Fielding—in a sane world, no conceivable motive."

Yet was it a sane world? Year in year out they must share the same life, say the same things to the same people, sing the same hymns. They had no money, no hope. The world changed, fashion changed; the women saw it second-hand in the glossy papers, took in their dresses and pinned up their hair, and hated their husbands a little more. Shane Hecht— did she kill Stella Rode? Did she conceal in the sterile omniscience of her huge body not only hatred and jealousy, but the courage to kill? Was she frightened for her stupid husband, frightened of Rode's promotion, of his cleverness? Was she really so angry when Stella refused to take part in the rat race of gentility?

Rigby was right—it was impossible to know. You had to be ill, you had to be sick to understand, you had to be there in the sanatorium, not for weeks, but for years, had to be one in the line of white beds, to know the smell of their food and the greed in their eyes. You had to hear it and see it, to be part of it, to know their rules and recognise their transgressions. This world was compressed into a mould of anomalous conventions: blind, pharasaical but real.

Yet some things were written plain enough; the curious bond which tied Felix D'Arcy and Terence Fielding despite their mutual dislike; D'Arcy's reluctance to discuss the night of the murder; Fielding's evident preference for Stella Rode rather than her husband; Shane Hecht's contempt for everyone.

He could not get Shane out of his mind. If Carne were a rational place, and somebody had to die, then Shane Hecht should clearly be the one. She was a depository of other people's secrets, she had an infallible sense for weakness. Had she not found even Smiley out? She had taunted him with his wretched marriage, she had played with him for her own pleasure. Yes, she was an admirable candidate for murder.

But why on earth should Stella die? Why and how? Who tied up the parcel after her death? And why?

He tried to sleep, but could not. Finally, as the Abbey clock chimed three, he put the light on again and sat up. The room was much warmer and at first Smiley wondered if someone had switched on the central heating in the middle of the night, after it had been off all day. Then he became aware of the sound of rain outside; he went to the window and parted the curtains. A steady rain was falling; by to-morrow the snow would be washed away. Two policemen walked slowly down the road; he could hear the squelch of their boots as they trod in the melting snow. Their wet capes glistened in the arc of the street lamp.

And suddenly he seemed to hear Rigby's voice: "Blood everywhere. Whoever killed her must have been covered in it." And then Mad Janie calling to him across the moonlit snow: "Janie seed 'im . . . silver wings like fishes . . . flying on the wind . . . there's not many seen the devil fly. . . ." Of course: the parcel! He remained a long time at the window, watching the rain. Finally, content at last, he climbed back into bed and fell asleep.

He tried to telephone Miss Brimley throughout the morning. Each time she was out and he left no message. Eventually, at about midday, he spoke to her:

"George, I'm terribly sorry—some missionary is in London —I had to go for an interview and I've got a Baptist Conference this afternoon. They've both got to be in this week. Will first thing tomorrow do?"

"Yes," said Smiley. "I'm sure it will." There was no particular hurry. There were one or two ends he wanted to tie up that afternoon, anyway.

CHAPTER XII

UNCOMFORTABLE WORDS

He enjoyed the bus. The conductor was a very surly man with a great deal to say about the bus company, and why it lost money. Gently encouraged by Smiley, he expanded wonderfully so that by the time they arrived at Sturminster he had transformed the Directors of the Dorset and General Traction Company into a herd of Gadarene swine charging into the abyss of voluntary bankruptcy. The conductor directed Smiley to the Sturminster Kennels, and when he alighted in the tiny village he set out confidently towards a group of cottages which stood about a quarter of a mile beyond the church, on the Okeford road.

He had a nasty feeling he wasn't going to like Mr. Harriman. The very fact that D'Arcy had described him as a superior type of person inclined Smiley against him. Smiley was not opposed to social distinctions but he liked to make his own.

A notice stood at the gate: "*Sturminster Kennels, proprietor, C. J. Reid-Harriman, Veterinary Surgeon. Breeder of Alsatian and Labrador Dogs. Boarding.*"

A narrow path led to what seemed to be a back-yard. There was washing everywhere, shirts, underclothes and sheets, most of it khaki. There was a rich smell of dog. There was a rusted hand-pump with a dozen or so dog leads draped over it, and there was a small girl. She watched him sadly as he picked his way through the thick mud towards the door. He pulled on the bell-rope and waited. He tried again, and the child said:

"It doesn't work. It's bust. It's been bust for years."

"Is anyone at home?" Smiley asked.

"I'll see," she replied coolly, and after another long look at him she walked round the side of the house and disappeared from view. Then Smiley heard from inside the house the sound of someone approaching, and a moment later the door opened.

"Good day to you." He had sandy hair and a moustache. He wore a khaki shirt and a khaki tie of a lighter shade; old Service dress trousers and a tweed jacket with leather buttons.

"Mr. Harriman?"

"Major," he replied lightly. "Not that it matters, old boy. What can we do for you?"

"I'm thinking of buying an Alsatian," Smiley replied, "as a guard dog."

"Surely. Come in, won't you. Lady wife's out. Ignore the child: she's from next door. Just hangs around; likes the dogs." He followed Harriman into the living-room and they sat down. There was no fire.

"Where are you from?" Harriman asked.

"I'm staying at Carne at the moment; my father lives over at Dorchester. He's getting on and he's nervous, and he wants me to find him a good dog. There's a gardener to look after it in the daytime, feed it and exercise it and so on. The gardener doesn't live in at night, of course, and it's at night that the old man gets so worried. I've been meaning to get him a dog for some time—this recent business at Carne rather brought it home to me." Harriman ignored the hint.

"Gardener good chap?"

"Yes, very."

"You don't want anything brilliant," said Harriman. "You want a good, steady type. I'd take a bitch if I were you." His hands were dark brown, his wrists too. His handkerchief was tucked into his cuff. Smiley noticed that his wrist-watch faced inwards, conforming with the obscure rites of the military *demi-monde* from which he seemed to come.

"What will it do, a dog like that? Will it attack, or what?"

"Depends how she's trained, old boy; depends how she's trained. She'll warn, though; that's the main thing. Frighten the fellers away. Shove a notice up, 'Fierce Dog', let her sniff at the tradesmen a bit and the word will get around. You won't get a burglar within a mile of the place."

They walked out into the garden again, and Harriman led the way to an enclosure with half a dozen Alsatian puppies yapping furiously at them through the wire.

"They're good little beasts, all of them," he shouted. "Game as hell." He unlocked the door and finally emerged with a plump bitch puppy chewing fiercely at his jacket.

"This little lady might do you," he said. "We can't show her—she's too dark."

Smiley pretended to hesitate, allowed Harriman to persuade him and finally agreed. They went back into the house.

"I'd like to pay a deposit," said Smiley, "and collect her in about ten days. Would that be all right?" He gave Harriman a cheque for five pounds and again they sat down, Harriman foraging in his desk for inoculation certificates and pedigrees. Then Smiley said :

"It's a pity Mrs. Rode didn't have a dog, isn't it? I mean, it might have saved her life."

"Oh, she *had* a dog, but she had it put down just before she was killed," said Harriman. "Damned odd story between ourselves. She was devoted to the beast. Odd little mongrel, bit of everything, but she loved it. Brought it here one day with some tale about it biting the postman, got me to put it down—said it was dangerous. It wasn't anything of the sort. Some friends of mine in Carne made enquiries. No complaints anywhere. Postman liked the brute. Damned silly sort of lie to tell in a small community. Bound to be found out."

"Why on earth did she tell it then?"

Harriman made a gesture which particularly irritated Smiley. He ran his forefinger down the length of his nose, then flicked either side of his absurd moustache very quickly. There was something shamefaced about the whole movement, as if he were assuming the ways of senior officers, and fearful of rebuke.

"She was trouble," he said crisply. "I can spot 'em. I've had a few in the regiment, wives who are trouble. Little

241

simpering types. Butter-wouldn't-melt, holier-than-thou. Arrange the flowers in the church and all that—pious as you please. I'd say she was the hysterical kind, self-dramatising, weeping all over the house for days on end. Anything for a bit of drama."

"Was she popular?" Smiley offered him a cigarette.

"Shouldn't think so. Thanks. She wore black on Sundays, I gather. Typical. We used to call them 'crows' out East, the ones who wore black—Sunday virgins. They were O.D. mostly—other denominations. Not C. of E.—some were Romans, mind. . . . I hope I'm not . . ."

"Not at all."

"You never know, do you? Can't stand 'em myself; no prejudice, but I don't like Romans—that's what my old father used to say."

"Did you know her husband?"

"Not so well, poor devil, not so well."

Harriman, Smiley reflected, seemed to have a great deal more sympathy for the living than the dead. Perhaps soldiers were like that. He wouldn't know.

"He's terribly cut up, I hear. Dreadful shock—fortunes of war, eh?" he added and Smiley nodded. "He's the other type. Humble origin, good officer qualities, credit to the mess. Those are the ones that cut up most, the ones women get at."

They walked along the path to the gate. Smiley said good-bye, and promised to return in a week or so to collect the puppy. As he walked away Harriman called to him:

"Oh—incidentally . . ."

Smiley stopped and turned round.

"I'll pay that cheque in, shall I, and credit you with the amount?"

"Of course," said Smiley. "That will do very well," and he made his way to the bus stop pondering on the strange byways of the military mind.

The same bus took him back to Carne, the same conductor railed against his employers, the same driver drove the entire distance in second gear. He got out at the station and made his way to the red-brick Tabernacle. Gently opening the Gothic door, made of thickly-varnished ochre pine, he stepped inside. An elderly woman in an apron was polishing the heavy brass chandelier which hung over the centre aisle. He waited a moment, then tiptoed up to her and asked for the Minister. She pointed towards the vestry door. Obeying her mimed directions, he crossed to it, knocked and waited. A tall man in a clerical collar opened the door.

"I'm from the *Christian Voice*," said Smiley quietly. "Can I have a word with you?"

Mr. Cardew led him through the side entrance and into a small vegetable garden, carefully tilled, with bright yellow paths running between the empty beds. The sun shone through the crisp air. It was a cold, beautiful day. They crossed the garden and entered a paddock. The ground was hard despite last night's rain, and the grass short. They strolled side by side, talking as they went.

"This is Lammas Land, belonging to the School. We hold our fêtes here in the summer. It's very practical."

Cardew seemed a little out of character. Smiley, who had a rather childish distrust of clergymen, had expected a Wesleyan hammer, a wordy, forbidding man with a taste for imagery.

"Miss Brimley, our editor, sent me," Smiley began. "Mrs. Rode subscribed to our journal; her family has taken it since it began. She was almost a part of the family. We wanted to write an obituary about her work for the Church."

"I see."

"I managed to have a word with her husband; we wanted to be sure to strike the right note."

"What did he say?"

"He said I should speak to you about her work—her refugee work particularly."

They walked on in silence for a while, then Cardew said, "She came from up North, near Derby. Her father used to be a man of substance in the North—though money never altered him."

"I know."

"I've known the family for years, off and on. I saw her old father before the funeral."

"What may I say about her work for the Church, her influence on the Chapel community here? May I say she was universally loved?"

"I'm afraid," said Cardew, after a slight pause, "that I don't hold much with that kind of writing, Mr. Smiley. People are never universally loved, even when they're dead." His North Country accent was strong.

"Then what may I say?" Smiley persisted.

"I don't know," Cardew replied evenly. "And when I don't know, I usually keep quiet. But since you're good enough to ask me, I've never met an angel, and Stella Rode was no exception."

"But was she not a leading figure in refugee work?"

"Yes. Yes, she was."

"And did she not encourage others to make similar efforts?"

"Of course. She was a good worker."

They walked on together in silence. The path across the field led downwards, then turned and followed a stream which was almost hidden by the tangled gorse and hawthorn on either side. Beyond the stream was a row of stark elm trees, and behind them the familiar outline of Carne.

"Is that all you wanted to ask me?" said Cardew suddenly.

"No," replied Smiley. "Our editor was very worried by a letter she received from Mrs. Rode just before her death. It was a kind of . . . accusation. We put the matter before the police. Miss Brimley reproaches herself in some way for not having been able to help her. It's illogical, perhaps, but there it is. I would like to be able to assure her that there was no connection between Stella Rode's death and this letter. That is another reason for my visit. . . ."

"Whom did the letter accuse?"

"Her husband."

"I should tell your Miss Brimley," said Cardew slowly, and with some emphasis, "that she has nothing whatever for which to reproach herself."

CHAPTER XIII

THE JOURNEY HOME

IT WAS MONDAY evening. At about the time that Smiley returned to his hotel after his interview with Mr Cardew, Tim Perkins, the Head of Fielding's house, was taking his leave of Mrs. Harlowe, who taught him the 'cello. She was a kindly woman, if neurotic, and it distressed her to see him so worried. He was quite the best pupil that Carne had sent her, and she liked him.

"You played foully today, Tim," she said as she wished him goodbye at the door, "quite foully. You needn't tell me—you've only got one more Half and you still haven't got three passes in A Level and you've got to get your remove, and you're in a tizz. We won't practise next Monday if you don't want—just come and have buns and we'll play some records."

"Yes, Mrs. Harlowe." He strapped his music-case on to the carrier of his bicycle.

"Lights working, Tim?"

"Yes, Mrs. Harlowe."

"Well, don't try and beat the record tonight, Tim. You've plenty of time till Boys' Tea. Remember the lane's still quite slippery from the snow."

Perkins said nothing. He pushed the bicycle on to the gravel path and started towards the gate.

"Haven't you forgotten something, Tim?"

"Sorry, Mrs. Harlowe."

He turned back and shook hands with her in the doorway. She always insisted on that.

"Look, Tim, what *is* the matter? Have you done something silly? You can tell me, can't you? I'm not Staff, you know."

Perkins hesitated, then said:

"It's just exams., Mrs. Harlowe."

"Are your parents all right? No trouble at home?"

"No, Mrs. Harlowe; they're fine." Again he hesitated, then: "Good night, Mrs. Harlowe."

"Good night."

She watched him close the gate behind him and cycle off down the narrow lane. He would be in Carne in quarter of an hour; it was downhill practically all the way.

Usually he loved the ride home. It was the best moment of the week. But tonight he hardly noticed it. He rode fast, as he always did; the hedge raced against the dark sky and the rabbits scuttled from the beam of his lamp, but tonight he hardly noticed them.

He would have to tell somebody. He should have told Mrs. Harlowe; he wished he had. She'd know what to do. Mr. Snow would have been all right, but he wasn't up to him for science any longer, he was up to Rode. That was half the trouble. That and Fielding.

He could tell True—yes, that's who he'd tell, he'd tell True. He'd go to Miss Truebody tonight after evening surgery and he'd tell her the truth. His father would never get over it, of course, because it meant failure and perhaps disgrace. It meant not going to Sandhurst at the end of next Half, it meant more money they couldn't afford. . . .

He was coming to the steepest part of the hill. The hedge stopped on one side and instead there was a marvellous view of Sawley Castle against the night sky, like a backcloth for *Macbeth*. He loved acting—he wished the Master let them act at Carne.

He leant forward over the handlebars and allowed himself to gather speed to go through the shallow ford at the

246

bottom of the hill. The cold air bit into his face, and for a moment he almost forgot. . . . Suddenly he braked; felt the bike skid wildly beneath him.

Something was wrong; there was a light ahead, a flashing light, and a familiar voice calling to him urgently across the darkness.

CHAPTER XIV

THE QUALITY OF MERCY

THE PUBLIC SCHOOLS Committee for Refugee Relief (Patroness: Sarah, Countess of Sawley) has an office in Belgrave Square. It is not at all clear whether this luxurious situation is designed to entice the wealthy or encourage the dispossessed—or, as some irreverent voices in Society whispered, to provide the Countess of Sawley with an inexpensive *pied-à-terre* in the West End of London. The business of assisting refugees has been suitably relegated to the south of the river, to one of those untended squares in Kennington which are part of London's architectural schizophrenia. York Gardens, as the square is called, will one day be discovered by the world, and its charm lost, but go there now, and you may see real children playing hopscotch in the road, and their mothers, shod in bedroom slippers, abusing them from doorways.

Miss Brimley, despatched on her way by Smiley's telephone call the previous morning, had the rare gift of speaking to children as if they were human beings, and thus discovered without difficulty the dilapidated, unnamed house which served the Committee as a collecting centre. With the assistance of seven small boys, she pulled on the bell and waited patiently. At last she heard the clatter of feet descending an uncarpeted staircase, and the door was opened by a very beautiful girl. They looked at one another with approval for a moment.

"I'm sorry to be a nuisance," Miss Brimley began, "but a friend of mine in the country has asked me to make some enquiries about a parcel of clothes that was sent up a day or two ago. She's made rather a stupid mistake."

"Oh goodness, how awful," said the girl pleasantly. "Would you like to come in? Everything's frightfully chaotic, I'm afraid, and there's nothing to sit on, but we can give you powdered coffee in a mug."

Miss Brimley followed her in, closing the door firmly on the seven children, who were edging gently forward in her wake. She was in the hall, and everywhere she looked there were parcels of every kind, some wrapped in jute with smart labels, some in brown paper, torn and clumsy, some in crates and laundry baskets, old suitcases and even an antiquated cabin trunk with a faded yellow label on it which read : "Not wanted on voyage."

The girl led the way upstairs to what was evidently the office, a large room containing a deal table littered with correspondence, and a kitchen chair. An oil stove sputtered in one corner, and an electric kettle was steaming in a melancholy way beside it.

"I'm sorry," said the girl as they entered the room, "but there just isn't anywhere to talk downstairs. I mean, one can't talk on one leg like Incas. Or isn't it Incas? Perhaps it's Afghans. However did you find us?"

"I went to your West End office first," Miss Brimley replied, "and they told me I should come and see you. I think they were rather cross. After that I relied on children. They always know the way. You are Miss Dawney, aren't you?"

"Lord, no. I'm the sort of daily help. Jill Dawney's gone to see the Customs people at Rotherhide—she'll be back at tea time if you want to see her."

"Gracious, my dear, I'm sure I shan't keep you two minutes. A friend of mine who lives in Carne—("Goodness! How grand," said the girl) she's a sort of cousin really, but it's simpler to call her a friend, isn't it?—gave an old grey dress to the refugee people last Thursday and now she's convinced she left her brooch pinned to the bodice. I'm sure she hasn't done anything of the sort, mind you—she's a scatter-brain creature—but she rang me up yesterday morning in a dreadful state and made me promise to come round at once and ask. I couldn't come yesterday, unfortunately—tied to my little paper from dawn till dusk. But I gather you're a bit behind, so it won't be too late?"

"Gosh, no! We're miles behind. That's all the stuff downstairs, waiting to be unpacked and sorted. It comes from the voluntary reps. at each school—sometimes boys and sometimes Staff—and they put all the clothes together and send them up in big parcels, either by train or ordinary mail, usually by train. We sort them here before sending abroad."

"That's what I gathered from Jane. As soon as she realised she'd made this mistake she got hold of the woman doing the collecting and sending, but of course it was too late. The parcel had gone."

"How frantic. . . . Do you know when the parcel was sent off?"

"Yes. On Friday morning."

"From Carne? Train or post?"

Miss Brimley had been dreading this question, but she made a guess:

"Post, I believe."

Darting past Miss Brimley, the girl foraged among the pile of papers on her desk and finally produced a stiff-backed exercise book with a label on it marked "Ledger". Opening it at random, she whisked quickly back and forth through the pages, licking the tip of one finger now and then in a harassed sort of way.

"Wouldn't have arrived till yesterday at the earliest," she said. "We certainly won't have opened it yet. Honestly, I don't know how we shall *ever* cope, and with Easter coming up we shall just get worse and worse. On top of that, half our stuff is rotting in the Customs sheds—hullo, here we are!" She pushed the ledger over to Miss Brimley, her slim finger pointing to a pencilled entry in the central column : "Carne, parcel post, 27 lb."

"I wonder," said Miss Brimley, "whether you would mind awfully if we had a quick look inside?"

They went downstairs to the hall.

"It's not quite as hideous as it looks," the girl called over her shoulder. "All the Monday lot will be nearest the door."

"How do you know where they come from if you can't read the postmark?" asked Miss Brimley as the girl began to forage among the parcels.

"We issue the volunteer reps. with our printed labels. The labels have an originator's number on. In other cases we just ask them to write the name of the school in capitals on the outside. You see, we simply can't allow covering letters; it would be *too* desperate. When we get a parcel all we have to do is send off a printed card acknowledging with thanks receipt of a parcel of such and such a date weighing so and so much. People who aren't reps. won't send parcels to this address, you see—they'll send to the advertised address in Belgrave Square."

"Does the system work?"

"No," replied the girl, "it doesn't. The reps. either forget to use our labels or they run out and can't be bothered to tell us. Ten days later they ring up in a rage because they haven't had an acknowledgement. Reps. change, too, without letting us know, and the packing and labelling instructions don't get passed on. Sometimes the boys will suddenly decide to do it themselves, and no one tells them the way to go about it. Lady Sarah gets as mad as a snake if parcels turn up at Head Office—they all have to be carted over here for repacking and inventories."

"I see." Miss Brimley watched anxiously as the girl foraged among the parcels, still talking.

"Did you say your friend actually *taught* at Carne? She must be terribly grand. I wonder what the Prince is like : he looks rather soft in his photographs. My cousin went to Carne—he's an utter wet. Do you know what he told me? During Ascot week they all . . . Hello! Here we are!" The girl stood up, a large square parcel in her arms, and carried it to a table which stood in the shadow of the staircase. Miss Brimley, standing beside her as she began carefully to untie the stout twine, looked curiously at the printed label. In its top left-hand corner was stamped the symbol which the Committee had evidently allocated to Carne: C4. After the four the letter B had been written in with ballpoint pen.

"What does the B mean?" asked Miss Brimley.

"Oh, that's a local arrangement at Carne. Miss D'Arcy's the rep. there, but they've done so well recently that she co-opted a friend to help with despatch. When we acknowledge we always mention whether it was A or B. B must be terribly keen, whoever she is."

Miss Brimley forebore from enquiring what proportion of the parcels from Carne had originated from Miss D'Arcy, and what proportion from her anonymous assistant.

The girl removed the string and turned the parcel upside down in order to liberate the overlap of wrapping paper. As she did so Miss Brimley caught sight of a faint brown smudge, no more, about the size of a shilling, near the join. It was consistent with her essential rationalism that she should search for any explanation other than that which so loudly presented itself. The girl continued the work of unwrapping, saying suddenly: "I say, Carne was where they had that dreadful murder, wasn't it—that master's wife who got killed by the gypsy? It really *is* awful, isn't it, how much of that kind of thing goes on? Hm! Thought as much," she remarked, suddenly interrupting herself. She had removed the outer paper, and was about to unwrap the bundle inside when her attention was evidently arrested by the appearance of the inner parcel.

"What?" Miss Brimley said quickly.

The girl laughed. "Oh, only the packing," she said; "The C4Bs are usually so neat—quite the best we get. This is quite different. Not the same person at all. Must be a stand-in. I thought so from the outside."

"How can you be so sure?"

"Oh, it's like handwriting. We can tell." She laughed

again, and without more ado removed the last wrapping. "Grey dress, you said, didn't you? Let's see." With both hands she began picking clothes from the top of the pile and laying them to either side. She was nearly half way through when she exclaimed "Well, *honestly*! They must be having a brain-storm," and drew from the bundle of partworn clothes a transparent plastic mackintosh, a very old pair of leather gloves, and a pair of rubber overshoes.

Miss Brimley was holding the edge of the table very tightly. The palms of her hands were throbbing.

"Here's a cape. Damp, too," the girl added in disgust, and tossed the offending articles on to the floor beside the table. Miss Brimley could only think of Smiley's letter: "Whoever killed her must have been covered in blood." Yes, and whoever killed her wore a plastic cape and a hood, rubber overshoes and those old leather gloves with the terra-cotta stains. Whoever killed Stella Rode had not chanced upon her in the night, but had plotted long ahead, had waited. "Yes," thought Miss Brimley, "had waited for the long nights."

The girl was talking to her again: "I'm afraid it really isn't here."

"No, my dear," Miss Brimley replied, "I see that. Thank you. You've been very sweet." Her voice faltered for a moment, then she managed to say: "I think, my dear, you should leave the parcel exactly as it is now, the wrapping and everything in it. Something very dreadful has happened, and the police will want to . . . know about it and see the parcel. . . . You must trust me, my dear—things aren't quite what they seem. . . ." And somehow she escaped to the comforting freedom of York Gardens and the large-eyed wonder of its waiting children.

She went to a telephone box. She got through to the Sawley Arms and asked a very bored receptionist for Mr. Smiley. Total silence descended on the line until the Trunks operator asked her to put in another three and sixpence. Miss Brimley replied sharply that all she had so far had for her money was a three-minute vacuum; this was followed by the unmistakable sound of the operator sucking her teeth, and then, quite suddenly, by George Smiley's voice:

"George, it's Brim. A plastic mackintosh a cape, rubber overshoes and some leather gloves that look as though they're stained with blood. Smudges on some of the wrapping paper too by the look of it."

A pause.

"Handwriting on the outside of the parcel?"

"None. The Charity organisers issue printed labels."

"Where is the stuff now? Have you got it?"

"No. I've told the girl to leave everything exactly as it is. It'll be all right for an hour or two.... George, are you there?"

"Yes."

"Who did it? Was it the husband?"

"I don't know. I just don't know."

"Do you want me to do anything—about the clothes, I mean? Phone Sparrow or anything?"

"No. I'll see Rigby at once. Goodbye, Brim. Thanks for ringing."

She put back the receiver. He sounded strange, she thought. He seemed to lose touch sometimes. As if he'd switched off.

She walked north-west towards the Embankment. It was long after ten o'clock—the first time she'd been late for Heaven knows how long. She had better take a taxi. Being a frugal woman, however, she took a bus.

Ailsa Brimley did not believe in emergencies, for she enjoyed a discipline of mind uncommon in men and even rarer in women. The greater the emergency, the greater her calm. John Landsbury had remarked upon it: "You have sales resistance to the dramatic, Brim; the rare gift of contempt for what is urgent. I know of a dozen people who would pay you five thousand a year for telling them every day that what is important is seldom urgent. Urgent equals ephemeral, and ephemeral equals unimportant."

She got out of the bus, carefully putting the ticket in the rubbish compartment. As she stood in the warm sunlight of the street she caught sight of the hoardings advertising the first edition of the evening papers. If it hadn't been for the sun, she might never have looked; but the sun dazzled her and made her glance downwards. And so she did see; she read it in the plump black of the wet newsprint, in the prepacked hysteria of Fleet Street: "All-night search for missing Carne boy."

CHAPTER XV

THE ROAD TO FIELDING

Smiley put down the receiver and walked quickly past the reception desk towards the front door. He must see Rigby at once. Just as he was leaving the hotel he heard his name called. Turning, he saw his old enemy, the night porter, braving the light of day, beckoning to him like Charon with his grey hand.

"They've been on to you from the police station," he observed with undisguised pleasure; "Mr. Rigby wants you, the Inspector. You're to go there at once. At once, see?"

"I'm on my way there now," Smiley replied irritably, and as he pushed his way through the swing doors he heard the old man repeat; "At once, mind; they're waiting for you."

Making his way through the Carne streets, he reflected for the hundredth time on the obscurity of motive in human action : there is no true thing on earth. There is no constant, no dependable point, not even in the purest logic or the most obscure mysticism; least of all in the motives of men when they are moved to act violently.

Had the murderer, now so near discovery, found contentment in the meticulous administration of his plans? For now it was clear beyond a doubt; this was a murder devised to the last detail, even to the weapon inexplicably far from the place of its use; a murder with clues cast to mislead, a murder planned to look unplanned, a murder for a string of beads. Now the mystery of the footprints was solved : having put the overshoes into the parcel, the murderer had walked down the path to the gate, and his own prints had been obscured by the subsequent traffic of feet.

Rigby looked tired.

"You've heard the news, sir, I suppose?"

"What news?"

"About the boy, the boy in Fielding's house, missing all night?"

"No." Smiley felt suddenly sick. "No, I've heard nothing."

"Good Lord, I thought you knew! Half-past eight last night Fielding rang us here. Perkins, his head boy, hadn't come back from a music lesson with Mrs. Harlowe, who lives over to Longemede. We put out an alert and started looking for him. They sent a patrol car along the road he should have come back on—he was cycling, you see. The first time they didn't see anything, but on the way back the driver stopped the car at the bottom of Longemede Hill, just where the water-splash is. It occurred to him the lad might have taken a long run at the water-splash from the top of the hill, and come to grief in the dip. They found him half in the ditch, his bike beside him. Dead."

"Oh, my dear God."

"We didn't let on to the press at first. The boy's parents are in Singapore. The father's an Army officer. Fielding sent them a telegram. We've got on to the War Office, too."

They were silent for a moment, then Smiley asked "How did it happen?"

"We've closed the road and we've been trying to reconstruct the accident. I've got a detective over there now, just having a look. Trouble is, we couldn't do much till the morning.

Besides, the men trampled everywhere; you can't blame them. It looks as though he must have fallen near the bottom of the hill and hit his head on a stone : his right temple."

"How did Fielding take it?"

"He was very shaken. Very shaken indeed. I wouldn't have believed it, to be quite honest. He just seemed to . . . give up. There was a lot that had to be done—telegraph the parents, get in touch with the boy's uncle at Windsor, and so on. But he just left all that to Miss Truebody, his house-keeper. If it hadn't been for her, I don't know how he'd have managed. I was with him for about half an hour, then he just broke down, completely, and asked to be left alone."

"How do you mean, broke down?" Smiley asked quickly.

"He cried. Wept like a child," said Rigby evenly. "I'd never have thought it."

Smiley offered Rigby a cigarette and took one himself.

"I suppose," he ventured, "it was an accident?"

"I suppose so," Rigby replied woodenly.

"Perhaps," said Smiley, "before we go any further, I'd better give you my news. I was on my way to see you when you rang. I've just heard from Miss Brimley." And in his precise, rather formal way, he related all that Ailsa Brimley had told him, and how he had become curious about the contents of the parcel.

Smiley waited while Rigby telephoned to London. Almost mechanically, Rigby described what he wanted done : the parcel and its contents were to be collected and arrangements made to subject them immediately to forensic examination; the surfaces should be tested for finger-prints. He would be coming up to London himself with some samples of a boy's handwriting and an examination paper; he would want the opinion of a handwriting expert. No, he would be coming by train on the 4.25 from Carne, arriving at Waterloo at 8.05. Could a car be sent to the station to collect him? There was silence, then Rigby said testily, "All right, I'll take a ruddy taxi," and rang off rather abruptly. He looked at Smiley angrily for a moment, then grinned, plucked at his ear and said :

"Sorry, sir; getting a bit edgy." He indicated the far wall with his head and added, "Fighting on too many fronts, I suppose. I shall have to tell the Chief about that parcel, but he's out shooting at the moment—only pigeon, with a couple of friends, he won't be long—but I haven't mentioned your presence here in Carne, as a matter of fact, and if you don't mind I'll . . ."

"Of course," Smiley cut in quickly. "It's much simpler if you keep me out of it."

"I shall tell him it was just a routine enquiry. We shall have to mention Miss Brimley later . . . but there's no point in making things worse, is there?"

"No."

"I shall have to let Janie go, I suppose. . . . She was right, wasn't she? Silver wings in the moonlight."

"I wouldn't—no, I wouldn't let her go, Rigby," said Smiley with unaccustomed vehemence. "Keep her with you as long as you can possibly manage. No more accidents, for heaven's sake. We've had enough."

"Then you don't believe Perkins' death was an accident?"

"Good Lord, no," cried Smiley suddenly, "and nor do you, do you?"

"I've put a detective on to it," Rigby replied coolly. "I can't take the case myself. I shall be needed on the Rode murder. The Chief will have to call the Yard in now; there'll be hell to pay I can tell you. He thought it was all over bar the shouting."

"And in the meantime?"

"In the meantime, sir, I'm going to do my damnedest to find out who killed Stella Rode."

"If," said Smiley slowly, "if you find fingerprints on that mackintosh, which I doubt, will you have anything . . . local . . . to compare them with?"

"We've got Rode's, of course, and Janie's."

"But not Fielding's?"

Rigby hesitated.

"As a matter of fact, we have," he said at last. "From long ago. But nothing to do with this kind of thing."

"It was during the war," said Smiley. "His brother told me. Up in the North. It was hushed up, wasn't it?"

Rigby nodded. "So far as I heard, only the D'Arcys knew; and the Master, of course. It happened in the holidays—some Air Force boy. The Chief was very helpful. . . ."

Smiley shook hands with Rigby and made his way down the familiar pine staircase. He noticed again the vaguely institutional smell of floor polish and carbolic soap, like the smell at Fielding's house.

He walked slowly back towards the Sawley Arms. At the point where he should have turned left to his hotel, however, he hesitated, then seemed to change his mind. Slowly, almost reluctantly, he crossed the road to the Abbey Close, and walked along the southern edge towards Fielding's house. He looked worried, almost frightened.

CHAPTER XVI

A TASTE FOR MUSIC

MISS TRUEBODY OPENED the door. The rims of her eyes were pink, as though she had been weeping.

"I wonder if I might see Mr. Fielding? To say goodbye."

She hesitated : "Mr. Fielding's very upset. I doubt whether he'll want to see anyone." He followed her into the hall and watched her go to the study door. She knocked, inclined her head, then gently turned the handle and let herself in. It was a long time before she returned. "He'll be out shortly," she said, without looking at him. "Will you take off your coat?" She waited while he struggled out of his overcoat, then took it from him and hung it beside the Van Gogh chair. They stood together in silence, both looking towards the study door.

Then, quite suddenly, Fielding was standing in the half-open doorway, unshaven and in his shirt-sleeves. "For Christ's sake," he said thickly. "What do you want?"

"I just wanted to say goodbye, Fielding, and to offer you my condolences."

Fielding looked at him hard for a moment; he was leaning heavily against the door; "Well, goodbye. Thank you for calling." He waved one hand vaguely in the air. "You needn't have bothered really, need you?" he added rudely. "You could have sent me a card, couldn't you?"

"I could have done, yes; it just seemed so very tragic, when he was so near success."

"What do you mean? What the devil do you mean?"

"I mean in his work . . . the improvement. Simon Snow was telling me all about it. Amazing really, the way Rode brought him on."

A long silence, then Fielding spoke: "Goodbye, Smiley. Thanks for coming." He was turning back into the study as Smiley called:

"Not at all . . . not at all. I suppose poor Rode must have been bucked with those exam. results, too. I mean it was more or less a matter of life and death for Perkins, passing that exam., wasn't it? He wouldn't have got his remove next Half if he'd failed in science. They might have superannuated him, I suppose, even though he was head of the house; then he couldn't have sat for the Army. Poor Perkins, he had a lot to thank Rode for, didn't he? And you, too, Fielding, I'm sure. You must have helped him wonderfully . . . both of you did, you and Rode; Rode and Fielding. His parents ought to know that. They're rather hard up, I gather; the father's in the Army, isn't he, in Singapore? It must have been a great effort keeping the boy at Carne. It will comfort them to know how much was done for him, won't it, Fielding?"

Smiley was very pale. "You've heard the latest. I suppose," he continued. "About that wretched gypsy woman who killed Stella Rode? They've decided she's fit to plead. I suppose they'll hang her. That'll be the third death, won't it? You know, I'll tell you an odd thing—just between ourselves, Fielding. I don't believe she did it. Do you? I don't believe she did it at all."

He was not looking at Fielding. He had clasped his little hands tightly behind his back, and he stood with his shoulders bowed and his head inclined to one side, as though listening for an answer.

Fielding seemed to feel Smiley's words like a physical pain. Slowly he shook his head:

"No," he said; "No. Carne killed them; it was Carne. It could only happen here. It's the game we play: the exclusion game. Divide and rule!" He looked Smiley full in the face, and shouted: "Now for God's sake go! You've got what you want, haven't you? You can pin me on your little board, can't you?" And then, to Smiley's distress, he began sobbing in great uncontrollable gulps, holding his hand across his brow. He appeared suddenly grotesque, stemming the childish tears with his chalky hand, his cumbersome feet turned inwards. Gently, Smiley coaxed him back into the study, gently sat him before the dead fire. Then he began talking to him softly and with compassion.

"If what I think is true, there isn't much time," he began. "I want you to tell me about Tim Perkins—about the exam."

Fielding, his face buried in his hands, nodded.

"He would have failed, wouldn't he? He would have failed and not got his remove; he'd have had to leave." Fielding was silent. "After the exam. that day, Rode gave him the writing case to bring here, the case that contained the papers; Rode was doing chapel duty that week and wouldn't be going home before dinner, but he wanted to correct the papers that night, after his dinner with you."

Fielding took his hands from his face and leant back in his chair, his great head tilted back, his eyes closed. Smiley continued:

"Perkins came home, and that evening he brought the case to you, as Rode told him to, for safe keeping. Perkins, after all, was head of your house, a responsible boy. . . . He gave you the case and you asked him how he'd done in the exam."

"He wept," said Fielding suddenly. "He wept as only a child can."

"And after breaking down he told you he had cheated? That he had looked up the answers and copied them on to his paper. Is that right? And after the murder of Stella Rode he remembered what else he had seen in the suitcase?"

Fielding was standing up. "No! Don't you see? Tim wouldn't have cheated to save his life! That's the whole point, the whole bloody irony of it," he shouted. "He never cheated at all. *I* cheated for him."

"But you couldn't! You couldn't copy his handwriting!"

"He wrote with a ball-pen. It was only formulae and diagrams. When he'd gone, and left me alone with the case, I looked at his paper. It was hopeless—he'd only done two out of seven questions. So I cheated for him. I just cribbed them from the science book, and wrote them with blue ball-point, the kind we all use. Abbots' sell them. I copied his hand as best I could. It only needed about three lines of figures. The rest was diagrams."

"Then it was you who opened the case? You who saw ..."

"Yes. It was me, I tell you, not Tim! He couldn't cheat to save his life! But Tim paid for it, don't you see? When the marks were published Tim must have known something was wrong with them. After all, he'd only attempted two questions out of seven and yet he'd got sixty-one per cent. But he knew *nothing* else, *nothing*!"

For a long time neither spoke. Fielding was standing over Smiley, exultant with the relief of sharing his secret, and Smiley was looking vaguely past him, his face drawn in deep concentration.

"And of course," he said finally, "when Stella was murdered, you knew who had done it."

"Yes," replied Fielding. "I knew that Rode had killed her."

Fielding poured himself a brandy and gave one to Smiley. He seemed to have recovered his self-control. He sat down and looked at Smiley thoughtfully for a time.

"I've got no money," he said at last. "None. Nobody knows that except the Master. Oh, they know I'm more or less broke, but they don't know *how* broke. Long ago I made an ass of myself. I got into trouble. It was in the war, when staff was impossible. I had a boys' house and was practically running the school—D'Arcy and I. We were running it together, and the Master running us. Then I made an ass of myself. It was during the holidays. I was up North at the time, giving a course of talks at an R.A.F. educational place. And I stepped out of line. Badly. They pulled me in. And along came D'Arcy wearing his country overcoat and bringing the Master's terms : Come back to Carne, my dear fellow, and we'll say no more about it; go on running your house, my dear fellow, and giving of your wisdom. There's been no publicity. We know it will never happen again, my dear fellow, and we're dreadfully hard up for staff. Come back as a temporary. So I did, and I've been one ever since, going cap in hand to darling D'Arcy every December asking for my contract to be renewed. And, of course—no pension. I shall have to teach at a crammer's. There's a place in Somerset where they'll take me. I'm seeing their Headmaster in London on Thursday. It's a sort of breaker's yard for old dons. The Master had to know, because he gave me a reference."

"That was why you couldn't tell anyone? Because of Perkins?"

"In a way, yes. I mean they'd want to know all sorts of things. I did it for Tim, you see. The Governors wouldn't have liked that much . . . inordinate affection. . . . It looks bad, doesn't it? But it wasn't that kind of affection, Smiley, not any more. You never heard him play the 'cello. He wasn't marvellous, but just sometimes he would play so beautifully, with a kind of studious simplicity, that was indescribably good. He was an awkward boy, and when he played well it was such a surprise. You should have heard him play."

"You didn't want to drag him into it. If you told the police what you had seen it would ruin Tim too?"

Fielding nodded. "In the whole of Carne, he was the one thing I loved."

"Loved?" asked Smiley.

"For God's sake," said Fielding in an exhausted voice, "why not?"

"His parents wanted him to go to Sandhurst; I didn't, I'm afraid. I thought that if I could keep him here another Half or two I might be able to get him a music scholarship. That's why I made him Head of House : I wanted his parents to keep him on because he was doing so well." Fielding paused; "He was a rotten Head of House," he added.

"And what exactly was in the writing-case," Smiley asked, "when you opened it that evening to look at Tim's exam. paper?"

"A sheet of transparent plastic . . . it may have been one of those pack-away cape things—an old pair of gloves, and a pair of home-made galoshes."

"Home-made?"

"Yes. Hacked from a pair of Wellington boots, I should think."

"That's all?"

"No. There was a length of heavy cable, I presumed for demonstrating something in his science lessons. It seemed natural enough in winter to carry waterproofs about. Then, after the murder, I realised how he had done it."

"Did you know," asked Smiley, "*why* he had done it?"

Fielding seemed to hesitate : "Rode's a guinea-pig," he began, "the first man we've had from a grammar school. Most of us are old Carnians ourselves, in fact. Focused when we start. Rode wasn't, and Carne thrilled him. The very name Carne means quality, and Rode loved quality. His wife wasn't like that. She had her standards and they were different, but just as good. I used to watch Rode in the Abbey sometimes on Sunday mornings. Tutors sit at the end of pews, right by the aisle, you know. I used to watch his face as the choir processed past him in white and scarlet, and the Master in his doctor's robes and the Governors and Guardians behind him.

Rode was drunk—drunk with the pride of Carne. We're heady wine for the grammar school men, you know. It must have hurt him terribly that Stella wouldn't share any of that. You could see it did. The night they came to dinner with me, the night she died, they argued. I never told anyone, but they did. The Master had preached a sermon at Compline that evening: 'Hold fast to that which is good.' Rode talked about it at dinner; he couldn't take much drink, you know, he wasn't used to it. He was full of this sermon and of the eloquence of the Master. She never came to the Abbey—she went to that drab tabernacle by the station. He went on and on about the beauty of the Abbey service, the dignity, the reverence. She kept quiet till he'd finished, then laughed, and said: 'Poor old Stan. You'll always be Stan to me.' I've never seen anyone so angry as he was then. He went quite pale."

Fielding swept his grey hair from his eyes and went on, with something like the old panache: "I've watched her, too, at meals. Not just here, but at dinner parties elsewhere, when we've both been invited. I've watched her do the simplest things—like eating an apple. She'd peel it in one piece, round and round till the whole peel fell off. Then she'd cut the apple and dice the quarters, getting it all ready before she ate it. She might have been a miner's wife preparing it for her husband. She must have *seen* how people do things here, but it never occurred to her that she ought to copy them. I admire that. So do you, I expect. But Carne doesn't—and Rode didn't; above all, Rode didn't. He'd watch her, and I think he grew to hate her for not conforming. He came to see her as the bar to his success, the one factor which would deprive him of a great career. Once he'd reached that conclusion, what could he do? He couldn't divorce her—that would do him more harm than remaining married to her. Rode knew what Carne would think of divorce; we're a Church foundation, remember. So he killed her. He plotted a squalid murder, and with his little scientist's mind he gave them all the clues they wanted. Fabricated clues. Clues that would point to a murderer who didn't exist. But something went wrong; Tim Perkins got sixty-one per cent. He'd got an impossible mark—he must have cheated. He'd had the opportunity—he'd had the papers in the case. Rode put his little mind to it and decided what had happened: Tim had opened the case and he'd seen the cape and the boots and the gloves. And the cable. So Rode killed him too."

With surprising energy, Fielding got up and gave himself more brandy. His face was flushed, almost exultant.

Smiley stood up. "When did you say you'll be coming to London? Thursday, wasn't it?"

"Yes. I had arranged to lunch with my crammer man at one of those dreadful clubs in Pall Mall. I always go into the wrong one, don't you? But I'm afraid there's not much point in my seeing him now, is there, if all this is going to come out? Not even a crammer's will take me then."

Smiley hesitated.

"Come and dine with me that evening. Spend the night if you want. I'll ask one or two other people. We'll have a party. You'll feel better by then. We can talk a bit. I might be able to help you . . . for Adrian's sake."

"Thank you. I should like to. Interview apart, I've got some odds and ends to clear up in London, anyway."

"Good. Quarter to eight. Bywater Street, Chelsea, number 9A." Fielding wrote it down in his diary. His hand was quite steady.

"Black tie?" asked Fielding, his pen poised, and some imp made Smiley reply:

"I usually do, but it doesn't matter." There was a moment's silence.

"I suppose," Fielding began tentatively, "that all this *will* come out in the trial, about Tim and me? I'll be ruined if it does, you know, ruined."

"I don't see how they can prevent it."

"I feel much better now, anyway," said Fielding; "much."

With a cursory goodbye, Smiley left him alone. He walked quickly back to the police station, reasonably confident that Terence Fielding was the most accomplished liar he had met for a long time.

CHAPTER XVII

RABBIT RUN

He knocked on Rigby's door and walked straight in.
"I'm awfully afraid you'll have to arrest Stanley Rode," he
began, and recounted his interview with Fielding.

"I shall have to tell the Chief," said Rigby doubtfully.
"Would you like to repeat all that in front of him? If we're
going to pull in a Carne master, I think the Chief had better
know first. He's just come back. Hang on a minute." He
picked up the telephone on his desk and asked for the Chief
Constable. A few minutes later they were walking in silence
down a carpeted corridor. On either wall hung photographs
of rugby and cricket teams, some yellow and faded from the
Indian sun, others done in a sepia tint much favoured by
Carne photographers in the early part of the century. At
intervals along the corridor stood empty buckets of brilliant
red, with FIRE printed carefully in white on the outside. At
the far end of the corridor was a dark oak door. Rigby
knocked and waited. There was silence. He knocked again
and was answered with a cry of "Come!"

Two very large spaniels watched them come in. Behind the
spaniels, at an enormous desk, Brigadier Havelock, O.B.E.,
Chief Constable of Carne, sat like a water rat on a raft.

The few strands of white hair which ran laterally across
his otherwise bald head were painstakingly adjusted to cover
the maximum area. This gave him an oddly wet look, as if
he had just emerged from the river. His moustache, which
lavishly compensated for the scarcity of other hair, was yellow
and appeared quite solid. He was a very small man, and he
wore a brown suit and a stiff white collar with rounded
corners.

"Sir," Rigby began, "may I introduce Mr. Smiley from
London?"

He came out from behind his desk as if he were giving

himself up, unconvinced but resigned. Then he pushed out a little, knobbly hand and said, "From London, eh? How d'you do, sir," all at once, as if he'd learnt it by heart.

"Mr. Smiley's here on a private visit, sir," Rigby continued. "He is an acquaintance of Mr. Fielding."

"Quite a card, Fielding, quite a card," the Chief Constable snapped.

"Yes, indeed, sir," said Rigby, and went on :

"Mr. Smiley called on Mr. Fielding just now, sir, to take his leave before returning to London." Havelock shot a beady glance at Smiley, as if wondering whether he were fit to make the journey.

"Mr. Fielding made a kind of statement, which he substantiated with new evidence of his own. About the murder, sir."

"Well, Rigby?" he said challengingly. Smiley intervened :

"He said that the husband had done it; Stanley Rode. Fielding said that when his head boy brought him Rode's writing-case containing the examination papers . . ."

"What examination papers?"

"Rode was invigilating that afternoon, you remember. He was also doing chapel duty before going on to dinner at Fielding's house. As an expediency, he gave the papers to Perkins to take . . ."

"The boy who had the accident?" Havelock asked.

"Yes."

"You know a lot about it," said Havelock darkly.

"Fielding said that when Perkins brought him the case, Fielding opened it. He wanted to see how Perkins had done in the science paper. It was vital to the boy's future that he should get his remove," Smiley went on.

"Oh, work's the only thing now," said Havelock bitterly. "Wasn't the way when I was a boy here, I assure you."

"When Fielding opened the case, the papers were inside. So was a plastic cape, an old pair of leather gloves and a pair of rubber overshoes, cut from Wellingtons."

A pause.

"Good God! Good God! Hear that, Rigby? That's what they found in the parcel in London. Good God!"

"Finally, there was a length of cable, heavy cable, in the case as well. It was this writing-case that Rode went back for, you remember, on the night of the murder," Smiley concluded. It was like feeding a child—you couldn't overload the spoon.

There was a very long silence indeed. Then Rigby, who seemed to know his man, said :

"Motive was self-advancement in the profession, sir. Mrs. Rode showed no desire to improve her station, dressed in a slovenly manner and took no part in the religious life of the school."

"Just a minute," said Havelock. "Rode planned the murder from the start, correct?"

"Yes, sir."

"He wanted to make it look like robbery with violence."

"Yes, sir."

"Having collected the writing-case, he walked back to North Fields. Then what does he do?"

"He puts on the plastic cape and hood, overshoes and gloves. He arms himself with the weapon, sir. He lets himself in by the garden gate, crosses the back garden, goes to the front door and rings the bell, sir. His wife comes to the door. He knocks her down, drags her to the conservatory and murders her. He rinses the clothes under the tap and puts them in the parcel. Having sealed the parcel, he walks down the drive this time to the front gate, following the path, sir, knowing that his own footprints will soon be obscured by other people's. Having got to the road, where the snow was hard and showed no prints, he turned round and re-entered the house, playing the part of the distressed husband, taking care, when he discovers the body, sir, to put his own fingerprints over the glove-marks. There was one article that was too dangerous to send, sir. The weapon."

"All right, Rigby. Pull him in. Mr. Borrow will give you a warrant if you want one; otherwise I'll ring Lord Sawley."

"Yes, sir. And I'll send Sergeant Low to take a full statement from Mr. Fielding, sir?"

"Why the devil didn't he speak up earlier, Rigby?"

"Have to ask him that, sir," said Rigby woodenly, and left the room.

"You a Carnian?" Havelock asked, pushing a silver cigarette-box across the desk.

"No. No, I'm afraid not," Smiley replied.

"How d'you know Fielding?"

"We met at Oxford after the war."

"Queer card, Fielding, very queer. Say your name was Smiley?"

"There was a fellow called Smiley married Ann Sercombe, Lord Sawley's cousin. Damned pretty girl, Ann was, and went and married this fellow. Some funny little beggar in the Civil Service with an O.B.E. and a gold watch. Sawley was damned annoyed." Smiley said nothing. "Sawley got a son at Carne. Know that?"

"I read it in the press, I think."

"Tell me—this fellow Rode. He's a grammar-school chap, isn't he?"

"I believe so, yes."

"Damned odd business. Experiments never pay, do they. You can't experiment with tradition."

"No. No, indeed."

"That's the trouble today. Like Africa. Nobody seems to understand you can't build society overnight. It takes centuries to make a gentleman." Havelock frowned to himself and fiddled with the paper-knife on his desk.

"Wonder how he got his cable into that ditch, the thing he killed her with. He wasn't out of our sight for forty-eight hours after the murder."

"That," said Smiley, "is what puzzles me. So does Jane Lyn."

"What d'you mean?"

"I don't believe Rode would have had the nerve to walk back to the house after killing his wife knowing that Jane Lyn had seen him do it. Assuming, of course, that he *did* know, which seems likely. It's too cool . . . too cool altogether."

"Odd, damned odd," muttered Havelock. He looked at his

watch, pushing his left elbow outwards to do so, in a swift equestrian movement which Smiley found comic, and a little sad. The minutes ticked by. Smiley wondered if he should leave, but he had a vague feeling that Havelock wanted his company.

"There'll be a hell of a fuss," said Havelock. "It isn't every day you arrest a Carne tutor for murder." He put down the paper-knife sharply on the desk.

"Those bloody journalists ought to be horsewhipped!" he declared. "Look at the stuff they print about the Royal Family. Wicked, wicked!" he got up, crossed the room and sat himself in a leather armchair by the fire. One of the spaniels went and sat at his feet.

"What made him do it, I wonder. What the devil made him do it? His own wife, I mean; a fellow like that." Havelock said this simply, appealing for enlightenment.

"I don't believe," said Smiley slowly, "that we can ever entirely know what makes anyone do anything."

"My God, you're dead right. . . . What do you do for a living, Smiley?"

"After the war I was at Oxford for a bit. Teaching and research. I'm in London now."

"One of those clever coves, eh?"

Smiley wondered when Rigby would return.

"Know anything about this fellow's family? Has he got people, or anything?"

"I think they're both dead," Smiley answered, and the telephone on Havelock's desk rang sharply. It was Rigby. Stanley Rode had disappeared.

CHAPTER XVIII

AFTER THE BALL

He caught the 1.30 train to London. He just made it after an argument at his hotel about the bill. He left a note for Rigby giving his address and telephone number in London and asking him to telephone that night when the laboratory tests were completed. There was nothing else for him to do in Carne.

As the train pulled slowly out of Carne and one by one the familiar landmarks disappeared into the cold February mist, George Smiley was filled with a feeling of relief. He hadn't wanted to come, he knew that. He'd been afraid of the place where his wife had spent her childhood, afraid to see the fields where she had lived. But he had found nothing, not the faintest memory, neither in the lifeless outlines of Sawley Castle, nor in the surrounding countryside, to remind him of her. Only the gossip remained, as it would while the Hechts and the Havelocks survived to parade their acquaintance with the first family in Carne.

He took a taxi to Chelsea, carried his suitcase upstairs and unpacked with the care of a man accustomed to living alone. He thought of having a bath, but decided to ring Ailsa Brimley first. The telephone was by his bed. He sat on the edge of the bed and dialled the number. A tinny model-voice sang: "Unipress, good afternoon," and he asked for Miss Brimley. There was a long silence, then, "Ah'm afraid Miss Brimley is in conference. Can someone else answer your query?"

Query, thought Smiley. Good God! Why on earth query —why not question or enquiry?

"No," he replied. "Just tell her Mr. Smiley rang." He put back the receiver and went into the bathroom and turned on the hot tap. He was fiddling with his cuff-links when the telephone rang. It was Ailsa Brimley:

"George? I think you'd better come round at once. We've got a visitor. Mr. Rode from Carne. He wants to talk to us." Pulling on his jacket, he ran out into the street and hailed a taxi.

CHAPTER XIX

DISPOSAL OF A LEGEND

THE DESCENDING ESCALATOR was packed with the staff of Unipress, homebound and heavy-eyed. To them, the sight of a fat, middle-aged gentleman bounding up the adjoining staircase provided unexpected entertainment, so that Smiley was hastened on his way by the jeers of office-boys and the laughter of typists. On the first floor he paused to study an enormous board carrying the titles of a quarter of the national dailies. Finally, under the heading of "Technical and Miscellaneous", he spotted the *Christian Voice*, Room 619. The lift seemed to go up very slowly. Formless music issued from behind its plush, while a boy in a monkey jacket flicked his hips on the heavier beats. The golden doors parted with a sigh, the boy said "Six", and Smiley stepped quickly into the corridor. A moment or two later he was knocking on the door of Room 619. It was opened by Ailsa Brimley.

"George, how nice," she said brightly. "Mr. Rode will be dreadfully pleased to see you." And without any further introduction she led him into her office. In an armchair near the window sat Stanley Rode, tutor of Carne, in a neat black overcoat. As Smiley entered he stood up and held out his hand. "Good of you to come, sir," he said woodenly. "Very." The same flat manner, the same cautious voice.

"How can I help you?" asked Smiley.

They all sat down. Smiley offered Miss Brimley a cigarette and lit it for her.

"It's about this article you're writing about Stella," he began. "I feel awful about it really, because you've been so good to her, and her memory, if you see what I mean. I know you wish well, but I don't want you to write it."

Smiley said nothing, and Ailsa was wise enough to keep quiet. From now on it was Smiley's interview. The silence didn't worry him, but it seemed to worry Rode.

"It wouldn't be right; it wouldn't do at all. Mr. Glaston agreed; I spoke to him yesterday before he left and he agreed. I just couldn't let you write that stuff."

"Why not?"

"Too many people know, you see. Poor Mr. Cardew, I asked him. He knows a lot; and a lot about Stella, so I asked him. He understands why I gave up Chapel too; I couldn't bear to see her going there every Sunday and going down on her knees." He shook his head. "It was all wrong. It just made a fool of your faith."

"What did Mr. Cardew say?"

"He said we should not be the judges. We should let God judge. But I said to him it wouldn't be right, those people knowing what she'd done, and then reading all that stuff in the *Voice*. They'd think it was crazy. He didn't seem to see that, he just said to leave it to God. But I can't, Mr. Smiley."

Again no one spoke for a time. Rode sat quite still, save for a very slight rocking movement of his head. Then he began to talk again:

"I didn't believe old Mr. Glaston at first. He said she was bad, but I didn't believe it. They lived upon the hill then, Gorse Hill, only a step from the Tabernacle; Stella and her father. They never seemed to keep servants for long, so she did most of the work. I used to call in Sunday mornings sometimes after church. Stella looked after her father, cooked for him and everything, and I always wondered how I'd ever have the nerve to ask Mr. Glaston for her. The Glastons were big people in Branxome. I was teaching at Grammar School in those days. They let me teach part-time while I read for my degree, and I made up my mind that if I passed the exam. I'd ask her to marry me.

"The Sunday after the results came out I went round to the house after morning service. Mr. Glaston opened the door himself. He took me straight into the study. You could see half the potteries in Poole from the window, and the sea beyond. He sat me down and he said : 'I know what you're here for, Stanley. You want to marry Stella. But you don't know her,' he said, 'you don't know her.' 'I've been visiting two years, Mr. Glaston,' I said, 'and I think I know my mind.' Then he started talking about her. I never thought to hear a human being talk like that of his own child. He said she was bad—bad in her heart. That she was full of malice. That was why no servants would stay at the Hill. He told me how she'd lead people on, all kind and warm, till they'd told her everything, then she'd hurt them, saying wicked things, half true, half lies. He told me a lot more besides, and I didn't believe it, not a word. I think I lost my head; I called him a jealous old man who didn't want to lose his housekeeper, a lying, jealous old man who wanted his child to wait on him till he died. I said it was him who was bad, not Stella, and I shouted at him liar, liar. He didn't seem to hear, just shook his head, and I ran out into the hall and called Stella. She'd been in the kitchen, I think, and she came to me and put her arms round me and kissed me.

"We were married a month later, and the old man gave her away. He shook my hand at the wedding and called me a fine man, and I thought what an old hypocrite he was. He gave us money—to me, not her—two thousand pounds. I thought perhaps he was trying to make up for the dreadful things he'd said, and later I wrote to him and said I forgave him. He never answered and I didn't see him often after that.

"For a year or more we were happy enough at Branxome. She was just what I thought she'd be, neat and simple. She liked to go for walks and kiss at the stiles; she liked to be a bit grand sometimes, going to the Dolphin for dinner all dressed up. It meant a lot to me then, I don't mind admitting, going to the right places with Mr. Glaston's daughter. He was Rotary and on the Council and quite a figure in Branxome. She used to tease me about it—in front of other people too, which got me a bit. I remember one time we went to the Dolphin, one of the waiters there was a bloke called Johnnie Raglan. We'd been to school together. Johnnie was a bit of a tear-about and hadn't done anything much since he'd left school except run after girls and get into trouble. Stella knew him, I don't know how, and she waved to him as soon as we'd sat down. Johnnie came over and Stella made him bring another chair and sit with us. The Manager looked daggers, but he didn't dare to do anything because she was Samuel Glaston's daughter. Johnnie stayed there all the meal and Stella talked to him about school and what I was like. Johnnie was pleased as punch and got cheeky, saying I'd been a swot and a good boy and all the rest, and how Johnnie had knocked me about—lies most of it, and she egged him on. I went for her afterwards and said I didn't pay good money at the Dolphin to hear Johnnie Raglan tell a lot of tall stories, and she turned on me fast like a cat. It was her money, she said, and Johnnie was as good as me any day. Then she was sorry and kissed me and I pretended to forgive her."

Sweat was forming on his face; he was talking fast, the words tripping over each other. It was like a man recalling a nightmare, as if the memory were still there, the fear only half gone. He paused and looked sharply at Smiley as if expecting him to speak, but Smiley seemed to to be looking past him, his face impassive, its soft contours grown hard.

"Then we went to Carne. I'd just started reading *The Times* and I saw the advert. They wanted a science tutor and I applied. Mr. D'Arcy interviewed me and I got the job. It wasn't till we got to Carne that I knew that what her father had said was true. She hadn't been very keen on Chapel before, but as soon as she got here she went in for it in a big way. She knew it would look wrong, that it would hurt me. Branxome's a fine big church, you see; there was nothing funny about going to Branxome Tabernacle. But at Carne it was different; Carne Tabernacle's a little out-of-the-way place with a tin roof. She wanted to be different, to spite the school and me, by playing the humble one. I wouldn't have minded if she'd been sincere, but she wasn't, Mr. Cardew knew that. He got to know Stella, Mr. Cardew did. I think her father told him; anyway, Mr. Cardew was up North before, and he knew the family well. For all I know he wrote to Mr. Glaston, or went and saw him or something.

"She began there well enough. The townspeople were all pleased enough to see her—a wife from the School coming to the Tabernacle, that had never happened before. Then she took to running the appeal for the refugees—to collecting clothes and all that. Miss D'Arcy was running it for the school, Mr. D'Arcy's sister, and Stella wanted to beat her at her own game—to get more from the Chapel people than Miss D'Arcy got from the School. But I knew what she was doing, and so did Mr. Cardew, and so did the townspeople in the end. She listened. Every drop of gossip and dirt, she hoarded it away. She'd come home of an evening sometimes—Wednesdays and Fridays she did her Chapel work—and she'd throw off her coat and laugh till I thought she'd gone mad.

" 'I've got them! I've got them all,' she'd say. 'I know all their little secrets and I've got them in the hollow of my hand, Stan.' That's what she'd say. And those that realised grew to be frightened of her. They all gossiped, Heaven knows, but not to profit from it, not like Stella. Stella was cunning; anything decent, anything good, she'd drag it down and spoil it. There were a dozen she'd got the measure of. There was Mulligan the furniture man; he's got a daughter with a kid near Leamington. Somehow she found out the girl wasn't married—they'd sent her to an aunt to have her baby and begin again up there. She rang up Mulligan once, something to do with a bill for moving Simon Snow's furniture, and she said "Greetings from Leamington Spa, Mr. Mulligan. We need a little co-operation." She told me that—she came home laughing her head off and told me. But they got her in the end, didn't they? They got their own back!"

Smiley nodded slowly, his eyes now turned fully upon Rode.

"Yes," he said at last, "they got their own back."

"They thought Mad Janie did it, but I didn't. Janie'd as soon have killed her own sister as Stella. They were as close as moon and stars, that's what Stella said. They'd talk together for hours in the evenings when I was out late on Societies or Extra Tuition. Stella cooked food for her, gave her clothes and money. It gave her a feeling of power to help a creature like Janie, and have her fawning round. Not because she was kind, but because she was cruel.

"She'd brought a little dog with her from Branxome, a mongrel. One day a few months ago I came home and found it lying in the garage whimpering, terrified. It was limping and had blood on its back. She'd beaten it. She must have gone mad. I knew she'd beaten it before, but never like that; never. Then something happened—I shouted at her and she laughed and then I hit her. Not hard, but hard enough. In the face. I gave her twenty-four hours to have the dog destroyed or I'd tell the police. She screamed at me—it was her dog and she'd damn' well do what she liked with it—but next day she put on her little black hat and took the dog to the vet. I suppose she told him some tale. She could spin a good tale about anything, Stella could. She kind of stepped into a part and played it right through. Like the tale she told the Hungarians. Miss D'Arcy had some refugees to stay from London once and Stella told them such a tale they ran away and had to be taken back to London. Miss D'Arcy paid for their fares and everything, even had the welfare officer down to see them and try and put things right. I don't think Miss D'Arcy ever knew who'd got at them, but I did—Stella told me. She laughed, always the same laugh: 'There's your fine lady, Stan. Look at her charity now.'

"After the dog, she took to pretending I was violent, cringing away whenever I came near, holding her arm up as though I was going to hit her again. She even made out I was plotting to murder her: she went and told Mr. Cardew

I was. She didn't believe it herself; she'd laugh about it some-times. She said to me : 'It's no good killing me now, Stan; they'll all know who's done it.' But other times she'd whine and stroke me, begging me not kill her. 'You'll kill me in the long nights!' She'd scream it out—it was the words that got her, the long nights, she liked the sound of them the way an actor does, and she'd build a whole story round them. 'Oh, Stan,' she'd say, 'keep me safe in the long nights.' You know how it is when you never meant to do anything anyway, and someone goes on begging you not to do it? You think you might do it after all, you begin to consider the possibility."

Miss Brimley drew in her breath rather quickly. Smiley stood up and walked over to Rode.

"Why don't we go back to my house for some food?" he said. "We can talk this over quietly. Among friends."

They took a taxi to Bywater Street. Rode sat beside Ailsa Brimley, more relaxed now, and Smiley, opposite him on a drop-seat, watched him and wondered. And it occurred to him that the most important thing about Rode was that he had no friends. Smiley was reminded of Büchner's fairy tale of the child left alone in an empty world who, finding no one to talk to, went to the moon because it smiled at him, but the moon was made of rotten wood. And when the sun and moon and stars had all turned to nothing, he tried to go back to the earth, but it had gone.

Perhaps because Smiley was tired, or perhaps because he was getting a little old, he felt a movement of sudden com-passion towards Rode, such as children feel for the poor and parents for their children. Rode had tried so hard—he had used Carne's language, bought the right clothes, and thought as best he could the right thoughts, yet remained hopelessly apart, hopelessly alone.

He lit the gas-fire in the drawing-room while Ailsa Brimley went to the delicatessen in the King's Road for soup and eggs. He poured out whisky and soda and gave one to Rode, who drank it in short sips, without speaking.

"I had to tell somebody," he said at last. "I thought you'd be a good person. I didn't want you to print that article, though. Too many knew, you see."

"How many really knew?"

"Only those she'd gone for, I think. I suppose about a dozen townspeople. And Mr. Cardew, of course. She was terribly cunning, you see. She didn't often pass on gossip. She knew to a hair how far she could go. Those who knew were the ones she'd got on the hook. Oh, and D'Arcy, Felix D'Arcy, he knew. She had something special there, something she never told me about. There were nights when she'd put on her shawl and slip out, all excited as if she was going to a party. Quite late sometimes, eleven or twelve. I'd never ask her where she was going because it only bucked her, but sometimes she'd nod at me all cunning and say, 'You don't know, Stan, but D'Arcy does. D'Arcy knows and he can't tell,' and then she'd laugh again and try and look mysterious, and off she'd go."

Smiley was silent for a long time, watching Rode and thinking. Then he asked suddenly: "What was Stella's blood group, do you know?"

"Mine's B. I know that. I was a donor at Branxome. Hers was different.

"How do you know that?"

"She had a test before we were married. She used to suffer from anaemia. I remember hers being different, that's all. Probably A. I can't remember for sure. Why?"

"Where were you registered as a donor?"

"North Poole Transfusion Centre."

"Will they know you there still? Are you still recorded there?"

"I suppose so."

The front door bell rang. It was Ailsa Brimley, back from her shopping.

Ailsa installed herself in the kitchen, while Rode and Smiley sat in the warm comfort of the drawing-room.

"Tell me something else," said Smiley, "about the night of

the murder. Why did you leave the writing-case behind? Was it absent-mindedness?"

"No, not really. I was on Chapel duty that night, so Stella and I arrived separately at Fielding's house. She got there before I did and I think Fielding gave the case to her—right at the start of the evening so that it wouldn't get forgotten. He said something about it later that evening. She'd put the case beside her coat in the hall. It was only a little thing about eighteen inches by twelve. I could have sworn she was carrying it as we stood in the hall saying goodbye, but I must have been mistaken. It wasn't till we got to the house that she asked me what I'd done with it."

"*She* asked *you* what you'd done with it?"

"Yes. Then she threw a temper and said I expected her to remember everything. I didn't particularly want to go back, I could have rung Fielding and arranged to collect it first thing next morning, but Stella wouldn't hear of it. She made me go. I didn't like to tell the police all this stuff about us quarrelling, it didn't seem right."

Smiley nodded. "When you got back to Fielding's you rang the bell?"

"Yes. There's the front door, then a glass door inside, a sort of french window to keep out draughts. The front door was still open, and the light was on in the hall. I rang the bell and collected the case from Fielding."

They had finished supper when the telephone rang.

"Rigby here, Mr. Smiley. I've got the laboratory results. They're rather puzzling."

"The exam. paper first: it doesn't tally?"

"No, it doesn't. The boffins here say all the figures and writing were done with the same ballpoint pen. They can't be sure about the diagrams but they say the legend on all the diagrams corresponds to the rest of the script on the sheet."

"All done by the boy after all in fact?"

"Yes. I brought up some other samples of his hand-writing for comparison. They match the exam. paper right the way through. Fielding couldn't have tinkered with it."

"Good. And the clothing? Nothing there either?"

"Traces of blood, that's all. No prints on the plastic."

"What was her blood group, by the way?"

"Group A."

Smiley sat down on the edge of the bed. Pressing the receiver to his ear, he began talking quietly. Ten minutes later he was walking slowly downstairs. He had come to the end of the chase, and was already sickened by the kill.

It was nearly an hour before Rigby arrived.

CHAPTER XX

THE DROSS OF THE RIVER

ALBERT BRIDGE WAS as preposterous as ever; bony steel, rising to Wagnerian pinnacles, against the patient London sky; the Thames crawling beneath it with resignation, edging its filth into the wharves of Battersea, then sliding towards the mist down river.

The mist was thick. Smiley watched the driftwood, as it touched it, turning first to white dust, then seeming to lift, dissolve and vanish.

This was how it would end, on a foul morning like this when they dragged the murderer whimpering from his cell and put the hempen rope round his neck. Would Smiley have the courage to recall this two months from now, as the dawn broke outside his window and the clock rang out the time? When they broke a man's neck on the scaffold and put him away like the dross of the river?

He made his way along Beaumont Street towards the King's Road. The milkman chugged past him in his electric van. He would breakfast out this morning, then take a cab to Curzon

Street and order the wine for dinner. He would choose something good. Fielding would like that.

Fielding closed his eyes and drank, his left hand held lightly across his chest.

"Divine," he said "divine!" And Ailsa Brimley, opposite him, smiled gently.

"How are you going to spend your retirement, Mr. Fielding," she asked. "Drinking Frankenwein?"

His glass still held before his lips he looked into the candles. The silver was good, better than his own. He wondered why they were only dining three. "In peace," he replied at last. "I have recently made a discovery."

"What's that?"

"That I have been playing to an empty house. But now I'm comforted to think that no one remembers how I forgot my words or missed an entry. So many of us wait patiently for our audience to die. At Carne no one will remember for more than a Half or two what a mess I've made of life. I was too vain to realise that until recently." He put the glass down in front of him and smiled suddenly at Ailsa Brimley. "That is the peace I mean. Not to exist in anyone's mind, but my own; to be a secular monk, safe and forgotten."

Smiley gave him more wine: "Miss Brimley knew your brother Adrian well in the war. We were all in the same department," he said. "She was Adrian's secretary for a while. Weren't you, Brim?"

"It's depressing how the bad live on," Fielding declared. "Rather embarrassing. For the bad, I mean." He gave a little gastronomic sigh. "The moment of truth in a good meal! *Übergansperiode* between *entrement* and dessert," and they all laughed, and then were silent. Smiley put down his glass, and said:

"The story you told me on Thursday, when I came and saw you . . ."

"Well?" Fielding was irritated.

"About cheating for Tim Perkins . . . how you took the paper from the case and altered it . . ."

"Yes?"

"It isn't true." He might have been talking about the weather. "They've examined it and it isn't true. The writing was all one person's . . . the boy's. If anyone cheated, it must have been the boy."

There was a long silence. Fielding shrugged.

"My dear fellow, you can't expect me to believe that. These people are practically moronic."

"Of course, it doesn't necessarily signify anything. I mean you could be protecting the boy, couldn't you? By lying for him, for his honour so to speak. Is that the explanation?"

"I've told you the truth," he replied shortly. "Make what you want of it."

"I mean, I can see a situation where there might have been collusion, where you were moved by the boy's distress when he brought you the papers; and on the spur of the moment you opened the case and took out his paper and told him what to write."

"Look here," said Fielding hotly, "why don't you keep off this? What's it got to do with you?" And Smiley replied with sudden fervour :

"I'm trying to help, Fielding. I beg you to believe me, I'm trying to help. For Adrian's sake. I don't want there to be . . . more trouble than there need, more pain. I want to get it straight before Rigby comes. They've dropped the charge against Janie. You know that, don't you? They seem to think it's Rode, but they haven't pulled him in. They could have done, but they haven't. They just took more statements from him. So you see, it matters terribly about the writing-case. Everything hangs by whether you really saw inside it; and whether Perkins did. Don't you see that? If it was Perkins who cheated after all, if it was only the boy who opened the case and not you, then they'll want to know the answer to a very important question : *they'll want to know how you knew what was inside it.*"

"What are you trying to say?"

"They're not really moronic, you know. Let's start from the other end for a moment. Suppose it was you who killed

283

Stella Rode, suppose you had a reason, a terribly good reason, and they knew what that reason might be; suppose you went ahead of Rode after giving him the case that night—by bicycle, for instance, like Janie said, riding on the wind. If that were really so, none of those things you saw would have been in the case at all. You could have made it up. And when later the exam. results came out and you realised that Perkins had cheated, then you guessed he had seen inside the case, had seen that it contained nothing, *nothing but exam. papers.* I mean that would explain why you had to kill the boy." He stopped and glanced towards Fielding. "And in a way," he added almost reluctantly, "it makes better sense, doesn't it?"

"And what, may I ask, was the reason you speak of?"

"Perhaps she blackmailed you. She certainly knew about your conviction in the war from when she was up North. Her father was a magistrate, wasn't he? I understand they've looked up the files. The police, I mean. It was her father who heard the case. She knew you're broke and need another job and she kept you on a hook. It seems D'Arcy knew too. She told him. She'd nothing to lose; he was in on the story from the start, he'd never allow the papers to get hold of it; she knew that, she knew her man. Did *you* tell D'Arcy as well, Fielding? I think you may have done. When she came to you and told you she knew, jeered and laughed at you, you went to D'Arcy and told him. You asked him what to do. And he said—what would he say?—perhaps he said find out what she wants. But she wanted nothing; not money at least, but something more pleasing, more gratifying to her twisted little mind : she wanted to command and own you. She loved to conspire, she summoned you to meetings at absurd times and places; in woods, in disused churches, and above all at night. And she wanted nothing from you but your will, she made you listen to her boasts and her mad intrigues, made you fawn and cringe, then let you run away till the next time." He looked up again. "They might think along those lines, you see. That's why we need to know who saw inside the case. And who cheated in the exam." They were both looking at him, Ailsa in horror, Fielding motionless, impassive.

"If they think that," asked Fielding at last, "how do they suppose I knew Rode would come back for the case that night?"

"Oh, they knew she was expecting you to meet her that night, after the dinner at your house." Smiley threw this off as if it were a tedious detail, "It was part of the game she liked to play."

"How do they know that?"

"From what Rode says," Smiley continued, "Stella was carrying the case in the hall, actually had it in her hand. When they arrived at North Fields she was without it; she flew into a rage and accused him of forgetting it. She made him go back for it. You see the inference?"

"Oh, clearly," said Fielding, and Smiley heard Ailsa Brimley whisper his name in horror.

"In other words, when Stella devised this trick to gratify her twisted will, you saw it as an opportunity to kill her, putting the blame on a non-existent tramp, or, failing that, on Rode, as a second line of defence. Let us suppose you had been meaning to kill her. You had meant, I expect, to ride out there one night when Rode was teaching late. You had your boots and your cape, even the cable stolen from Rode's room, and you meant to lay a false trail. But what a golden opportunity when Perkins turned up with the hand-case! Stella wanted her meeting—the forgotten hand-case was agreed upon as the means of achieving it. That, I fear, is the way their minds may work. And you see, they *know* it wasn't Rode."

"How do they know? How *can* they know? He's got no alibi." Smiley didn't seem to hear. He was looking towards the window, and the heavy velvet curtains stirring uneasily.

"What's that? What are you looking at?" Fielding asked with sudden urgency, but Smiley did not answer.

"You know, Fielding," he said at last, "we just don't know what people are like, we can never tell; there isn't any truth about human beings, no formula that meets each one of us.

285

And there are some of us—aren't there?—who are nothing, who are so labile that we astound ourselves; we're the chameleons. I read a story once about a poet who bathed himself in cold fountains so that he could recognise his own existence in the contrast. He had to reassure himself, you see, like a child being hateful to its parents. You might say he had to make the sun shine on him so that he could see his shadow and feel alive."

Fielding made an impatient movement with his hand. "How do you know it wasn't Rode?"

"The people who are like that—there really are some, Fielding—do you know their secret? They can't feel anything inside them, no pleasure or pain, no love or hate; they're ashamed and frightened that they can't feel. And their shame, this shame, Fielding, drives them to extravagance and colour; they must make themselves feel that cold water, and without that they're nothing. The world sees them as showmen, fantasists, liars, as sensualists perhaps, not for what they are : the living dead."

"How do you know? How do you know it wasn't Rode?" Fielding cried with anger in his voice, and Smiley replied : "I'll tell you."

"If Rode murdered his wife, he had planned to do so long ago. The plastic cape, the boots, the weapons, the intricate timing, the use of Perkins to carry the case to your house— these are evidence of long premeditation. Of course one could ask : if that's so, why did he bother with Perkins at all— why didn't he keep the case with him all the time? But never mind. Let's see how he does it. He walks home with his wife after dinner, having deliberately forgotten the writing-case. Having left Stella at home, he returns to your house to collect it. It was a risky business, incidentally, leaving that case behind. Quite apart from the fact that one would expect him to have locked it, his wife might have noticed he hadn't got it as they left—or you might have noticed, or Miss Truebody —but luckily no one did. He collects the case, hurries back, kills her, fabricating the clues which mislead the police. He thrusts the cape, boots and gloves into the refugees' parcel, ties it up and prepares to make good his escape. He is alarmed by Mad Janie, perhaps, but reaches the lane and re-enters the house as Stanley Rode. Five minutes later he is with the D'Arcy's. From then on for the next forty-eight hours he is under constant supervision. Perhaps you didn't know this, Fielding, but the police found the murder weapon four miles down the road in a ditch. They found it within ten hours of the murder being discovered, long before Rode had a chance to throw it there.

"This is the point, though, Fielding. This is what they can't get over. I suppose it would be possible to make a phoney murder weapon. Rode could have taken hairs from Stella's comb, stuck them with human blood to a length of coaxial cable and planted the thing in a ditch *before* he committed the murder. But the only blood he could use was his own—which belongs to a different blood group. The blood on the weapon they found belonged to Stella's blood group. He didn't do it. There's a rather more concrete piece of evidence, to do with the parcel. Rigby had a word with Miss Truebody yesterday. It seems she telephoned Stella Rode on the morning of the day she was murdered. Telephoned at your request, Fielding, to say a boy would be bringing some old clothes up to North Fields on Thursday morning—would she be sure to keep the parcel open till then? . . . What did Stella threaten to do, Fielding? Write an anonymous letter to your next school?"

Then Smiley put his hand on Fielding's arm and said : "Go now, in God's name go now. There's very little time, for Adrian's sake go now," and Ailsa Brimley whispered something he could not hear.

Fielding seemed not to hear. His great head was thrown back, his eyes half closed, his wine glass still held between his thick fingers.

And the front-door bell rang out, like the scream of a woman in an empty house.

Smiley never knew what made the noise, whether it was

Fielding's hands on the table as he stood up, or his chair, falling backwards. Perhaps it was not a noise at all, but simply the shock of violent movement when it was least expected; the sight of Fielding, who a moment before had sat lethargic in his chair, springing forward across the room. Then Rigby was holding him, had taken Fielding's right arm and done something to it so that Fielding cried out in pain and fear, swinging round to face them under the compulsion of Rigby's grip. Then Rigby was saying the words, and Fielding's terrified gaze fell upon Smiley.

"Stop him, stop him, Smiley, for God's sake! They'll hang me." And he shouted the last two words again and again: "Hang me, hang me," until the detectives came in from the street, and shoved him without ceremony into a waiting car.

Smiley watched the car go. It didn't hurry, just picked its way down the wet street and disappeared. He remained there long after it had gone, looking towards the end of the road, so that passers-by stared oddly at him, or tried to follow his gaze. But there was nothing to see. Only the half-lit street, and the shadows moving along it.